Science Ficti
the Two Cu

CRITICAL EXPLORATIONS IN SCIENCE FICTION AND FANTASY
(a series edited by Donald E. Palumbo and C.W. Sullivan III)

Science Fiction and the Two Cultures

Essays on Bridging the Gap Between the Sciences and the Humanities

Edited by
GARY WESTFAHL *and*
GEORGE SLUSSER

CRITICAL EXPLORATIONS IN
SCIENCE FICTION AND FANTASY, 16
Donald E. Palumbo *and* C. W. Sullivan III, *series editors*

McFarland & Company, Inc., Publishers
Jefferson, North Carolina, and London

ALSO OF INTEREST
Hugo Gernsback and the Century of Science Fiction
by Gary Westfahl (McFarland, 2007)

LIBRARY OF CONGRESS CATALOGUING-IN-PUBLICATION DATA

Science fiction and the two cultures : essays on bridging the gap
 between the sciences and the humanities / edited by Gary
 Westfahl and George Slusser.
        p.   cm.   — (Critical explorations in science fiction
        and fantasy ; 16)
     Includes bibliographical references and index.

   ISBN 978-0-7864-4297-3
   softcover : 50# alkaline paper ∞

    1. Science fiction, English — History and criticism.   2. Science fiction,
 American — History and criticism.   3. Science and the humanities in
 literature.   4. Science and literature.   I. Westfahl, Gary.   II. Slusser,
 George Edgar.
 PR830.S35S34   2009
 823'.087609 — dc22   2009010114

British Library cataloguing data are available

On the cover: *Vitruvian Man*, Leonardo da Vinci, Galleria dell'Accademia,
Venice; background image ©2009 Shutterstock

Manufactured in the United States of America

McFarland & Company, Inc., Publishers
  Box 611, Jefferson, North Carolina 28640
  www.mcfarlandpub.com

Table of Contents

II. CASE STUDIES: SCIENCE FICTION AS AN EXPRESSION OF TWO CULTURES

Introduction: Science Fiction at the Crossroads of Two Cultures

Gary Westfahl

In 1959, scientist and novelist C. P. Snow ignited a fierce debate when he gave a famous lecture lamenting the emergence of "two cultures":

> I believe the intellectual life of the whole of western society is increasingly being split into two polar groups.... Literary intellectuals at one pole — at the other scientists, and as the most representative, the physical scientists. Between the two a gulf of mutual incomprehension — sometimes (particularly among the young) hostility and dislike, but most of all lack of understanding. They have a curious distorted image of each other. Their attitudes are so different that, even on the level of emotion, they can't find much common ground.[1]

Certainly, it is possible to dispute the accuracy of Snow's claims, as many have done. One can say, for example, that these two purportedly monolithic cultures are in fact each splintered into scores of separate subcultures, some of them as antithetical to each other as the two broad groups that Snow discerns (a point Snow himself conceded in his 1963 follow-up essay, "The Two Cultures: A Second Look"). One can also note that, in some areas at least, experts in the sciences and the humanities have indeed found some "common ground": both scientists and humanists, for example, have long stood at the forefront of efforts to stem nuclear proliferation, and more recently they have joined forces to call attention to the looming threat of global warming.

Overall, however, most would concede that there is at least a degree of truth in Snow's arguments that there is a gap between these two cultures, and that this division has been, and continues to be, a significant social problem. The issue to discuss would then become possible ways to confront and improve this sorry situation. On the fiftieth anniversary of Snow's original lecture, this volume will be exploring one apparently obvious solution to Snow's dilemma:

the genre of science fiction, which in its very name proclaims itself to be a meeting ground for persons devoted to science and persons devoted to the humanities.

Speaking in 1959, Snow can certainly be forgiven for overlooking science fiction as a means of bridging the gap between the two cultures. At the time of his lecture, the genre remained largely centered in science fiction magazines which attracted relatively few readers; science fiction book publishing, still in its infancy, was emerging as a profitable niche market, but science fiction novels were never reviewed in major periodicals and never appeared on best-seller lists; and science fiction films and television programs, also less than a decade old as a recognized category, were generally low-budget productions primarily aimed at an audience of children. Because of science fiction's low reputation, both literature and film scholars, and commentators outside of academia, regularly ignored science fiction, unaware of the genre's increasing maturity and quality. In the late 1950s, then, someone like Snow would understandably feel that such a marginalized and debased form of literature merited little attention, and would be utterly incapable of playing any role in addressing a major societal division.

Today, of course, the status of science fiction is very different. Its authors now include a number of famous figures who regularly command million-dollar advances and enjoy huge sales and prominent positions on best-seller lists; and science fiction films and television programs have become a dominant, perhaps *the* dominant, presence in western popular culture, as best evidenced by the enormous successes of the *Star Trek* and *Star Wars* franchises. Now appreciating the value of science fiction, increasing numbers of scholars and commentators are analyzing its texts, which have also become regular assignments in high school and college classes. With so many people reading or watching science fiction, and everyone fully aware of its existence, the genre now seems poised to make a significant contribution to society — such as, perhaps, helping to bring together the still-dueling factions of the sciences and the humanities, to break down stereotypical preconceptions which hinder communication, and to achieve some measure of reconciliation and commonality between these two disparate cultures.

Surprisingly, however, the scholars who write about Snow's two cultures have continued to ignore science fiction, despite its heightened quality, visibility, and respectability. Within the field, there have been occasional discussions of science fiction as a bridge between the two cultures — as early as 1962, a young college student and future Pilgrim Award–winning science fiction scholar, David N. Samuelson, wrote his bachelor's thesis on "Science Fiction and the Two Cultures" — but other critics and commentators have consistently ignored the genre. Consider, for example, two collections of essays expressly focused on the problem of the gap between cultures — Joseph W. Slade and Judith Yaross Lee's *Beyond the Two Cultures: Essays on Science, Technology, and Literature* (1990) and Richard E. Lee and Immanuel Wallerstein's *Overcoming the Two Cultures: Science Versus the Humanities in the Modern World Systems* (2004). The first collection contains precisely one reference to science fiction — in an introductory flourish to an essay about images of scientists in the nineteenth century — and the second collection contains not a single reference to science fiction. Thus, when a number of science fiction scholars and writers gathered at the Twentieth J. Lloyd Eaton Conference on Science Fiction and Fantasy Literature to discuss the topic of "Science Fiction at the Crossroads of Two Cultures," they were belatedly addressing a significant weakness in responses to Snow's dilemma; and now, on the fiftieth anniversary of Snow's lecture on the subject, they have revised and updated their contributions so as to bring their provocative conclusions to a wider audience.

And how, precisely, might the desirable goal of bridging the gap between Snow's two cultures be attained? As it happens, this has been a longstanding preoccupation of many science fiction commentators. It was central, for example, to the vision of Hugo Gernsback, the man who first promulgated the term and the idea of "science fiction" and established the genre as a recognized category of literature. Gernsback is often misrepresented as a tireless advocate of science, inextricably tied to the interests of the scientific community, but the true situation is rather more complex. Despite his lifelong devotion to practical science, Gernsback never received any formal scientific education and hence could not claim membership in the scientific community; thus, it was as an excluded outsider that he viewed the credentialed scientists who taught classes, conducted research at universities, published peer-reviewed articles, and lectured on the radio, and he complained that those scientists were all too often close-minded and unreceptive to new perspectives from outside their cloistered community.

Science fiction, then, could serve as a way to convey some productive input from non-scientists to scientists: writers would come up with intriguing new scientific ideas, and scientists reading their stories would be inspired to transform those ideas into actual new inventions and discoveries. The insularity of the scientific community would thus be reduced, and its work would be continually reinvigorated by helpful suggestions from persons who were not members of that circle. As for communication in the other direction, scientists and others with scientific knowledge could employ science fiction to educate readers who were less well informed by presenting accurate scientific information in the palatable context of an entertaining story. So, non-scientists could become better aware of, and presumably more sympathetic to, science by reading science fiction, just as scientists could become more productive by reading science fiction. Gernsback even proposed that this productive inter-action could have the effect of improving human society, a goal not unrelated to Snow's broader social concerns; as he argued in one editorial, "Science Fiction Week,"

> Not only is science fiction an idea of tremendous import, but it is to be an important factor in making the world a better place to live in, through educating the public to the possibilities of science and the influence of science on life which, even today, are not appreciated by the man on the street.... If every man, woman, boy and girl, could be induced to read science fiction right along, there would certainly be a great resulting benefit to the community, in that the educational standards of its people would be raised tremendously. Science fiction would make people happier, give them a broader understanding of the world, make them more tolerant.[2]

As a way to resolve the division between the two cultures, needless to say, Gernsback's vision had some definite limitations. The messages to be conveyed to scientists were only to be ideas for new inventions; outsiders, it seemed, were not permitted to offer, say, criticisms of the scientific community or proposals to reform the way that scientists conducted their business. And the messages to be conveyed to non-scientists were only to involve correct and up-to-date scientific facts, with nothing to be said about the broader philosophy and world-view of the scientist and how that differs from the perspectives of literary intellectuals and other outsiders. It is also clear that the often pedestrian science fiction stories found in Gernsback's magazines, which failed to attract vast numbers of readers, were doing little to actually achieve any of his grandiose ambitions, and when he abandoned the field of science fiction publishing in 1936, it would be left to others to carry on the business of explaining and promoting science fiction as a meeting ground of the two cultures.

Gernsback's most prominent successor, John W. Campbell, Jr., generalized and expanded upon Gernsback's ideas. According to Campbell, science fiction stories could be written either by scientists or by non-scientists; both could employ their stories to present scientific ideas; and, more significantly, both could discuss not only the inner workings of new inventions, but the ways that these new inventions might affect society at large. Presumably, scientist writers and readers might be more interested in the science of new inventions, whereas non-scientist writers and readers would be more interest in the social ramifications of new inventions; but everyone could offer and respond to ideas of all kinds, and science fiction could thus become a forum where both scientists and non-scientists could come together to discuss matters of common interest — namely, forthcoming scientific advances and how they might have a positive or negative impact on human society. As Campbell once explained, science fiction was "a way of considering the past, present, and future from a different viewpoint, and taking a look at how else we *might* do things ... a convenient analog system for thinking about new scientific, social, and economic ideas — and for re-examining old ideas."[3]

Some essays in this volume will be exploring the validity and value of Gernsback's and Campbell's ideas, and other suggestions as to how science fiction might have functioned in the past, or might function in the future, to resolve the problem identified by Snow and help to bring the cultures of the sciences and the humanities closer together. It must be acknowledged, though, that there have also been commentators on science fiction who would argue that such communication is not the proper role of the genre. Brian W. Aldiss, later a major figure in science fiction's avant-garde "New Wave" of the 1960s, famously proclaimed in 1961 that "Science fiction — the fact needs emphasizing — is no more written for scientists and technologists than ghost stories were written for ghosts,"[4] and just as he saw they were not the intended readers of science fiction, he also had little interest in recruiting them to be science fiction writers. To leading figures of the New Wave such as Aldiss, Michael Moorcock, and Harlan Ellison, science fiction was purely and simply another form of literature, which needed to display no special awareness of or interest in scientific matters; indeed, to emphasize that science fiction was largely unrelated to science, many in the New Wave even sought to rename the genre "speculative fiction." While acknowledging that science fiction stories did contain scientific ideas, those ideas could now be regarded, as Ursula K. Le Guin argued in 1976, merely as "metaphors," literary devices deployed to convey some theme or concern about human nature and society.[5] Such a literature would not, then, have any unique ability to bridge Snow's cultural gap.

Needless to say, these attitudes were not universally embraced, and as one response to the New Wave, there emerged a new subgenre, hard science fiction, particularly devoted to the presentation and exploration of scientific ideas, which has remained a prominence presence in the field, with writers and readers who today tend to congregate in the magazine formerly edited by Campbell, *Analog: Science Fiction/Science Fact*. There, at least, some version of Gernsback's and Campbell's limited dreams lives on, as scientist and non-scientist readers and writers do come together to vigorously debate the merits of new scientific ideas presented in science fiction stories.

But can science fiction play a broader role in bridging the gap between the two cultures, beyond this sort of sometime-derided shoptalk? This volume will be striving to answer that question, or at least to suggest some directions for further investigations into answering that question.

The first section of this volume, "Overviews: Science Fiction in the Context of Two Cultures," offers seven chapters that specifically focus on the problem identified by Snow and on science fiction as a potential solution to that problem. Carl Freedman's "Science Fiction and the Two Cultures: Reflections after the Snow-Leavis Controversy" closely examines the original C. P. Snow–F. R. Leavis debate and presents several science fiction authors as exemplary solutions to Snow's dilemma. Bradford Lyau's "Science Fiction, Mediating Agent between C.P. Snow's Two Cultures: A Historical Interpretation" mounts a similar argument, although he places the Snow-Leavis controversy in a broader historical context and focuses on three exemplary writers — H. G. Wells, Robert A. Heinlein, and Ursula K. Le Guin — to represent three sorts of science-fictional responses to Snow's concerns. Howard V. Hendrix's "Fighting Out of Context: Culture Wars Within and Without Science Fiction from Snow to Sokal" approaches the original Snow-Leavis argument, and the more recent controversy surrounding Alan Sokal's hoax, from the personal perspective of someone who has worked as both a science fiction critic and a respected science fiction writer, while Stephen Potts's "A Tale of Two Cultures: Science Studies and Science Fiction" focuses specifically on the Sokal affair and its relationship to science fiction. Moving in another direction, my essay "The Rich and the Poor: Science Fiction and the Other Two Cultures" confronts the issue of whether science fiction has addressed or can address the core concern behind Snow's original lecture — naming, lessening the technological and economic gap between the developed and the underdeveloped nations of the world. Finally, two chapters employ Snow's ideas as a basis for far-ranging explorations of science fiction: the late Frank McConnell's "The Science of Fiction and the Fiction of Science: A Storytelling Animal in an Inhospitable World" wittily relates Snow's argument to a characteristically eclectic range of texts, including *2001: A Space Odyssey, Star Wars,* and *Gilligan's Island,* while George Slusser's "Dimorphs and Doubles: J. D. Bernal's 'Two Cultures' and the Transhuman Promise" considers Snow's dilemma in the context of the groundbreaking ideas of J. D. Bernal and several science fiction works that focus on new forms of humanity.

The second section of this volume, "Case Studies: Science Fiction as an Expression of Two Cultures," offers nine chapters which rarely make specific reference to Snow and his ideas but more broadly illustrate the diverse ways in which works of science fiction can be regarded as expressions of both literary and scientific values, thus functioning to bridge the gap between the two cultures even if that was not the author's purpose. The section begins with two essays that explore recurring tropes in a variety of science fiction texts: Carol MacKay and Kirk Hampton's "Discontinuity: Spaceships at the Abyss" discerns a different sort of disquiet behind Snow's essay, as illustrated by a range of science fiction texts featuring spaceships, and Pekka Kuusisto's

"Gregory Benford's *Against Infinity* and the Literary, Historical and Geometric Formation of the Encyclopedic Circle of Knowledge" connects works by Dante, H. G. Wells, Jorge Luis Borges, and Gregory Benford as efforts to imagine encyclopedic compilations of knowledge and geometrically envision alien realms and the infinite. Next come two chapters which consider the works of H. G. Wells, the writer who perhaps best exemplified the ideal of combining the perspective of the scientist and the humanist: John S. Partington's "Utopia and Utopianism in the Life, Work, and Thought of H. G. Wells" explores the ways in which Wells epitomized utopianism, while Gareth Davies-Morris's "The Alien Eye: Imperialism and Otherness in H. G. Wells's *The First Men in the Moon*" closely analyzes the Wells novel which perhaps offers his most provocative vision of a technologically advanced alien civilization and the strange society it has evolved. Shifting to more modern texts, George Atkins's "Killer Robots, Laws of Robotics, and Pernicious Humans" discusses a fascinating dialogue between literature and science involving robotics, as Isaac Asimov's proposed Three Laws of Robotics inspire thoughtful responses from both computer scientists actively working in robotics and later science fiction writers. Noah Mass's "Philip K. Dick's Conversion Narrative" documents how, at a time when science fiction was visibly moving away from a focus on scientific matters, a major writer was able to employ the genre as a way to express his new religious feelings and to comment on developments in the era's counterculture. Jake Jakaitis's "The Terror of Nature Not Understood: Science, Mysticism, and the Unknowable in Don DeLillo's *Ratner's Star*" explains how a major novel "probes the assumptions sustaining scientific and humanistic discourses," and Sharon D. King's "When the Caesura Ceases: Two Romanian Authors Gauge the Place of Writers in the Age of Computers" shows how Romanian writers have pondered the ways in which computers now challenge human values. To conclude this section, Gregory Benford's "A Creature of Double Vision" presents a thoughtful meditation on the human condition from a writer who, like Wells, bridges the gap between the two cultures in his own person, since Benford has spent his life both working as a physicist at the University of California, Irvine, and writing and analyzing works of science fiction; his provocative ideas thus prove Snow was right in discerning that there would be valuable results from heightened communication between the sciences and the humanities.

It is difficult to summarize what all of these diverse contributions have to say about science fiction and the two cultures, but a few observations might be proffered. First, by means of a rough chronological arrangements, these essays function as historical survey of science fiction, demonstrating how early writers like Dante and Blaise Pascal reveal a gradual shift from medieval attitudes to the genuine understanding of science necessary for science fiction;

how H. G. Wells first showed the world the fascinating possibilities of a literature which would combine scientific and humanistic perspectives; how writers influenced by Gernsback's ideas like Isaac Asimov illustrated how the literature of science fiction might indeed function to interact with science and assist in its progress; and how more recent writers like Dick and DeLillo have shifted more to offering critiques of science and its practitioners.

Second, while the original call for essays included no instructions of the kind, the experts who wrote these chapters have focused almost exclusively on science fiction literature, not science fiction films and television; as evidence, the final bibliography of works cited in the chapters includes 113 science fiction novels and stories, but only 16 science fiction films and television programs, so that about 88 percent of the texts discussed by contributors were science fiction novels or stories while only about 12 percent of the discussed texts were science fiction films or television programs. Thus, although science fiction criticism now features ever-increasing attentiveness to its media incarnations, the contributions suggest that improving dialogue between the sciences and the humanities remains one function of science fiction that is still mostly performed by science fiction literature; in contrast, films and television programs, seeking to appeal to mass audiences, in general, apparently, display little commitment to this goal.

Third, one might imagine that a topic of this kind would most privilege the writers of hard science fiction who most conspicuously display their knowledge of, and interest in, scientific matters. But the critics in this volume display no such preference, analyzing both writers known for their scientific acumen like Wells, Benford, and Hendrix and writers like DeLillo, Dick, and Samuel R. Delany who have no scientific credentials. This would indicate that works in the genre of science fiction can serve to bridge the gap between the two cultures even if their authors lack explicit connections to, or a strong interest in, both of the factions.

I will conclude this introduction, for the first time in my tenure as an Eaton Conference volume co-editor, on a more personal note. All but three of the essays in this volume were originally presented at the Twentieth J. Lloyd Eaton Conference on Science Fiction and Fantasy Literature (held on the campus of the University of California, Riverside, in January 1999). Since it is probably the last Eaton volume that I will co-edit, I deemed it appropriate to append to this volume my own tribute to the Eaton Conferences. It is relevant to the theme of this volume because it documents, among other things, how the Eaton Conferences themselves consistently functioned as a bridge between the two cultures, as both scientists and literary scholars gathered to discuss texts and issues of common interest. This would interestingly suggest that science fiction criticism such as that found in this volume, along with science fiction literature, may itself be helping to resolve the ruinous division between cultures that C. P. Snow so fervently decried fifty years ago.

Notes

1. C. P. Snow, "The Two Cultures," *The Two Cultures*, by Snow, introduction by Stefan Collini (Cambridge, UK: Cambridge University Press, 1993), 9–10.

2. Hugo Gernsback, "Science Fiction Week," *Science Wonder Stories*, 1 (May 1930), 1061.

3. John W. Campbell, Jr., "Introduction," *Prologue to Analog*, edited by Campbell (Garden City, NY: Doubleday, 1962), 9–16.

4. Brian W. Aldiss, "Introduction," *Penguin Science Fiction*, edited by Aldiss (Hammondsworth, UK: Penguin, 1961), 10.

5. Ursula K. Le Guin, "Introduction," *The Left Hand of Darkness*, by Le Guin (New York: Ace, 1976), [xvi].

I. OVERVIEWS: SCIENCE FICTION IN THE CONTEXT OF TWO CULTURES

1. Science Fiction and the Two Cultures: Reflections after the Snow-Leavis Controversy

Carl Freedman

More than four decades after C. P. Snow's famous (or notorious) Rede Lecture on "the two cultures," the bitter dispute that it provoked between him and F. R. Leavis retains considerable currency.[1] And this is true despite the fact that the Snow-Leavis controversy, in and of itself, is far from one of the most distinguished moments in the history of intellectual debate. Indeed, the dispute — marred by much shallow glibness on Snow's part and by much unargued vituperation on Leavis's — looks shabby when set beside the most obviously pertinent term of comparison: namely, the Victorian debate about education between T. H. Huxley and Matthew Arnold, who might well be considered the intellectual grandfathers, respectively, of Snow and Leavis.[2] It is not just that Huxley and Arnold respect one another in a way that Snow and Leavis clearly do not. It is also that, as Huxley argues for an enhanced role for science in education, and as Arnold defends the traditional priority of the literary humanities, each is often at his strongest when affirming what the other does not profoundly deny; for each was able to see a good deal of sense in the other's position. Arnold, after all, was no enemy to science, about which he seems to have been better informed than most literary people of his day or later (emphatically including Leavis, whose ignorance of science appears to have been practically total); while Huxley, so far from being philistine or anti-literary, was (like Ruskin, like Newman, like Arnold himself) one of the major contributors to what still looks like the most artistically golden age in the history of English nonfictional

This essay first appeared in Extrapolation *42:3 (Fall 2001): 207–217. Reprinted with permission of the Kent State University Press.*

prose. It is a good bet that Huxley's writing will continue to be read with pleasure when Snow's novels are even more forgotten than they already are.

But my point is not simply that Huxley and Arnold are greater figures than Snow and Leavis — a plausible though perhaps not irresistible contention. If Huxley and Arnold are able genuinely to speak to each other's concerns — rather than merely talking past one another and posing for public effect, as Snow and Leavis so often do — the explanation is also to be found in their very different historical situations. Though intellectual specialization was certainly well advanced in many ways during the Victorian era, there was nonetheless still some life in the old humanistic notion that an educated person was one with interest in and knowledge of *all* branches of learning. Furthermore, specialization was and had been proceeding in a fairly *gradual* way. The intellectual climate in which Huxley and Arnold moved was more specialized than that which had prevailed a century earlier — when Samuel Johnson conducted serious chemical experiments in his home, and when Erasmus Darwin published botanical speculations in heroic couplets -but the difference was probably not felt as an actual break in continuity. Though Huxley and Arnold were aware of increased intellectual diversification, it seems likely that they were able to think of themselves and of each other not only as advocates of particular kinds of knowledge but also as *generally* educated men. In Snow's language, they occupied the same culture, however determined they may have been to establish different positions within it.

Between the era of Huxley and Arnold and that of Snow and Leavis lie at least two intellectual revolutions that are strictly incomparable to anything that had taken place in the century or two previous: twentieth-century physics and literary modernism. Wishing to characterize his "two cultures," Snow is fond of contrasting the personality of Lord Rutherford with that of his contemporary T. S. Eliot: the buoyant secular optimism of the one, as against the thin-blooded irrationalist gloom of the other.[3] The comparison is fair enough as far as it goes; but it is not the only or most interesting conclusion that the collocation of those two names suggests. For Rutherford and Eliot were, of course, key figures in the radical reconfigurations of their respective fields. The discoverer of the atomic structure and the author of *The Waste Land* (1922) were engaged (perhaps without quite realizing it immediately) in enterprises that would very soon make much of modern science and modern literature decreasingly accessible to people of general education: which is another way of saying that they were destroying general education itself in the sense of rendering it forever obsolete. This is the situation that Snow and Leavis inherit and with which they struggle. Snow makes only a dubiously rigorous argument for the existence of "two cultures"; yet the blank incomprehension with which he and Leavis often regard one another is certainly evidence that *some* sort of disjunction and dysfunction has taken place. But their situation is our own too. This, indeed, is the reason that, for all its faults, the Snow-Leavis dispute remains fascinating. However inadequately they may engage the problem of the "two cultures," they do engage it; and the problem is one that we are still unsuccessfully grappling with today.

Though Snow has most often been criticized for an imperfect understanding of literature and literary culture, his notion of a scientific culture is also far from unassailable. An excellent example is provided by the most famous point in his Rede Lecture: the contention that the ability to describe the second law of thermodynamics is the equivalent of having read a work of William Shakespeare's (14–15). What can this mean? Shakespeare is presumably to be taken as the summit of literary excellence, and everyone who values literature at all must indeed agree that reading Shakespeare can develop the mind in desirable ways (though there is no consensus among literary critics as to what, exactly, those ways are). It seems a curious reduction of science to suggest that its nearest equivalent to reading the greatest literature is, in effect, the ability to answer a simple examination question. Is such positivistic knowledgeableness really what binds scientists into a "culture"? Leavis, in his Richmond Lecture, hotly proclaims the very idea of a scientific equivalent to Shakespeare to be nonsense — "[E]quations between orders so disparate are meaningless" (61) — and this is perhaps the most fully rigorous statement on the matter. Yet, even without going quite so far as that, one can still object to Snow's glib vulgarity. The ability to think logically; the ability to draw conclusions supported by a specific body of evidence; appreciation of the epistemological distinction between the anecdote and the controlled experiment; perhaps the ability to think in mathematical symbolism as well as in words — if, as Snow rightly insists, a scientific training cultivates the mind as positively as a literary one does, then surely it is capacities of this sort, and not mere gobbets of information, that, on the scientific side, are at least roughly comparable to the cultivation achieved by reading Shakespeare. How many dilettantes under Snow's influence have memorized the second law of thermodynamics with the conviction of being henceforth scientifically literate?[4]

But the more serious problems with Snow's exposition of "the two cultures" do indeed concern his understanding of literature and what he calls the literary culture (or "the traditional culture," as he also terms it). The basic argument of the Rede lecture, we must recall, is not only that literary people tend to be ignorant of thermodynamics and the other glories of science. He also indicts the literary culture for being instinctively hostile to science and technology, hostile even to democracy itself and especially to rational social planning, and at times not far from fascistic irrationalism; and he further maintains that the literary culture tends to be politically hegemonic and so prevents the scientists and engineers from achieving the scientific social planning that England and the world so desperately need.

It is hard to know where to begin disentangling the confusions here. The notion that literary intellectuals run the world, or even England, is bizarre. One suspects some historic class resentment to be at work here. The lower-middle-class Snow rose from provincial obscurity to the metropolitan elite by scientific and, much more, by administrative aptitude; and he would have had every right to be scornful of the old Tory notion that well-born gentlemen who had studied classics at public school and at Oxford were those naturally best fitted to administer Britain and its dominions. But, by 1959, the dominance of Oxford Greats was even more of a dead horse than the British Empire to which it had been so closely linked. And Snow, indeed, never even mentions Greek and Latin in his denunciations of the literati; his real target is literary modernism, which he takes to be most notably represented by W. B. Yeats, Eliot, Ezra Pound, and Wyndham Lewis.

This move raises a whole new crop of confusions. In the first place, about the highest earthly reward for which a knowledge of modernist literature has ever qualified anyone is tenure in an English Department in California. The idea that literary intellectuals with heads full of Yeats's *The Tower* (1928) and Pound's *The Cantos* (1954) are regularly obstructing technocrats from eliminating hunger and disease is just ludicrous. Yet even more serious, in some ways, is Snow's almost total failure to understand modernism itself. His list of representative authors, with the persistent inclusion of so minor a figure as Lewis ("brutal and boring," as Leavis called him [53]), is of course tendentiously selective. Against the arch-conservatism of Yeats, the theocratic royalism of Eliot, and the fascist anti–Semitism of Pound, one might set the secular democratic humanism of James Joyce; the radical Liberalism of C. M. Forster and the feminism of Virginia Woolf; the left-wing Celtic nationalisms of Sean O'Casey and Hugh MacDiarmid; the Marxism of the young W. H. Auden and even the democratic centrism of the later Auden; the profound anti-fascism of Samuel Beckett; and, of course, much else. But Snow's ignorant hostility to modernism is intensive as well as extensive. In particular, he seems unable to see any cognitive value in literature beyond its most overt and "official" ideologies. It is symptomatic, for instance, that, in admitting that there is perhaps something to be said for Yeats despite his reactionary politics, Snow takes his evidence not from Yeats's poetry but from unnamed "friends whose judgment I trust," who certify Yeats to have been "a man of singular magnanimity of character" (8). This is to reduce literary study to gossip. Actually to *read* the poems of Yeats (whom MacDiarmid, incidentally, considered a friend and comrade) is to be aware that, however unfortunate and wrong-headed his extreme conservatism may have been, it was partially motivated by a genuine sympathy for the Irish poor, by a sensitive revulsion from the cultural ravages caused by capitalist property relations, and by an entirely proper contempt for the philistine vulgarity of Ireland's Catholic middle class. Indeed, philistine vulgarity and the cultural ravages of capitalism in general are problems that Yeats ponders with considerable subtlety, depth, and force — and that Snow himself almost entirely ignores.

It may well be, and has been, felt that Snow's attitude toward modernism — that is, toward most of the most important literature produced in Snow's language during Snow's lifetime — amounts to a hostility toward literature itself. There is some truth to this, though the whole truth, as I will argue shortly, is a little more complex. First, however, it is time to consider Leavis not merely as Snow's antagonist but as a major thinker of remarkable ignorances himself.

The most serious general charge to be leveled against Leavis is not his breach of good manners. It is simply that, although he often, despite his shrill tone, succeeds in exposing Snow's shortcomings, he never really contributes anything positive of his own. He himself repeatedly insists just the opposite — "I *have* a positive theme, and ... it and my attitude are truly positive" (20), he writes rather plaintively — but, upon examination, the "positive" values of his Richmond Lecture and its successor pieces turn out to be only the usual unargued clichés of late–Leavisite vitalism: especially "life" and D. H. Lawrence, two categories that become increasingly interchangeable for Leavis.[5] In particular, he has nothing of conceptual substance to say about the place of science in modern schooling or about the gulf that Snow points out between scientific and literary education. Sometimes Leavis's lack of scientific knowledge on even the most elementary level is virtually comical. For example, in attempting to refute any notion that he himself is "Luddite" or anti-scientific, he repeatedly expresses his whole-hearted admiration for one Daniel Doyce. And who is Daniel Doyce? Not an actual scientist at all, but a character in Dickens's *Little Dorrit* (1855–1857), where he is an inventor whose work is frustrated by the inanities of government bureaucracy. Leavis is right enough to note that Dickens portrays Doyce as an admirably creative and disinterested applied scientist, and thus that Dickens himself can hardly be considered an intellectual Luddite (a charge, however, that Snow, despite Leavis's insinuations on the matter, never actually makes). But the crucial point here is not only that Leavis is, evidently, unable to think of a real-world scientist whose creativity he admires; it is also that the intellectual horizons of *Little Dorrit* (arguably Dickens's greatest novel, as Leavis would probably agree) are so alienated from the scientific imagination that Dickens is quite unable to represent anything of Doyce's work. We are *told* that Doyce is a great inventor but never given any concrete sense of his inventing. Though Dickens has perhaps the largest representational range of any English writer after Shakespeare, it is not large enough to include the science and applied science that were such vital social forces in Dickens's own time and place. The character of Doyce, then, far from proving anything for Leavis's side, really amounts to an early or anticipatory instance of the disjunction between "the two cultures" that Snow notices: and this *despite* Dickens's abstractly positive attitude toward scientific inventing.

It might be objected, though, that Leavis, unlike Snow, never claims to speak with authority on both science and literature and that it is strictly as a literary critic that he ought to be judged. But here his blanknesses and evasions are perhaps even more disturbing. The curious windiness of the Richmond Lecture and its sequels largely results from the fact that a truly literary-critical response to Snow would foreground a principled defense of the modernism that Snow so distorts and undervalues: and yet this is exactly what Leavis does not do. He is, indeed, disabled from doing so by his general critical principles. Though Leavis is not flatly anti-modernist in Snow's fashion — he ardently admires Eliot and, of course, Lawrence — the great bulk of modernism does indeed lie outside Leavis's warmest sympathies. He recognizes writers like Yeats, Joyce, Pound, Marcel Proust, Franz Kafka, Bertolt Brecht, and Beckett either grudgingly or not at all, while, on the other hand, the essential Leavis canon (insofar as nineteenth- and twentieth-century literature is concerned) is occupied by such very different authors as Jane Austen, George Eliot, Nathaniel Hawthorne, Mark Twain, Dickens, Henry James, Lawrence at his most realistic and least modernist (hence Leavis's exaltation of *Women in Love* [1920] and his dismissal of *The Plumed Serpent* [1926] and *Lady Chatterley's Lover* [1928]), and, above all, the Leo Tolstoy of *Anna Karenina* (1875–1877). Indeed, if one were to select a single text, composed after the seventeenth century, that best exemplifies what Leavis values in literature, it would, almost certainly, be Tolstoy's greatest novel.[6]

Yet here we seem to hit on a perhaps unexpected point of agreement between Snow and Leavis: for scattered remarks in Snow's writings indicate that for him, too, Tolstoy represents the apex of modern literature. Though few would wish to dispute this shared enthusiasm for Tolstoy — probably the greatest of all literary realists — it provides a specific clue to a much larger underlying similarity between the otherwise so violently contrasting intellectual personalities of Snow and Leavis: namely, that, as their respective failures adequately to engage literary modernism may tend to imply, for both Snow and Leavis it is realistic prose fiction of the type that reached its most powerful expression in the nineteenth century that constitutes not only the greatest achievement in post–Renaissance letters, but, to a considerable degree, the essential model for what all modern literature ought to be. Leavis's bias toward realism has, indeed, been somewhat camouflaged by his early and influential role as a critical advocate for Eliot and Lawrence, a role that made him appear to be at least a fellow-traveler of the modernist revolution. Yet, as we have seen, Leavis's taste for modernism was always tentative and highly selective, and never really triumphed over his sense that realistic works like George Eliot's *Middlemarch* (1874), *Little Dorrit, Anna Karenina,* Henry James's *The Portrait of a Lady* (1908), Mark Twain's *Huckleberry Finn* (1884), and *Women in Love* provided the most reliable literary touchstones from the middle nineteenth century onwards. As for Snow, his critical insistence on the primacy of realism was considerably more blatant — in some circles, indeed, Snow's anti-modernist and pro-realist stance become almost scandalous during his career as a London book reviewer — but is most memorably recorded in his own fiction, the immense *Strangers and Brothers* cycle of novels. Leavis, I think, was perfectly right to be astounded at the inflated conventional reputation that this work once enjoyed, and to insist on the almost unreadable flatness of Snow's characters and situations; indeed, *Strangers and Brothers* provides a textbook Lukácsian example of the degeneration of high realism into a depthless and lifeless naturalism. What Leavis chose not to remark, however, was that Snow's novels are failed attempts to write precisely the *kind* of literature that he himself most approved. Almost perfectly antipathetic to one another, Snow and Leavis seem incapable of acknowledging their largest area of agreement: the notion that, whether literature is valued too little (as arguably for Snow) or too exclusively (as arguably for Leavis), and whether one is thinking of the brilliance of *Anna Karenina* or the banality of *Strangers and Brothers*, realistic prose fiction is the literature that matters.

How is the pro-realist ideology of Snow and Leavis connected to the inadequacy with which they argue the problem of the "two cultures"? I will not here pursue what nonetheless seems to me an intriguing fact: that, at least in English and the other Western European languages (for the situation may be different in Russian), the major realistic novelists seem seldom to have taken the kind of interest in science displayed by great poets from Virgil and Lucretius, through Dante and John Milton, to Alfred Lord Tennyson and Auden. Instead, I will pursue a possibly more straightforward contention: that Snow's and Leavis's massive bias towards realism helped to blind them to the genre — science fiction — that could have shed some real light on their shared problem. Though Leavis's neglect of science fiction is entirely unsurprising — for in addition to his preference for realism one must recall his contempt for nearly all twentieth-century writing either American or putatively "popular" in provenance — it is more puzzling that Snow, the apostle of scientific culture and the follower of H. G. Wells, should have failed to notice, for example, the significance of the series of pioneering science fiction novels that Wells began in 1895 with *The Time Machine*. Despite his elaborate contempt for England's traditional literary culture, in his failure to appreciate science fiction Snow concurs with one of that culture's most disabling prejudices.

To be sure, we should not exaggerate the maturity of the science fiction tradition with regard either to literary or to scientific culture, especially vis-à-vis the defining revolutions of modernist literature and modern physics. Much science fiction, even by authors with some professional scientific training, sets fairly low standards of scientific rigor, while the number of science fiction novelists who have managed to write as though Joyce never wrote is downright embarrassing: A novel like Gregory Benford's *Timescape* (1980), which intervenes in cutting-edge physical speculation, is an exceptional masterpiece, as is Samuel Delany's *Dhalgren* (1975), one of the major achievements of the post–Joycean avant-garde. Yet not only is it as fair to let Benford and Delany represent twentieth-century science fiction as it is to let George Eliot and Tolstoy represent nineteenth-century realism, but, furthermore, *all* genuine science fiction, even when far below the level of its highest masterworks, must at least attempt to illuminate the issues raised by the concept of the "two cultures." After all, the fundamental problem announced by Snow is, in one sense, the response on the level of human feeling and perception to the changes, intellectual and practical, wrought by the development of science: and such is the concern too of nearly every science-fictional text. Indeed, one reliable test of whether a particular text is only weakly science-fictional is precisely whether it fails to establish any genuine connections between the "two cultures": as witness the innumerable dreary instances in which the reader is transported to a remote galaxy or a distant century only to witness an adventure story or a love story that might, in all essentials, have equally well (or better) been staged in the mundane here-and-now.

By contrast, strongly science-fictional works — i.e., those by which the genre is to be judged — interrogate the limits of the human in ways inaccessible (or less efficiently accessible) in the absence of scientifically based estrangement. I do not mean that scientific prediction or even speculation is the central aim of science fiction. On the contrary, the estrangements of the genre ultimately function to demystify our empirical here-and-now, and the great Ballardian maxim — that the future which matters in science fiction is never more than five minutes away — thus holds.[7] But such demystification, in strong science fiction, depends upon estrangements that in some way take the epistemological challenges of science seriously. The science in science fiction need not necessarily be empirically correct, and it may even incorporate a few discrete elements (like travel into the past) that scientists and scientifically oriented philosophers generally regard as impossible. But the general conceptual framework of science fiction is defined by the scientific project of producing rational, cognitive knowledge of the universe. And, in the finest works of scientific fiction, the disposition of plot, character, and theme are inextricably bound up with specific instances of scientific cognition, or, at least, the literary effect of scientific cognition. Thus, for example, the environmentalist insights of *Timescape* could hardly have been enforced so powerfully in the absence of the text's speculations on the nature of time enabled by quantum physics. Or, again, the demystifications of war in Joe Haldeman's *The Forever War* (1974), or of imperialism in Ursula K. Le Guin's *The Word for World Is Forest* (1972), or of species being itself in Octavia Butler's *Xenogenesis* trilogy (1987–1989), crucially depend upon possibilities of (respectively) time travel, space travel, and genetic engineering that are strictly unthinkable below a certain level of scientific understanding. Furthermore, science fiction can remind us — as Arnold, indeed, reminded Huxley — that the concept of science need not be always confined to the narrow English sense of the physical sciences but can also encompass everything suggested by the German word *Wissenschaft*: *Dhalgren* makes clear that urban sociology is a science, and Philip K. Dick's *The Man in the High Castle* (1962) and Joanna Russ's *The Two of Them* (1978) do much the same for political historiography and for gender studies, respectively. Indeed, one might go so far as to maintain that these texts by Delany, Dick, and Russ amount to substantial *contributions* to those fields of learning as well.

Adequately to display what might be termed the "bi-cultural" nature of science fiction would be fully to investigate the cognitive resources of the genre; and this would require a book — which, in fact, I have already written.[8] In conclusion here, I will only examine in a bit more detail two works less well-known than any mentioned above, for they are by an author who has only very recently emerged as one of our more interesting science fiction writers: Howard V. Hendrix's *Lightpaths* (1997) and *Standing Wave* (1998). The largest significance of these texts (each of which is a free-standing story but which together also constitute two-thirds of a trilogy in progress) is found, I think, in the recent history of the utopian novel. As is widely appreciated, such major works of the 1970s as Russ's *The Female Man* (1975), Le Guin's *The Dispossessed* (1974), Marge Piercy's *Woman on the Edge of Time* (1976), and Delany's *Triton* (1976; later retitled *Trouble on Triton*) represent the successful revival of the authentic utopia after decades of occlusion by the kind of negative utopia associated with the names of Yevgeny Zamyatin, (Aldous) Huxley, and George Orwell — a revival, however, that was itself largely occluded in the following decade, mainly by cyberpunk but also by the comeback of the more conventional negative utopia typified by Margaret Atwood's *The Handmaid's Tale* (1985) — and despite such brave exceptions as Delany's *Stars in My Pocket Like Grains of Sand* (1984). Hendrix, then, can be understood (along with more veteran authors like Piercy herself in *He, She and It*,

[1991] and Kim Stanley Robinson in the Mars trilogy [1993–1997]) as one of the writers who, in the 1990s, revived the utopian revival and insisted again on the indispensability of utopian speculation.

Lightpaths is set in an orbital complex that is authentically utopian, its society organized according to principles that, in view of the book's debt to *The Dispossessed*, might be called neo-Odonian. *Standing Wave*, a more wide-ranging if less intense and tightly organized novel, maintains a focus on this orbiting utopia (known as HOME, for High Orbital Manufacturing Enterprise) while also including views of other places, including some fascinating glimpses of a negative utopia based mainly on today's Christian Right. Ultimately, Hendrix's socio-political-economic speculations shade into metaphysical ones, as a post–Stapledonian materialist spirituality becomes the most encompassing world-view of the text. The point to be stressed here, however, is that both the politics and the metaphysics of these novels are concretized through a dynamic melding of the humanistic and the technical. In the context of utopia and of transcendence, Hendrix closely and "realistically" draws characters involved in ambiguous family relations, professional routine, resentful personal manipulation, sexual love, and much else. We see, for instance, how the personal ambivalence of a mother-son pair can be overdetermined, even in a utopia, by relations of bureaucracy. We see how the most violently bigoted forms of sub-fascist irrationalism may be closely linked to wholly understandable family tragedy. We glimpse the filiations between vegetarianism and certain varieties of sexual attraction, and between professional ambition and mind-altering drugs. Consistently, the light shone on such problems of what Leavis would call the human world is directly dependent on estrangements enabled by the novel's sophisticated handling of natural sciences from cosmology to botany, of human sciences like anthropology and political economy, and, above all (and in a way that owes much to William Gibson while finally, I think, going beyond him), of information science — a branch of learning that itself deconstructs the natural/human binary and so challenges any dichotomy of "two cultures." I end having hardly begun to do justice to Hendrix's work. But I think it incontestable that these novels, as works of genuine science fiction, provide both the kind of close human observation demanded by Leavis (though in a form beyond Leavis's comprehension) *and* the deeply progressive scientific and technological understanding that Snow finds so alien to the modern literary imagination.

Notes

1. C. P. Snow, *The Two Cultures* (Cambridge, UK: Cambridge University Press, 1993), and F. R. Leavis, *Nor Shall My Sword: Discourses on Pluralism, Compassion and Social Hope* (New York: Harper and Row, 1972). The former contains Snow's original Rede Lec-

ture of 1959 and his essay of four years later, "The Two Cultures: A Second Look." The latter contains "Two Cultures? The Significance of Lord Snow," Leavis's Richmond Lecture of 1962 in which he delivered his first counterblast to Snow, plus five subsequent addresses and an introductory overview of the matter as Leavis saw it. Unless otherwise noted, later parenthetical page references to Snow and Leavis are to these editions.

2. The key texts in the Huxley-Arnold debate are "Science and Culture," a lecture that Huxley gave in 1880 at the opening of Mason College, Birmingham (an institution established specifically to provide scientific training), and "Literature and Science," the Rede Lecture (!) that Arnold gave two years later in reply. I have designated Huxley and Arnold the intellectual grandfathers rather than fathers of Snow and Leavis, respectively, and it does seem possible to identify the pertinent individuals of the intervening generation. On one side, it is clearly H. G. Wells, who was Huxley's student and, much later, something of a mentor and hero to the young Snow. On the other side, the lines of descent are not quite so obvious; but Leslie Stephen, a Cambridge critic much admired by Leavis (and, incidentally, the father of Virginia Woolf), conveniently marks the point in English criticism between Arnold and Leavis.

3. *The Two Cultures*, 4–5; see also C. P. Snow, *Variety of Men* (Scribner's, 1966), 4.

4. In "The Two Cultures: A Second Look," Snow does somewhat qualify the shallow positivism of his use of the second law (72). Still, Leavis (46–47) goes so far as to maintain that, on the evidence of his novels and his Rede Lecture, Snow's mind has enjoyed no real discipline either scientific or otherwise, and that science exists for him merely as a matter of external reference without psychological depth. Doubtless this, like so much in Leavis's assaults on Snow, is too harsh. Yet it may be recalled that, though Snow was professionally trained as a scientist, and though (as he later delighted to recall) he participated in the glory days of the Cavendish Laboratory under Rutherford during the 1920s and 1930s, he never became a scientist of real distinction; and he had abandoned scientific research altogether for more than two decades by the time of the Rede Lecture. Of course, he remained a vigorous propagandist for science and for what he took to be the scientific culture; but working scientists have by no means always felt well represented by Snow.

5. See George Steiner, *Language and Silence* (Atheneum, 1970), 234: "What had been advertised as a responsible examination of the concept of 'the two cultures' dissolved -as so much else in Leavis's recent work has done — into a ceremonial dance before the dark god, D. H. Lawrence."

6. For instance: "*Anna Karenina* one of the great European novels?— it is, surely, *the* European novel. The completeness with which Tolstoy, with his genius, was a Russian of his time made him an incomparably representative European, and made the book into which his whole experience, his most comprehensive 'relatedness,' went what it is for us: the great novel of modern — of our — civilization" (F. R. Leavis, *Anna Karenina and Other Essays* [Simon and Schuster, 1969], 32).

7. J. G. Ballard has been reported as saying, "The future in my work has never been more than five minutes away"— a remark that seems to me such a brilliant insight not only into Ballard's own fiction but into science fiction as a whole that I have generalized it into the "maxim" above. I have been unable to determine the original location of the quoted comment.

8. The advertisement is for Carl Freedman, *Critical Theory and Science Fiction* (Hanover, CT: Wesleyan University Press, 2000).

2. Science Fiction, Mediating Agent between C.P. Snow's Two Cultures: A Historical Interpretation

Bradford Lyau

There is a supermarket in Cambridge, Massachusetts, as the familiar academic joke goes, that has an express checkout lane. Above it is a sign that reads, "Six Articles or Less Only." Late one night a student shows up in the lane with a shopping cart containing more than ten items. The exasperated cashier looks up at the student and remarks, "Either you must be from M.I.T. and can't read or from Harvard and can't count!"

This in a nutshell presents the problem in post–World War II education as described by C. P. Snow.[1] To him the sciences and humanities have become two mutually exclusive fields — hence two cultures. He views Western scholars as being so specialized in their formal training that one discipline of scholars has little or no idea what another is doing. What is not as well known, however, is the second part of his observation, which should be viewed with equal importance. Snow saw this gap between the sciences and humanities as being much more than bad education policy. He saw this chasm of knowledge as having catastrophic political, economic, and social consequences.

Describing the rich industrialized countries getting wealthier at the expense of the non-industrialized poor ones, the international community must get together and exploit the best uses of science and technology to feed the hungry, clothe the naked, shelter the homeless, etc. For that to happen, those involved with public policy must be familiar with what is going on in the sciences and apply their latest developments to much needed social improvement. In democratic governments, then, this knowledge must also be passed on to the general population as well as to the government officials. So education in both the sciences and humanities is no longer just a good idea; it now becomes a prerequisite for global survival.

Bringing up Snow's two-part mid twentieth-century observation at the beginning of the twenty-first century hardly qualifies as an astounding revelation. Volumes been written on this subject. Much overlooked, however, have been the various responses contained in the literary branch of science fiction. A close look at this field reveals that many of its offerings on this matter belong to the central intellectual and cultural lines of Western thought and therefore should not be viewed as either tangential or trivial. This applies to both its treatment of Snow's two cultures and its examination of Snow's political and social ramifications.

This paper will attempt to identify important works by science fiction's major representative figures and examine their works in light of both Snow's two-pronged dilemma and the central intellectual trends of Western thought.

Snow's education problem is certainly not a new one. Ever since the eighteenth-century Enlightenment's attempts to come to terms with the Scientific Revolution of the previous century, many thinkers have wrestled with the problems of how society should integrate the traditional, or humanistic, knowledge with the new scientific fields. They also understood the emerging dilemma of a society stymied by the limitations originating from its own citizens' lack of understanding of those new fields of knowledge. Since these thinkers readily realized that knowledge — regardless of its shape and scope — means power, this issue becomes more than one of mere epistemological aesthetics.

These thinkers anticipated that the very structure of society would depend on how the knowledge emerging from the new sciences was to be applied. So the aim of finding common ground where the two sides can meet had to be accompanied with the aim of finding or devising a political structure that would best be suited to exploit the new fields of science and technology.

A case in point of the latter goal is the concept of enlightened despotism. At first glance this phrase looks to be a contradiction in terms, for how can the new and enlightened concepts of rational constitutional authority deal with the demands for supra-constitutional powers that would-be despots claim they need? Leonard Krieger, in his provocative work *An Essay on the Theory of Enlightened Despotism*, argues that the political thinkers of the eighteenth century were well aware of this paradox, but remained proponents of the concept nonetheless.

They, according to Krieger, should not be condemned out of hand as dishonest charlatans who were willing to accommodate their ideas to those in power. Considering the historical period in which these thinkers lived, they had to contend with an ultra-hierarchical society where the noble elite; the small, but rising bourgeoisie; and the vast multitudes of the illiterate masses rarely came into contact with each other and hence could not communicate with each other across class lines. More particularly, it was these particular thinkers who were more familiar with the class of literate, but unlettered reading public than with the elitist (in social origins and not necessarily in political convictions) constitutional liberals, whom today we would usually identify and canonize as the great thinkers, or *philosophes*, of the Enlightenment. So it can be said that the thinkers of enlightened despotism became the middle agents for all these disparate groups. As Krieger puts it:

> In the sociology of culture, the proponents of enlightened despotism may indeed be accorded a mediatory role between the collective mentality of the mass and the high culture of the philosophes.[2]

Krieger concludes his essay with the warning that enlightened despotism is indeed still with us. The notion just takes on different appearances. Since the Eighteenth Century various rulers have claimed superior enlightenment (regardless of the ideological base or public policy) and therefore have argued the need for more power in order to increase their promised beneficence to the people. And the possibility for this type of leadership remains a very real one today.

Given that today's science and technology are developing at such a rate that even scientists from various specialties have problems understanding each other, the temptation becomes even greater for a "savior" to rescue the people from this confusion. However, the claims to power of these would-be messiahs still possess the same paradoxical relationship of legitimacy and power that faced their counterparts of two centuries ago. As Krieger admonishes at the end of his essay, "Let the voter beware" (91).

Like Snow, Krieger has some practical reasons and advice to give along with his analysis of intellectual middle agents. The same can be said for that branch of literature that is also identified by a phrase that seems to be a contradiction in terms: science fiction.

Science fiction has provided an entry point for millions of people to appreciate the world of science and to ponder upon both the potentialities and the dangers that advanced developments could bring about. Along with being the mediator between the sciences and humanities, science fiction also acts as a warning beacon against what may happen if either field of human endeavor is wrongfully applied. Furthermore, as with the theory of enlightened despotism, science fiction's thematic roots as mediator between the two cultures can also be traced back to the eighteenth-century Enlightenment. Unlike the theory, however, science fiction lays no claims to a privileged knowledge for solving the world's ills. There may be utopian projections by some writers, but this field as a whole is characterized by speculations and extrapolations — and not prescriptions.

Of course, there is more than just a methodological parallel that this paper shares with Krieger's work, for warnings of future societies gone wrong have provided science fiction with one of its major and most recognizable themes. Furthermore, the future societies in question oftentimes take on a form of enlightened despotism. And so it can be said that, in response to Snow's problem of the two cultures and its political implications, science fiction serves as both mediator and watchdog.

Three categories of response to the Snow's two cultures can be detected. Their intellectual roots can be traced back to the three major intellectual expressions of the Enlightenment period itself.[3] Science fiction possesses significant representatives in each.

The first consists of those thinkers who were optimistic, believing that there exist universal laws of human society and culture that can be found to operate in the same way as scientific laws govern the behavior of objects in the natural world. This is probably the most familiar characteristic that most people have of the Enlightenment. Baron de Montesquieu, Anne-Robert-Jacques Turgot, and Marquis de Condorcet best characterize this group. H. G. Wells is science fiction's most noted example of this outlook.

The second category of response comprises of those products of Dave Hume's skepticism and the Scottish Enlightenment. Here Adam Smith and Edward Gibbon typify the view that the search for and adherence to universal social laws are too constricting and actually unverifiable for productive analysis. Wide-reaching conclusions can still be made, but absolute ones are impossible. A version of this approach made its way to the American colonists, who added a more non-systematic approach to this philosophy and a more practical emphasis due to their frontier experiences. Robert A. Heinlein can be used as the most significant representative of this group.

Of course characterizing the impact of the Enlightenment in America is problematic as the first category of response also had a very strong presence. The division among American thinkers between the Anglophiles and the Francophiles is well known. However, due to America's more pragmatic view of reality and its sometimes disdain for comprehensive theoretical structures, elements of the Scottish Enlightenment could be viewed as the more dominant mode in America — especially in light of its frontier tradition stressing pragmatic observations and solutions.

Finally, the third category centers on the ideas of Jean-Jacques Rousseau. His critique of his contemporaries' ideas focuses on his insistence on the rediscovery of humanity's true nature, which has been obscured and almost destroyed by a civilization that has lost its original moorings. For him rational thinking is a corruption of humanity's way of explaining the world. Only after finding its true nature could humanity go forward. Ursula K. Le Guin has produced perhaps the best example of this category.

H. G. Wells could be considered a direct descendant of those optimistic proponents of finding universal laws for governing society. Though he is a born and bred Englishman and brought up in the land heavily influenced by the Scottish Enlightenment, he was shaped more by the intellectual trends of the late nineteenth century that found their inspirations from the mid-century works of Karl Marx and Charles Darwin, which inspired all-encompassing systematic treatises of human reality. In this light, the work of Herbert Spencer (perhaps the most read sociological thinker among late–Victorian intellectuals) and especially the ideas of T. H. Huxley — under whom Wells actually studied — could be said to have a most profound impact on Wells and his promulgations for the search for universal laws.

Wells was not an instant believer in the optimistic view of better society through science and technology. In his earlier, more famous science-fiction novels he was not so sure about humanity's future. As displayed in his *The Time Machine* (1895), the laws of evolution meant the end of humanity — in other words, its extinction. After the publication of his *Anticipations* (1901) he became prophet of progress, explaining how the human race as a whole must take control of its own social evolution — which included the discovery of and mastery over the natural laws that govern the world around them and their proper application through technology.

Subsequently, both his fiction and non-fiction serve to emphasize his concerns about how to educate society to the new ways of science and technology. His warnings about how either the ignorance or misuse of new science could result in total catastrophe are often accompanied by his vision of great promises that await humanity if intelligent applications of science can take place.

Of these three writers, Wells is the only writer with a personal connection with C. P. Snow. Snow viewed Wells as one of his early major influences. When Snow became a scholar and writer in his own right, he reviewed Wells's books, joined him at various talks and presentations, and was considered by many as one of his supporters.[4] And like Wells he was scientifically trained, a novelist, and a public political figure.

Wells's non-fiction work is no less than encyclopedic in range. After World War I he published a trio of tomes, *The Outline of History* (1920), *The Science of Life* (1929), and *The Work, Wealth, and Happiness of Mankind* (1931), in which he attempted to explain the whole range of human existence in light of the new scientific age. In 1938 his *World Brain* called for no less than a new comprehensive and interdisciplinary approach to the organization of human knowledge. In this last volume, he even proposed a field of study that would comprise a total integration of the physical sciences and which he labeled "environmental sciences."

If humanity does not learn to educate itself properly, its experiences of terror from World War I will become merely a foreshadowing of even worse disasters as long as the new powers derived from the sciences remain in the hands of those who understand nothing about them. A basic reorganization of knowledge and the teaching of it must be developed. As he wrote in *Outline of History*, "Human history becomes more and more a race between education and catastrophe."[5]

These notions of knowledge certainly do permeate his fiction, as do his speculations on the required structure of society that should organize and apply new human knowledge. The latter especially dominate a majority of his post–1900 science fiction. Works such as *The Shape of Things to Come* (1933) clearly place him in the tradition of Turgot and Condorcet as exhortations for a society governed by scientific principles and administered by enlightened technocrats. However Wells insisted that his leaders be well versed in the arts as well.

This point is made quite clearly in his earlier *A Modern Utopia* (1905).[6] Here Wells divides the ruling elite of his utopia, called samurai, into two groups: The Poietic and the Kinetic. The former are the creative and intelligent people who reinvigorate society, thus preventing his utopia from reaching any final stage (which to Wells meant stagnation and corruption). The latter are the non-creative, yet still intelligent clear-thinking people on whom this society depends for proper administration. While the Kinetic run society, the Poietic experiment with ideas about society. It is this tension of cooperation between the Poietic and Kinetic that Wells saw as the mechanism that would prevent his modern utopia from becoming a technocratic nightmare (265–270).

The education of the Poietic must be as wide-ranging as possible. The founders of Wells's utopia made sure that every individual who displays poetic potentials be given "a full development in art, philosophy, invention, or discovery" (274–275). The work that these people would do could range in scope from the particular as "the art of Whistler or the science of a cytologist" to most comprehensive where "at last both artist and scientific inquirer merge in the universal reference of the true philosopher" (266). Finally, the utopian state would provide the proper support and incentives for universities to produce great discoveries in both the sciences and the arts. No promising person is to be neglected (276).

This combination of Poietic and Kinetic classes constitutes Wells's only check against the possibility of a technocratic dictatorial nightmare. During the latter part of his life, he rarely questions his vision of a government based on technocratic principles and governed by highly educated and trained elites. His warnings instead focus on how the power of science and technology is abused when in the hands of the wrong group of elites. Perhaps the most graphic examples are *The War in the Air* (1908), in which air power would only prolong wars and make them more devastating (this went against the common wisdom of the time) and *The World Set Free* (1914), in which Wells presents the first fictional account of atomic war and coins the term, "atomic bomb." The latter book, along with *A Modern Utopia*, also composes his earliest visions of the technocratic elites who know how to save humanity from itself.

Wells's future societies are basically elitist. The hierarchical society described in *A Modern Utopia* calls to mind Plato's *Republic* more than Thomas Jefferson's *Declaration of Independence*. His new governing elite does respond to Snow's crisis of bifurcated knowledge. But they could also be seen as falling under Krieger's category of reemerging enlightened despots.

The opposite can be said about Robert A. Heinlein. A libertarian by political conviction, Heinlein would see Wells's statist solutions as anathema to human progress and development. However, Heinlein does share with Wells the concern about the division between science and the humanities. In both his non-fiction and fiction Heinlein remains constant.

In "The Happy Days Ahead" (1980), Heinlein sharply criticizes the state of American public higher education in an article containing his opinions on the state of American society.[7] Like Wells, he comments on the lack of a general education available to students, pointing out how his father had a more well-rounded education in nineteenth-century "back-country" schools than he had; he views late twentieth-century schools as even worse (521). He, unlike Wells, does not attempt to set up a systematic regimen of organized subject matter.

Heinlein purposely avoids making complete philosophical generalizations in education. In fact, he even describes the field of philosophy itself as "Easy and lots of fun and absolutely guaranteed not to teach you anything.... In more than twenty-five centuries of effort *not one* basic problem of philosophy has *ever* been solved" (531, emphasis Heinlein's).

What he does offer is a method of how to accomplish this task: learn the three basic tools of understanding — history, languages, and mathematics. Mastering these fields will enable one to learn anything he or she wants to learn. All three must be learned. As he puts it, "But if you lack *any one* of them you are just another ignorant peasant with dung on your boots" (519, emphasis Heinlein's).

Heinlein's consequences of a failure to attain a proper education for society mirror that of Wells's, for Heinlein views the present dismal state of public education as one of the "increasingly pathological trends of our culture that show us headed down the chute of self-destruction" (519). In fact, he later views this dilemma as enough to cause all by itself the fall of American society (535).

This attitude is also prevalent in his fiction. A novel that is useful in this analysis is *Time Enough for Love* (1973).[8] Centering on Heinlein's Methuselah-like character, Lazarus Long, the novel follows Long's attempts to discover new experiences. Throughout the novel Long expounds on the need to know as much as one can. Do not specialize and always be open to new experiences. As Long reminds the reader in one of his aphorisms,

> A human should be able to change a diaper, plan an invasion, butcher a hog, conn a ship, design a building, write a sonnet, balance accounts, build a wall, set a bone, comfort the dying, take orders, give orders, pitch manure, program a computer, cook a tasty meal, fight efficiently, die gallantly. Specialization is for insects [265].

While describing the education of his children by his own family, which has settled on a newly discovered planet, Long states the case for learning as many disciplines as possible. Here he claims that one of his daughters who "can shape a comfortable and handsome saddle ... solve quadratic equations in her head ... spout page after page of William Shakespeare ... can't be called ignorant" (346). These apparently helter-skelter lists show Heinlein's approach to education is quite different from Wells's. The latter strove for a very systematic approach to education and knowledge in his fiction, the former much less so.

Note that Heinlein's view of knowledge does not mean that one cannot come up with any substantive conclusions. Like his forbearers of the Scottish Enlightenment, Heinlein does make far-reaching statements on what constitutes the best realistic alternative for the betterment of humanity's future. He definitely makes quite clear his views on the relationships between advancing knowledge and the individual, government, and society in general.

With his libertarian views no one would ever accuse Heinlein of espousing any form of enlightened despotism, or almost any other form of government claiming that more centralization is needed.

However, Heinlein still views an elite group of people as the vanguard of human progress. It is just that these people are not products of any centralized planning as Wells's samurai were. They may still be the ones who make the great advances in knowledge, but their knowledge should not necessarily translate into political power. Again, referring to one of Lazarus Long's aphorisms,

> Throughout history, poverty is the normal condition of man. Advances which permit this norm to be exceeded ... are the work of an extremely small minority,

frequently despised, often condemned.... Whenever this minority is kept from creating or ... is driven out of a society, the people then slip into abject poverty. This is known as "bad luck" [262].

As Wells desired to control the population under one government, Heinlein remains skeptical about such enterprises. Heinlein's elite should be left alone to be creative and not weighed down by any oppressive government or society. If not, then they should leave — even to another world. As his character Lazarus Long once put it, "When a place gets crowded enough to require ID's, social collapse is not far away. It is time to go elsewhere. The best thing about space travel is that it made it possible to go elsewhere" (262).

Of course, Heinlein is aware that science is a two-edged sword. It can also be used to suppress individual freedoms, as his novels "'If This Goes On —'" (1940), Between Planets (1951), and The Moon Is a Harsh Mistress (1966) will attest. In these novels it is an overbearing government that is the root of all political problems. In Time Enough for Love, however, he has no final solution outside of leaving and recreating somewhere else the American frontier experience. If Wells seems unwilling to examine the downside of his technocratic elite, Heinlein has no doubts about the possible threats of the misuse of science by any government. If the human race is to succeed here on Earth, then let those individuals who can innovate and progress so the rest of humanity can benefit.

Ursula K. Le Guin would disagree with both Wells and Heinlein about the need for a hierarchical society, whether centrist or anarchic. Like Snow, Wells, and Heinlein, she too has expressed in both her nonfiction and fiction her concern for education and its relation to political power.

In her Bryn Mawr Commencement Address delivered in 1986, Le Guin describes in no uncertain terms her ideas about education, the nature of knowledge, and both fields' relation to power.[9]

She divides knowledge into three groups or languages, as she labels them. The first is the "father tongue," the language of power. This is the reason why people go to college: to learn the language of power and then take their place in the hierarchy that is the patriarchic society that exists today. The written dialect of this tongue is the subject matter on which the colleges want their students to focus. Citing Isaac Newton, René Descartes, Immanuel Kant, Karl Marx, and others, Le Guin says that this is an excellent dialect, for this type of knowledge seeks objectivity.

However, she refuses to call this the sum total of rational thinking, as reason encompasses much more than the search for objectivity. Objective thought, for her, means separation: subject/object, mind/body, active/passive, dominant/deferential, Man/Nature, man/woman, etc. The application of this split has led to the emphasis on science and technology and also to the rise of the Industrial Revolution, which made the divisions between rich and poor, powerful and powerless even more extreme.

When the father tongue is dedicated to the service of justice or clarity or ideas, Le Guin calls it "noble and indispensably useful." However, when it claims to have a "privileged relationship with reality," then it becomes "dangerous and potentially destructive" (149).

There is an alternative: the second language or sphere of knowledge, what Le Guin calls the "mother tongue." As the father tongue separates, the mother tongue unites. The former focuses on communication, the latter relationships. The language of power talks of dividing, the other speaks of binding. The first talks in analytic and objective terms, the other expresses itself in subjective experiences.

This language also provides "the womb" for literature. But even this has been taken over by the patriarchal society that has removed women and their expressions from canon of approved literature. So even the arts are now male oriented. These are acknowledged by present society as the "High Arts" (153).

Le Guin later extends the meaning of literature and the arts to include the "low arts," usually what men do not want to do. These include how one lives his or her life in day-to-day activities, e.g., cooking, housekeeping, making clothes, etc. Art is now meant to encompass "living well, living with skill, grace, and energy" (154).

The mother tongue is what people learn first. They do so from their mothers. Only when the children slowly begin to leave home does their language start to change. However, this is a voice that must be heard, for if the father tongue is the language of power then the mother tongue is that of the powerless — poor men, women, and children. For Le Guin, the present education system teaches people to discount the mother tongue, to keep it silent.

Both of these approaches to knowledge must have their rightful place in a person's education, for both are needed to form a synthesis — Le Guin's third language, the "native tongue." This she calls, "the true discourse of reason. A wedding and welding back between the alienated consciousness that I have been calling the father tongue and the undifferentiated engagement that I have been calling the mother tongue" (153).

Le Guin does not divide knowledge exactly the way Snow envisioned the split, but her division between the objective study and the arts do make for a compelling parallel. Her synthesis of her first two types of knowledge, however, does place her alongside both Wells and Heinlein when it comes to the urging for the reunification of knowledge.

Her ideas outlined in her address do echo in her fictional works. *The Dispossessed* (1974) brings out in stark detail two differing utopian models that deal with philosophy and power. But the novel that really focuses on knowledge and the type of society it could produce is *Always Coming Home* (1985).[10]

This novel portrays a pastoral society in a distant-future northern California where its members live in harmony with nature as well as each other. They possess a cyclical outlook on life and constantly search for new spiritual experiences. There is a passage that reveals succinctly the pastoral society's approach to perceiving reality by describing how difficult it is to explain it with our current language and viewpoint.

> It is very difficult to be sure of these meanings when dealing with a language and a way of thought in which no distinction is made between human and natural history or between objective and subjective fact and perception, in which neither chronological nor causal sequence is considered an adequate reflection of reality, and in which time and space are so muddled together that one is never sure whether they are talking about an era or an area [153].

Le Guin's native tongue comes through quite clearly.

However, Le Guin does not totally abandon the science and technology of the past. In the novel there is a place of called "City of Mind," a place described as a network of eleven thousand sites located all over the planet operated by independent and self-sustaining cybernetic devices whose reason for existing is to collect and store the sum total of human knowledge. All have access to this information. As humanity continues to learn, this entity will continue to grow. This growth is described as proceeding "consistently in the direct linear mode" (151).

Besides farming and crafts, such sophisticated devices as solar panels, electric heaters, washing machines, printing presses, and generators (282, 292, 302, and 316) are mentioned in a constructive light. When the universe is described as being one, a single entity, even an existing electronic network extending into outer space is included (290–291). Le Guin is certainly not a Luddite (i.e., as the term is popularly perceived). She just does not place a primacy of importance on the technology of the Industrial Revolution in her future society.

The antagonists to this way of life are embodied in a warrior group called the Condors. They are male, thus representing the ways of the Le Guin's father tongue, carry with them the social diseases of aggression, exploitation, and domination. They eventually fail to conquer the harmonious valley people. The book offers several possibilities why (lack of natural resources to build advanced weapons, The City of Mind's cybernetic caretakers withholding crucial information, etc.), but in the end it suggests that, "Very sick people tend to die of their own sickness" and that "Destruction destroys itself" (379–381).

So there remains a place for the sciences in Le Guin's utopian exercise.

However one must first engage in the Rousseau-like process of rediscovering one's original and true nature first before deciding where science fits in one's life.

Wells, Heinlein, and Le Guin all agree that Snow's problem of the two cultures must be reconciled. Where Wells and Heinlein stress the study of both fields of knowledge, Le Guin proposes a basic reexamining of human nature before settling on the type of education to be taken.

When it comes to warning about the possibility of a reemerging enlightened despotism in modern-day guise, only Wells remains relatively silent. As Wells argues for more education and central organization, Heinlein views advanced technology as both a threat and a boon to individual freedoms and potentialities while Le Guin proposes for less emphasis on the sciences and for a redefinition of the individual in a communal context.

Wells, Heinlein, and Le Guin represent the three major traditions of the eighteenth-century Enlightenment. In this context, one could label these three as mainstream critics, their differing ideologies and solutions notwithstanding. Meanwhile, there obviously exist other ways of responding to Snow's thesis and Krieger's warnings.

By way of conclusion, two more recent writers who also deal with this twin issue of knowledge and power will be discussed: Mary Doria Russell and Howard V. Hendrix. The former reaches back to a far older tradition than the Enlightenment while the latter uses cutting-edge ideas on human consciousness and cosmology.

Mary Doria Russell's two-novel series, *The Sparrow* (1996) and *Children of God* (1998), uses the centuries-long traditions of the Roman Catholic Church, especially the Jesuitical one, to examine the consequences of new knowledge and its use with power.[11] A worthy successor to James Blish's classic, *A Case of Conscience* (1958), Russell's novels tell of a first contact with an alien race in a neighboring star system.

Though she never discusses specifically her solution to the problem of the two cultures, she does examine a possible approach for analysis in the first novel through the nature of the crew (who will be the first to touch down on the planet Rakhat) and their ongoing discussions. Composed of both Jesuits and lay people, the crew has fields of expertise encompassing a wide range of subjects: astronomy, archaeology, medicine, biology, chemistry, linguistics, agriculture, music, artificial intelligence, philosophy, anthropology, and (of course) theology. Despite this impressive arsenal of knowledge, the crew experience incredible difficulties understanding even the most basic facts of Rakhat culture and society. Throughout these two novels, when all of human understanding cannot explain things and events threaten to challenge the crew's sanity, questions about the power of faith and God's purposes for humanity enter the picture. Russell does not proselytize, but matters of faith become the fall-back field of discussion for every problem.

The two novels also focus on power, through the machinations of the Jesuits as they attempt to fulfill their roles as the intellectual, political, and military soldiers of Christ. When evidence of intelligent life first emerges, it is the Jesuits who make the first move for first contact. While the United Nations debate back and forth about forming an expedition, the Jesuits — being answerable only to the Pope (and he only to God) — use their world-wide resources to build and supply the first ship to Rakhat with an efficiency reminiscent of Wells's United Airmen from his film, *Things to Come* (1936).

After the first expedition ends in a scandalous and tragic manner, the church and the Jesuit's prestige and power decline tremendously back on Earth. So, in the same manner as the first, they immediately send a second expedition to find out what went wrong and possibly to repair the damage both on Rakhat and at home. When the purposes behind this expedition are discussed, the labyrinthine connections to power in the secular world — not all of them legal — that the Jesuits and the Pope share due to their privileged positions are also revealed. Economic and political issues, not just spiritual ones, take center stage. The Jesuits and their Church become swallowed up in their own corruption. So for Russell contemporary enlightened despotism could even appear in the form of the Roman Catholic hierarchy.

Howard V. Hendrix, in his two-novel sequence *Lightpaths* (1997) and *Standing Wave* (1998), admirably updates the themes of consciousness, cos-mology, and evolution examined during the 1950s by Arthur C. Clarke's *Childhood's End* (1953), Theodore Sturgeon's *More Than Human* (1953), and Alfred Bester's *The Stars My Destination* (1956) by filtering them through the high-tech, cyberspace world of William Gibson's *Neuromancer* (1984).[12]

Basing its ideas about consciousness on an unpublished manuscript by a philosopher, Bruce Albert, *Lightpaths* hypothesizes that the different fields of knowledge, which are divided by whether they examine the physical world or the mental/spiritual world, really describe one single reality. As the novel explains, "The energy that fuels the black hole furnaces in quasars and the galactic cores in the physical universe is the same energy that archetypes fuel within psyche — moving systems beyond causation, to dynamicality" (221). It is the human mind, consciousness, that can unite these two planes of real-ity. One of the novel's characters says, "the mind is a co-evolutionary proj-ect between physical and non-physical elements. A cooperation between biological, psychological, and spiritual dimensions" (205). Using a concept of Stapledonian proportions, the novel posits that the universe itself is on the verge of attaining consciousness (363–365). At the present stage of evolution, however, humans can perceive reality only in multiple levels.

The solution to attaining true knowledge then lies not in the increase of research and experimentation (as Wells and Heinlein would have it), or a rediscovery of one's original true nature (as Le Guin would espouse), or even in a contemplation of faith (as Russell perceives the issue); but rather it involves human consciousness transcending the material world and integrating itself with the cosmos as a whole, thus taking the next step in evolution. And it is through the technologies of cybernetics and computer interface that humanity will be able to accomplish this.

Unity is crucial for the survival of the human race. The future that the novel presents is a divided and bloody one. In a world overpopulated and ecologically falling apart, militant religious theocracies, rapacious transnational corporations, and corrupt governments struggle amongst each other for the power to control the world's resources. Each of these groups claims the right to dictate to others what should be done. For Hendrix there are many enlightened despots for which the people should watch out and prevent from succeeding.

Of course, there are other approaches to this theme. With the recent literary developments of cyberpunk and postmodernism in science fiction, writers continue to examine the themes of epistemology and social structures in light of the new ideas emerging from the sciences and humanities. And there remain those who write in the traditional modes of the genre who also remain interested in the exploration of new knowledge and its consequences of social organization.

These five writers demonstrate both the scope and depth of science fiction's responses to Snow's educational dilemma and Krieger's political admonitions. As the new fields of knowledge are constantly being created and existing ones expanded, the challenges to comprehensive understanding become more daunting and the threats to proper government more intimidating. As long as science fiction remains a branch of popular literature, it will continue to serve as a valuable teaching tool for the population at large to understand the ever-increasing complexity of our future. As long as its writers keep up with political and cultural traditions, both old and new, this field will continue to warn its readers about new forms of power that could threaten more than help in the name of enlightenment. Let the reader beware.

Notes

1. C. P. Snow, *The Two Cultures*, introduction by Stefan Collini (Cambridge, UK: Cambridge University Press, 1993).

2. Leonard Krieger, *An Essay on the Theory of Enlightenment Despotism* (Chicago: University of Chicago Press, 1975), 90. Later parenthetical page references are to this edition.

3. See Ernst Cassirer, *The Philosophy of the Enlightenment* (Boston: Beacon, 1955); Peter Gay, *The Enlightenment: An Interpretation*, 2 volumes (New York: Vantage, 1966–1969); and Leonard Krieger, *Kings and Philosophers, 1689–1789* (New York: Norton, 1970).

4. Stefan Collini, Introduction, *The Two Cultures*, xxiii–xxiv; David C. Smith, *H. G. Wells: Desperately Mortal* (New Haven, CT: Yale University Press, 1986), 472.

5. H. G. Wells, *The Outline of History*, Third Edition (New York: Macmillan, 1921), 1100.

6. H. G. Wells, *A Modern Utopia* (Lincoln: University of Nebraska Press, 1967). Later parenthetical page references are to this edition.

7. Robert A. Heinlein, "The Happy Days Ahead," *Expanded Universe* (New York: Grosset and Dunlap, 1980), 514–582. Later parenthetical page references are to this edition.

8. Robert A. Heinlein, *Time Enough for Love* (New York: G. Putnam's Sons, 1973). Later parenthetical page references are to this edition.

9. Ursula K. Le Guin, "Bryn Mawr Commencement Address," *Dancing at the Edge of the World* (New York: Grove, 1989), 147–160. Later parenthetical page references are to this edition.

10. Ursula K. Le Guin, *Always Coming Home* (New York: Harper and Row, 1985, Science Fiction Book Club Edition). Later parenthetical page references are to this edition.

11. Mary Doria Russell, *The Sparrow* (New York: Villiard, 1996); *Children of God* (New York: Villiard, 1998).

12. Howard V. Hendrix, *Lightpaths* (New York: Ace, 1996); *Standing Wave* (New York: Ace, 1998). Later parenthetical page references are to this edition of *Lightpaths*.

3. Fighting Out of Context: Culture Wars Within and Without Science Fiction from Snow to Sokal

Howard V. Hendrix

As a graduate of the University of California, Riverside and a long-time participant of the Eaton Conferences held at UCR, I was honored to have the opportunity to present a keynote address at the 1999 conference on "Science Fiction at the Crossroads of Two Cultures," now revised as this paper. I approached this assignment with some considerable trepidation. Because discussion of the Two Cultures has a tradition of being tendentious to the point of academic tribalism — no offense to any actually tribal people intended — I kept my remarks as relevant and humble as I could manage, knowing that my original audience would include both physicists and literary intellectuals, the traditional opponents in the Two Cultures contest.

Issues of both context and authority were very much on my mind as I did my research. After downloading a bunch of material from sources on the web, I then dutifully went to my local university library and checked out numerous articles and a number of books: C. P. Snow's *The Two Cultures and the Scientific Revolution* (1959) and *The Two Cultures: A Second Look* (1963), R. D. Leavis's *Two Cultures?* (1962), George Levine and Owen Thomas's *The Scientist vs. the Humanist* (1963), W. T. Jones's *The Sciences and the Humanities* (1965), Mark R. Hillegas's *The Future as Nightmare* (1967), Wylie Sypher's *Literature and Technology* (1968), and William H. Davenport's *The One Culture* (1970). During the 1970s the Two Cultures debate quieted somewhat, but grew louder again with George Levine's work in the 1980s (particularly his *One Culture: Essays in Science and Literature* [1987]). The Two Cultures struggle became raucous again once it was subsumed into the broader "culture wars" debate, in works such as Paul R. Gross and Norman Levitt's *Higher Superstition* (1994) and the Sokal Text/*Social Text* affair, which ultimately led to the publication of Alan Sokal and Jean Bricmont's *Fashionable Nonsense* (1998)—which appeared under the title *Impostures Intellectuelles* a year earlier in France.

From my time in graduate school during the 1980s and my early years as a professor soon thereafter, I was familiar already with the works of the "evil relativist subjectivist perspectivist poststructuralist postmodernists": Jacques Derrida, Michel Foucault, Jean Lyotard, Jean Baudrillard, Jacques Lacan, Julia Kristeva, Luce Irigaray, Gilles Deleuze, Felix Guattari, Stanley Aronowitz, Donna Haraway, Andrew Ross, and N. Katherine Hayles. The articles by and about these authors which I encountered during the long strange research trip for this chapter—from the publication of Snow's initial book on the topic in 1959 to the present—are too numerous to recount except in an extended bibliography.

What struck me in this review of the Two Cultures literature, and which I know has also struck many readers, is the relative paucity of references in that literature to the genre the Eaton Conference deals with: science fiction. Among the postmodern critics, when science fiction comes up at all, the tone is generally along the lines of "Thank heavens for cyberpunk! At last, science fiction worth paying attention to"—as if nothing had come before or since. Among the scientist-critics writing in the Two Cultures debate—people with "the future in their bones," mind you—when science fiction comes up at all (which is rarely), the reference is generally dismissive, as when Gross and Levitt use Ursula K. Le Guin's *Always Coming Home* (1985) and its Kesh people to introduce a chapter concluding, basically, that "literary intellectuals are natural Luddites" (as Snow phrased it).[1] In a similar vein Sokal and Bricmont write, "if a science-fiction writer uses secret passageways in space-time in order to send her characters back to the era of the Crusades, it is purely a question of taste"—and therefore unworthy of serious discussion.[2]

To suggest that the Two Cultures problem is utterly solved in the works of one writer or even in a single genre is glib and facile, but I think no one who seriously considers the question of the Two Cultures can afford to dismiss science fiction out of hand.

After reading so much of the Two Cultures material from all sides, I do wonder about how seriously the question has actually been considered. One could talk about the various posturings involved—particularly about academics presenting themselves as either heretics or defenders of the faith—yet ultimately the debate has not been even that lofty. Despite myself I can't help but see a perverse similarity between the Two Cultures debate and the art and science of demolition derby.

In a faulty analogy that I know will be decried by both postmodernists and their scientist critics, I submit to you that demolition derby stands in the same relation to automobile racing as the Two Cultures debate stands in relation to the usual business of academia. Academic years, with their cycles of classes and committees and grants and publication and tenure and promotion, are fairly patterned and predictable, year after year being rather like the lap after lap of stock car or enduro racing, the mundane business of watching cars go round in circles, jockeying for position, with rarely a wreck to spice up the proceedings. The Two Cultures debate, however, stands outside the usual round of academic life. Scholars leave gentility behind, pop on their crash helmets, chain down the hoods and trunks of their twenty-year old theoretical frameworks, strap themselves into those theoretical vehicles and run into each other backwards, again and again, "cut to the crash, cut to the crash, cut to the crash, until the track is littered with smoldering auto parts and only one car is still moving"— this last description being taken from Richard Conniff's fine *Smithsonian* article on demolition derby, "Crash, Slam, Boom!"[3]

Perhaps my fondness for such an analogy comes of reading too much of this material. Yet, despite the way in which my sacred clown/melancholy fool/naïf/"evil twin" may have just undercut my own authority in this context, I have come to see, through the course of my review of the Two Cultures literature, that much of what it has all been about is context and authority and symmetry — or the lack thereof. I have argued, in previous Eaton chapters and elsewhere, that science functions as an important "authority source" for science fiction. Dedicated science fiction readers commonly make a distinction not only between "hard" science fiction and "soft" science fiction, but also between "story" or "style" writers (say, J. G. Ballard or, to a lesser extent, William Gibson) and "idea" writers (say Hal Clement or Greg Egan in some of his books). The fact that I have a difficult time coming up with writers who are primarily "story" writers or primarily "idea" writers — the fact that the majority of SF writers mingle both — says something about the way in which science fiction as a genre has long since begun integrating both the humanist values and the scientific values of the Two Cultures, about which more later.

Suffice to say for now that, in general, literary critics have not responded kindly to those textual instances where this emphasis on scientific "ideas" and speculation (as opposed to "style") have occurred. Despite the SF writer's argument that such "idea" emphasis is essential to the SF writer's claim of "scientificity" as an authority source for his or her fictions, this emphasis on ideas rather than style has meant that most SF writers have ended up being accused of the same sin that literary critic F. R. Leavis lays to the charge of C. P. Snow: "bad writing."

Yes, Leavis is probably right in thinking it a bit arrogant of Snow to imply that he (Snow) is the "New Man" (or as we would say in our more politically correct age, "New Human"). As Leavis tells us in his acerbic manner, "there are two uncommunicating and indifferent cultures, there is the need to bring them together, and there is C. P. Snow, whose place in history is that he has them both, so that we have in him the paradigm of the desired and necessary union."[4] The good Cambridge don says further that Snow's "incapacity as a novelist is what I say it is — total. He seems to me almost unreadable" (19). Leavis predicts that Snow's novels will not last. In this prediction, Leavis is generally correct: Snow's novels are read less and less every year. Nonetheless, Snow is remembered for *The Two Cultures*. Snow's weaknesses as a novelist and his "crass Wellsianism" (43) do not by themselves render useless and a "nullity" (30) every word Snow wrote — nor do Snow's supposed weaknesses as a writer, in themselves, come near to refuting the ideas presented in *The Two Cultures*.

If we are willing to admit that the charge of "bad novelist" is not enough to disqualify all of Snow's work from consideration, we must also at least entertain the possibility that the same holds on the other side of the coin. Gross and Levitt in *Higher Superstition* and Sokal and Bricmont in *Fashionable Nonsense* chart courses for us through the most science-dependent sections of the postmodern theorists they examine. These scientist-critics largely make their case that the French postmodernists and poststructuralists they attack are "bad physicists" and "bad mathematicians." Yet, as Ronald Shusterman of the Universite Michel de Montaigne in Bordeaux points out, in an article in *Philosophy and Literature*, Sokal and Bricmont's reasoning is

> fallacious at times. Just because poststructuralists talk nonsense when they talk about science doesn't prove that poststructuralism itself is entirely nonsense. One would have to prove that all of these erroneous borrowings from science are not just accidental and auxiliary to poststructuralism, but its very essence. One would also have to prove that within the framework in which poststructuralism operates (philosophy, theory, literary criticism) the poststructuralist arguments don't stand up. Sokal and Bricmont sometimes imply that the very fact these French thinkers misuse science is enough to prove that the rest of their work is nonsense.[5]

This implication is found in Gross and Levitt and other scientific critics of postmodernism, as well as in Sokal and Bricmont. The idea that all the work of the poststructuralists is *prima facie* nonsense because they are at times quite guilty of "bad science" is a sort of intratextual guilt-by-association. The idea that postmodern theory is "entirely nonsense" is no more proved than that we should reject all Snow's work (fiction and non-fiction) because he's a "bad novelist" — or that we should reject all science fiction simply because it too has often fallen short of the glory of God.

Let me admit that I have never been much of a fan of postmodern theory. I have often found it an unnecessarily jargon-laden, precious, trendy, and still-born intellectual activity. Yet the anti-"po-mo" books by the scientist-critics probably had an effect on me just the opposite of what those scientist-critics intended. After seeing all those trendy theorists lambasted for their ineptitude as scientists, I was suddenly swept by a wave of fellow-feeling for them. As a science fiction writer, I too have speculated about scientific matters on which I was not expert. I too have sinned, or at least fallen short of the glory of Wittgenstein in the *Tractatus* when he said "What we cannot speak about we must pass over in silence,"[6] or, as Sokal and Bricmont put it, "One can ... either speak about the natural sciences knowing what one is talking about, or else not speak about them and concentrate on other things" (193–194).

Science fiction has long been attacked by literary critics for being "bad literature"—and here I found postmodern theory being attacked by scientists for being "bad science." Suddenly, it seemed a looking-glass world, Alice. If postmodernism at its worst is "fashionable nonsense," then perhaps science fiction at its best could be "unfashionable sense." As a science fiction writer, I wanted to welcome my looking-glass doubles, these postmodern theorists, these writers of non-science non-fiction — or at least see whether, when I waved my right hand, one of them might wave her left.

Alas, that cannot be the case. As you may recall, it is precisely the "experiment at Columbia by Yang and Lee" which Snow mentions so particularly in *The Two Cultures*—"the contradiction of parity" (17)—that refutes the notion of a looking-glass universe. Actually, Yang and Lee came up with the idea that parity — mirror-symmetry — was not respected by the weak force and they proposed likely candidates for a test of mirror-symmetry. Leon Lederman *et al.* actually provided the first experimental proof of what Yang and Lee had argued. The mathematically and intuitively beautiful theory of mirror-symmetry was transformed into merely a "higher superstition" by the ugly fact that left handed muons don't exist. Lederman's discussion of that experiment is one of the highlights of his book *The God Particle*, from which I've adapted this account.[7]

I'm careful to cite that source because, in reviewing the literature of the Two Cultures, I have been made painfully aware of how inexpert I am in so many different fields. Initially I tried to anesthetize myself against that realization with rationalizations. "Specialization," I told myself, "necessarily also results in a diminution of context, a flatlandization of perspective, even of consciousness itself— a failure to consider larger vistas, bigger pictures, other dimensions of a problem." Or, in turn, I tried to write the controversy off by shrinking the context of the Two Cultures debate itself, thinking that, after all, the conflict between Snow and Leavis was a Cambridge University thing, just as the conflict between Sokal and Ross (editor of *Social Text*) is an NYU "thang." I reminded myself that all politics is ultimately local, and I thought again of a button I had once read at a science fiction convention that said "Academic infighting is so vicious because there's so little at stake" (a quote variously attributed to experts ranging from Woodrow Wilson to Henry Kissinger).

None of those palliatives worked, however. Ultimately, I do think there *is* something significant at stake. It's not enough to simply say that the Two Cultures are really one culture, or three cultures, or tending toward an infinity of cultures. Or to say, with equal merit, that the Two Cultures are, by strict sociological definition, actually Two Subcultures. I must return to the issue of asymmetry — if I may be allowed to do so, even if I am not a professional physicist.

The French postmodernist theorists, in terms of their power, are not the mirror image of science fiction writers. Where Snow in 1959 could write with an almost gracious condescension about how "Now and then one used to find poets conscientiously using scientific expressions, and getting them wrong" (17–18) and how bizarre it is that so "very little of twentieth century science has been assimilated into twentieth century art" (17), by the time we get to the end of Gross and Levitt's *Higher Superstition* in 1994, the tone has changed:

> ... if scientists perceive that a spate of nonsense concerning science has been coming out of the mouths of their young humanist colleagues, then they have the right to raise questions about the mechanisms that give a fair wind to such shaky scholarship. It will be argued immediately that this is an asymmetric, and therefore inequitable, proposition. If physicists are to judge scholars of English, why shouldn't English professors judge physicists? The fallacy here is that the asymmetry originates in the pretensions, legitimate or otherwise, of members of the English (or sociology or cultural studies or women's studies or African American studies) department to qualification on scientific questions.... To put it bluntly, it is the humanists of the academic left who have transgressed the boundaries — as they are eager in most circumstances to proclaim. That's their privilege; but they are not (or should not be) exempt from the customs duties! ... Plainly there is no direct way to enjoin our counterparts in these fields to abandon the pleasures of subjective narrativity for the fuddy-duddy rigors of empirical and statistical research. Still, "hard" scientists should find some way of supporting those of their colleagues in these areas who are willing to honor the principle that the right to make knowledge claims in a university has to be earned by the methodologically sound sweat of one's brow. It's fine to argue about competing methodologies; it is not fine to congratulate oneself on having abandoned method [256].

I think the shift here, from Snow's disgruntled bemusement to Gross and Levitt's sense of being genuinely embattled, is clear enough that I will not belabor the point.

Of course, I am quoting out of context. That is what literary critics do. Quotes are our authority sources. Yet perhaps the scientists "quote out of context" too. Any experiment must be performed on only a subset of the entire universe, after all. If the context is the entire text, or if the universe is as fully interconnected a whole as Bell's Theorem and the Aspect experiments suggest, then what both the literary critic and the physical scientist does is "quote out of context"— though the scientist's "quote" is experimental proof and evidence from the authoritative "primary text" of Nature, the physical and material world.

Because I am not a professional physicist, I am aware that some will think it wrong of me even to mention Bell's Theorem or the Aspect work. I know from reading about "postmodern intellectuals' abuse of science" that interconnectedness is among the scientific concepts most often abused by post-modernists — along with Kurt Gödel's Incompleteness Theorem, Werner Heisenberg's Uncertainty Principle, and Niels Bohr's complementarity. And yes, I have used scientific ideas metaphorically in my fiction too, for which I beg your forgiveness.

I am not here trying to suggest that the scientific method is the same methodology as that used by literary critics. Quite the contrary. Underdetermination of theory by evidence — namely, that "the set of all our experimental data is finite, but our theories contain a potentially infinite number of predictions" (Sokal and Bricmont 69)— that's a *conundrum* for the sciences. In literary criticism, it's the *basic method of operation*: primary texts are finite, but interpretations are potentially infinite. Readings of a primary text, however, can be seen as "overinterpreted" if there is not enough textual evidence backing up that reading, just as a scientific theory is weak if experimental data are particularly lacking.

Nor am I suggesting here that the universe is just a "text" or "story" or that reality is "chimerical or at best completely inaccessible to human cognition" (Gross and Levitt 74). Against the relativist postmodernists, I am epistemologically fuddy-duddy enough to agree with the scientist-critics that science, though it *has* a story, is not *just* a story — that it does refer not merely to human constructions, languages, and discourses, but also to a "thing," the physical world. Even if we only understand it *as* a world through the subjectivity of individual human consciousness, human beings did not *create* that thing we choose to call a world.

Science, like consciousness itself, is of course to some extent culturally constructed and constrained. Though I'm not above taking a jab or two at the haughtiness of science and have been known to play around with language and with relativism in my novels, in the end I do not believe the idea that "there is no reality but language" or that "all human awareness is a creature and prisoner of the language games that encode it" (Gross and Levitt 74). In my second novel, *Standing Wave* (1998), for instance, you'll find a long argument against the work of Clifford Geertz and other postmodern theorists' ideas that "consciousness is essentially all words and concepts. Words and concepts are all social. The consciousness of any individual, therefore, is inherently and absolutely a social construct, a mere nexus or space where social forces play themselves out."[8] That argument among characters in that book is there because that book's author — who is also the author and speaker of this chapter, if consciousness is at all unitary — believes that the idea that consciousness is a *fundamentally* social phenomenon is itself an essentially fascistic (or at least dangerously totalizing) concept.

Although I am not a professional philosopher, I hold that language does not precede consciousness. Following from the biological work on autopoiesis by Humberto Maturana and Francisco Varela, from the philosophy of D. Bruce Albert (particularly his as-yet-unpublished master work *Spontaneous Human Consciousness*, which I have had the good fortune to read in manuscript), and from my own experiences of the ineffable — I hold that consciousness precedes language. So too science does not precede the physical world; the physical world precedes science. In my admittedly nonprofessional philosophical view, an analogy can be drawn between the way consciousness stands in relation to language and the way the physical world stands in relation to science. As a literary critic, I might even go so far as to say that consciousness is the "primary text" which language interprets, comments upon, elaborates upon — just as the physical world or "nature," as I have already suggested, stands as "primary text" to science.

In advancing this analogy, have I again committed the sin of "metaphor-mongering," as Gross and Levitt (116) term it? Probably. I'm sure it will please no one. Through my fictions I have in some small way attempted to restore a proper valuation to the idea of individual consciousness — and have run directly counter to the postmodernists' denial of the actuality of individual consciousness. In *Standing Wave*, however, I counter the postmodernists with something equally repugnant to physical scientists, namely D. Bruce Albert's elucidation of "portal experiences." Albert argues for the *necessity* of non-physical events, of mystical and spiritual experiences — subjective, but real — which, at the same time, can't, at the moment of experiencing them, be put into words. This situation of fundamental "unwordableness" is what is traditionally meant by "the ineffable."

(I have received some criticism for this stance: a techie fan who was also a very nice person approached me at an autographing session in Monterey in November, 1998, and said: "I liked *Lightpaths* and *Standing Wave*, except for the endings. Too mystical. On a mystic woo-woo scale of 1 to 10, those went to 11." As I recall, at the time I muttered something about technomysticism, Arthur C. Clarke, and Olaf Stapledon in response.)

Here in the realm of words and academic criticism, however, things are even more slippery. Sokal and Bricmont state forthrightly that

> Science is not a text ... scientific theories are not like novels; in a scientific con-
> text words have specific meanings which differ in subtle but critical ways from
> their everyday meanings, and which can only be understood within a complex
> web of theory and experiment. If one uses them only as metaphors, one is easily
> lead to nonsensical conclusions [187].

But what does "only as metaphor" mean? In the long quote far above, are Gross and Levitt using the word "asymmetry" only as metaphor, or some-how in the correct physical-science sense? And what of that wonderful mixed metaphor of theirs — "methodologically sound sweat" of one's brow? Should they fall into silence too, rather than commit the sin of "metaphor-mongering?"

Most of the other scientific critics of postmodernism say much the same thing. They emphasize again and again the distinction between fiction and fact, story and substance, relativism and empiricism, subjectivity and objectivity. They diligently patrol the borders between "the pleasures of subjective narrativity" and "the fuddy-duddy rigors of empirical and statistical research," as Gross and Levitt put it above. I must admit that I agree with their argument, generally — despite its grumpy-white-guy tone.

Yes, there is a distinction between *poiein* and *tekhne*, between fictive creation and material skill, between storytelling and scientific methodology. The discourse of the humanities is at root narrative, telling a story — while scientific discourse is at root explanatory, elaborating ideas about phenomena. I would never assert that what science is explaining (the physical world) is any less real than what literature is often attempting to narrate (the subjective experience of consciousness). Yet I fear that the push for "scientific correctness" in non-scientific discourse may be as prone to unanticipated pernicious effects as has been the push for "political correctness" in academic speech generally.

The solution to speech one does not agree with is not the "final solution" of driving one's opponents into silence, but more speech, hopefully more carefully reasoned and effective speech. The dark effects of "scientific correctness" on non-scientific discourse concern me because I have already seen the dark effects of "literary correctness" when applied to science fiction. I'm sure any number of science fiction scholars could write any number of articles about the negative consequences of the "ghettoization" of science fiction as a "subliterary" form throughout most of the twentieth century.

And yet — and yet, I hear this little *déjà-vu* voice telling me not to worry so much. Not for any mystical "woo-woo" reason, but because, as a science fiction fan, scholar, and writer, I've already been there, I've already done that.

The scientific critics of postmodernism warn us again and again in their texts of the "revolutionary, apocalyptic, millenarian" aspects of postmodern theory. Yet science fiction has already survived a "revolutionary, apocalyptic" movement within its ranks, a movement emphasizing language and discourse, literary-style-story values as against scientific speculative "idea" values. Science fiction's revolution was called the New Wave — more than forty years ago. Like the postmodern theorists, the New Wavers presented themselves as more revolutionary than they actually were, and the science fiction old guard — like the scientific critics railing against postmodernism today — presented themselves and their work as more static and unyielding than is actually the case.

Those who do not know the past of science fiction are condemned to repeat it in the Two Cultures war. Because I know something of that history — and because my doctoral dissertation was on apocalyptic literature and my first book-length work of science fiction was a utopian novel — I feel almost qualified to speak on this. Postmodernists place the "doom" of Western science too soon, while their scientist critics place it too far away. Postmodernists trumpet for an apocalyptic endtime to the world of science that will usher in a new utopian millennial era; their scientist-critics counter that the millennium actually began three hundred years ago, with the ascendancy of the scientific method and the beginning of the Enlightenment.

The millennium, or any static vision of utopia, is to the body politic as immortality is to the individual physical body: a denial of final change, the ultimate triumph of stasis. The left hand of apocalypse is the right hand of utopia. I submit to you that yes, science has lasted three centuries, in one form and another — far longer than any single theoretical school in the arts and humanities. Yet religious systems have already lasted far longer, and ancient Egypt lasted forty centuries, in one form and another.

Western science will likely outlive postmodernism. It may already have. Yet I think it is wrong to hold with Albert Einstein, as the scientific critics do, that "Politics is for the moment, while ... an equation is for eternity."[9] Tell that to the ghosts of those who died in Hiroshima and Nagasaki, from the ephemeral political exploitation of the eternal equation $E = mc^2$. I think that David W. Hawkins's view — that science is about better and better approximations to truth, about "replacing one theory that is wrong with one that is more subtly wrong"[10] — is nearer the mark. Many of the scientific critics of postmodernism evince a fear of history — that "muddled," "dreary," "wrongheaded" and "muddleheaded" thing that humans engage in. Gross and Levitt in particular present us with the notion that human beings are somehow unworthy of the scientific method human beings themselves created. For these authors, science is the dream, not of a final theory, but of a final methodology — outside time, outside history.

Although I am no professional scientist, I submit to you that *that* is an unscientific concept. Science, existing in time and history, evolves, and may perhaps achieve its greatest effect when it has created the conditions by which it will itself be superseded, giving way to something larger in which the scientific method will be subsumed — the way Newtonian mechanics was subsumed into relativity, only much more profoundly.

What will it look like? Arthur C. Clarke, a writer in that genre which survived its own postmodern "revolution," in a phrase known to most of you, suggests that any sufficiently advanced science and technology is indistinguishable from magic. Recently, I heard a magician being interviewed on TV, who said that magic is "secular mysticism." Sokal and Bricmont argue that the postmodernists are guilty of "secular mysticism" as well — they use that same oxymoronic, paradoxical phrase. Perhaps literary critics generally, and scientists writing in the Two Cultures debate specifically, have both overlooked science fiction not because it is so different from what they are doing, but because it is so very similar: a blending of the worlds of "story" and "idea."

As a science fiction writer, I revel in paradox. Although I am no physicist, I see complementarity in story and idea, in literary and scientific values; in the "inner world" subjective descriptions of literature and speculative philosophy, and the "outer world" objective descriptions of the sciences. As an academic I believe that, although different discourses have different jobs to do, they are all necessary to knowledge. As a person I assent to physicist Wolfgang Pauli's intriguing suggestion that physics and mysticism are complementary aspects of a single reality.[11] I could do worse, we could do worse, than being called "magicians," if by magicians we mean secular mystics, the power of whose illusions comes from how carefully we have practiced to make our practice *invisible*. The greatest illusionists, after all, are also the greatest believers in any particular system or method — those individuals, it might be said, for whom their practice has become invisible even to themselves.

Notes

1. Paul R. Gross and Norman Levitt, *Higher Superstition: The Academic Left and Its Quarrels with Science* (Baltimore, MD: Johns Hopkins University Press, 1994), 149–150; C. P. Snow, *The Two Cultures* (Cambridge, UK: Cambridge University Press, 1993), 22; later parenthetical page references are to this edition.

2. Alan Sokal and Jean Bricmont, *Fashionable Nonsense: Postmodern Intellectuals' Abuse of Science* (New York: Picador, 1998), 10. Later parenthetical page references are to this edition.

3. Richard Conniff, "Crash, Slam, Boom!," *Smithsonian*, 29:10 (January 1999), 92.

4. F. R. Leavis, *Two Cultures?* (New York: Pantheon Books/Random House, 1963), 31. Later parenthetical page references are to this edition.

5. Ronald Shusterman, "Ravens and Writing-Desks: Sokal and the Two Cultures," *Philosophy and Literature*, 22:1 (April 1998), 128–129.

6. Ludwig Wittgenstein, *Tractatus Logico-Philosophicus*, translated by D. F. Pears and B. F. McGuinness, introduction by Bertrand Russell (London and New York: Routledge, 1974), 89.

7. See Leon Lederman with Dick Teresi, *The God Particle* (New York: Delta/Bantam Doubleday Dell, 1994), 256–273.

8. Howard V. Hendrix, *Standing Wave* (New York: Ace, 1998), 203.

9. Albert Einstein, cited in Stephen Hawking, "A Brief History of Relativity," *Time*, 154:27 (December 31, 1999), 81.

10. David W. Hawkins, cited in Henry L. Bussey, "Problems with Monitoring Heparin Anticoagulation," *Pharmacotherapy*, 19:1 (January 1999), 4.

11. "It would be most satisfactory of all if physics and psyche could be seen as complementary aspects of the same reality," Wolfgang Pauli, "The Influence of Archetypcal Ideas on the Scientific Theories of Kepler," *The Interpretation of Nature and the Psyche; Synchronicity: An Acausal Connecting Principle, C. G. Jung. The Influence of Archetypal Ideas on the Scientific Theories of Kepler, W. Pauli* (New York: Pantheon, 1955), 210.

4. A Tale of Two Cultures: Science Studies and Science Fiction

Stephen Potts

Alan Sokal's 1996 hoax at the expense of postmodern critique has now slipped into academic history, but it has not been forgotten. Indeed, Oxford University Press has just published (in 2008) the volume *Beyond the Hoax,* a definitive collection of Alan Sokal pieces beginning with his infamous parody, proceeding with other essays on the topic, previously published and unpublished, and concluding with some new material on antiscientific thinking in the new century. At this distance — and with the assistance of the information provided in the new publication — it is worth reviewing the details of Sokal's prank and its place in the so-called "science wars."

Alan D. Sokal has been for most of his professional career a mathematical physicist at New York University. Inspired in 1994 by a reading of Paul Gross and Norman Levitt's *Higher Superstition: The Academic Left and Its Quarrels with Science,*[1] he took it upon himself to absorb as much postmodern critique of science as he could and to produce a parodic article in that vein, which he ended up submitting to the progressive postmodern journal *Social Text.* He claims to have been only half surprised when the editors, led by Scottish-born culture theorist Andrew Ross, accepted it for a special issue on the "Science Wars" — Ross's own term for the attacks on postmodern critique of science that, in his view, had been coming mainly from the political right. "Transgressing the Boundaries: Toward a Transformative Hermeneutics of Quantum Gravity" begins with the premise that the Enlightenment imposed upon Western thought the concept of an exterior world with physical laws independent of individual consciousness, then argues for a new egalitarian science and mathematics liberated from such outdated elitist concepts as "reality" and more in line with multiculturalism, feminism, and queer theory.

Fully half the article consists of extensive footnotes that sweep in every name in the modern history of science studies, from Thomas S. Kuhn to Donna Haraway, sweetened by unsubtle praise for the ideas of Ross and journal founder Stanley Aronowitz. Sokal outed himself soon after its publication in a follow-up essay that was turned down by *Social Text* but published a few weeks later in *Lingua Franca*.[2]

In 1997 Sokal published a sequel, a full-length criticism of the humanistic study of science co-authored by Belgian physicist Jean Bricmont and entitled *Impostures Intellectuelles*[3]; an English version appeared a year later in North America as *Fashionable Nonsense: Postmodern Intellectuals' Abuse of Science*.[4] In this volume Sokal begins by deconstructing his parody, pointing to several levels of satire. Most obvious, of course, is the element of "political correctness" in his advocacy of a science of liberation, modeled on concerns of the postmodern left. More subtle are the intentional inaccuracies Sokal slipped into his hoax. He notes, for instance, that — contrary to the article's assertions — Einstein's non-linear equations do *not* have a solid foundation in traditional mathematics, and that the equations of quantum mechanics are linear, not non-linear expressions. The parody intentionally confuses the concepts of chaos and complexity — all to demonstrate that postmodern scholars of science do not understand their subject. While a non-scientist like Andrew Ross might understandably miss some of these subtleties, he is also guilty, according to Sokal, of overlooking a deliberate misquotation of Noam Chomsky, underlining another complaint against postmodern critique — that it is intellectually sloppy. Indeed, the very fact that Ross and his colleagues at *Social Text* could not distinguish a parody of postmodern critique from the real thing certainly seems damning, both of their intellectual rigor and that of the academic discipline they represent.

In the remainder of their book, Sokal and Bricmont go on to attack "postmodernists, relativists, and radical social constructivists" (2). Citing the work of such postmodern critics as Jacques Lacan and Jean Baudrillard, Gilles Deleuze and Felix Guattari, Luce Iriguay and Julia Kristeva, they criticize the literary license that confuses "the technical meaning of words such as 'uncertainty' or 'discontinuity' with their everyday meanings," as well as the postmodern "fondness for the most subjectivist writings of Werner Heisenberg and Niels Bohr, interpreted in a radical way that goes far beyond their own views." As though to clinch their objections, they add rhetorically, "But postmodern philosophy loves the multiplicity of viewpoints, the importance of the observer, holism, and indeterminism" (261). Sokal seems particularly troubled that postmodern critique is so closely associated with the literary Left. As a well-credentialed leftist himself— for example, he taught math as a volunteer in Nicaragua after the triumph of the Sandinista revolution — he views the postmodern left as representing "not the triumph of politics over intellectual inquiry but rather a retreat from real politics into careerism disguised as progressive politics."[5]

Sokal and Bricmont's reference to "relativists" includes both cultural relativists — mostly in the field of anthropology, where scientism is sometimes treated as merely one worldview, equivalent to Zuni or Hindu cosmology — and cognitive relativism, applied to philosophers of science like Karl Popper, Thomas S. Kuhn, and Paul Feyerabend, and the critics who follow them. In Chapter 4 of their 1997 book — expanded in Sokal's 2008 volume *Beyond the Hoax* into the essay "Cognitive Relativism in the Philosophy of Science"— Sokal targets the radical skepticism that casts doubt on the ability of the scientific enterprise to certify "truth" or to guarantee that what science defines as truth in fact speaks to a reality independent of human cognition. At the same time they take on "radical social constructivists," specifically, advocates of the Strong Programme of sociological science studies represented by David Bloor and Barry Barnes and, at one remove, by Bruno Latour. For these thinkers, "truth" is viewed as "belief": "knowledge for the sociologist is whatever people take to be knowledge. It consists of those beliefs which people confidently hold to and live by [...]."[6]

Sokal spends considerable time on Latour's Third Rule of Method from *Science in Action*, which asserts that the settlement of a scientific controversy *creates* a representation of Nature that is not necessarily supported by the natural world, an assertion that Sokal sees as either trivial or absurd, depending on how one interprets it. As Sokal elsewhere declares, he is "a stodgy old scientist who believes, naively, that there exists an external world, that there exist objective truths about that world, and that my job is to discover some of them." And he has "gleefully invited anyone who believed that the laws of physics were mere social conventions to jump out of his apartment window on the 21st floor."[7]

However, as one cultural relativist, Princeton anthropologist Emily Martin, has responded, "What did we ever write that gave Alan Sokal the impression that you could jump out of the 21st story and not have anything happen?"[8] Her comment reflects the main objection made by the critics of science to the critics of the critics of science: that their criticism represents a misunderstanding rooted in the differences between disciplinary objectives and language, not to mention honest philosophical differences with considerable precedent in the history of science. Broadly speaking, this conclusion is reinforced by the chain reaction in academic publishing following 1996, the year not only of the Sokal hoax but of editor Andrew Ross's own essay collection *Science Wars*.[9]

Differences of opinion, however, do not neatly break down along the conventional divide between the two cultures. For example, philosopher of science Christopher Norris, although a humanist, echoes Sokal when he charges any relativist who consents to fly at 30,000 feet of being a hypocrite. He lays out the positions of philosophical realism in his 1997 book *Against Relativism: Philosophy of Science, Deconstruction and Critical Theory*.[10] Like Sokal, Norris, who calls himself a "causal realist," spends considerable space on Paul Feyerabend, Richard Rorty, and the Strong Programme of the sociology of science, questioning their practice of setting aside all questions of objective reality in favor of focusing on the means by which cultures, including scientific subcultures, "create" truth through interaction and negotiation. Like other realists in the science debate, Norris traces the roots of such relativism back to Kuhn, whose *The Structure of Scientific Revolutions*, first published in 1962, was republished in 1996, coincident with Kuhn's death and the fallout from Sokal's hoax.

Kuhn is credited — or blamed — for the notion that as scientific interpretations of the natural world change over time in his famous "paradigm shifts," multiple visions of reality may succeed one another or even co-exist. He cites as examples the contrast between the deterministic universe of Newton and the relativistic one of Albert Einstein, or the different definitions of "molecule" used by physicists and chemists, or the different, if equally heuristic, descriptions of gravity offered by relativity and quantum theory. Kuhn harks back to the phenomenology of Ernst Mach and the empirical psychology of William James when he observes that, while the external stimuli available in the real world may be identical from individual to individual, the processing of these stimuli into empirical sensations and observations may not be, such that "two groups, the members of which have systematically different sensations on receipt of the same stimuli, do *in some sense* live in different worlds."[11]

Like Sokal and other realists, Norris acknowledges some value in Kuhn's theory of scientific progress, but believes Kuhn goes too far when he apparently asserts that a change in theoretical gestalt effectively replaces one reality with another:

> One contains constrained bodies that fall slowly, the other pendulums that repeat their motions again and again. In one, solutions are compounds, in the other mixtures. One is embedded in a flat, the other in a curved, matrix of space. Practicing in different worlds, the two groups of scientists see different things when they look from the same point in the same direction.

Kuhn, however, immediately and decisively clarifies this assertion in terms that acknowledge an independent reality.

> *Again, that is not to say that they can see anything they please. Both are looking at the world, and what they look at has not changed.* But in some areas they see different things, and they see them in different relations one to the other [Kuhn 150; italics mine].

In the process of attacking relativism, Norris cites the distinction between the different truth-seeking strategies of science and critique. Both depend to some extent on rhetoric and metaphor to formulate problems and suggest answers, but while critique remains at the rhetorical stage, relying on linguistic rationalizations and internal authority, science must establish parallels with the real world. Paraphrasing Jacques Derrida's "White Mythology," Norris states,

> on the one hand ... there is no escaping the ubiquity of metaphor as a vital resource — in Derrida's Heideggerian phrase, a perpetual "standing reserve" — for those speculative advances in science which as yet lack the means of adequate proof or rigorous conceptualization. Yet on the other, there can be no science (or indeed philosophy of science) in the absence of certain criteria and decision procedures for establishing the point at which speculative metaphors give way to adequate concepts [23].

For Norris, the error that relativists make is not recognizing this distinction: "in the case of scientific metaphors, knowledge comes about through a more exact grasp of their explanatory powers and limits, along with a variety of relevant procedures — experimental, theoretical, hypothetico-deductive and so forth — for determining their validity conditions in any given case" (25). Accustomed to making purely rhetorical claims themselves, postmodern cultural critics of literary background tend to see all theoretical pronouncements as purely rhetorical; bound by the practice of analyzing truth through the various lenses of cultural and social forces, anthropologists and sociologists who study science cannot help but regard the field as culturally formed. Even a scientific relativist like Kuhn misses the point of science, in this view. As Nobel-winning physicist Steven Weinberg, a strong scientific realist, has complained, "Kuhn did not deny that there is progress in science, but he denied that it is progress *toward* anything," to wit, an ultimate portrait of deep reality.[12]

Although intended as a criticism, Norris's complaint about the disciplinary prejudices of science critics really just highlights their different motives and objectives in approaching science. Indeed, as if in direct response to Norris, Derridan scholar Gregory Desilet best represents the humanist side of this debate when he maintains that these disciplinary approaches do not oppose the scientific method, that in fact they all contribute to the scientific endeavor. One does not deny the objective existence of reality simply by insisting that science operates not just in relationship to the natural world but to human communities and rhetorical strategies: "scientists are not merely listening to nature but are engaged in a dense and complex communication between themselves — as well as a more general public — in finding accommodation and winning support for various analyses and hypotheses concerning the object-world."[13] If every fact or theory must be posed as a description, one that must convince a scientific community and often a larger public of its truth, "then the *last* criterion, the court of *final* appeal, has become persuasiveness — the court of rhetoric and argument rather than the court of brute facts and objectivity" (352–353).

Significantly, the different worldviews of the science wars strongly suggest Kuhn's paradigms: in approaching the objects of study through their various disciplinary objectives and philosophies, the disputants in fact represent different epistemological realities — in some sense, different worlds. The literature that appeared in the aftermath of the Sokal hoax certainly demonstrates this conflict of realities, philosophies, and rhetorical approaches, and again not just along the divide between the two cultures. In 1998 Sokal and Bricmont reiterated and refined their own views in a collection that included many others critical of science studies — *A House Built on Sand: Exposing Postmodernist Myths About Science*, edited by Noretta Koertge.[14] Defenders of science and science studies alike replied in *The One Culture?*, edited by Jay A. Labinger and Harry Collins, respectively chemist and sociologist.[15] Also published in 2001, seemingly the culminating year of the science wars, is another collection that brings together essayists from various disciplines in a search for common ground: *After the Science Wars*, edited by Keith M. Ashman and Philip S. Baringer.[16]

A reading of these essay collections reinforces the idea already expressed that a significant part of this debate derives from miscommunication. Many disagreements arise from different interpretations of terms such as "reality," "truth," and "knowledge." In other words, "[d]ifferent styles of language use appear to be at the root of many of the disputes" between scientists and science scholars.[17] For example, as one essayist notes, "'objectivity' is usually meant in the metaphysical sense by the scientists and in the epistemic sense by the critics."[18] In other words, when scientists speak of objectivity, they are thinking of the relationship of their hypotheses and evidence to external reality, while the critics are referring to the scientists' degree of independence from the assumptions of their scientific community and to social and cultural prejudices. As sociologist Trevor Pinch explains,

> We ask not why science is more true than other accounts of the world or why the scientific method is the only valid method for generating truth, but rather how do scientists reach agreement about what *counts* as truth and as valid scientific method and how have these notions arisen historically? Asking these sorts of questions inevitably means putting aside epistemologically loaded terms like "truth."[19]

Thus, when cognitive relativists speak of the social construction of truth, they are referring not to the relationship of a scientific theory to deep reality, as a scientific realist might do, but to the various factors that convince a community, especially a scientific community, to agree to embrace a particular theory as "true." For cultural or sociological students of science, therefore, "truth" has an epistemological, not an ontological, meaning; their approach distinguishes "knowledge" from "reality." Indeed, confessing that much of his disagreement with sociologists of science has been a mere failure to communicate across disciplinary lines, physicist N. David Mermin sets out a list of rules for continuing the discussion between the cultures: (1) focus on substance, not motive, (2) acknowledge these difference in disciplinary terminology, and thus (3) recognize you may be missing a point.[20] Even speaking as a realist who believes "that the goal of science is to find out how things really are" (Sokal 2008: 229), Sokal is willing to acknowledge that theory "is constrained in part by the prevailing attitudes of mind, which in turn arise in part from deep-seated historical factors" among them "political, economic, and to some extent ideological considerations, as well as by the internal logic of scientific inquiry."[21]

In fact, much of the rhetoric of the debate between scientists and science critics resembles arguments within science itself. According to Steven Shapin, scientists themselves have made most of the claims attacked as antiscience in this debate, assertions such as "New knowledge is not science until it has been made social" and "Scientists do not find order in nature, they put it there." In the interest of preserving their image as objective seekers of truth, however, most scientists just don't like outsiders saying these things.[22] Indeed, even the more *ad hominem* arguments advanced in the science wars — not just questioning the merits of an opponent's stance but attacking her motives or ridiculing his intellect — reflect a commonplace of the history of science, as any student of that history can avow.

Thus, some of the irritation and contempt expressed toward postmodernism and relativism by a modest realist like Sokal or a strong realist like Steven Weinberg reflect to a degree their disagreement with non-realist philosophical trends within science. While Weinberg argues that all physics is teleological, working toward an ultimate explanation of the natural world that is universal and permanent[23] and that will thus put physicists "out of business,"[24] Sokal demarcates a respectful distance between realists and those he calls "pragmatists" or "instrumentalists." The latter dismiss the entire notion of uncovering an ultimate reality as "an illusion," content "that science should aim at empirical adequacy" (Sokal 2008, 231). For the pragmatist, "[s]cience works precisely because its results are always tentative"[25]; no matter how confident one was that one had reached Weinberg's goal, "it would still be impossible to claim that no inexplicable anomaly could emerge at even higher levels of accuracy."[26] This view accords with that of one pair of science critics, who observe that "[s]cientists remain the foremost experts on the natural world," but "often that expertise can deliver only the best available advice, not truth."[27]

For the strong pragmatists, scientific tools such as mathematics may offer applications and predictions, but they cannot provide essentialist explanations of reality. According to founding philosopher of science Karl Popper, like Kuhn an inspiration for the recent debate,

> a mathematical hypothesis does not claim that anything exists in nature which corresponds to it — neither to the words or terms with which it operates, nor to the functional dependencies which it appears to assert. It erects, as it were, a fictitious mathematical world behind that of appearance, but without the claim that this world exists.[28]

This view accords with one of the most extreme versions of the pragmatic approach: the Copenhagen interpretation of quantum theory, famously formulated by Niels Bohr and Werner Heisenberg, who in their most theoretical mode remain *bêtes noirs* for Sokal and Bricmont. The Copenhagen interpretation has survived into the present in the scientific worldview of John Wheeler, Nobel-winning quantum theorist and coiner of the term "black hole." In comments published by *Science News* to mark his April 2008 death, Wheeler approvingly quotes Leibniz ("This world may be a dream. And existence may be an illusion. But to me, this dream or illusion is real enough if by using reason well we are never deceived by it") and Niels Bohr ("To be? To be? What does it mean to be?"). He criticizes Einstein for thinking the universe exists "out there," and he engages the problem of human descriptions of the physical world: "we run into puzzles about the concept of time and then we say, oh, what a terrible thing. We don't realize we're the source of the puzzles because we invented the word."[29]

This philosophical split within science, and especially within physics, has considerable provenance. In truth, history does not support the assertion made in Sokal's parody and left unchallenged by the editorial board of *Social Text* that Enlightenment thinkers agreed on the independent existence of an objective reality. For example, Immanuel Kant, who outlined the philosophical parameters of epistemology and ontology for the century to follow, foreshadowed the role of the observer in both quantum theory and relativity when he asserted that "self and object are not independent entities but reciprocal elements in experience."[30] George Berkeley, outlining his idealist philosophy in *A Treatise Concerning the Principles of Human Knowledge* (1710), doubted that anything in the world could be proved to exist independently of the mind that perceives it. He went on to express a mistrust of abstract ideas, scientific explanations included, charging that all theories rested ultimately upon language and "the abuse of words." He complained of scientific controversies which were "*purely verbal;* the springing up of which weeds in almost all the sciences has been a main hindrance to the growth of true and sound knowledge."[31]

Berkeley's complaint could apply to the "science wars" debate that surrounded the Sokal hoax. In fact, the very existence of this debate supports contentions of Kuhn, the sociology of science, and postmodernism alike: our grasp of reality is hopelessly mediated by social and subjective forces, by mindset and language. Science itself has had to deal with the growing divide between what our perceptions tell us and what theory tells us is true. Kant could praise Isaac Newton for coming up with mathematical explanations that accorded with our intuitive sense of the world, but twentieth century physics was not so favored. Ernst Mach, after all, rejected both the concept of atoms and Einstein's relativity for the very reason that neither could be confirmed by experience. Einstein, in his turn, asserted that quantum theory — despite its internal consistency — was ontologically underdetermined, and that its mysteries would eventually be resolved in favor of some *Weltbild* more in line with rational expectations. Indeed, Mach, Bohr, and Einstein were all conscious of Kant and the subsequent thread of philosophical speculation when they debated their own approaches to epistemology and ontology. Even when mathematical proofs receive theoretical confirmation in experiment, we continue to be faced with phenomena that defy reality, such as that which Richard Feynman cited as "a phenomenon which is impossible, *absolutely* impossible to explain" and "the *only* mystery [...] [at the core] of all quantum mechanics" — to wit, that electrons passing through a pair of slits to a detector screen behave as though each electron knows whether both slits are open and whether it is being observed, and behaves accordingly as a particle or a wave.[32]

For the genuinely curious, modern physics begs for philosophical interpretation, no matter how much that partakes of uncertainty, discontinuity, and the role of the observer. If the mysteries of relativity and quantum theory have lent themselves to a range of popularizations, New Age extrapolations, and postmodern discourses, many of the most prominent speculations have been penned by scientists themselves. For example, physicist Paul Davies has gone on record endorsing the Everett "Many Worlds" thesis as the only reading of quantum theory that satisfies all the requirements of mathematics.[33] Mathematician Roger Penrose has argued that consciousness influences matter at the quantum level because consciousness itself is a function of quantum gravity.[34] The postmodern theories burlesqued by Alan Sokal were far less fantastic than these. And while not generally subscribed to by the scientific community, the theses of Davies and Penrose can be argued with some degree of scientific and mathematical rigor. They are just not testable at our stage of knowledge, if indeed they could ever be. As suggested already, it is in fact this aspect of science that opens the field to science studies.

Such ideas on the edge, like the "theory" of postmodern literary critics, are not theories in the scientific sense. As once suggested to me by science fiction author Kim Stanley Robinson, possessor of a Ph.D. in literature and a disciple of postmodern critic Fredric Jameson, critical "theory" would better be termed "speculation." As Kuhn observes, it is precisely when a paradigm is in flux, when evidence falls short of theory or vice versa, that such philosophical speculation occurs in the productive space between the known and the unknown. Postmodernism — it must be noted — arose after the humanities lost faith in the scientism of modernism, which had led to the problematic embrace of Karl Marx and Sigmund Freud; it is therefore not surprising that postmodern critique has come to question scientism in general. Postmodernism, in this view, may not actually represent an intellectual paradigm so much as a transition between paradigms. To draw an underdetermined parallel with science, it is the thought experiments that take place in this twilight zone that make possible the formation of a new vision of reality, something that better deserves the name "theory." Indeed, taking postmodern critics at their word, we should regard the more literary extrapolations of the field as speculative fictions, exercises in *jouissance,* and evaluate them to the degree that they are rhetorically interesting or entertaining, if not grounded in objective truth.

The boundary space between certainty and uncertainty is also where science fiction thrives, throwing off its own virtual realities at various removes from scientific knowledge. Due to its embrace of the scientific model, or perhaps in spite of it, science fiction has a long history of exploring the way science works and of questioning paradigms of reality. More often than not science fiction strays far from accepted truths; more often than not it sides with cognitive and cultural relativism. For example, we find many cases in science fiction of the relativistic stance that the apprehension of reality is mediated by biology, culture, and language; indeed, this thesis offers one of the genre's favorite themes. During the genre's post–World War II Golden Age, as most scholars of the genre know, the Sapir-Whorf thesis became a favorite of the circle of hard sf authors surrounding editor John W. Campbell, Jr. This thesis — that language not only determined one's picture of the physical world but essentially created its own reality — influenced A. E. van Vogt's *Slan* (1940, 1946), Robert A. Heinlein's *Stranger in a Strange Land* (1960) and L. Ron Hubbard's *Dianetics* (1950), turning up later as the prime plot mover in Samuel R. Delany's *Babel-17* (1966).

Of course, none of these works can be considered "hard" science fiction, that branch of the genre which extrapolates most rigorously from the mathematical sciences like physics and astronomy. Fortunately, scientific popularizers like Davies, Penrose, and John Gribbin have shown that even a more or less scientific treatment of modern theory can venture into philosophically challenging territory. Rare, however, is the work of hard science fiction that simultaneously explores such territory in a convincingly human — read "literary" — manner, straddling the two cultures. The best such novel is Gregory Benford's *Timescape* (1980), a Nebula-winning work that not only explores the philosophical implications of quantum theory but in the process provides a wholly convincing picture of the scientific process, including the purely human factors involved in the creation of new knowledge and a new reality in the Kuhnian sense.

A career physicist on the faculty of the University of California at Irvine, Benford himself has long been an advocate of bridging the divide between science and the humanities, and he sees science fiction as a primary means for doing so. For example, in a 1992 review of a book that revisits the famous C. P. Snow–F. R. Leavis "two cultures" debate, Benford observes that the author "rightly urges a view of science and art as mutually dependent, each needing the insights of the other. What we should seek is some mediation beyond mere popularization, cross-talk not quite so cross, which reconciles 'practitioners of different intellectual disciplines to the reality of different intellectual demands.'"[35] At the same time, Benford has been openly skeptical, if not contemptuous, of the postmodern enterprise, sharing with most of his scientific colleagues the impression that postmodern critique does not make sense and thus cannot make sense of science. On the other hand, he used to cite and recommend Thomas Kuhn.[36]

Briefly summarized, *Timescape* takes place in two timelines equidistant from the year of its publication: one in the early 1960s, mostly on and around the newly founded University of California at San Diego (where/when Benford was a graduate student) and the other the late 1990s, centered at Cambridge University but expanding elsewhere as the plot requires. Faced with an incipient ecological disaster caused by agricultural chemicals, the *fin-de-siècle* characters attempt to send a coded message back in time via faster-than-light tachyons, hoping their message will be picked up as interference in a few experiments taking place in the past, one a graduate student project at the UCSD of 1963. There the chief protagonist is assistant professor of physics Gordon Bernstein, supervisor of said student, who must come to terms with his own scientific skepticism regarding the apparent message before overcoming the logical skepticism of his scientific community.

The speculations arising from physical theory saturate the novel, speculations in the same camp as those by Paul Davies, who is actually named in the novel. As Benford announces on his acknowledgments page,

> Many scientific elements in this novel are true. Others are speculative, and thus may well prove false. My aim has been to illuminate some outstanding philosophical difficulties in physics. If the reader emerges with the conviction that time represents a fundamental riddle in modern physics, this book will have served its purpose.[37]

The philosophical conundra spun off by theory, especially quantum theory, are most explicitly discussed in the 1990s thread of the story. And in these discussions Benford, through his scientist characters, takes a philosophical stance more in line with the quantum instrumentalist Wheeler than the strong realist Weinberg. In fact, Wheeler gets specific mention during one conversation in which American physicist Gregory Markham, who shares many characteristics with the author, talks to British bureaucrat Ian Peterson about the problem of time.

> Look, the point here is that our distinctions between cause and effect are an illusion. This little experiment we've been discussing [to send messages into the past] is a causal *loop*—no beginning, no end. That's what Wheeler and Feynmann [*sic*] meant by requiring only that our description be logically consistent. *Logic* rules in physics, not the myth of cause and effect. Imposing an order to events is *our* point of view. A quaintly human view, I suppose. The laws of physics don't care. [...] *We* think we're moving along in time, but that's just a bias [101].

Over the course of the story, as it becomes clear that the physical world operates in ways the human mind cannot fully fathom, the reader must conclude with Peterson that the "landscape of the scientist was ultimately unreal" (146). Again and again it is emphasized that, as Markham phrases it, "Theories are based on pictures of the world — human pictures" (225). This sounds much like the belief shared by Enlightenment thinkers and postmodern critics alike that scientific theories are primarily human inventions. Even if per the scientific method they must be tested against the external world and some version of reality, we can never be completely certain of the extent to which that reality is determined or delimited by human understanding.

The issues of frame of reference — key to relativity theory — and the place of the observer, which relativity shares with quantum theory, turn up not only in the actual discussions of these theories but metaphorically in cleverly constructed scenes. For example, Cambridge physicist John Renfrew, sender of messages in the doomed world of 1998, takes time from his laboratory to build a set of shelves to hold his wife's jars of preserves. Because they live in a centuries-old English cottage, however, the walls have settled and become crooked; even though Renfrew has used all the tools at his disposal to make sure the shelves are level, they do not appear to be so. As he watches his wife worriedly rearrange the jars, he cannot displace the observation that

> the shelves did seem at a tilt. He had made them on a precise radial line extending dead to the center of the planet, geometrically impeccable and absolutely rational and quite beside the point [....] This kitchen was the true local reference frame, the Galilean invariant [....] [H]e saw that it was the shelves which stood aslant now; the walls were right [90].

Given the problems of the role of the observer, frame of reference, and the multiplicity of points of view, Benford does show that physics, at least, has an advantage over other methods of plumbing the world's mysteries: the objectivity of mathematics. As Markham tells himself, "Theories were more elegant if they could be transformed mathematically to other frames, other observers" (357). Of course, whether the mathematics describe a "real" world is beside the point; pragmatically speaking, in line with the aforementioned stances of Bohr, Heisenberg, and Wheeler, all that matters is that they describe a self-consistent one, even if that includes faster-than-light tachyons and the symmetry of time.

While social factors propel the science of the 1998 plot thread, they do not have much influence on the scientific conclusions of that timeline, only on implementation, as the looming ecological catastrophe makes it possible for Renfrew's experiment to go forward. It is the 1963 branch of the story which best displays the sociology and methodology connected to scientific theorizing. No sooner does Gordon Bernstein recognize the intentional pattern in what he had dismissed as simple noise in his graduate student's molecular resonance experiment than we get our first echo of Thomas Kuhn: the physicist admits to his student that they had missed the signal for so long because "[w]e 'knew' it was garbage, and why study garbage?" (39). In his study, Kuhn marks the beginning of a paradigm shift with a phenomenon inherited from the empirical psychology of Mach and James: what you are psychologically prepared to find influences what your senses actually perceive. Kuhn cites as evidence an experiment in which the suits of a card deck are painted in the opposite colors (i.e., black hearts, red spades), making it difficult for subjects to identify them correctly until they get used to them (Kuhn 63). As Bernstein later reflects, "If you were damned certain you weren't looking for something, there was a very good chance you wouldn't see it" (229).

Benford draws attention to the relevance of mindset at various points throughout his novel. During one discussion between Bernstein and his own faculty supervisor Isaac Lakin about the apparent coded message in the experimental results, the latter mentions by way of warning the episode of Percival Lowell's Martian canals:

> He "discovered" canals of Mars. Saw them for years, decades. Other people reported seeing them. Lowell had his own observatory built in the desert [...]. He had excellent seeing conditions there. The man had time and fine eyesight. So he discovered evidence of intelligence [....]
>
> The only mistake was that he had the wrong conclusion. The intelligent life was on *his* side of the telescope, not the Mars end. His mind [...] saw a flickering image and then imposed order on it. His own intelligence was tricking him [113–114].

Ironically, the reader already knows what these characters do not, that the future is attempting to send a message back to their very laboratory. Bernstein's scientific curiosity has overcome his own skepticism and opened his mind to new evidence, while it is Lakin who is stubbornly clinging to an established paradigm that prevents him from even considering this evidence honestly. Indeed, as an administrator of a young science program that is endeavoring to establish its reputation, Lakin's priorities are social and economic, primarily issues of grant renewal and favorable publicity. Lakin, in fact, is not only incapable of seeing any code in what Bernstein brings to him but unwilling to even consider the possibility because it does not fit any scientifically established paradigm. To maintain the respect of the scientific community in the face of the evidence, Lakin invents a wholly spurious if more acceptable explanation for the interference in the graduate experiment — "spontaneous resonance" — which better fits the expectations of professional journals and organizations. Benford thus shows us scientific methodology being skewed by non-scientific factors.

Bernstein's professional problems with Lakin, like his relationship with his graduate student Cooper, reflect the assertion of social scientist Keith Ashman (in his contribution to the volume he edited) that a number of personal factors influence the conduct of science, such as personal animosity, professional competition, and student-advisor or faculty-administrator interactions.[38] Benford, as an academic insider, does a wholly credible job of dramatizing departmental politics and their effect on science. For example, in a scene that Benford — faced with the inertial politics of publishing — had to fight to preserve in the manuscript, we watch Cooper being examined by his graduate committee, which consists of Lakin and two other senior faculty members, with Bernstein, as Cooper's advisor, naturally sitting in. While Cooper is not a stellar student, the exam becomes a test of Bernstein's merits as an assistant professor and researcher, based not just on Cooper's preparation but on the problematic discovery of the message in his results. Still rejecting out of hand the entire notion of a message, Lakin uses his part of the exam to press his "spontaneous resonance" theory. Ultimately, the results of the oral are inextricably bound up with the anomaly and Gordon Bernstein's interpretation of it.

> Gates and Carroway and Lakin thought the message hypothesis was bullshit, pure and simple. They weren't going to let the issue slide by. Cooper couldn't explain all his data, not the interesting parts, anyway. As long as that riddle hung in the air, this committee wasn't going to pass on a thesis [262].

Thus, the committee fails Cooper, foreshadowing the department's later decision not to grant Bernstein a pro forma step increase.

The process that Bernstein and his colleagues eventually undergo over the course of the novel perfectly mimics the history of a paradigm shift as outlined by Kuhn. When Bernstein decodes the warning of the future environmental crisis, he himself regards the result skeptically, but as a good scientist he keeps an open mind and a low profile, reaching outside of his field to biologists and astronomers for confirmation of his evidence. In the process, word gets to the Carl Sagan–like character Saul Shriffer, a popularizer who makes a theoretical leap of faith, in line with his own obsessions, and publicizes Bernstein's coded messages as possible extraterrestrial communiqués.

This publicity, unfortunately, draws in the media and the UFO fanatics but turns Bernstein's entire scientific community against him. As one colleague tells him, Shriffer "puts a black eye on the whole game" (215). When Bernstein alludes to the message during a departmental colloquium, the audience of scientists cannot objectively evaluate the evidence Bernstein presents because they cannot separate it from Shriffer's underdetermined thesis, even though Bernstein has disavowed it. Furthermore, as yet another scientist character observes to Bernstein, "In science you usually can't convert your opponents [...] you have to outlive them" (357–358). This is a paraphrase of a statement Kuhn quotes from Max Planck: "a new scientific truth does not triumph by convincing its opponents and making them see the light, but rather because its opponents eventually die, and a new generation grows up that is familiar with it."[39] As Kuhn documents, the history of science is replete with proofs of this assertion, backing up his insistence that scientists on either side of a paradigm inhabit different epistemological worlds.

Ultimately, the truth — per the novel — wins out, when Bernstein solicits and receives independent confirmation of the content and future origin of the messages from other scientists. At this stage in the plot, Benford provides a splendid metaphor for the different worlds on either side of a paradigm shift, in the process also resolving the story's time paradoxes. Making use of Everett's Many Worlds thesis, he has the world actually split at the moment that the information in Bernstein's messages is scientifically validated, laying the groundwork for the implementation of the warnings imbedded in them. The environmentally catastrophic future in which Renfrew continues to send — and incidentally receive — tachyon messages has been averted, although the characters we have gotten to know in 1998 will not enjoy the fruits of their success. In other words, acceptance of the existence of tachyons and the reality of the message literally leaves Bernstein and everyone around him in a different world with a different future, one we soon discover is not actually our own.

In his superb treatment of the psychological and social factors that go into the making of science, in his exploration of the epistemologically challenging and "ultimately unreal" landscape of modern physics, Benford finds himself in the same relativistic territory as some of the science scholars attacked by Sokal, Norris, and their fellow realists. It should be underlined that among the scientific premises in Benford's novel are some suggested by mathematics and theory but contradicted so far by experience, experiment, and probability: the existence of tachyons, the symmetry of time, the Many World thesis. In fact, Benford has confessed in conversation that he does not accept Everett's thesis himself and that he has no reason to doubt the impossibility of faster-than-light travel. Ultimately, therefore, *Timescape* is less about scientific truths than it is about the sociology and philosophy of science. That it so possesses the ring of truth is a tribute not only to Benford's understanding of science in theory and practice but to his rhetorical skills as an author.

As a speculative fiction straddling the two cultures, Benford's work arguably lies on a spectrum that includes the sociological, philosophical, and rhetorical products of science studies. Far from undermining respect for scientific truth, as its detractors claim, practitioners of science studies insist they can foster the appreciation of science by showing how it works, and even improve science itself by inspecting the means — especially the non-scientific ones — by which scientific knowledge advances. Sociologists of science investigate sexism and racism in science, for example, in order to help exorcise such prejudices,[40] or study the personal relationships and social organization of scientists to determine how such factors as personal animosity and departmental politics influence results.[41] Ultimately, the humanistic study of science is motivated by "a desire to integrate science into larger intellectual currents, institutional practices, and personal lifestyles."[42] From Kuhn to Latour, the belief persists among science critics that science remains a superior methodology for producing knowledge of the natural world, one that theorists in humanistic studies can only envy.[43] Even epistemological anarchists like Paul Feyerabend have suggested that, if we cannot regard scientific theories as definitive descriptions of reality, still less can we make such claims for critical theory. Fundamentally, it is this admiration of science and the scientific method that drives many science scholars.

Even at its most wrongheaded or shortsighted, it is difficult to imagine science studies doing any harm to science, any more than science fiction does. Labinger and Collins conclude as much at the end of their essay collection, noting that "the authors appear to converge in the opinion that science studies is *not* hostile to the interests of science, either deliberately or as an unintended byproduct" (296). At its worst, critique merely makes itself irrelevant. At its best, however, it can awaken us to the philosophical and historical context of scientific theories, and enlighten us to the social and other human factors that affect the practice of science. To deny that such factors have any bearing on the pursuit of knowledge about the natural world, as some realists would do, is to throw Archimedes out with the bathwater. As Kuhn observes at the conclusion of his landmark study, "Scientific knowledge, like language, is intrinsically the common property of a group or else nothing at all" (210). Especially if critique is willing to imitate the scientific ideal and learn from its mistakes, science studies — like science fiction — can reinforce the bridge between the two cultures.

Notes

1. Paul Gross and Norman Levitt, *Higher Superstition: The Academic Left and Its Quarrels with Science* (Baltimore, MD: Johns Hopkins University Press, 1994); 2nd ed., 1998.

2. Alan Sokal, "A Physicist Experiments with Cultural Studies," *Lingua Franca* 6/4 (May/June 1996): 62–64.

3. Paris: Editions Odile Jacob.

4. New York: St. Martin's, 1998.

5. Alan Sokal, *Beyond the Hoax: Science, Philosophy and Culture* (Oxford and New York: Oxford University Press, 2008), 131. Cited hereafter as Sokal 2008.

6. Quoted in Sokal 2008, 205 n.87. From David Bloor, *Knowledge and Social Imagery*, 2nd ed. (Chicago: University of Chicago Press, 1991), 5.

7. Quoted by Liz McMillen in "The Science Wars," *The Chronicle of Higher Education* 42 (28 June 1996), A9.

8. Quoted by McMillen in "The Science Wars," A9.

9. Durham and London: Duke University Press, 1996.

10. Oxford: Blackwell, 1997.

11. *The Structure of Scientific Revolutions*, 3rd ed. (Chicago: University of Chicago Press, 1996), 193.

12. Steven Weinberg, "Physics and History," *The One Culture?: A Conversation About Science*, edited by Jay A. Labinger and Harry Collins (Chicago: University of Chicago Press, 2001), 125.

13. "Physics and Language — Science and Rhetoric: Reviewing the Parallel Evolution of Theory on Motion and Meaning in the Aftermath of the Sokal Hoax," *Quarterly Journal of Speech*, 85/4 (November 1999): 354.

14. Oxford and New York: Oxford University Press, 1998.

15. Cited hereafter as Labinger.

16. London and New York: Routledge. Cited hereafter as Ashman.

17. Peter R. Saulson, "Life Inside a Case Study" (Labinger 73–82), 79.

18. Ann E. Cudd, "Objectivity and Ethno-Feminist Critique of Science" (Ashman 80–97), 81.

19. "Does Science Studies Undermine Science?" (Labinger, 13–26), 18–19.

20. "Conversing Seriously with Sociologists" (Labinger 83–98), 97.

21. "Science and Sociology of Science: Beyond War and Peace," Labinger, 30.

22. "How to Be Antiscientific," Labinger 100–101.

23. "Physics and History" (Labinger 116–127), 127.

24. "Physics and History," Labinger 124.

25. Robert L. Park, "Voodoo Medicine in a Scientific World" (Ashman 140–150), 144.

26. Kenneth G. Wilson and Constance K. Barsky, "Beyond Social Construction" (Labinger 291–295), 293.

27. Wilson and Barsky, Labinger 300.

28. *Conjectures and Refutations: The Growth of Scientific Knowledge* (New York and London: Basic Books, 1962), 169.

29. 24 May 2008: 32.

30. *Kant and the Nineteenth Century,* 2nd ed., edited by W. T. Jones (New York: Harcourt Brace Jovanovich, 1969), 38.

31. In *The Empiricists* (Garden City, NY: Doubleday, 1961), 149.

32. Quoted by John Gribbin, *In Search of Schrödinger's Cat: Quantum Physics and Reality* (New York: Bantam, 1984), 164.

33. *Other Worlds: A Portrait of Nature in Rebellion: Space, Superspace and the Quantum Universe* (New York: Simon and Schuster 1980), Chapter 7.

34. *The Emperor's New Mind: Concerning Computers, Minds, and the Laws of Physics* (New York and London: Viking 1991), Chapter 10.

35. "Science and Art Mutually Dependent," review of Tom Sorrell, *Scientism: Philosophy and the Infatuation with Science* (London and New York: Routledge, 1991), *Science-Fiction Studies* 19/1 (March 1992), 140.

36. Kuhn's work is regarded as past its prime by many of the philosophers of science represented in the essay collections cited earlier. At best, according to Wilson and Barsky, his signature book must be regarded as merely "an initial, highly tentative proposal" (Labinger 154). On the other hand, five years after this conclusion, Kuhn remains the starting point in Edwin H-C. Hung, *Beyond Kuhn: Scientific Explanation, Theory Structure, Incommensurability and Physical Necessity* (Hants, UK, and Burlington, VT: Ashgate, 2006). It may be worth noting that Benford's novel appeared halfway in time between the 1962 first edition of Kuhn and the centerpoint of the science wars debate.

37. *Timescape* (New York: Bantam, 1980).

38. "Measuring the Hubble Constant: Objectivity under the Telescope," Ashman 110–111.

39. From Planck, *Scientific Autobiography and Other Papers,* trans. F. Gaynor (New York 1949). Quoted by Kuhn, 151.

40. Ann E. Cudd, "Objectivity and Ethno-Feminist Critique of Science" (Ashman 80–97), 81–82.

41. Keith M. Ashman, "Measuring the Hubble Constant: Objectivity under the Telescope" (Ashman 98–119), 110–111.

42. Steve Fuller, "The Reenchantment of Science: A Fit End to the Science Wars?" (Ashman 182–208), 182.

43. Robert Koch, "The Case of Latour," *Configurations: A Journal of Literature, Science, and Technology,* 3/3 (Fall 1995), 108.

5. The Rich and the Poor: Science Fiction and the Other Two Cultures

Gary Westfahl

Everyone familiar with the career of C. P. Snow knows that, in a famous 1959 lecture, he decried a growing gap between the "two cultures" of the sciences and the humanities, and that he called for vigorous efforts to bridge that gap. Yet few people recall Snow's expressly stated *reason* for improved communication between the two cultures: that it would help reduce the disparity between the rich nations and poor nations of the world. As he stated in the final section of his essay, subtitled "The Rich and the Poor,"

> The main issue is that the people in the industrialized countries are getting richer, and those in the non-industrialised countries are at best standing still: so that the gap between the industrialized countries and the rest is widening every day.... Education isn't the total solution to this problem: but without education the West can't even begin to cope.... Closing the gap between our cultures is a necessity in the most abstract intellectual sense, as well as in the most practical.[1]

Snow returned to this point with even greater emphasis in his 1963 follow-up essay, "The Two Cultures: A Second Look":

> The scientific revolution is the only method by which most people can gain the primal things (years of life, freedom from hunger, survival for children) — the primal things which we take for granted and which have in reality come to us through having had our own scientific revolution not so long ago ... we can educate a large proportion of our better minds so that they are not ignorant of imaginative experience, both in the arts and in science, not ignorant either of the endowments of applied science, of the remediable suffering of most of their fellow humans, and of the responsibilities which, once they are seen, cannot be denied.[2]

We are even told that Snow originally intended to title his first lecture "The Rich and the Poor" to emphasize this issue.

If this aspect of Snow's argument is unfamiliar to many people, that may be because that Snow does not do a particularly good job of explaining precisely *why* this lack of communication between cultures is hindering the economic progress of poorer nations and *why* better communication between the humanities and the sciences would help the economic progress of poorer nations. The following seems to represent the essence of his argument. First, literary intellectuals are "natural Luddites" ("The Two Cultures" 22), inclined to be willfully ignorant of and opposed to scientific advances, even seeming at times to believe in a "pre-industrial Eden from which our ancestors were, by the wicked machinations of science, brutally expelled" ("The Two Cultures: A Second Look" 83–84). Second, because of this unfortunate attitude, these humanists have been indifferent to, or even opposed to, improvements in scientific education and efforts to speed technological progress in underdeveloped countries. Third, if literary intellectuals had more contact with scientists, and a better understanding of science and its beneficial effects, they would first of all assist in achieving stronger scientific education in the Western countries, which would have the result of producing more qualified scientists and engineers to assist the poorer countries in their economic advancement. Fourth, they would also, presumably, join in efforts to, in Snow's words, "nag away" at political leaders to do more to help the underdeveloped world ("The Two Cultures" 49). Correcting one common misperception of his views, Snow acknowledges in "The Two Cultures: A Second Look" that humanists have little direct power over their societies, that they are not "the main decision-makers of the western world"; however, he goes on to assert that they "represent, vocalise, and to some extent shape and predict the mood of the non-scientific culture: they do not make the decisions, but their words seep into the minds of those who do" (61). Thus, their support for efforts to bring out scientific progress in non-western societies would indeed have some tangible effects.

An apparent omission in Snow's argument involves how scientists could better help humanity if they had more contact with humanists. However, one idea to build upon might be Snow's comment that "I can't see the political techniques through which the good human capabilities of the West can get into action" ("The Two Cultures" 49). In addition to the indirect influence they could have on political leaders, perhaps, literary intellectuals, with stronger interpersonal skills and knowledge of human history, might be able to assist and advise scientists, who at times seem anti-social and cloistered in their awareness of the wider world, in navigating through complex political realities to achieve their technological goals.

If this indeed represents the totality of Snow's argument, then someone living in the twenty-first century might justifiably dismiss it as outdated. That is, simply by living in nations where one scientific advance after another has been introduced to, popularized in, and thoroughly integrated into the culture at large, the literary intellectuals of the western world, even without much direct contact with scientists, have unavoidably become aware of scientific progress and its beneficial effects on society. It would be hard to find anyone in the world today who would seriously maintain, for example, that non-western countries would be better off without advanced technology. Furthermore, far from being Luddites, literary critics of the past two decades, especially those devoted to postmodernism, have consistently displayed a fascination with scientific matters; while one can still say that they remain insufficiently knowledgeable about science — one point of the Sokal affair — they certainly are no longer hostile toward scientific progress. Finally, whatever indirect influence over society that humanists might have once enjoyed is, today, surely less than it once was. Thus, inspiring literary intellectuals to support scientific progress throughout the world would now appear to be both unnecessary and unimportant.

Nevertheless, in a volume devoting to examining Snow's argument after half a century of debate and relating his ideas to the genre of science fiction, it seems appropriate to address what he announced to be his chief reason for making that argument. That is, if Snow could somehow return to life today and consider some of the chapters in this volume, he probably would concede that, yes, in some respects, science fiction has played a role, and will continue to play a role, in bridging the gap between the cultures of the sciences and the humanities. However, he might go on to say: but achieving that goal in and of itself, after all, was never my primary concern. Rather, he would ask, how exactly has the improved communication between cultures effected through science fiction contributed to helping to reduce the gap between the rich nations and the poor nations of the world? And indeed, regardless of any desire to remain focused on Snow's original goals, one could also argue that it remains a question worth asking. That is, science fiction is a category of literature which has become the focus of a large community of people throughout the world, people who by some accounts are often unusually intelligent or talented; it seems fair to ask, how has this literature, and how have the people devoted to this literature, helped to make the world a better place to live in?

It is a question easy enough to ask, but vexingly difficult to answer, and certainly no single essay, or even a series of essays, could possibly come close to providing a definitive answer. All I can do, in the space available here, is to outline a few approaches one might take to address the question and offer some very preliminary conclusions.

At this time, I can envision three ways to test the hypothesis that science fiction has helped, is helping, or will help to bridge not only the gap between the two cultures but also the gap between the rich and the poor. First, one might consider the standard argument that science fiction is uniquely able to generate and present valuable new ideas in order to contribute to human progress — as John W. Campbell, Jr., put it in one letter, "science fiction needs to fulfill its job of stimulating people to try for something better than we have, or have had"[3] — and see if the literature is offering any intriguing suggestions that could help to improve living conditions in underdeveloped nations. Second, one might investigate the members of the science fiction community created by this genre of writing to see if those individuals have been especially energetic or effective in addressing the problems that Snow identifies. Finally, one might attempt to establish a statistical correlation between a country's economic development and its attentiveness in science fiction, which would provide evidence that, in some unspecified fashion, science fiction is indeed contributing to technological and economic progress.

In conceiving of science fiction as a database of ideas for reducing global poverty, I will admit that scores of texts did not spring to mind; as I have argued elsewhere, science fiction generally has displayed little interest in economics,[4] and I also suspect that its stories are rarely set in, or involve, Third World countries. Still, I immediately thought of one novel that I had read as part of my research into space stations in science fiction —*Manna* (1983), by Lee Correy (the fiction-writing pseudonym of G. Harry Stine) — as one example of a science fiction story providing potentially valuable advice for the leaders of underdeveloped nations.

The novel, which takes place in the year 2050, is about a fictitious African nation named the United Mitanni Commonwealth, which is an island of freedom and prosperity surrounded by impoverished totalitarian regimes. The country seems analogous to Kenya, in that it is also located on the east coast of Africa, has a highly multiethnic population, is roughly rectangular in its dimensions, and is about the size of California, although the 2050 population of the United Mitanni Commonwealth is said to be only about one-tenth of the current population of Kenya. This and other information is presented in the form of an introductory map and an appendix with several paragraphs of data about the United Mitanni Commonwealth, purportedly taken from a future reference book, all of which provides this fictitious nation with an aura of realism presumably designed to contribute to its persuasive effect as an exemplary model for actual African nations.

Although the virtues of the United Mitanni Commonwealth include a culture fiercely devoted to libertarian ideals and free enterprise, the main reason for its prosperity is that, for the last fifty years, it has been home to a spaceport, profiting from its own ventures into space and its business arrangements with the Free Traders who inhabit space. The philosophy that has brought wealth to the United Mitanni Commonwealth, referenced in the novel's title, is explained several times, at greatest length by the nation's patriarch, General Vamori:

> The human race has evolved in a peasant economy where, if things were the best they could possibly be, everyone had a little of everything but no one had very much of anything.... Now it isn't necessary to live that way! There's plenty for everyone! There will always be plenty for everyone from now on. By using our minds and applying technology wisely, we're using the Earth and, at last, the Solar System. What happens to greed when manna falls from the sky in such great abundance that it becomes senseless to hoard it?[5]

Thus, poverty remains a problem in the other African nations of 2050 because they still do not realize that access to space has permanently altered the human condition, and they have failed to take advantage of the limitless opportunities available to those who travel into space.

As a message to contemporary African countries, it is hard to deny that, from one perspective, *Manna* definitely has a point. Scientists agree that the best place to launch vehicles into space is on or near the Equator, and Africa by far offers the largest geographical area for spaceports that would meet that criterion. If one can find practical ways to exploit them, outer space does indeed offer limitless resources of various kinds which would be enormously profitable for those who gain access to them. With numerous private entrepreneurs now making plans to launch vehicles into space in order to earn money, an equatorial African nation might wisely make a vigorous effort to attract their business, or might endeavor to assemble its own team of experts to venture into space, and in these ways that nation might indeed lay the groundwork for great prosperity in the future.

Still, there are also reasons for African nations to resist Correy's implicit plan of action. In the first place, his motives are definitely suspect: prior to writing *Manna*, Correy had long been a vigorous advocate of space exploration, and under his own name, G. Harry Stine, he had written two books, *The Space Enterprise* (1975) and *The Third Industrial Revolution* (1980), arguing that space initiatives represented a guaranteed road to riches.[6] Thus, his true interest in writing *Manna*, rather obviously, was getting people to go into space, not to improve the lives of people in Africa; the promises of profits were clearly intended to encourage those who lacked his visionary impulse to spread humanity throughout the cosmos to put some money into space travel anyway, merely as a way to make a buck. And for that reason, all of his arguments seem overly optimistic, as he severely underestimates the expense and difficulty of getting into space and greatly overestimates the easy money to be made by doing so. Needless to say, if an African nation in 1983 had decided to model itself on the United Mitanni Commonwealth and seek prosperity through space travel, it likely would today still be waiting to earn its first profits from its investments.

Even if one accepts the sincerity of Correy's desire to assist underdeveloped nations and believes in the practicality of his proposals, the novel is not painting an entirely desirable picture of the fate of an African nation which commits itself to space travel. For, by transforming itself into an island of prosperity in a struggling continent, the United Mitanni Commonwealth has attracted the enmity both of the governments and corporations of the developed world — described in the novel as the "Tripartite Coalition" (15) — and of its impoverished, dictatorial neighbors. The novel focuses on the United Mitanni Commonwealth's newly recruited space pilot — American Sandy Baldwin — who joins his new African colleagues in confronting an unending series of violent attacks, on Earth and in space, aimed at bringing this upstart nation to its knees. The people of this country, it seems, can never pause to enjoy their prosperity, as they must constantly run away from burning buildings, dodge missiles aimed at their spacecraft, or take up arms to rescue kidnapped allies. An African leader might well read *Manna* and ask: if such constant violence is the price one must pay for these riches from outer space, are they really worth having?

There are, of course, a few other science fiction stories which might be regarded as valuable advice for Third World Nations. An earlier science fiction story about Africa, Mack Reynolds's *Blackman's Burden* (1972), with its sequels *Border, Breed nor Birth* (1972) and *The Best Ye Breed* (1978),[7] argues that a future African continent abandoned by the rest of the world might achieve prosperity if it were unified and brought under the control of a benevolent dictator — here, African-American sociologist Homer Crawford, who under the name of El Hassan strives for "the uniting and modernization of the continent of my racial heritage."[8] The desirability of modernization need no longer be argued, to be sure, but given the turmoils that have afflicted that continent, a policy of unifying the continent under one government might indeed be wise, although it is hard to see how this might be realistically achieved through the sort of gradual, small-scale tactics that Crawford employs. Providing an argument against rapid technological development at all costs, Bruce Sterling's "Green Days in Brunei" (1985) heterodoxically suggests that people in underdeveloped countries might, overall, be much happier lives if they vehemently reject advanced science and instead work toward a simpler, more environmentally-friendly lifestyle, albeit with a touch of high technology as revealed in the end.[9] Snow himself might reject such a view as "Luddite," but developing nations struggling with problems like ruinous pollution and rapid urbanization might find this approach to be appealing. Overall, I cannot honestly report that I regard this line of investigation as promising, but science fiction remains, as I have said elsewhere, a vast and largely unexplored territory, and there may well be more food for thought about economic and scientific progress in underdeveloped countries than my own limited knowledge of the field has so far suggested.

The next issue to consider is whether the people who form the community created by science fiction have been a significant force in improving living conditions throughout the world, and almost immediately, a number of their charitable efforts come to mind. Internet searches will bring to light many local science fiction organizations that volunteer their services to worthwhile causes; one unique example is T'Mar, a group based in the state of Washington. Their website describes their mission in this way:

> We are a group of Science Fiction fans dedicated to establishing a positive presence in our community through volunteer service and fund raising activities. We make ourselves available to provide assistance at charity events and fundraisers, and visit hospitals, schools, movie premieres and book stores — anywhere we can help.[10]

What makes this group unusual is that its members dress up and act like Klingons, the warlike aliens of the *Star Trek* universe, which admittedly might be a bit disconcerting to some of the people they are dedicated to helping. Still, it is clear that their hearts are in the right place.

Turning to national and international fan organizations, one finds a number of worthwhile traditions of giving. The Trans-Atlantic Fan Fund, established in 1953, collects donations so that a deserving American or British science fiction fan can attend a major science fiction convention on the other side of the Atlantic Ocean; nineteen years later, the Down Under Fan Fund was set up to send Australian fans to North American conventions, and sometimes to send North American fans to Australian conventions. Due to the advocacy of the late Robert A. Heinlein — a beloved author whose life was once saved by a blood transfusion — virtually all major science fiction conventions now include a blood drive, and campaigns to collect toys for poor children and canned food for poor families are also common.

One can also readily find examples of charitable initiatives in response to particular problems, whether these are small or large. When horror writer and editor Charles L. Grant was diagnosed with chronic obstructive pulmonary disease, he faced daunting medical expenses due to a lack of health insurance. Upon hearing the news, over fifty writers, including major figures like Clive Barker, Neil Gaiman, Stephen King, and Dean Koontz, donated items for a vast charity auction to raise funds to assist him. On a larger scale, after an enormous tsunami devastated many regions of southern Asia in December, 2005, science fiction and fantasy authors came together and donated original stories to an anthology, *Elemental: The Tsunami Relief Anthology*

(2006), specifically designed to raise money to provide relief for victims of the tsunami. The book featured an introduction by Sir Arthur C. Clarke and stories by noteworthy authors like Brian W. Aldiss, Kevin J. Anderson, David Drake, Esther M. Friesner, David Gerrold, Joe Haldeman, Larry Niven, and Sean Williams.[11]

A minor example of science fiction charity that should be of special interest to readers of this volume involves the 1996 World Science Fiction Convention, held in Anaheim, California, which like most events of this kind ended up earning a modest profit. In the course of disbanding the organizations set up to stage these conventions, the tradition is to donate all leftover funds to worthwhile causes. Now, in the late 1990s, the University of California, Riverside, had temporarily withdrawn all financial support for the J. Lloyd Eaton Conferences on Science Fiction and Fantasy Literature, and it was very uncertain whether we would be able to have our envisioned 20th Eaton Conference. Fortunately, two of the people closely connected to the 1996 World Science Fiction Convention, the late Bruce Pelz and Ed Green, had also become firm friends of the Eaton Conferences, and when they were apprised of the situation, they quickly arranged to have the 1996 convention organization donate $3000 to support the next Eaton Conference — which, as it happens, turned out to be the conference that addressed the topic of "Science Fiction at the Crossroads of Two Cultures" and attracted the papers which, revised and updated, now make up this volume. Quite literally, then, this volume would not exist had it not been for the charitable spirit that has so frequently proved to be characteristic of the science fiction community.

One could easily devote several more pages to listing the various sorts of charitable activities that members of the science fiction community have engaged in; but enough has been said, perhaps, to indicate that most of these efforts, however admirable they might be, have not directly addressed Snow's desire to achieve progress in underdeveloped countries. Quite understandably, science fiction fans have been mostly concerned with helping their own, whether it is other people in their vicinity or other science fiction fans. Indeed, in a conversation I recall having with Bruce Pelz, he said that while the World Science Fiction Conventions would consider any meritorious applicants for their leftover funds, their organizers always preferred to donate money to causes related to science fiction — which is why they were happy to support a conference devoted to science fiction research and scholarship. Considering the broad question of making the entire world a better place, then, one must struggle to see the work of the science fiction community as a significant factor in achieving that goal.

A third avenue of investigation, as already indicated, would be to move beyond scattered and anecdotal data to seek statistical verification of the impact of science fiction: specifically, can one establish a strong correlation between a nation's interest in science fiction and its technological and economic progress? If such a correlation could be found, it would demonstrate that the dialogue between the science and the humanities carried on through science fiction can in fact help to improve the lives of people in underdeveloped countries.

To test this hypothesis, I decided to focus on the nation of Taiwan — for two reasons. First, as a nation which during the last fifty years effectively managed to advance from the status of a Third World country to that of an economic powerhouse, Taiwan represents a success story, which invites examination of how it achieved that success and what lessons it might provide for other nations which have not yet achieved such success. Second, while I was attending the Hong Kong 2003 Conference, Danny J. Han–Chang Lin kindly gave me a copy of a book he had compiled and self-published, entitled *The Complete Bibliography of Taiwanese Science Fiction* (2003).[12] This valuable compendium of information included tables listing every science fiction book that had ever been published in Taiwan, including both original works and translations as well as critiques and dissertations on science fiction. This volume, then, would provide half of the data I would need in my efforts to establish a statistical correlation between science fiction and scientific and economic progress. The other data I would need — the annual Taiwanese Gross Domestic Product during the last fifty years, to measure its economic growth, could be easily obtained from the Global Financial Data database.[13]

With this information in hand, I was prepared to compute what is known as the Pearson r — a number between 1 and -1 which for two sets of data can indicate either a strong positive correlation (when r is near 1), no correlation at all (when r is near 0), or a strong negative correlation (when r is near -1). There are two computationally equivalent methods for determining the Pearson r for given sets of data. First, one compiles the data to be compared in pairs, finds the product of each pair, and finds in each case the sum, the square of the sum, the sum of each item individually squared, and the sum of the products; with these numbers, a formula can be used to find the Pearson r. Second, one converts each datum into a z-score (a way of standardizing a set of numerical data so that the highest possible score is about 3, the average score is 0, and the lowest possible score is about -3), and for each pair finds the product of the z-scores. Then, by dividing the sum of the products by the number of pairs, one finds the Pearson r. Properly computed, the results from both methods should be identical, but I employed both methods as a way to check for a possible error. In the tables at the end of this chapter, I provide all of my data, the formulas I used, and the results I obtained. Using the first method, I found r = 0.897401824; using the second method, I found r = 0.897601825. The small deviation in the ten-thousandth place can be attributed to the fact that all calculations were done using a hand-held calculator which could only handle numbers up to ten digits, generating small rounding errors in several of the calculations.

As statisticians know, a Pearson r in the vicinity of 0.897 constitutes proof positive of a strong positive correlation, regardless of which level of significance one chooses to employ. Unquestionably, then, there is a strong positive correlation between the growth in Taiwan's Gross Domestic Product from 1953 to 2002 and the growth in Taiwan's publication of science fiction books during the same period. However, the precise *reason* for this strong positive correlation remains very much up in the air.

In general, there are three possible explanations for a strong positive correlation. One, the first factor caused the second factor, or in this case, the scientific and economic progress that Taiwan achieved during this period had, as one of its effects, a growing interest in science fiction, as measured by increasing numbers of science fiction books. Two, the second factor caused the first factor, or in this case, a growing interest in science fiction among citizens of Taiwan somehow spurred them to achieve more and more scientific and economic progress (and this, of course, is the explanation that would be most desirable to persons seeking to demonstrate that science fiction does indeed address Snow's concerns). Third, both factors are caused by a third, unidentified factor; or in this case, as one possibility, it might be that improvements in Taiwanese education during this period had, as two effects, scientific and economic progress, and a growing interest in science fiction.

It has also occurred to me that there is another way to explain my findings. In general, since books cannot be considered a necessity, one does not expect poorer countries to be publishing a lot of books; however, as technological and economic conditions improve, one predictable result would be the publication of more and more books. Although I have no data at hand, it seems logical to assume that during the last fifty years, as a natural accompaniment to its scientific and economic progress, Taiwan would be publishing more and more books of all sorts, which would be measured by someone with an obsessive interest in science fiction only by an observed, and proportionate, increase in the numbers of science fiction books. Thus, the figures I compiled from Lin's book may be documenting not an increasing interest in science fiction, but rather an increasing number of book publications in general. Strong positive correlations can result from the use of two different measurements of the same phenomenon; in this case, then, my two sets of data may simply represent two different ways of measuring the economic growth of Taiwan — a higher and higher Gross Domestic Product, and more and more books being published in the country.

Still, it must be recalled that, at the very beginning, I noted that I could not expect to achieve any definitive results from the limited investigations I would be engaging in; rather, my purpose was simply to provide some preliminary hints as to what might be achieved by more extended, and extensive, research. In concluding, though, I can offer some suggestions for anyone who might be interested in pursuing the question of whether or not science fiction has helped, is helping, or might in the future help to make the world a better place.

First, in considering science fiction as a potential source of valuable suggestions for achieving scientific and economic progress in underdeveloped countries, one would obviously have to commit oneself to more extensive research into the literature. I am reminded of a project that I once worked for, Innovative Technologies from Science Fiction for Space Applications (ITSF), which was supported by a grant from the European Space Agency. The idea was to hire science fiction researchers, such as myself, to survey science fiction stories to locate innovative ideas that might be helpful to future efforts to explore and colonize outer space.[14] One can easily envision a similar initiative to search for innovative ideas that might be helpful to future efforts to improve economic conditions throughout the globe. Perhaps I am simply unfamiliar with any number of relevant texts; perhaps there is a greater need to survey the science fiction that is now actually being written by residents of underdeveloped countries, who understandably might have more interest in potential ways to improve conditions in countries like their own.[15]

Second, in considering science fiction as a community that often appears dedicated to helping others, one might work with members of the science fiction community to compile a comprehensive and detailed listing of all the charitable activities that have been undertaken by science fiction writers, readers, and fans. As one suggestion, *Locus* magazine, which every year conducts a detailed survey of its readers to determine, among other things, their reading interests, average income, and average level of education, might be persuaded to add a question or two about the amount of money they annually donate to charity or the types of charitable work they engage in. Such data, if compared to data from Americans as a whole, might demonstrate that reading science fiction, in some fashion, makes people more likely to be engage in volunteer work, more likely to contribute to worthwhile causes, and more likely to be altruistic to others; and even if some specific connection to the needs of underdeveloped nations could not be established, a simple link between science fiction and a strong charitable impulse might show that science fiction is, at least in a general sense, contributing to the noble cause that Snow once articulated.

Third, in considering science fiction as a force that might in some statistically significant fashion serve to drive scientific and economic progress, one might seek out data similar to my own from other counties throughout the world to see if similar correlations can be found. To address the particular concern that I raised, one might employ, instead of the numbers of science fiction books published annually, the annual *percentage* of total books published in a country which can be classified as science fiction. If, say, the annual percentage of science fiction books being published rises from 5 percent to 15 percent in tandem with technological and economic progress during the same period, that might be a more persuasive indicator that a growing interest in science fiction does indeed correlate to such progress. It would also be valuable to recruit a professional statistician — something that I am not — to employ more sophisticated methods to test my hypothesis.

In the end, however, one might ask: does such research really *matter?* Certainly, there is no need to prove there is some sort of tangible economic benefit associated with science fiction in order to validate the genre as a worthwhile activity for writers and readers; simply by providing stimulating entertainment for generations of readers, science fiction has unquestionably demonstrated its enormous value. Still, as I have documented elsewhere, the history of science fiction is characterized by recurring arguments that the genre, in fact, is capable of affecting the world in a positive way, arguments frequently offered to debunk the annoying charge that imaginative stories represent little more than a form of "escapism," an evasion of real-world problems. If one could establish with solid evidence that, in some fashion, science fiction is indeed helping to improve conditions in the real world, then that would at least provide a measure of comeuppance to some of the genre's traditional opponents, and a sense of satisfaction for its many writers and readers.

Table 1. Taiwan Gross Domestic Product in Constant 2001 Dollars Per Year, 1953–2002

(Taken from Global Financial Data Online Database)

Year	Gross Domestic Product	Year	Gross Domestic Product
1953	233,769.0000	1965	622,593.3125
1954	256,071.0000	1966	678,086.4375
1955	276,827.0000	1967	750,717.9375
1956	292,062.0000	1968	819,564.2500
1957	313,561.0000	1969	892,901.9375
1958	334,602.0000	1970	994,432.8125
1959	360,202.0000	1971	1,122,666.0000
1960	382,924.0000	1972	1,272,173.2500
1961	423,150.3125	1973	1,435,427.7500
1962	456,594.8438	1974	1,452,108.1250
1963	499,304.4375	1975	1,523,673.6250
1964	560,214.2500	1976	1,734,864.2500

Year	Gross Domestic Product	Year	Gross Domestic Product
1977	1,911,641.3750	1990	5,400,623.5000
1978	2,171,508.2500	1991	5,808,584.5000
1979	2,349,006.2500	1992	6,243,500.0000
1980	2,520,512.5000	1993	6,681,408.5000
1981	2,675,843.7500	1994	7,156,324.5000
1982	2,770,869.2500	1995	7,616,050.0000
1983	3,004,922.0000	1996	8,088,068.0000
1984	3,323,433.5000	1997	8,621,225.0000
1985	3,488,027.0000	1998	9,013,354.0000
1986	3,893,929.2500	1999	9,531,425.0000
1987	4,390,205.0000	2000	10,081,059.0000
1988	4,734,416.0000	2001	9,862,183.0000
1989	5,124,175.5000	2002	10,280,971.0000

Table 2. Number of Taiwanese Science Fiction Books Published Per Year, 1953–2002

(Taken from *A Bibliography of Taiwanese Science Fiction*)[16]

Year	Original sf	Original critiques of sf	Original children's sf	Translated sf	Translated critiques of sf	Translated children's sf	Novels from films	Dissertations on sf	TOTAL
1953				1					1
1954									0
1955									0
1956									0
1957				1					1
1958						1			1
1959						1			1
1960									0
1961									0
1962									0
1963									0
1964									0
1965									0
1966									0
1967			1						1
1968				2		2			4
1969				1		4			5
1970	2					6			8
1971				1					1

Year	Original sf	Original critiques of sf	Original children's sf	Translated sf	Translated critiques of sf	Translated children's sf	Novels from films	Dissertations on sf	TOTAL
1972	1			2		1			4
1973				3					3
1974						2			2
1975	1		1	3		1			6
1976						4			4
1977		1			2	13	1		17
1978	1		2	1		18	4		26
1979	1			4					5
1980	6	1	3	10	1	4	3		28
1981				35		2			37
1982	1			1		1			3
1983	2	1		11		1	2		17
1984	4			4		3			11
1985	5		1	1		2	2		11
1986	8			4		4			16
1987	4		1	2			1		8
1988	3		5	1		8			17
1989	3		1			1	1	1	7
1990	3	1		2		18			24
1991	6	2	1	2		4			15
1992	6	1	2	23		5	2	2	41
1993	1	1	4	7		12	1	1	27
1994	2		4	16			2	1	25
1995	6	2	2	16		6	8	1	41
1996	5	1	2	27		3	7	1	46
1997	5	1	3	5		6	12	2	34
1998	4	1	5	10	1	4	22	5	52
1999	9	1	2	14		1	8		35
2000	20	2	2	35			2	4	65
2001	20	6	1	14	1	4	1	3	50
2002	27			17	1			7	52
TOTALS	156	22	43	278	4	142	79	28	752

Table 3. Taiwan Gross Domestic Product Per Year, Number of Taiwanese Science Fiction Books Per Year, and Product of Those Numbers Per Year, 1953–2002

Year	X = GDP	Y = Taiwanese sf	XY
1953	233,769.0000	1	233,769.0000
1954	256,071.0000	0	0
1955	276,827.0000	0	0
1956	292,062.0000	0	0
1957	313,561.0000	1	313,561.0000
1958	334,602.0000	1	334,602.0000
1959	360,202.0000	1	360,202.0000
1960	382,924.0000	0	0
1961	423,150.3125	0	0
1962	456,594.8438	0	0
1963	499,304.4375	0	0
1964	560,214.2500	0	0
1965	622,593.3125	0	0
1966	678,086.4375	0	0
1967	750,717.9375	1	750,717.9375
1968	819,564.2500	4	3,278,257.0000
1969	892,901.9375	5	4,464,509.6875
1970	994,432.8125	8	7,955,462.5000
1971	1,122,666.0000	1	1,122,666.0000
1972	1,272,173.2500	4	5,088,693.0000
1973	1,435,427.7500	3	4,306,283.2500
1974	1,452,108.1250	2	2,904,216.2500
1975	1,523,673.6250	6	9,142,041.7500
1976	1,734,864.2500	4	6,939,457.0000
1977	1,911,641.3750	17	32,497,903.3750
1978	2,171,508.2500	26	56,459,214.5000
1979	2,349,006.2500	5	11,745,031.2500
1980	2,520,512.5000	28	70,574,350.0000
1981	2,675,843.7500	37	99,006,218.7500
1982	2,770,869.2500	3	8,312,607.7500
1983	3,004,922.0000	17	51,083,674.0000
1984	3,323,433.5000	11	36,557,768.5000
1985	3,488,027.0000	11	38,368,297.0000
1986	3,893,929.2500	16	62,302,868.0000
1987	4,390,205.0000	8	35,121,640.0000
1988	4,734,416.0000	17	80,485,072.0000
1989	5,124,175.5000	7	35,869,228.5000
1990	5,400,623.5000	24	129,614,964.0000
1991	5,808,584.5000	15	87,128,767.5000
1992	6,243,500.0000	41	255,983,500.0000
1993	6,681,408.5000	27	180,398,029.5000
1994	7,156,324.5000	25	178,908.112.5000

Year	X = GDP	Y = Taiwanese sf	XY
1995	7,616,050.0000	41	312,258,050.0000
1996	8,088,068.0000	46	372,051,128.0000
1997	8,621,225.0000	34	293,121,650.0000
1998	9,013,354.0000	52	468,694,408.0000
1999	9,531,425.0000	35	333,599,875.0000
2000	10,081,059.0000	65	655,268,835.0000
2001	9,862,183.0000	50	493,109,150.0000
2002	10,280,971.0000	52	534,610,492.0000
TOTALS	164,431,757.1560	752	4,960,325,273.5000

Table 4. Taiwan Gross Domestic Product Per Year, and Number of Taiwanese Science Fiction Books Per Year, Both Expressed as Z-Scores, and the Product of Those Z-Scores, 1953–2002

Year	Z_X = GDP	Z_Y = Taiwanese sf	$Z_X Z_Y$
1953	-0.966221552	-0.800785695	0.773736397
1954	-0.959167667	-0.857821713	0.822794851
1955	-0.952602766	-0.857821713	0.817163336
1956	-0.947784098	-0.857821713	0.813029778
1957	-0.940984194	-0.800785695	0.753526681
1958	-0.93432915	-0.800785695	0.748197417
1959	-0.926232143	-0.800785695	0.7471345
1960	-0.919045417	-0.857821713	0.788377113
1961	-0.906322264	-0.857821713	0.777462917
1962	-0.895744116	-0.857821713	0.768388752
1963	-0.882235527	-0.857821713	0.756800791
1964	-0.862970404	-0.857821713	0.74027475
1965	-0.843240572	-0.857821713	0.723350071
1966	-0.825688689	-0.857821713	0.708293685
1967	-0.802716121	-0.800785695	0.642803586
1968	-0.780940767	-0.62967764	0.491740939
1969	-0.757744839	-0.572641622	0.433916233
1970	-0.725631707	-0.401533568	0.291365488
1971	-0.685072919	-0.800785695	0.548596593
1972	-0.637785372	-0.62967764	0.401599187
1973	-0.586149716	-0.686713659	0.402517016
1974	-0.580873892	-0.743749677	0.432024769
1975	-0.558238488	-0.515605604	0.287830892
1976	-0.491441147	-0.62967764	0.309449501
1977	-0.43552843	0.111790595	-0.048687982
1978	-0.353335311	0.625114759	-0.220875117
1979	-0.297194588	-0.572641622	0.17018599
1980	-0.242948992	0.739186795	-0.179584686
1981	-0.193819376	1.252510959	-0.242760892
1982	-0.163763825	-0.686713659	0.112458855
1983	-0.089735438	0.111790595	-0.010031578

Year	Z_X = GDP	Z_Y=Taiwanese sf	$Z_X Z_Y$
1984	0.011006348	-0.230425513	-0.002536143384
1985	0.063065515	-0.230425513	-0.014531903
1986	0.191448064	0.054754577	0.010482657
1987	0.348414787	-0.401533568	-0.139900232
1988	0.457285052	0.111790595	0.051120168
1989	0.580561821	-0.458569586	-0.266227993
1990	0.667999373	0.511042722	0.341376217
1991	0.797033082	-0.002281440727	-0.001818383155
1992	0.934592212	1.480655032	1.383808662
1993	1.073097997	0.68215077	0.732014633
1994	1.223308858	0.568078741	0.694935755
1995	1.368715127	1.480655032	2.02659494
1996	1.518009382	1.765835123	2.680554284
1997	1.68664125	1.081402905	1.823938747
1998	1.810667467	2.108051232	3.816979785
1999	1.974527794	1.138438923	2.247879295
2000	2.148371161	2.849519469	6.12182545
2001	2.079143019	1.993979196	4.145767925
2002	2.211601193	2.108051232	4.66216862
Total $Z_X Z_Y$			44.88009127

Table 5. Figures and Formulas Used to Calculate Pearson r Using Two Methods (X = Taiwanese Gross Domestic Product Per Year; Y = Number of Taiwanese Science Fiction Books Published Per Year; 1953–2002)

Method 1.

ΣX	=	164,431,757.156
$(\Sigma X)^2$	=	27,037,802,761,400,000
ΣX^2	=	1,040561,443,630,000
$\overline{X}$	=	3,288,635.14312
ΣY	=	752
$(\Sigma Y)^2$	=	565,504
ΣY^2	=	26,680
$\overline{Y}$	=	15.04
ΣXY	=	4.960,325,273.5
N	=	50

$$r = \frac{N\Sigma XY - \Sigma X \Sigma Y}{\sqrt{[N\Sigma X^2 - (\Sigma X)^2][N\Sigma Y^2 - (\Sigma Y)^2]}} = 0.897401824$$

Method 2.

δ_{nX}	=	3,161,662.18436

$$\sigma_{nY} = 17.532780726$$

$$Z_X = \frac{x - \overline{X}}{\sigma_{nX}} \qquad Z_Y = \frac{y - \overline{Y}}{\sigma_{nY}}$$

$$r = \frac{\Sigma Z_X Z_Y}{N} = 0.897601825$$

Notes

1. C. P. Snow, "The Two Cultures," *The Two Cultures*, introduction by Stefan Collini (Cambridge, UK: Cambridge University Press, 1993), 41, 50. Later parenthetical page references are to this edition.

2. Snow, "The Two Cultures: A Second Look," *The Two Cultures*, introduction by Stefan Collini (Cambridge, UK: Cambridge University Press, 1993), 79–80, 98, 100. Later parenthetical page references are to this edition.

3. John W. Campbell, Jr., letter to Lurton Blassingame, March 4, 1959, *The John W. Campbell Letters, Volume 1*, edited by Perry A. Chapdelaine, Sr., Tony Chapdelaine, and George Hay (Franklin, TN: AC Projects, 1985), 364.

4. Gary Westfahl, "In Search of Dismal Science Fiction," *Interzone*, No. 189 (May/June 2003), 55–56.

5. Lee Correy, *Manna* (New York: DAW, 1983), 81–82. Later parenthetical page references in the text are to this edition.

6. G. Harry Stine, *The Space Enterprise* (New York: Ace, 1980); Stine, *The Third Industrial Revolution* (New York: Ace, 1979).

7. Mack Reynolds, *Black Man's Burden*, published dos-à-dos with Reynolds, *Border, Breed nor Birth* (New York: Ace, 1972); Reynolds, *The Best Ye Breed* (New York: Ace, 1978). The first novel was originally published in *Analog* in 1961; the second was originally published in *Analog* in 1962.

8. Reynolds, *Border, Breed Nor Birth*, 143.

9. Bruce Sterling, "Green Days in Brunei," *The Ultimate Cyberpunk*, edited by Pat Cadigan (New York: Pocket/iBooks, 2002), 276–340. Story originally published in 1985.

10. "The IKV T'Mar," at *http://www.ikvtmar.com/purpose.html*.

11. *Elemental: The Tsunami Relief Anthology: Stories of Science Fiction and Fantasy*, edited by Steven Savile and Alethea Kontis (New York: Tor Books, 2006).

12. Danny J. Han–Chang Lin, *The Complete Bibliography of Taiwanese Science Fiction* (Taipei, Taiwan: privately published, 2003).

13. Global Financial Data online database, accessed at the University of California, Riverside in September, 2008, at *https://www.globalfinancialdata.com/index_tabs.php3?action=user_homepage&message=true*.

14. Information about this project can be found at the Innovative Technologies in Science Fiction for Space Applications website, *http://www.itsf.org/*.

15. Gerald Gaylard's essay "Black Secret Technology: African Technological Subjects," *World Weavers: Globalization, Science Fiction, and the Cybernetic Revolution*, edited by Wong Kin Yuen, Gary Westfahl, and Amy Kit-sze Chan (Hong Kong: Hong Kong University Press, 2005), 191–204, which discusses several works of South African science fiction, provides one indication that Third World science fiction might represent a rich field for explorations of these kinds.

16. This table exactly replicates Lin's categories, though I note that one could dispute some of his classifications; for example, in the category of translated children's science

fiction, he includes Mary Shelley's *Frankenstein* (1818), Robert Louis Stevenson's *Strange Case of Dr. Jekyll and Mr. Hyde* (1886), Sir Arthur Conan Doyle's *The Lost World* (1912), Edgar Rice Burroughs's *A Princess of Mars* (1917), Isaac Asimov's *The Caves of Steel* (1954), and several novels by Jules Verne and H. G. Wells, all of which would not normally be considered "children's science fiction."

6. The Science of Fiction and the Fiction of Science: A Storytelling Animal in an Inhospitable World

Frank McConnell

I really think it's all the fault of William Wordsworth. I could be wrong, of course: since I wrote my first book, on Wordsworth's *Prelude*, I've tended to assume that a lot of what's good and almost all of what's not in the modern imagination is finally, somehow, his fault — the Ronald Reagan of our visionary climate. To paraphrase Frank Kermode on John Milton, he made it possible to write and think badly in a whole new way; and this, like inventing a really *new* sin, is a remarkable accomplishment.

But here — "here," by the way, is the whole, sublimely, inconsequential, "two cultures" debate — I've got, I think, the smoking gun. In the preface to the 1800 edition of *Lyrical Ballads*, Wordsworth — was any poet, by the way, ever more ironically named? — famously redefines the classicist idea of "poetic diction" as the mere language of ordinary men, raised to sublimity by the heightened — but universally available — perceptions of the poet himself.

Now at its overwhelming — I want to say, Shakespearian — pitch of energy, this attitude accounts for an amazing amount of the best writing in English (or must we now say "Anglophone"?) of the last two hundred years. Revising and inverting Milton in the preface to *The Excursion*, he asks why the myths of Paradise should be only unattainable memories or a "mere history of what never was?" "For," he says in what for me is his most unavoidably exalted and exalting passage:

This essay first appeared in Sniper Logic 7 *(Winter, Fall 1999): 113–120.*

> For the discerning intellect of Man,
> When wedded to this goodly universe
> In love and holy passion, shall find these
> A simple produce of the common day.
> — I, long before the blissful hour arrives,
> Would chant, in lonely peace, the spousal verse
> Of this great consummation: — and, by words
> Which speak of nothing more than what we are,
> Would I arouse the sensual from their sleep
> Of Death....[1]

We could be reading William Blake here — Blake who despised Wordsworth — except that Blake's language never achieved this fusion of the cosmic and the quotidian. So much becomes possible in a passage like this: Charles Dickens; Thomas Hardy; Wallace Stevens; William Carlos Williams; Thomas Pynchon; Theodore Sturgeon; Isaac Asimov; Arthur C. Clarke; *The Three Stooges Go to Mars*; *Gilligan's Island*.

Perhaps I should explain.

To reenter — actually, recapture — Eden through "words which speak of nothing more than what we are" is the crucial effort of romanticism, and by now I think we can all admit that we are still living in the romantic era. It is also, as I've written often, a variety of the ancient "heresy" of Gnosticism — the faith that this world, or this scripture — any scripture — properly understood, contains a hermetic meaning that is the key to arouse the sensual from their sleep of Death. And what we mistakenly call "science fiction" is part of the same urge — is, in fact, the furthest reach of romanticism in popular culture (as opposed, by the way, to what? *Un*popular culture?). As is, to use a word almost irrevocably degraded by current academic critics, the discourse of science. We talk about "two cultures," in other words, not because there really *are* two cultures — there aren't — but because *believing* that there are preserves our comfortable Gnostic faith in the infinite promise of the everyday, our faith that words which speak of nothing more than what we are actually do speak of something more than what we are.

Not that any of this is all that new: God, is anything? The first romantics, as far as I can discern, had names like Thales, Heracleitus, Anaximenes, and Parmenides, folks who in a stunning leap of imagination argued that world is exactly what it is and subtly not what is. Think about Ludwig Wittgenstein's famous, corrosive opening to the *Tractatus:* "the world is all that is the case."[2] Everything is really water; everything is really fire; everything is really — shades of Alan Guth — a vacuum fluctuation; everything is really — shades of Haight-Ashbury — everything, man. It can't be denied, though, that we've turned the cottage industry of pre–Eleatic speculation into a heavy industry.

But enough history of ideas, already. What do Wordsworth, Gilligan, and Stephen Hawking have to do with one another?

Well, think about the difference between Dave Bowman at the end of *2001: A Space Odyssey* (1968) and Luke Skywalker at the end of the first *Star Wars* movie (1977). In both films, technology reaches a pitch of crisis where it must either collapse in on itself or be lifted — G. W. F. Hegel's term was *aufgehoben*—into spirituality. But one *Aufhebung* is what I, Chestertonian to the core, would call "orthodox," while the other is definitively gnostic. Perpend.

Dave Bowman, on a mission to discover the source of extraterrestrial communications from Jupiter, finds himself rapt — in St. Paul's sense of "rapture" through a stargate by alien entities — just call them God — who give him a second birth as the enigmatic, embryonic, starchild orbiting Earth, in the unforgettable last shot of the film, with that quizzical smile, the inevitable end-product of an evolutionary process that began before the dawn of time. Man, through no conscious effort of his own, has become more than man: in a way, it's a Christmas story, ending with the birth of a babe.

Luke Skywalker, on the other hand, has to learn to reject technology completely, to switch off his radar or whatever and use "the Force" as he launches his bomb into the heart of the malevolent Death Star. It's the moment for which the entire film has been waiting, and it's, to risk an oxymoron, transcendently gnostic. Nature, technology, things as they are not to be collaborated with, but to be overcome. Dave Bowman emerges as a newborn humanity; Luke emerges as a conqueror. I'm not sure about Wordsworth, but I am reasonably certain that Blake, Percy Shelley, Wolfgang Pauli, and Hawking would prefer Luke to Dave.

Now let me be clear. I find most of feminist criticism hopelessly silly. Hell, I find most of *everything* hopelessly silly. Nevertheless, there's a point to the feminist argument that post–Enlightenment science is "male" in that it assumes a rhetorical stance of dominance over and — I shudder as I write this — penetration into the secrets of Nature — a word that, by the way, takes the feminine case in all Indo-European languages.

Not, as Seinfeld would say, that there's anything wrong with that. The Pythagorean Theorem holds whether or not you have a Y chromosome; light still hits you at 186,000 miles per second; and quarks and hadrons and leptons and all their tiny pals are no respecters of gender — or do you want to try and describe a quarkette?

What I'm trying to describe, rather clumsily I fear, is a habit of speech that we've all, poets and physicists alike, acquired over the last couple of centuries. And a large part of my problem is that this habit of speech is a good thing, even despite the abuses to which it has given cause. Let's call it, with a nod to George Orwell, one of this century's patron saints, gnostispeak.

And gnostispeak is precisely why some of us labor under the delusion that there are two cultures. (I am, by the way, explaining what Wordsworth, Gilligan, and Hawking have to do with one another; have a little faith, can't you?)

C. S. Lewis remarks somewhere that the Renaissance is brooded over by two contrasting figures of power, the astrologer and the alchemist. The astrologer, rooted in the age of faith, assumes the world to be comprehensible, reading, but essentially unalterable: Dave Bowman, realizing that the cosmos is going to take him precisely where it wants him to go. The alchemist, rooted in the age of inquiry, assumes that the world is his playground, to be manipulated according to the demands of his own quest for selfhood: rather like Luke Skywalker, giving himself to and then using the Force.

Now I want to suggest that these two magi, the astrologer and the alchemist, brood over not only the Renaissance but also our current thought. And I also want to suggest that their antagonism is very much the stuff— or at least the speech — our dreams are made of. Poetry — whatever "poetry" is — and science — whatever "science" is — are not "two cultures," but simply two dialects of the same language, which happens to be the discourse of our happy discontent.

In what I more and more believe to be the single most inexhaustible of poems, *King Lear,* Gloucester, the good but gullible old Earl, articulates the orthodoxy of the astrologer: "These late eclipses in the sun and moon portend no good to us. Though the wisdom of Nature can reason it thus and thus, yet nature finds itself scourged by the sequent effects." And his bastard son Edmund — an even more wonderful villain than Iago — immediately afterwards articulates the stance of the alchemist, the Cartesian to his father's Thomist: "An admirable evasion of whoremaster man, to lay his goatish disposition on the charge of a star. My father compounded with my mother under the dragon's tail and my nativity was under Ursa Major, so it follows I am rough and lecherous. Fut! I should have been that I am had the maidenliest star in the firmament twinkled on my bastardizing."[3]

Now immediately after this remarkable *Kulturkampf* another character comes on the stage: Edgar, Gloucester's legitimate son, whom Gloucester will, terribly, disown and banish and who will ultimately redeem his father and sanction (I love tradecraft words) his half-brother. Edgar is very important — perhaps even as much so as Gilligan or as, to stir one more name into the soup, Prospero. But for the moment let him rest.

The astrologer and the alchemist attack reality from distinctly different angles; yet they seem to share — they do share — one essential assumption. That assumption, to quote Wittgenstein once again, is that the world is everything which is the case. Maybe we don't realize what a world of trouble that implies.

Martin Heidegger, that brilliant and vile man, observes that the central question of metaphysics is, *Wacht ist überhaupt Seiendes und nicht vielmehr Nichts?* Why is there something instead of nothing?[4]

Seems reasonable, right?

But then consider one of the first, and most important, koans — meditative riddles — given a Zen student by his master. It's the question of *u* and *mu*: *u* means "nothing" and *mu* means "something." The question, the koan, is, simply, "Is everything nothing or something?"

Now don't worry. This is not going to turn out to be one of those wow-we-knew-it-in-the-sixties-the-wisdom-of-the-East-shall-shake-the-West-awake-and-what's-in-the-fridge? Bits of hippie retrocrap. Nevertheless, you can surely hear the difference between Heidegger's question and that of the sensei. It's a difference of *timbre* as much as of thought.

Why is there something instead of nothing? Is everything nothing or something? The first question — the protognostic question, I'd say — assumes that there is something, and that it can be read and reasoned thus and thus. It's the wisdom of Gloucester and also of his bastard Edmund: reality and can be known and seized — Clarke's *Childhood's End* (1953) or Alfred Bester's *The Stars My Destination* (1956) (and is there a more definitively gnostic title anywhere?) — but reality is *there*. Something *is*: even Parmenides, the first purely theoretical physicist, had to admit that. Actually, you have to assume that — that something is — if you want to tell a story at all, whether your story is the *Mahabharata*, Charles Darwin's *On The Origin of Species* (1859), Mickey Spillane's *Kiss Me Deadly* (1952), or Albert Einstein's Special Theory of Relativity.

But what about the koan? If nothing else it gives us a new perspective — if I were looking for tenure I'd call it something like a "paradigm shift" or, worse, "episteme" — on the relation between the mind and the world of things, i.e. on the motive for both storytelling and science altogether. Let me now violate all decorum by actually trying to explain a koan.

Is everything something or nothing? The point of the question is that it really isn't a question at all; it simply will not *tolerate* a binary yes/no, on/off response. It teaches you, by its unanswerability, that "this goodly universe" and "words that speak of nothing more than what we are" can — not must, but can — be regarded not as two different things, but aspects of a single, seamless process. You've solved the question when you *get* the question. Presumably, you stare at your Zen master, your eyes light up, you say "Oh, wow. Is everything something or nothing? *Yeah!*" And he smiles, you hug and whoop and holler, and go out for a drink or something.

The riddle carries the same kind of kick as Bertrand Russell's paradox (is the set of all sets which are not members of themselves itself a member of itself?); as Kurt Gödel's Incompleteness Theorem; as Werner Heisenberg's so-often-misconstrued Uncertainty Principle; and as St. Augustine's assertion, at the beginning of the *Confessions*, that we can know God only by first calling upon him. Moment by moment, we make the world by whispers; or as Wallace Stevens titles one of his last poems, "Reality Is an Activity of the Most August Imagination."[5]

Mysticism? You bet. But the splendid paradox here — and when we think about thinking, we're, Hansels and Gretels all, hopelessly lost in paradox — is that mysticism of this sort is actually a good deal more realistic than realism — at least than what I've been calling gnostic "realism."

Look. This isn't a good guys/bad guys thing. But the fact is that the mystic — the guy who thinks about how he knows as much as about what he knows — is in some important ways a little more in tune with The Way Things Are than his gnostic cousin. Remember the old gag about the difference between a psychotic and neurotic. The psychotic knows, with absolute certainly, that two plus two equals five; the neurotic knows that two plus two equals four — but the fact makes him nervous. My very favorite legend of the Baal Shem Tov is this one:

"The Baal Shem Tov and his disciples were traveling. While they were riding along the road a leaf floated down and settled upon the lap of the Baal Shem Tov. A bit further on a wind came and blew the leaf from the lap of the Baal Shem Tov to the ground; and there a worm came and crawled onto the leaf and used it for shelter and food. The Baal Shem Tov stopped the wagon and called his disciples. 'Look here,' he said. 'When the world was created, even then did the Almighty decree that this leaf should fall on my lap and that a wind should come and take it from my lap and blow it onto the ground where this worm would use it for food and shelter.'"[6]

What? You want to say. That's it? Well, actually, yes: that's it. *Die Welt ist alles, was der Fall ist.* Or — the Besht goes Wittgenstein one better here — *Die Welt ist nur alles, was der Fall ist.* Dave Bowman would get it; the most gnostically named Skywalker, not.

Wordsworth really wants to rouse the sensual from their sleep of Death. And Stephen Hawking, an authentic hero of consciousness, wants, as he says in *A Brief History of Time* (1998) (wonderful title!) to know the mind of God.[7] These are both exhilarating, Promethean desires without which our culture would be impoverished. Gilligan, on the other hand, good mystic — if not outright Taoist — that he is, does not seek to know the mind of God so much as he simply wants to dwell there. Everybody else, the Skipper, the millionaire and his wife, the movie star, the professor and Mary Ann, Faustians all, sees the island of exile as a problem to be solved, a place to leave. Gilligan sees it as a place to be, at least until events take him somewhere else. Is everything nothing or something, *u* or *mu*? His response is in effect another word, perhaps the most meaning-fraught word I know: *u* or *mu*? *nu*?

A completely Gilliganized world would, of course, be hell on Earth: nothing would work (you are welcome to ask my wife about this). But how sad a world it would be without him. He's the spirit of acceptance. He's (to invoke what I think the most fascinating, maddeningly complicated character in all of Shakespeare) the Fool who cures or at least salves the madness of the King. He's the necessary angel of earth, the mystic, the teller of shaggy dog jokes — since all real mystics are tellers of shaggy dog jokes.

All fiction, which is to say all human knowledge of any conceivable value, is to be found in jokes you know. And there are only two sorts of jokes, representing, as Blake said of Innocence and Experience, two contrary states of the human soul: punch-line and shaggy dog. Which type of joke you prefer is a rather strong indication of what sort of person you are, what sort of stories you like, and whether you think the "two cultures" debate is a serious issue or just another pretext for a conference.

The punch line joke implies that the universe is ordered, and either knowable or controllable. Whether it's "to get across the road" or the law of inverse squares, the punch line explains why there is something rather than nothing. Punch line folks like chess and bridge and Wolfgang Amadeus Mozart and books like *Childhood's End*. Shaggy dog folks, at home with the concept of indeterminacy, like poker and backgammon and Charles Mingus and books like Lewis's *Perelandra* (1944).

And if course it's clear that everybody — at least everybody not certifiable — is, alternately, both sorts of person. Some years ago I asked a friend of mine from Tokyo what his religion was (after the third sake you can ask that sort of thing). He laughed. "It depends," he said. "If things are going well for me, I'm a Confucian. If I'm confused, I'm a Taoist. And some day — well, some days I'm almost a Christian."

Sir Arthur Eddington once summarized quantum theory in the observation that "*Something unknown is doing we don't know what.*"[8] At the moment of that utterance Eddington was being a shaggy dog person — Eddington, who usually was one of the most punch line people of the century. Einstein's more celebrated saying — "The Lord God is subtle, but he is not malicious"[9] — comes close to this but, for me at least, just misses the force of the final, definitive shrug: *nu*? But then Einstein, the definitive gnostic of the age, was notoriously distressed at quantum mechanics, spending his later years in quest of the Grail, the Philosopher's Stone of the Universal Constant that would put everything back in place again.

The point of the shaggy dog view of the world, though, is that there *is* no Grail; that the point of the quest is just getting back to where you started from. In my favorite, really favorite tale, Sir Gawain journeys into the other world and confronts the daunting Green Knight only to find out that it's been an elaborate practical joke all along. And in my second favorite story, Gilgamesh, the anti–Dante, voyages into the otherworld questing for a cure for mortality only to find that there is none, that the world is — well — everything which is the case. The same sensibility permeates what is certainly one of the best sf novels written, Walter M. Miller, Jr.'s *A Canticle for Leibowitz* (1959), as well as, as well as I understand chaos theory, chaos theory.

I must confess that, until I began to contemplate this topic, it hadn't occurred to me that the quest stories I like best are the ones where the quest is a bust. The common, and inaccurate definition of the shaggy dog story is that it's a story with no point. The point of the story, in fact, is that *you listened to it*, all the way to the end. It's a model for the expectation of meaning, always deferred but always seductively there: faith, if you prefer the term, instead of certainty.

I don't want, in other words, Fermat's Last Theorem to be proved. I don't want a Grand Unified Theory. No more do I want an irrefutable demonstration of the existence of God, or to read a novel with absolutely no flaws.

Nor is this perversity. It's simply a conviction that consciousness is, as Wallace Stevens never tires of telling us, consciousness of imperfection, that the imperfect is our paradise. Two cultures? Not at all. Only one, which is, to quote Stevens again, "the poem of the mind in the act of finding/What will suffice."[10] The idea that the discourse of science and that of the humanities are growing farther apart holds true *only* if you're thinking about the compartmentalization of the modern university where people from different disciplines don't talk to one another because they never get the chance; or if you're thinking about the by-now-irreversible decline of academic literary discourse into hopelessly zero-meaning jargon. Let's face it: the prose of Fredric Jameson, J. Hillis Miller, or Gerald Graff makes the prose of science writers like Roger Penrose and Paul Davies sound positively lyrical. And then there's Ilya Prigogine.

But the professors of literature, having splendidly reduced themselves to self-parody (who would have thought one would ever long for the comparative lucidities of Kenneth Burke?) do not even deserve a voice in the debate: let them speak when they learn to speak plainly; for the rest of us, poor bastards crawling between Heaven and Earth, cosmic amphibians all, there is only the search, already doomed, for finality or, as a dear friend once wrote about scholarship, "A thrust to fill a bright gold ring/Whose challenge is its own defense."[11]

I was going to conclude with an elegant, really classy discussion of Mary Shelley's *Frankenstein* (1818): believe me, you'd have loved it. But, as the immortal phrase goes, the hand of fate stepped in. About two weeks ago, walking to our car with my wife in Santa Barbara, I tripped over an irregular piece of pavement and launched, headfirst, into the side of a parked SUV. Dislocated shoulder; thirty-two stitch gash over the left eye; concussion; and the entire torso one large bruise (actually, I looked like a giant plum with no nipples).

And there was no reason at all for it. I'd done nothing to bring it on myself, it had no antecedents or consequences — except, to be sure, considerable discomfort for me — and was my own little private demonstration that the world is everything which is the case.

And we don't like that: at least I know I don't. So we make up stories — myths or enthymemes — to reassure us, in effect, that shit *doesn't* happen.

And all the while — this is the real glory of our species — we know that it does. I'd suggest that the most salient characteristic of humankind is its enormous capacity for radiant self-delusion about its own importance. Stars die, galaxies explore, Leo Tolstoy's Anna Karenina throws herself under a train, Bester's Gully Foyle finds himself the most important man in the universe. And our way is to make up tales to explain why those absurdities are not, really, absurd — as, in fact, I've just done by turning my fall in the parking lot into an intro to a theory of fiction.

We are the storytelling animal. And whether we call our stories *Principia Mathematica* or *Blade Runner* makes, finally, little difference. They are our assertions — like Lear, like Job — that we exist in an inhospitable universe but nevertheless choose to make sense of it. A tragic species, since aware of our own mortality, we have invented comedy to tell us that everything will be okay, anyway. And on that truth and on that brilliant lie are founded all the worthwhile stories — novels or theorems — ever told. They're our glory.

And they shine.

Notes

1. William Wordsworth, "The Recluse," in *Selected Poems and Prefaces,* edited by Jack Stillinger (Boston: Houghton Mifflin, 1965), 46.

2. Ludwig Wittgenstein, *Tractatus Logico-Philosophicus*, translated by D. F. Pears and B. F. McGuinness, introduction by Bertrand Russell (London and New York: Routledge, 1974), 5.

3. William Shakespeare, *King Lear*, Act I, Scene 2, edited by R. A Foakes (London: Thomas Nelson, 1997), 185–187.

4. Martin Heidegger, *Einführung in die Metaphysik* (Tübingen: Max Neimeyer Verlag, 1957), 1; McConnell's translation.

5. Wallace Stevens, "Reality Is an Activity of the Most August Imagination," in *Collected Poetry and Prose* (New York: Library of America, 1997), 471–472.

6. Jerome R. Mintz, *Legends of the Hasidim: An Introduction to Hasidic Culture and Oral Tradition in the New World* (Chicago and London: University of Chicago Press, 1968), 337.

7. Stephen Hawking, *A Brief History of Time* (New York: Bantam, 1998).

8. Sir Arthur Eddington, *The Nature of the Physical World* (1928; Cambridge, UK: Cambridge University Press, 1953), 291; author's italics.

9. Albert Einstein, cited in J. M. Cohen and M. J. Cohen, compilers, *The Penguin Dictionary of Twentieth-Century Quotations* (New York: Penguin, 1980), 115.

10. Wallace Stevens, "Of Modern Poetry," in *The Collected Poems of Wallace Stevens* (New York: Alfred A. Knopf, 1954), 239.

11. At this time, the editors have been unable to locate a source for this quotation.

7. Dimorphs and Doubles: J. D. Bernal's "Two Cultures" and the Transhuman Promise

George Slusser

J. D. Bernal published *The World, the Flesh, and the Devil: An Enquiry into the Future of the Three Enemies of the Rational Soul* (1929) 30 years before C. P. Snow's 1959 Rede Lecture on "The Two Cultures." In this treatise, Bernal not only sketched the master plot for the development of SF across the 20th century but also located the two cultures gap as culminating moment in the narrative of scientific advancement, placing it at the crux of transhuman promise. Bernal sees humanity, by means of science and technology, transforming both its environment and physical being to the point where it is ready to advance to a new state of being. At this juncture Bernal finds a two cultures gap hard wired into human circuitry: the "rational soul," the motor of change leading humanity to transgress boundaries and aspire to the more-than-human, proves divided against itself. Science, in this case psychology, cannot fix this problem. Eventually, however, the species' evolution will result in a "dimorphic split" generating, in turn, two scenarios for the future of *homo sapiens*: radical change, the forward looking half of humanity leaving behind home and human form, evolving into something totally different; and retreat to ecotopia, a stay-behind humanity husbanding and conserving its well-tended "human zoo."[1]

If Bernal's reader is humanity at the transhuman crossroads, it finds itself at the edge of knowability and the limit of storytelling as well. In relation to human norms, the changing dimorph reaches the point, at the moment it shoots the gulf, where it logically no longer needs to communicate with what it once was. Similarly, old humanity, unable to conceive of its new form, cannot

96

understand what it will become. If SF is the genre recounting Bernal's story of humanity advancing beyond itself, then its task is to find the means whereby narrative negotiates this ultimate two cultures gap between story and non-story. How SF strives to tell Bernal's transhuman story is the subject of this essay.

SF's solution to this dilemma lies in the process of dimorphism itself. For at each moment of dimorphic split, the evolving dimorph generates its double, a comprehensible analogue to a destiny that has become incomprehensible. Humanity at this crux is not given John Cabal's choice: which shall it be? The material forces of evolution resolve the impasse of divided humanity. Yet at this moment the old mind-matter duality that defined humanity's position in the universe, from Christian "soul" to Cartesian "mind," repositions itself to generate a ghost in the material machine. Bernal claims to speak of enemies of the material mind, as entity engaged with evolutionary forces of change. Yet in using the term "rational soul," he echoes a residual Cartesian faith in the immutable uniqueness of the human mind. As humanity moves beyond itself, it invariably generates an alternate form that both domesticates the unknown and retrieves a conventional image of humanity at the instant humanity is losing that image forever.

There are two models for evolutionary dimorphism — catastrophe and continuity. An example of catastrophic transformation is Arthur C. Clarke's Overmind in *Childhood's End* (1953). Humanity and its Earth are consumed in a transfer of energy, resulting in an entity bearing no apparent resemblance to the humanity that generated it. J. H. Rosny's *La Mort de la Terre* (1910) exemplifies the continuity model. When Rosny's Last Man Targ offers up the last remaining carbon molecules to his ferromagnetic successor, there is continuity between one kingdom of life and another. Yet in the evolutionary gap between humanity's dying mind and the remotest possibility of the development of ferromagnetic intelligence, the possibility of transhuman communication seems as remote as contact with the Overmind. Bernal's concept of dimorphic evolution, however, suggests the possibility of a continuity-in-catastrophe scenario allowing the human body and mind to cross the threshold, to become another state, while maintaining contact with its former state: that of us the reader. Bernal's split generates the dimorph, a post-human entity changed beyond recognition, thus (logically) beyond communication. Simultaneously, however, the dimorph generates its double — the (i.e. *our*) old form to which it remains improbably attached. For example, Robert A. Heinlein's advancing humans, as they evolve to a state of being radically different from their origins, keep looking back to the "green hills of Earth." The dimorph-double dynamic allows SF the possibility of "pushing the envelope" of human advancement, glimpsing the undiscovered country, yet returning with stories still relevant to our wish for human continuity. It also allows SF to narrate situations that otherwise would be lost to non-narrativity.

Bernal's Three Enemies of the Rational Soul

On the eve of the 20th century, Paul Gauguin's famous painting asks the question: "Who are we? Where do we come from? Where are we going?" Placing this in an evolutionary perspective, we rephrase the question: *What* are we? Two significant restatements of this question, across the 20th century, are crystallographer Bernal's *The World, the Flesh, and the Devil,* and Donna Haraway's "A Cyborg Manifesto" (1985). Despite the span of time and technological change separating them, they offer essentially the same story of human advancement, a story quite improbable if we consider the material *facts* of any mutation process, of constancy in change. Bernal's treatise is an evolutionary challenge to the static idea of humanity Western science has had to contend with, as expressed in Alexander Pope's claim that the proper study of mankind is Man. At the same time, Bernal's use of a term like "rational soul" suggests Christian and Cartesian systems in which humanity retains centrality and immutability. Thus, his sequence of "enemies"—world, flesh, and devil—sets predictable limits to future-oriented change, sheltering advancing humanity from too-radical transformation. "World" remains the Cartesian *res extensa.* Driven by resource depletion and population explosion, the rational mind expands its habitat to moons, planets, and beyond. Such expansion, however, raises the problem of the body. To go farther into hostile physical environments, we must alter our bodily limitations. Bernal's "flesh," then, is René Descartes' "machine," to be altered by mechanical or biological engineering. This second "enemy" forces awareness of the third term in the Cartesian system — the body as interface between mind and world.

Descartes in a sense minimized the problem of the body by declaring it a machine—part of *res extensa,* not *res cogitans.* Evolutionary advancement, in contrast, gives body a central role, making it the necessary connection not simply between mind and world, but between our past and future. True to his time, Bernal cites the evolutionary need to transform the human body, as vehicle of mind, to allow it expanded access to new physical environments. He speaks of prosthetic devices; later scientists and SF writers envision electronic and bionic means of transformation — the "cyborg"—while pursuing the ultimate dream of freeing mind from its imperfect and mortal "machine" completely and forever. Such radical transformation should, in the reciprocal process of evolution, cause mind to mutate radically as well. In Bernal, however, it does not. His "devil" enters at this point as a Cartesian governor to control such radical change. What Bernal means by "devil" is an innate form of division or duality within mind itself, untouchable either by mechanical or psychological alteration. In his scenario, mind resists change until finally, through sheer material pressures of evolution, dimorphism occurs, at which time one form moves beyond humanity to interstellar reaches while the other remains on Earth to perfect the conventional habitat: "The conflict between the humanizers and the mechanizers will be solved not by the victory of one or the other, but by the splitting of the human race — the one section developing a fully balanced humanity, the other groping unsteadily beyond it" (56). The progressive form is "the fanatical but useful people who chose to distort their bodies or blow themselves into space" (70).

We wonder, however, whether such dimorphism of humanity is an advancement or retreat. In the name "devil," Bernal doubles the Cartesian dualism with another form of division: the Fall. Here, Lucifer and his "fanatical but useful people," once cast from heaven, look back, even in their defiant transformation, with envy on the perfect form they once had. For Bernal, then, dimorphism is both irreversible change *and* unavoidable nostalgia for the lost form. Yet, however radical the process of transformation, this new humanity always retains a sense of its old physical locus. For example, Bernal speculates on the effects of freeing the brain from its "locomotor organs" (41), going beyond prosthetic alteration of the flesh to envision a chemical dispersion of individuality as multiple organisms — anticipating the dream of later 20th century scientists and SF writers, itself Cartesian, to convert all matter into a conscious entity, self-replicating "dematerialized modes of organization" such as the electron plasma of Fred Hoyle's *The Black Cloud* (1957). Yet for Bernal, even such an entity retains the need to look homeward to what it once was (what we as readers *currently* are), as if to some lost perfection. As new mankind leaves for parts unknown, "old mankind — would be left in undisputed possession of the earth, to be regarded by the inhabitants of the celestial spheres with a curious reverence" (73). The world new humanity leaves behind must serve as a "human zoo, a zoo so intelligently managed that its inhabitants are not aware they are there merely for purposes of observation and experiment" (73). Whatever dimorph we envision, it must have its human double. For this form gives it not only a story to tell — the distance traveled between us and it, the succession of forms separating us from our possible future — but the means of telling that story, providing the transformed entity and its (necessarily future) narrator with an audience still interested in the tale. The adventure Descartes began by decentering the classical *mens sana in corpore sano* creates this dynamic of dimorph and double. We think that, once body and mind are given up to the physical process of evolution, human transformation would be rapid, in new and unpredictable ways. Yet, however great our imaginative or speculative reach, it cannot, in Bernal's formulation, surpass our *desire* to remain human. Again, on the horns of this Cartesian dilemma, if we do transform, there is simply no story to tell.

The Spacetime Odysseys of Arthur C. Clarke

The work of Arthur C. Clarke offers near-perfect examples of Bernal's dimorphic split. His novels and stories retreat from the radical dimorphism of his early *Childhood's End* toward an almost Swiftian affirmation of a human mean in "A Meeting with Medusa" (1971), finally to the stylized interplay of dimorph and double, transcendence and homecoming, in his sequels to *2001: A Space Odyssey* (1968). These works (*3001: The Final Odyssey* appeared in 1997) represent the culmination of Clarke's career. *Childhood's End* presents dimorphism as a cataclysmic rather than continuous process. The novel is set in a near future, where potential atomic holocaust is averted by the arrival of mysterious "Overlords" who impose a reign of peace and plenty. The figures, whom earlier humanity named devils, return to bring a foreshortened millennium, from which emerges the utopian boredom of New Atlantis. Here dimorphism suddenly erupts, as human children mysteriously lose contact with adults, developing an internal chain reaction that consumes their (and all human and Earthly) forms. As a result, a catastrophic energy transfer creates the Overmind, an entity retaining no vestiges of its former state. Following the logic of evolution, Clarke depicts the dimorph Overmind as forever closed to its human antecedents and the star-roaming "mechanizer" Overlords. These latter, whose tails and wings place them, in a bodily sense, as proportionately below the human norm as the Overmind is above it, are cosmic museum keepers, retaining the defunct human form to place it, again in a median position, between the Earth sea monsters and interstellar oddities it collects. In the novel, this museum centerpiece is provided by Jan, the "last man" who recounts the death of the Earth and all its marvels in elegiac accents, captured and stored by the Overlords, perpetual exiles between stars, worlds, and forms of sentient life. Once seen as devils, these Overlords appear later to be guardian "angels." In relation to humans and Overmind, however, it is finally revealed that they are reprobate after all. They can be keepers of Bernal's well-tended "zoo," but they are an evolutionary dead end, forever outside the line of advancement.

If *Childhood's End* unfolds in the arena Bernal calls "world," "A Meeting with Medusa" is ostensibly about transformation on the level of "flesh." Badly mangled in the crash of dirigible *Queen Elizabeth*, "rebuilt" protagonist Howard Falcon undertakes to explore the Jovian atmosphere and its "aerial sea" in a hot-hydrogen device he names the *Kon Tiki*. This appears a classic example of Bernalian advancement. The move from luxury liner to explorer's raft implies high adventure, where an enhanced human leaves over-domesti-cated Earth to chart Jupiter, "lord of the Solar System."[2] There are ironic hints, however, that this journey is no straight line. The name *Kon Tiki* invokes Thor Heyerdahl's "inverted" approach to the problem of Polynesian explor-ers, positing that they did not sail in the direct line of linguistic evidence, from South Seas to New World, but rather came from the other direction, a roundabout one from South America. The analogy between dirigible use on Earth and in Jupiter's atmosphere is equally tricky. On Earth, we rise to extend our exploratory reach, to go to some distant location and land; on Jupiter, we rise to *stay away* from the planet's surface, to escape its gravity, hence nei-ther to land nor explore. Falcon's journey to greater-than-human powers and possible transcendence is continuously offset so that as he becomes more than a man, he simultaneously becomes less.

This story is, in every detail, an exercise in dimorphism, where every movement promising to exceed the human form and norm in some way pro-duces a mirroring event restating our familiar world. For example, the Jov-ian atmosphere is compared to the seas of Earth. The two situations are vastly different (the new world "could hold a hundred Pacifics" [141]), yet strangely analogous: "At the level where the *Kon Tiki* was drifting now ... the pressure was five atmospheres. Sixty-five miles farther down it would be as warm as equatorial Earth, and the pressure about the same as the bottom of one of the shallower seas" (142–143). Such analogies render the strangeness of Jupiter banal, while also rendering our familiar world uncertain, elusive. On closer look, for instance, we see the *Queen* is more out of its element on Earth than is its counterpart in deep space. For if the new version now sails the air, not the seas, it does so only at the whims of a bored, post-industrial humanity, seeking pleasure in increasingly unnatural fashion, as if Bernal's well tended "zoo" were losing its balance. On the other hand the *Kon Tiki*, which appears initially all wrong and out of place for the immense task of Jovian exploration (just as its Earth original came at its problem the wrong way), in fact proves to work perfectly. When Falcon maneuvers to meet the alien, it turns out to be a "medusa," a South Seas creature Heyerdahl could have encountered on his voyage. In the same manner, Falcon acts to name the alien; his doing so, however, reveals severe limits in humanity's vision, its tendency to domesti-cate the unknown. Yet Clarke, by incessant undulation between dimorph and double, confounds comfortable solutions. In another striking reversal, it is on Earth, the heart of the familiar, that Falcon has his most intense encounter with the uncanny. Again, however, the meeting proves anticlimactic, and apprehension of the new resolves into banality. Inside the air sack of the *Queen* as it begins its fatal fall, Falcon discovers a landscape stranger than Jupiter, an inverted land with a "curiously submarine quality" where, in a flash, sea and air merge, the huge translucent gasbags become "harmless jellyfish, pulsing their mindless way above a shallow tropical reef" (128). In this environment, moreover, he faces his crash with heroic equanimity, sole witness to an extraordinary event that must surely kill him, a moment Clarke instantly deflates with a phrase: "One of the most spectacular wrecks in history was occurring — without a single camera to record it" (133). In contrast, Falcon seems in full control of his fall on Jupiter. But now, where the expectation is genuine alien contact, what occurs is the exact opposite of human "advancement." Here Falcon, the first human to realize the Prime Directive, finds himself out of control, dropping toward Medusa, with only one act of "heroic" will possible — to let the ship rise. Where on Earth to fall, in one sense, is to rise, here on Jupiter to rise is to fall. The Falcon soars only to fail at the juncture of both alien encounter and transhuman possibility.

One thinks first, in this counterbalancing play of dimorphs and doubles, of Swiftian deflation, the need to measure any pretense at human advancement by a fixed human norm. The process here, however, is more complex, indeed (befitting Clarke's modern sense of the temptations and perils of scientific advancement) more Pascalian. Pascal is the first thinker to link scientific advancement to the question of how such change defines a "human condition." His *Pensée* 420 provides a perfect gloss for the career of "enhanced" human Falcon: "S'il se vante, je l'abaisse; s'il s'abaisse, je le vante, et le contradis toujours, jusqu'à ce qu'il comprenne qu'il est un monstre incompréhensible" [if he praises himself, I lower him ; if he lowers himself, I praise him, and contradict him ever, until he comprehends that he is an incomprehensible monster].[3] In this light, Falcon's culminating (and arrogant) assertion of his advancement beyond humanity as we know it only reveals his monstrosity. His friend Webster attests to Falcon's advancement: "*Men,* thought Webster. He said 'men.' He's never done that before. And when did I last hear him use the word 'we'? He's changing, slipping away from us" (167). Yet this advancement is only a grotesque act of compensation: "The leather mask of his face was becoming more and more difficult to read. Instead, he rolled back from the Administrator's desk, unlocked his undercarriage so that it no longer formed a chair, and rose on his hydraulics to his full seven feet of height. It had been good psychology on the part of the surgeons to give him that extra twelve inches, to compensate somewhat for all that he had lost" (167).

Childhood's End openly asserts radical dimorphism. But, to appease readers, it retreats from its consequences by giving us Jan's narrative and the Overlords as recording angels. The Overmind itself has moved beyond the single human form as norm toward what John Barrow and Frank Tipler in *The Anthropic Cosmological Principle* call "the Omega Point" where intelligence has "gained control of *all* matter and forces, not only in a single universe, but in all universes whose existence is logically possible."[4] In Clarke's version, however, the birth of matter as intelligence, wherever it is going, simply ceases to communicate, to tell a story. In "A Meeting with Medusa" this paradigm is adjusted so that advanced humanity now finds itself in the position of not the Overmind but the Overlords, a median position between dimorph and normative human double. At the end of the story Falcon, from his more-than-human perspective, revisits his encounter, at the beginning of the story, with the "superchimp." It becomes clear that the uplifted animal, terrified by the falling *Queen*, is Falcon's true double, who like him (if in different circumstances) flees upward to avoid the crash of the dirigible. His words now resonate ironically against his own retreat upward as he approaches the Medusa: "He felt sorry for the creature, involved in a man-made disaster beyond its comprehension.... He felt that strange mingling of kinship and discomfort that all men experience when they gaze thus into the mirror of time" (132). Chimp and man, two "advanced" forms still in thrall to their original forms, are alike in being "incomprehensible monsters." Falcon, striving to leave humanity behind, can do no more than reposition himself with the chimp in relation to his Pascalian condition: "He now knew why he had dreamed about that superchimp aboard the doomed *Queen Elizabeth*. Neither man nor beast, it was between two worlds; and so was he" (168). Thus encapsulated, his destiny reflects back on *Childhood's End*. For from this perspective, Jan's world is effectively dead, and that of the Overlords powerless to be born: "Some day the real masters of space would be machines, not men — and he was neither. Already conscious of his destiny, he took a somber pride in his unique loneliness — the first immortal midway between two orders of creation" (168).

Clearly, in "Medusa," Clarke is writing against the classic Cartesian vision of stories like John W. Campbell, Jr.'s "Twilight" (1934). Here, machines have supplanted humanity in the future. These machines and their world, however, are futile, material constructs without mind. Yet, thanks to intervention by the time traveler, the evolutionary process is reopened when he reprograms a machine to become "A curious machine."[5] This unique quality of human mind is thus rekindled, but now in matter organized in a superior manner. After a false start, and necessary resurrection of the human double, we again approach the Omega Point. In "Medusa," however, Clarke envisions something like Pascal's two orders. On one hand, dimorphic split yields alien "machines," higher entities requiring no reintroduction of human traits. On the other hand, because as humans we must tell the story of dimorphism from our side of transformation —*this* order of creation — we remain prisoner to our aspirations and failings — Pascal's "man without god," forever deprived of vision beyond formal limits of body and mind.

Later Clarke novels, especially the "space odyssey" series which revisits the possibility of transcendence in each work as humanity inches chronologically into its future, do little more than reiterate this contrariety of the human condition. The original *2001: A Space Odyssey*, ostensibly, is a tale of human advancement from prehistory to transcendence. The origin of human intelligence launching us on our evolutionary journey remains, as in Christian history, the moment of the fall — caught clearly in Stanley Kubrick's image of the bone-weapon tossed in the air that becomes a spaceship weapon orbiting the Earth, an arc that elides and encapsulates all known human history. The play of dimorphs and doubles resonates through film and book alike. In the book, we advance from Moonwatcher to Starchild. Yet each, at the height of their powers, utters the same words: "For though he was master of the world, he was not quite sure what to do next. But he would think of something."[6] In the film, Kubrick presents the morphologically transcendent Star Child as, literally, a human child, encased in its embryo-mandala. This being is Janus-faced: the baby face looks forward but the knowing eyes look backward, to the original sin that still holds human advancement in thrall.

In Clarke's version of *2001*, the human form as template for future transformation abides in the "rectangle" that goads future humanity to seek transcendence: a quadratic sequence 1:4:9, where human proportionality serves as "loom" on which a "weaver" constructs a future. This future may be of a "finer texture," but, as this image implies, it remains made of the same stuff, in fact fashioned after the same form. This vision is reaffirmed at the end of *2061: Odyssey Three* (1987). Here a transformed Bowman, a reconstituted HAL, and a mysterious apparition of Heywood Floyd are involved in a vast terraforming operation, again in the Jupiter sector. However, the moon they choose, Europa, points back to known origins rather than to unknown futures. Further, the destiny of the future Floyd seems less transhuman than transcendent — as with the Overmind dimorphic split, total loss of continuity: "You are both equally real. But he will soon die, never knowing that he has become immortal."[7] Yet in typical Clarke fashion, movement forward is matched by equal movement backward. As in the seminal story "The Sentinel" (1951), the monolith, serving as "catalyst of intelligence," appears to lead humanity forward but has seemingly brought little advancement. Nor do we still, as in Clarke's previous odysseys, have any idea who created it or to what end. We still face Pascal's two incommunicable orders of being: though always promised future advancement, we never achieve a higher order of existence; or if we do, we never return to tell about it. Humanity remains in Pascal's realm of reason without God, never escaping the anthropic factor, where the human form is measure of all things. Thus, in *Odyssey Three*, the Pascalian gambit of the thinking reed is again invoked to proclaim human parity with the vast transformational forces of the monolith. To Floyd's question "But how can *we* match ourselves against the monolith — the devourer of Jupiter?" Bowman replies: "It is only a tool; it has vast intelligence — *but no consciousness*. Despite all its powers, you, Hal, and I are its superior" (271). A human-based geometry — in this case a "triad" — still limits the possibility of dimorphism. As with Pascal's reed, whom a drop of water suffices to crush, but *who knows that it is crushed, while the universe does not know it crushes*, a mutated but recognizable humanity still remains, in *Odyssey Three*, fulcrum between past and future, the zoo and the stars: "We three must be the administrators of the unforeseen, as well as the guardians of this world" (271).

Clarke's last novel in this series, *3001: The Final Odyssey*, proves not to be final, as its action, situated again at the crux of a dimorphic split, promises transformation only to reaffirm the centrality of the human original. On one hand, the novel appears to end with spectacular change. Now on Ganymede, yet more advanced forms of HAL, Bowman, and Poole witness a total eclipse of Lucifer (the old Jupiter transformed into a sun) by "a disk of perfectly black material, just over ten thousand kilometers across, so thin it shows no visible thickness."[8] Poole sees this as the result of our "infect[ing] the Monolith" (229), unleashing new forces and unpredictable change in the future. Here, seemingly, is a transformation of the physical form of the monolith itself, changing from human-like proportions to the "impossible" form of disk: "If you attempt to make a disk out of rectangular blocks — whether their proportions are 1:4:9 or any other — it cannot possibly have a smooth edge" (231). Yet this new adventure of the Odyssean Bowman is like all the others, where what first seems strange and new in the end exists only to reveal the centrality of the initial, fundamentally human, form, in this case the ubiquitous "rectangle": the disk "was composed of millions of identical rectangles, perhaps the same size as the Great Wall of Europa. And now they were splitting apart: it was as if a gigantic jigsaw puzzle was being dismantled" (231). Clarke's final novel only repeats, at another thousand-year interval, the same pattern of promise and preservation that informs the initial novel. Bowman, in *2001*, is said to move "into a realm of consciousness that no man had experienced before" (216). Yet he experiences forward movement as time running backward, until he realizes that, co-existent with advancement, his experiences are his own memory "unreeling like a tape recorder playing back at ever-increasing speed" (216). In Kubrick's film, a similar "playback" deprogramming of HAL is ambiguous, for whatever regret the machine feels as its memory reels back to songs of lost innocence, what is recovered is a condition central to human consciousness, the sense of having fallen from Eden into humanity. In contrast, Clarke's Bowman finds solace in the possibility of total transformation. He can do so because he now sees change as dimorphic, where the loss of humanity entails its simultaneous recapture: "He was ... being drained of knowledge and experience as he swept back toward his childhood. But nothing was being lost; all that he had ever been, at every moment of his life, was being transferred to safer keeping. Even as one David Bowman ceased to exist, another became immortal" (216). In *3001*, dimorphism has been modified, but not abolished. It is now Poole who glimpses "entities — far superior to the Monoliths, and perhaps even their makers" (224). Still, the solution to whatever promise of human transformation these powers bring remains dimorphism. The agent is the mutated "Halman," a fusion of HAL and Bowman into a single cybernetic entity that can be stored on a "petabyte memory tablet" (225). Again, as Pascal's gambit strikes parity between the vastness of universal spacetime and the human reed, Clarke preserves his spark of human consciousness, to be stored in a vault on Earth's moon, the same site where the original space odyssey was launched in "The Sentinel." In dimorphic fashion, the tablet serves as both a way to protect and assure human advancement in the future ("This tablet contains programs that we hope will prevent the Monolith from carrying out any orders that threaten mankind" [225]) and a memory bank to conserve the consciousness of Hal and Bowman, as repository for the history of familiar humanity, on the brink of being lost to evolutionary transformation: "'Ten to the fifteenth bytes is more than sufficient to hold all the memories and experiences of many lifetimes. This will give you one escape route'.... Halman was willing to cooperate: he still had sufficient links with his origins" (225–226). The "final" Odyssey merely inscribes another elliptical path, wider in its dimorphic reach perhaps, but still anchored at its human center. Humanity buries its past, knowing that doing so sends another message to its future, which in turn will cause that past to be resurrected. The best we can have is another millennium, a thousand year reprieve, for humanity: "Poole had often cursed Einstein in the past; now he blessed him. Even the powers behind the Monoliths ... could not spread their influence faster than the speed of light. So the human race should have almost a millennium to prepare for the next encounter" (235). Poole hopes the post-millennial future will not need to reawaken Halman. He knows however that the human zoo must always be ready to anchor future advancement. Indeed, it is Poole, the least "advanced" of these future hybrids, who with his ordinary human memory must stand guard as the final preserving machine. For as Halman tells him: "If we are unable to download, remember us" (229).

The Promise of the Cyborg: Haraway's "Manifesto"

Clarke's wrestling with the problem of dimorphism in his narratives of human advancement may seem predictable. He and Bernal share both the nationality and vision of another influential contemporary, Olaf Stapledon, whose *Last and First Men: A Story of the Near and Far Future* appeared in 1930, one year after Bernal's essay. One expects less to find the dimorph-double pattern at work in American SF, nominally committed to the "straight line" ideology of technological progress. Surprisingly, dimorphism abides in two dissimilar writers, though both advocate a human drive toward morphological change: Donna Haraway and Robert A. Heinlein. Except for the fact that their names begin with an "H," one may see little affinity between them. Examining their visions of human advancement reveals otherwise.

An air of Frankensteinian monstrosity hovers over Bernal's alterations of flesh and Clarke's Falcon alike. Haraway's revalorization of the "cyborg" as positive next step in human evolution, however, rests on a "postmodern" vision demanding deconstruction of the human form divine. But "postmodernism" in this sense proves less than "post" when one finds suggestive ambiguity about a like project in a work more-or-less contemporary to *Frankenstein*: Honoré de Balzac's story of the painter Frenhofer, "Le Chef d'oeuvre inconnu" (1831). Frenhofer's "masterpiece," his vision of the ideal woman constructed from sittings with living models, when unveiled is an incoherent welter of lines and colors. The painting however is not entirely incoherent; in one corner an exquisite human foot (described as "un pied *vivant*," a "living foot") emerges from the chaos. All that remains for Haraway to do is ask the question: in what direction did Frenhofer's making proceed? Did he work away from the human form, toward its destruction? The foot then serves, like Clarke's utopian children, as jumping-off place toward a vision of transcendent humanity. To Frenhofer's onlookers, "old humanity" like Clarke's Jan, "here ends our art on Earth." To them, the foot is a "fragment échappé à une incroyable, à une lente et progressive destruction" [a fragment that has escaped from some incredible process of slow, progressive destruction].[9] The postmodernist merely takes sides with Frenhofer: his dismantling of the normative or classic "human form divine" is a necessary move away from defining humanity as "presence," as self-defined consciousness. Postmodern evolution must move away from identity; the work of art depicting it can no longer represent the individual subject; when a Hermione steps from the postmodern pedestal, she no longer bears a human name or form. In this light, Frenhofer's welter of lines must be celebrated as "advanced" form, no longer subsumable by dichotomies like subject/object, mind/body, or animate/inanimate. So it is for the gestalt Haraway calls the "cyborg"; despite her celebration of the cyborg's newness, dimorphism still holds sway at this postmodern juncture with humanity's future.

Haraway makes great claims for her new being. Unlike Bernal's cyborg, hers is born of disorder, in the interstices and across the boundaries of our rational projects for an ordered, technology-directed future. For Haraway, the cyborg cannot be categorized (as in early "male" SF) as "black" or "white," nor as a "perversion" (Frederik Pohl's "Day Million" [1966]) nor even as a grotesque yet functionally positive transformation (Heinlein's "Waldo" [1942]). The cyborg, she claims, is not simply another hybrid of flesh and metal, or mixture of natural and "artificial" memory. The workshop where it is created is one of universal atomization or etherealization of all forms, where dualist categories of animal/machine or physical/non-physical are utterly confounded. The technologies of the cyborg are miniaturization and dispersion, aimed at reducing solid forms to a flow of information "bytes," transgenetic codings, micro- and nano-electrical impulses: the pixels and quanta from which simulacra are created. As Haraway puts it, "microelectronics is the technical basis of simulacra; that is, copies without originals." But politics creeps into its making as well, for as our best machines "are made of sunshine ... all light and clean because they are nothing but signals," so the cyborg is "ether, quintessence."[10]

This statement is however too radical for Haraway to sustain. Her cyborg is not Clarke's Overmind, the product of complete rupture, of total transfer of energy from one form to another. Despite its ethereal promise, there remains resistance, re-coupling; nodules form, arteries harden, proof that, even here, the dimorph sustains a continuous link with its human double, with the reader's normative "humanity." Haraway's very definition of the cyborg offers a litany of doublings: "The cyborg is a kind of disassembled and reassembled, postmodern collective and personal self" (163). Moreover, she feels obliged to spend a whole page on a "chart of transitions," making sure all links are articulated from the "old hierarchical dominations to the scary new networks I have called the informatics of domination" (161). Haraway, in inspired spurts, describes her cyborg's newness in terms of its formal elusiveness as a "mosaic," a "chimera." But as her essay proceeds, her descriptions are increasingly dimorphic; over and over she doubles lyrical evocations of new techno-transformations with disquisitions on surprisingly conventional political causes. Emerging in the mirror of the cyborg is a classic Leftist portrait of what Haraway (in an un-cyborg-like manner) calls a "bimodal society," a world marked less by transgressed boundaries than by the unchallenged dualisms of "left" and "right," domination and non-domination. Again and again, her advanced being is reclaimed by the "obsolete" human form it purportedly abandons. Indeed, the face behind the welter of signals and bytes is increasingly that of "Man, the embodiment of Western logos." Her simulacrum reveals itself to be little more than another hybrid, cobbled together from what Istvan Csicsery-Ronay, Jr. calls "the Great Paradigmatic Pool of Aliens": machines, animals, women, people of color.[11]

Csicsery-Ronay offers two significant comments on Haraway's cyborg, both bolstering her claim that the cyborg represents the advancement of humanity: first, its creation represents a "full-catastrophe model" (511); second, children are absent from the pool of aliens that comprises its doubles. Indeed, Haraway implies catastrophic separation by qualifying her new form of humanity as "about transgressed boundaries, potent fusions and dangerous possibilities." Even so, a dimorphic split clearly must not occur, lest the postmodern privilege of her entity be lost. In Haraway's final striking image, the monstrously regenerating salamander body, not only does the old form remain, but that form acts as both ground and limit for any possible future transformation: "cyborgs have more to do with regeneration and are suspicious of the reproductive matrix and of most birthing. For salamanders, regeneration after injury, such as the loss of a limb, involves regrowth of structure and restoration of function with the constant possibility of twinning or other odd topographical productions at the site of former injury. The regrown limb can be monstrous, duplicated, potent. We have all been injured, profoundly" (181). Despite claims to morphological transformation, Haraway still works this side of what I call the Frankenstein barrier. When Frankenstein refused his creature a bride, the possibilities of procreation and of creating a new evolutionary form, the creature can never become more than a similar self-generating monstrosity. Haraway too denies her cyborg this "reproductive matrix," and with it any real evolutionary future. Inverting Shelley's formula, it is Eve without an Adam. Balzac's Frenhofer indulges in his welter of lines, making monstrous claims that new life lies within them. Haraway does likewise. In painting her triumphant picture of the etherealized cyborg, all "nodes" and links, she does little more than conjure the old specter of a human form as something grotesquely distorted, stillborn.

The Lives and Loves of Lazarus Long

Haraway's vision, she admits, owes much to science fiction's cyborg entities. She makes no mention of Heinlein, for obvious political reasons. Yet Heinlein, surprisingly, develops a vision analogous to hers, where the extent of future change remains grotesquely tied to the hegemony of the old bodily form. Differences are glaring, but instructive. In light of Bernal and Clarke, Haraway's models for future transformation — cyborgs and salamanders — remain regressive in the evolutionary sense. Heinlein's model, though hardly postmodern, is equally regressive — the individual "God-given" body of Lazarus Long, his genetically and evolutionarily chosen protagonist. "Chosen" here retains a quasi–Calvinist sense. Heinlein may proclaim fascination with future advancement of humanity, yet he shares with Haraway the desire that such advancement not violate the limits of an individual body and identity, be that a cyborg or a chosen human prototype. In this sense, the group entity, offered as possible next stage in human evolution, is anathema to Heinlein. The group entity is a well-developed trope in SF, running from Bernal's speculation on "chemical dispersion" of individual being through Stapledon and Clarke to scores of modern imaginings. Haraway's next cyborgian step — her "hope for a monstrous world without gender" — reflects the ambiguity prevalent among SF authors as they ponder a future when human particularities are fused or leveled. Attitudes range from the caution of Theodore Sturgeon's *More than Human* (1953) to the skepticism and black humor of Serge Brussolo's "Trajets et itinéraires de l'oubli" (1981). Heinlein flatly rejects advancement in this direction. He proclaims this in *Have Space Suit, Will Travel* (1958), where just such an "evolved" entity sits in judgment on a "primitive" human race. The entity defines itself: "I am older than that, but no part of me is that old. I am partly machine, which part can be repaired, replaced, recopied; I am partly alive, these parts die and are replaced. My living parts are more than a dozen dozens of dozens of civilized beings from throughout Three Galaxies...."[12] For Heinlein, the fatal flaw of such a being is blindness to what he sees as the prime motor of evolution, the creative unpredictability of the individual human. The group entity of *Space Suit* is a dimorph that has lost contact with its double, for in its pluralistic existence, it conceives of humans only as parts of a single organism ("From three samples of the organism you call the human race I can predict the future potentialities and limits of that race" [232]). The judges are stymied when protagonist Kip asserts that humans "have no limits" (232), declaring them alien creatures to be "pondered," but never understood.

Human advancement then, for Heinlein, cannot occur in a more-than-human context, but must evolve within the limits of a single individual existence. What is more, he refuses claims, like those of Haraway, that hybridization of the human form or consciousness is the way to transhumanity. Heinlein admits the transhuman alterations that mark Bernalian advancement. Their field of expansion however must occur within the boundaries of an endlessly preserved human form. The "omega point" is reached within the circumference inscribed by such an expanded individual — here the extended body and mind of Lazarus Long. Long's progress, if it seems radically opposite to that of Haraway's cyborg, is in fact its re-encapsulation within a human body. Lazarus may undergo a full gamut of physical and biological transformations. Yet because dimorphic possibility is ever circumscribed by its expanding double, Lazarus is even more than Haraway's cyborg excluded from any possibility of evolutionary advancement by the barrier of the body-as-it-is, the tyranny of a "conventional," strikingly postlapsarian, human form. The many and frantic metamorphoses of Heinlein's protagonist, dispersing his being along chemical and genetic pathways, only underscore the fact that he, like every individual, has but one body, wherein is found his origin, cause, and end. Lazarus's name (however infinite his capacity for disguises, he has but one "real" name) itself enfolds a dynamic, whereby the power to expand (Long — longevity, not immortality, a dynamic not static state) is ever circumscribed by the limits of the individual — the endless Lazarus-like regeneration of a single bodily form that each time becomes, to use Haraway's word, more grotesquely "potent."

Heinlein introduces Lazarus early in his career, in *Methuselah's Children* (1941), as patriarch of the Howard Family. Favored by genes, he and his kin use rational planning and "serendipity" (Heinlein's secular form of grace) to broadcast their seed and flesh over the entire universe. In the novel, longevity is aided by time dilation, as Lazarus tours the stars at near-light speeds and returns to Earth barely aged to find that science has, during Earth's long span of time, developed means to keep his body alive indefinitely. Centered in his own being, with its unique "life line," Lazarus can conceive of advancement solely through endless resurrections of his own body. This becomes clear when Lazarus recoils in horror at friend Mary Sperling's capitulation to the "Little People" on planet Elysium. Rather than age and die as an individual, she becomes part of their group consciousness. This "translation" becomes painfully clear to Lazarus when he hears Mary's voice grotesquely coming from another body. In later SF, such situations, though presented as cyborg-like improvements on the condition of human flesh, usually create forms of human existence almost invariably revealed to be monstrous distortions of the norm, beings less-than-human. An example is William Gibson's Dixie Flatline in *Neuromancer* (1984), a downloaded personality construct able to speak from any hardware capable of slotting his "memory." Yet if Dixie has a name, he has no local habitation and remains at the mercy of any finger in the "meat" world that can throw the switch.

Lazarus's way of advancing his progeny, far in his fictional future, and thirty years across Heinlein's opus in *Time Enough for Love* (1973), is to use technology not merely to preserve, but physically to extend his individual bodily form until, like some great sensorium, it fills all future evolutionary spacetime. Contained within the circumference of Lazarus's dispersed body, each of "humanity's" next steps is merely an avatar, more properly speaking a clone, of Lazarus's original form. As such, as in Haraway, the "love" of the title is — despite the pretext of family lines and gene transmission — more a process of regeneration than reproduction. For example, Lazarus's love for the dead "ephemeral" Dora finds a new location in human flesh, yet as with all such resurrected creatures at a degree less than human. Lazarus's Pygmalion statue is a computer named Minerva. Like HAL in *2001*, Minerva has human yearnings because "she" is made in humanity's image, thus wants to experience Eros, or lust. Rejecting machine immortality, she embraces mortality, but unlike Pinocchio this new mortal has endless capacity to regenerate itself. Ever obedient to her creator, Minerva asks Lazarus what her fleshly form should look like. He gives Dora's portrait, and the new Minerva, springing full-born from the head of her Zeus, takes Dora's form, resurrecting it in a grotesque manner next to which natural processes of birth and death seem simple.

Heinlein's novel does not take Lazarus to the point of dimorphic split, for that moment is its opening premise. Lazarus has already reached *his* omega point; he and his universe are co-extensive. The result is the utopian impasse, where no further striving is possible and boredom reigns. There remains but one possible breakthrough to the new — death — which in the case of this one-man universe is suicide. The break offered is as radical as that which produced Clarke's Overmind. Heinlein's novel offers a hundred reasons for not making the break, all sophistic. Indeed, members of his cosmos, spun entirely out of Lazarus's entrails, must keep him alive to ensure their own existence. One by one, "family" members and advanced constructs of his making offer technologies and "sacrifices" that promise ways of generating new, but equally solipsistic, forms. Cloning, for instance, lets Lazarus "flesh" out his family in striking ways, even give himself twin "sisters" he never had. In all such creations, however, every new, often preposterous, form in turn generates the double that roots it in the conventional structures, and strictures, of Lazarus's sole body. In the case of the "sisters," Lazarus, not content with creating simulacra, insists on giving them a feigned biological origin as well. He has the cloned cells implanted in host mothers who are also his mistresses. With lovemaking divorced from conception, Lazarus produces a travesty of the process of reproduction while retaining its external forms. The ensuing children both are and are not biological products of Lazarus, part of his common gene pool perhaps, but divorced from any open line of procreation. In external form both his sisters and daughters, these creatures finally are neither — only sterile re-creations of Lazarus himself. His subsequent demands that these clones be raised like "real" daughters, with the cultural trappings of a "next generation," are pure theater, a theater of masturbation. As clones, pieces of a same genetic makeup, Lazarus is "free" to make love to them because, as lovers, they offer no risk or consequence. For Lazarus, the power to repeat his life cycle endlessly becomes the curse of endless re-enactment of life *in the same body*, a being doomed to take up again and again the various roles in what should be the successive and finite process of human existence.

If, as Heinlein proclaims, the advancement of Lazarus is an evolutionary process, it should be open-ended. It has an apparent first cause — the instant of genetic chance (or grace) from which the Howard Family emerges. Likewise, it simulates an ongoing dynamic of change. Natural selection appears guided (if we ignore strokes of too-good fortune along the way) by Bernal's rational soul. Seemingly through acts of human intelligence, Lazarus overcomes the suicide temptation (as if to say "Life is too long when one is not enjoying it now") and articulates a need to pass to a next stage in human evolution. Even so, the final section in *Time Enough for Love*, entitled *da capo* (the novel is constructed, in Heinlein's musical analogy, as Lazarus's symphony of himself), brings new humanity back to confront the old, in an extraordinary act of doubling that sets the limits of human transformation as those of the protagonist's original body. From his far future, through time travel, Lazarus regenerates as a young man to return to the Missouri of his (and Heinlein's) childhood and court and make love to his own mother. Lazarus possesses amazing future technologies allowing him to regenerate from his own flesh and memory, like Haraway's salamander, family members and loved ones lost to death and destiny. But in relation to the simple act of procreation, it is equally monstrous. For Lazarus does not transcend his condition; he merely defers what remains inevitable — his death. Now, in this final scene with his mother, Lazarus demonstrates the extent to which he remains in thrall to his personal moment of creation, to the mystery of the mother who launched him into the stream of time, once and forever. For Lazarus, the ultimate technology is that which would allow him to control this first cause and generational energy it produces. The dilemma however is that, as striving monad, he must take control without creating himself, making a tautology that lifts him out of the stream of evolution. Lazarus again offers high theater. As Sgt. Theodore Bronson, he returns to pre–World War Missouri, where he meets himself as young boy and courts his mother as lover. Long is now the master artist of time displacement, sculpting a family portrait that never was or could be, which he insists on grotesquely casting in flesh. In the scene of seduction, Heinlein titillates readers with the possibility that Lazarus could, if he wished, sire himself, ending the story and novel at will. What actually happens is more an Oedipal dream made flesh. The drama of seduction is elaborately acted out. The mother falls in love with Bronson and insists on having him at the same spot, and in the same clothes, as on the night she conceived Lazarus. This is, however, but another copy of a lost original. In this fantasy theater, not only is dress-up substituted for *the* moment, but the ersatz lovemaking is itself thwarted as little Lazarus (who sneaked a ride in the car and was watching all the while) steps forth, in the nick of time, to spoil the party.

Such complex play of dimorph and double only reinforces the tyranny of Lazarus's body as center whose circumference, in striving to encompass the entire spacetime universe, remains in thrall to its original form. This bodily circle offers no way to pass beyond original form to a new morphology. In the final pages, Bronson, despairing of ever controlling his first cause, suicidally throws himself into battle in World War I France and is literally blown to bits. The sophism is triggered; the future process of self-preservation Lazarus created in his own image *must* now intervene to preserve the original. Two of Lazarus's time-traveling mistress-clones swoop down *in extremis*, scrape his remains from the battlefield; as with the salamander limb, the original form regrows itself. Upon awakening, Lazarus hears a "Gray Voice" he thinks might be that of God. Asking, as resurrected or "new" man, to see God's face, he is told: "Try a mirror." Lazarus (as well as Lazarus's maker and double, Heinlein himself) now learns the grotesquely solipsistic condition of all such self-artificers: "You are you, playing chess with yourself, and again you have checkmated yourself."[13]

Almost the Same: The Strugatskys' Future History

The examples above are catastrophic in nature. Impatient with the creeping pace of his "future history," Heinlein abandons continuity for the big leap, from the slow time of *Methuselah's Children* to the Lazarus of *Time Enough for Love*, who appears to reach the end of human morphological change as we know it, poised at the instant of final, irrevocable transformation. Yet Lazarus, haunted by his origins, refuses this leap. Likewise, if Haraway sees her radically advanced form as a copy without an original, the very fact that it is a copy means it can only exist at a lesser degree of being than the original. As dimorph is driven to seek its double in its "original," the possibility of human advancement mutates into monstrosity. The Frankenstein limit remains. Each new Adam (or Eve), denied a mate of their evolved kind, thus the possibility of sustained transformation, is forced back upon the original form of its creator, to whom it forever remains a grotesque travesty of that form. The end of *Frankenstein* is emblematic of catastrophic tales of dimorphism: the "advanced" creature endlessly pursuing its original form, in the person of its creator, in icy limbo, the landscape of perfect solipsism.

Dimorphism, however, need not be catastrophic. Another model modifies the alternating rhythm of dimorph and double to allow, within rises and collapses, a continuous sense of human advancement. This is Ralph Waldo Emerson's "transcendentalist" dynamic, both non-linear and progressive. Here the rational soul, instead of separating, as in Bernal, the impulsions of fate and desire, understands them as working together in an interactive, "undulatory" relationship. In Emerson's dynamic of power and form, if fate inscribes formal limits, these exist as an elastic circumference generated by human actions. Now, desire in turn becomes the power permitting the human agent to launch successive undulations, launching a process of responsive transformation, both at the center and on the circumference. A work fitting this model is the story cycle of Arkady and Boris Strugatskys' future history: *Noon: 22nd Century (Polden: 22 vek)* (1962, revised in 1967, stories written in the late 1950s–early 1960s).

This story comes from a different ideological sector — Marxist dialectical materialism rather than Heinleinian individualism. We expect, therefore, any sustained advancement their future history reveals will be the product of dialectical continuity: thesis, antithesis, synthesis. Yet Soviet SF writers, under the dominant influence of forerunner Ivan Efremov, inherit a surprisingly "ahistorical" model of advanced humanity, in which all possibility of dimorphic evolution remains prisoner to the human double. Efremov clearly presents his static vision in *Heart of the Serpent* (1958), which describes the encounter of a future classless humanity with an alien race that looks exactly like them, except that it breathes fluorine, not oxygen. Efremov's thesis is that human organs and brain, as they are perfected by this utopian future race, are the summum of all evolutionary possibility for intelligent life in any universe: "I do not expect to find monsters with horns and tails in the space ship we shall meet. Only the lower forms of life differ greatly from one another; the higher the form the closer it is bound to be to us Earth-dwellers."[14] In an anti–Bernalian sense, Efremov argues (in a way oddly analogous to Heinlein) that the human body and mind provide the sole possible template for the advancement of life forms, a space waiting to be filled out as humanity realizes its potential: "Man is a microcosm. Thinking follows the laws of the Universe which are the same everywhere.... There cannot be any other entirely different thought process" (55). Any claim to human advancement, through either dimorphic transcendence or synthesis with alien life forms, must prove illusory, as the human form cannot be surpassed. Meeting the fluorine breathers offers nothing except inferior copies of our original form. These aliens look exactly like humans, but in the evolutionary sense they are inferior: fluorine is far rarer than oxygen in the universe. In the final scene, the two races, perfect mirror images except for their metabolisms, see each other through a transparent glass that separates them. Narcissus-like, Earth woman Afra Devi first throws herself at the glass, then retreats to offer the other race the means of joining ours, the key to let them evolve into humans: "She crossed out the symbol of the fluorine atom with its nine electrons that she had drawn and replaced it with a symbol of the oxygen atom" (111).

The Strugatskys, as Soviet SF writers, may be ideologically bound to this anthropocentric future, where the human form remains the "microcosm" containing all limits of possible advancement. But since they read SF writers such as Stapledon, Clarke, Heinlein, even Bradbury, the lure of advancement and dimorphism is on their fictional horizon. Curiously, then, in *Noon: 22d Century,* their chronicle of human advancement develops in a manner closer to Emersonian undulation than official dialectics. Movement is back and forth from a central point (Efremov's perfected humanity, basking in the sun of a classless future world) to an ever-expanding circumference, as humanity beyond our solar system, toward possible contact with "real" aliens, beings more than mirror images of humanity. At such points of human limitation, contact entails reciprocal adaptations, each of which rebounds in turn to bring change at the human center. It is interesting to speculate on the SF conduit whereby this "Emersonian" rhythm reached the Strugatsky brothers. Given their fascination in this story cycle with returning spacemen, and with temporal dislocations caused by the "twins paradox," Heinlein may offer a precise locus. There is no firm evidence, but a novel like Heinlein's *Time for the Stars* (1956) was not only widely available but, because it was ostensibly "juvenile" adventure, ideologically acceptable as well, able to pass censorship. In this novel, one twin, Pat Bartlett, sweeps around the galaxy at near-light speeds, gathering many lifetimes of experience and scientific data, yet barely ageing in relation to brother Tom, who remains on Earth. Experiences at the circumference, however, offering contact and possible "advancement," do not escape the center; Pat does return to his original spacetime location (where he finds Tom an old man). Moreover, because these twins are telepathic, and telepathy here is faster than light, all data gathered by Pat and broadcast back to Tom feed a scientific apparatus that, relative to Pat's weeks, has many years to do research, generating scientific breakthroughs that make Pat on his return a scientific and social relic. The Strugatskys, Heinlein's Soviet counterparts in terms of mastery of the SF juvenile, use this same trope of the returning spaceman and its doubling rhythm to perfection.

The two stories in the first section of *Noon,* set in the early 21st century, tell of two early space explorers: Sergei Kondratev and Evgeny Slavin. "Night on Mars" chronicles a very short step in human advancement, the doctors' trek through the dangers of the Martian night to deliver the first Earth child born on the newly colonized planet. That child is Slavin himself. The second story, "Almost the Same," is an anecdotal account of Kondratev's cadet days, where a low-key dimorphic split is enacted between Sergei and a certain Panin. The latter, describing himself as "a simple man, a guileless man," questions the need to go to the stars. Kondratev, for whom space travel is more important than all Earthly attachments, even love, articulates the difference between them: "As for whose sake will we find out about the stars ... [it is] for our own, for everyone's. Even for yours. But you won't take part in it.

You'll make your discoveries in the newspapers."[15] But Panin, it turns out, is neither an exhibit in the Bernalian zoo, nor the Heinleinian sacrificial twin. His role proves equally dynamic, in a way radically different from, yet in mirror fashion equivalent to, Kondratev's heroic flight: "All right.... So I'll become a teacher. I'll plumb the depths of children's souls for the sake of everyone" (36). Children are a way to the future as valid as individual heroics.

The second section, "Homecoming," presents the narrative of human advancement not as straight line outward, but as a space-time twist that brings Slavin and Kondratev back, as relics of the past, to an Earth that in their absence evolved technologically and socially. The seven stories in this section are mostly understated narratives of daily efforts made by the "Two from the Taimyr" (the title of the sixth story) to readapt to this new, utopian Earth. Long thought dead, they are literally resurrected in a time that does not reject them, but in Bernal's sense, studies them as curiosities, miraculously living forms of the old revered humanity. Though treated with respect, they are nevertheless forbidden to leave Earth.

The key story in this section is "Homecoming," where dimorph and double meet and engage in dialogue. The idle, depressed Kondratev is visited by Gorbovsky, a new breed of space explorer, whose adventures will unfold in later sections of *Noon*. Gorbovsky treats his double's "heroic" landing on a murderous planet much as one would an event in a *chanson de geste* — something magnificent yet quaintly archaic. Gorbovsky, however, though a space scientist rather than a pioneer, positions himself in analogous manner on the far circumference of his new frontier. For where other spacemen engage the hard sciences of planetology and astrophysics, or do D-principle (near-light-speed drive) research — the field Kondratev would choose if he could — Gorbovsky pursues the arcane "fourth problem" (118), which seeks traces of visits by aliens on distant planets. For this space mystic, things far and near offer the same mirror attraction they did for the earlier generation of spacers. When on Earth, Gorbovsky takes meals lying down like his "classic" ancestors. He sprawls in Earth's green grass, at water's edge, and catches an old-fashioned cold. In between trips to the far frontier on a D-ship, he flies settlers on a tame shuttle to nearby Venus (what was a death planet for Kondratev is now a suburb of Earth). He sees himself, like Kondratev, as all-too-rapidly superannuated by progress: "Now we're all ferrying volunteers. Even proud researchers of the D-principle. Now we're like the streetcar coachmen of your time" (119). Kondratev in turn, who cannot return to space, is offered work exploring ocean depths — as in Clarke a "new" frontier that was always there, once one grasps the fact that inner doubles outer space.

Here as in other stories of this section, the interplay of dimorphs and doubles weaves a firm thread of continuity between meetings that might otherwise be catastrophic. Kondratev realizes that his encounter with Gorbovsky and the oceanographer was not fortuitous: "They're intelligent people ... they came to help me. I need only one thing" (120). What he needs is a future, and these stories explore the undulations between desire and fate that get us there, the rhythm of one step backward for two steps forward. In "The Moving Roads," Slavin discovers that, though these "great-grandchildren" seem to live very much as he did, there has been change and movement, however imperceptible. The symbol of this is the "moving roads." Unlike Heinlein's rolling roads, these are slow moving conveyers of people and goods. But if they are not a "breakthrough" technology — where "rolling" implies a precise technology, these simply "move" — they offer a significant advance over the old form of road. The same slow but inexorable flow to the future is generated by the story "The Conspirators," located at the center of the section. Here, in what appears simply the perennial story of teacher and pupils, a new generation of space explorers emerges. Komov, Siderov, Sasha Kostylin, Pol Gnedykh: these are names we hear in stories in the next two sections. Now, however, they act out in childish games roles they will take on later as adults. They are future aspiring dimorphs; but their doubles, as they proclaim here, are the "heroes" of the first cycles. They are, figuratively, Panin's "children."

The group of stories featuring our "conspirators" are of two mutually mirroring sorts. In the first category, "breakthrough" projects — attempts to engineer new forms of humanity — collapse in grotesque failure. In "The Mystery of the Hind Leg," Slavin, now a journalist, encounters a fantastic horde of cybernetic creatures in Australia. But these, he discovers, do not represent some future evolutionary step, but are products of a Sorcerer's Apprentice prank. At the center of this story is a formidable artificial intelligence — CODD, Collector of Dispersed Data. This underground computer, gathering "traces" of past events and transforming them into images, resurrects the past as a "data base." At the same time, as sentient machine, it can expand its faculties, create and combine new elements, and thus advance toward some transhuman future. Yet the fact that CODD remains subject to human masters is comically vivid. Given a statistical problem to solve — which trough among several troughs a certain merino sheep will choose and why — the computer generates models — simulacra. While inputting data, however, programmers amuse themselves by giving the sheep seven legs. The result is a maker of forms gone berserk: "It piles absurdity upon absurdity" (207).

The mood is more somber in "Candles Before the Control Board." Here the next step in human advancement is personal immortality in the form of a Great Encoding, the downloading of a great Academician's personality into computer memory. The recipient of this data however is a massive structure: "twenty-six squat buildings, each with a frontage, each extending six levels underground" (228). Not only is too much space needed, but there is not enough time to do the job, and only 98 percent of the individual biomass is downloaded before natural death occurs. The "candles" here are simultaneously progressive and regressive: a substitute for the electricity that must be diverted to the experiment, and conventional sign of a wake. In the final image, glimmers from sputtering candles, a funeral for the futile labor devoted to the experiment, are reflected by the control board that was to make it happen. In this play of reflections, the dimorphic urge proves to be never free of its human double, present to set fatal limits to transhuman aspirations.

"Pilgrims and Wayfarers" similarly offers ironic mirrorings of extraordinary and common humanity, where our future again proves slightly more than reflected forms of our past. Here, "astroarcheologist" Gorbovsky meets Ivanov, an oceanographer who has discovered a lifeform that is primitive, previously unknown, but also undergoing a formal evolution. These "septipods" manifest potent changes in heart and muscle structure; and for some inexplicable reason (they are all males so reproduction is not the cause) they leave their former habitat and move onto land. It is spacer Gorbovsky who draws the analogy between these creatures and the new humanity he believes he represents: "They stayed in the depths for ages, and now they've risen up and entered an alien, hostile world. And what drives them? An ancient, dark instinct? ... Or an information-processing capacity which had risen up to the level of unquenchable curiosity?" (251). In the dialogue between Gorbovsky and Ivanov, there is mirroring of the realms of sky and water as well. Gorbovsky reveals he too has been "tagged" by some alien force, made to emit strange radio signals, and wonders whether he and the septipod, at different stages of evolution, are not living analogous fates. The force that marked him (the signal goes on "day and night. Whether we're happy or sad" [252]) is as indifferent to his desires as Ivanov is to the creatures he tags. The story ends with a statement by Ivanov's "forward-looking" daughter that, ironically, summons its own mirroring question: "There's a difference between an interstellar ship and wet slime in a gill bag" (253). Is there?

In other stories in this section an evolving humanity seeks out the alien, hoping this encounter will lead to a further step. For skeptics like Stanisław Lem, alien encounter merely reflects our desire to see our familiar selves mirrored in the cosmic mystery. Thus, in *Solaris* (1961), Kelvin's exploration of the alien "ocean" simply results in his conjuring an image of his dead wife Rheya from the analogous ocean of his unconscious mind. In the Strugatskys' work, however, the search for such encounters offers a more tentative undulation between dimorphic possibility and human stasis. In the story "The Planet with All the Conveniences," scientists reach distant planet Leonida in the wake of Gorbovsky's Pathfinders. In comparison with other alien worlds, this one does not seem to need "virophages" or other terraforming devices: the place is so clement that the visitors, ignoring the strangeness of its structures, make themselves "at home." Head of Mission Komov suspects this may be (echoing Bradbury's "Mars Is Heaven") a trap. The trap however is that this world *is* so close to being another Earth — another utopian world "with all the conveniences" — that possible differences go unheeded. The humans swim, run barefoot, trample the fauna. They even take the liberty to shoot the strange "animals" apparently stealing their belongings only to realize that these are intelligent beings. We set forth assuming aliens, by definition, must be radically different and miss the alien in the familiar. Here, what proves most alien is what most resembles the beholder. Ironically, when the explorers finally realize they are in the presence of uncanny beings, they do so only because they can associate them with humans. Again, in Cartesian and Efremovian fashion, humans can only take humans seriously: "They're people! Animals can steal, but only people can bring back what they've stolen" (274). There is double irony in the fact that, as perceptions undulate from alien to familiar to alien again, only when the observers see these aliens as "people" can they glimpse the possibility of an evolutionary "next step." They reason thus: the place has no machines or cities, only organic entities; but as its inhabitants have morals like people, culture has taken an alternate path here; if this is not a technological civilization, it must be a *biological* one. As with all such doublings in the Strugatskys, there is neither clear advance nor retreat. For in the end, these "best minds of humanity" see themselves, in this alien mirror, as little more than blunderers and spoilers: "We look for brothers in reason for 300 years, then run away as soon as we find them" (275). Yet for each step backward, two tentative ones go forward. In this case, one of the party, Komov, at least wishes to stay, to ask questions that might lead to a next step in human evolution. Given what has gone before, however, will not such pretense lead again to blindness, and beyond blindness to further negotiations between familiar things without and alien things within?

The final story, "What We Will Be," if its assertive title proves ironic, nevertheless expresses impatience with the slow undulatory pace of human advancement. Its tilt is forward, suggesting the need, if not necessity, of a dimorphic leap beyond humanity to post-human experience. In the well-kept zoo of twenty-second century Earth, Kondratev, Slavin and Gorbovsky gather at the seaside for a tranquil barbecue before the latter leaves for planet Tagora. On the threshold of the new, Gorbovsky tells a story of an old, past event. His story, however, is one of transcendent possibility. During a near-fatal accident in space, Petr Petrovich, a man claiming to be their "remote descendent," appears miraculously inside the ship. He is described as of "average height, thin pleasant face," and "dressed like a spacer," except that his jacket is buttoned from right to left, "like a woman's, or, according to rumor, like the Devil's" (316). Or is it the human figure seen in a mirror? Our mysterious mirror image doubles again: is it Saint Peter, or the Devil? Petrovich is a Janus-faced presence as enigmatic as Bernal's dimorph or Clarke's Monolith — depicting the lure of the human future in which twin impulsions toward domesticity and transcendence join in riddling tautology. Petr's "prediction" of human advancement is just such a riddle: "if you are what you plan on being, then we'll become what we are. And what you, accordingly, will be" (318). The circularity of this promise is subsequently skewed toward possible transcendence in an unpredictable future during a seemingly innocent, half-joking, exchange of views about the future. The spacers' views range from the quasi-mystical to facetious; yet buried in each lies a promise of dimorphic split — from Slavin's seriously uttered, post–Marxian prediction of a new, "completely fantastic" turn of history's spiral to Kondratev's whimsical invitation to his comrades to dive into the ocean to see "the Golden Grotto," a man-made amusement park with a mystical name. Thus, whether the future yields a commonplace at the heart of something inconceivably new (as in the banality of Slavin's exclamation of visionary awe, "you haven't seen anything like it"), or something startlingly new in an undiscovered corner of the thoroughly familiar, such as the "Grotto," the possibility of future transcendence haunts this story. Indeed, the event that inspires his friends' predictions is a real, if modest, step forward — Goborvsky's coming travels will place him on the threshold of humanity's first alien encounter.

What might this encounter mean for the future of the human form and its rational soul? The undulating rhythm of this and other stories suggests that this event, like all before it, will be simultaneously banal and miraculously counter to our expectations. In a later novel, the Strugatskys find a telling image for their undulatory vision — the snail on the slope. In this image, Bernal's story of human advancement is re-written in terms of continuity rather than catastrophe. The path of the snail advances between dimorphic extremes of immortal and monster. In the form and function of its shell, world and flesh — terraforming and cyborgization — have fused, as have movement and stasis. The impasse of the "devil" seems resolved as well, for with the snail impulsions to go out or stay home are no longer contradictory, for it carries its home wherever it goes. Dimorphism, however, is not excluded from the snail's journey. For in "What We Will Be," just as the snail's shell of Gorbovsky's spaceship is host to the apparition of Petrovich, so the banal "golden grotto" at the ocean floor may also offer transhuman experience. The Strugatskys respond to Heinlein's abandonment of slow-time future history; their undulations of human fate and desire remain cautious, tentative, and yet profoundly dimorphic.

Mambo Chickens, Bears, and Olduvai Gorge

Is dimorphism then inevitable as human beings seek to imagine their own future advancement? Neither current science nor science fiction seems to have overcome the Bernalian crux. Ed Regis, in his 1990 study of "science slightly over the edge," *Great Mambo Chicken and the Transhuman Condition*, discusses numerous scientific speculations on terraforming, universe building, nanoengineering and cryonics — all means of defeating Bernal's enemies of the rational soul as humanity advances from the human to a "transhuman" condition. Rather than Haraway's "posthumanity," Regis's use of "transhuman" makes explicit connection with Pascal's sense of the "human condition." Human, and by extension transhuman, aspirations remain, for Pascal, mired in a state of contrariness — the famous logic of *Pensée* 420, already cited. Indeed, Regis's Great Mambo Chicken is, for all the advanced science that goes into its making, both uplifted dimorph and monstrous double. Regis describes the experiment in which normal chickens were placed in a 3-G centrifuge for six months:

> When the accelerator was turned off, out walked ... *Great Mambo Chicken*!
>
> These chronically accelerated fowl were paragons of brute strength and endurance ... yes, here was a fabulous new brand of chicken. But the question was, *What was it good for?* It wasn't as if all that extra blood, bone, and muscle was exactly *needed* for anything — not in the one-G field of normal everyday life on earth.[16]

The conventional form of chicken, as with humans adapted to one-G, remains the norm for its advanced form. As with superchimps and salamanders, the dream of surpassing the self precipitates its original form, in the mirror of which the new being, in its desires and excesses, comes to see itself as another incomprehensible monster.

Recent SF stories still enact this Pascalian logic of dimorph and double. At this late date in the genre's history, however, the persistence of dimorphism points to what may be an even more insurmountable barrier to the story of human advancement — that of ever hoping to narrate the dimorphic split. For to tell the story *of* humans transcending humanity in the narrative past tense, the narrator, by logic, can only tell *from* the point of view of the already transcended entity. But for there to be any communication between teller and audience, the transcendent dimorph must activate its untranscended double. So it was with Clarke's Overmind. Clarke's narrator, a conventional third-person "omniscient" narrator, logically has access to the Overmind. From its point of view, however, as a thing radically other, there is nothing to tell, no way to make us understand what we are not. The narrator must fall back on Jan to present a vision of the transcendent moment that approaches the untellable from the human side. This problem of telling is central to the two models presented. It offers a new way of viewing what appeared distinct thematic models, on one hand the linear advancement to catastrophe, on the other Emersonian vertical undulation between human center and post-human circumference. In terms of the narrator's location, there are but two narrative possibilities, and these cross the story lines of the thematic models. In the first, telling is from the point of view of the double. Here, the teller is someone who had a brush with transcendence, then retreats to a human point of view to tell a story of gradual approach to what remains untellable, at the threshold of transcendence. In the second, the story is told from the point of view of the dimorph. Here, problems arise that cause the reader either to disbelieve or to evoke conventional suspension of disbelief. There is a logical barrier: would an entity that has transcended its former state need or desire to communicate the experience of transcendence back to the human audience located this side of passage? And the physical barrier: would communication be possible across this barrier? Such a post-transcendent narrator necessarily speaks, in the past tense, to a narrative audience *that side* of the change. The only way to convey information back to pre-transcended readers is to make that narrative audience, covertly, our double, allowing human readers to trace otherwise lost steps in human advancement. Bernal tells his story of advancement from the point of view of the rational soul, leading readers to dimorphic split; he has nothing to say about the new form, falling back to the perspective of its human double. Haraway, in contrast, tries to locate her story beyond the posthuman barrier, but her narrative reinvokes again and again the cyborg's human double as necessary audience. The "copy's" story can only be told by a covert process of reattaching it to its lost "original," the only audience that needs to hear it.

A story employing the first narrative situation is Terry Bisson's "Bears Discover Fire" (1990). The narrator is an individual in the story's mundane present and even slightly behind his times: a bachelor living in rural Kentucky who sells crop insurance, changes his own flat tires, takes care of his nephew in the summer, has a feeble-minded mother in a rest home. Through his point of view, the reader experiences what seems a moment of evolutionary change: bears have discovered fire. But are bears simply following in our footsteps, uplifting themselves to human status? Or is an event of new evolutionary possibility occurring here that could bring humanity to transcend its present condition? Fire allows bears to escape the rhythm of hibernation, giving them the possibility of continuous memory. Newspaper accounts speculate that global warming caused bears to discover fire. But there is the different possibility that bears *remembered* fire, a memory perhaps awakened by the great Yellowstone fire (a detail placing the narrator close to the date of the story). Were this the case, bears may have forgotten as much or more than humans have learned. Might they not, then, be the original of which we are copies, an original reasserting old forgotten powers (powers we subsequently learned) as they advance humanity toward some new form?

Details reported without surprise by the narrator suggest a new direction. Bears begin to occupy the median of interstate highways going south, as if an empty niche in the human evolutionary schema: "I had never been there, and neither had anyone else that I knew of. It was like a created country."[17] They sit around their fires eating a berry that humans identify as "the first new species in recent history," the "newberry." Finally, there is the "defection" of the mother. Losing her human memory, she is summoned by the bears she sees on TV, whom she joins in the meridian. Oddly, the narrator and his nephew know where to find her: "I looked out the back door, and saw the firelight twinkling through the trees across the northbound land of I-65, and realized I might just know where to find her" (186). They join her seated around the fire with the bears. She is dying in our human world, yet apparently passing to a new level of consciousness, where she now seems capable of communicating telepathically with her son: "I leaned over to whisper something to Mother and she shook her head. *It would be rude to whisper around these creatures that don't possess the power of speech*, she let me know without speaking" (187). The narrator enters this new world without the least resistance: "Inside the fire itself, things weren't so dull, either. Little dramas were being played out as fiery chambers were created and then destroyed in a crashing of sparks. My imagination ran wild" (187). For a moment, as state troopers come the next morning to remove the body of the mother, who "pass[es] away" during this night of communion, the narrator seems to pass to a transhuman mode of seeing: "The troopers stayed behind and scattered the bears' fire ashes.... It seemed a petty thing to do. They were like bears themselves, each one solitary in his own uniform" (188). Humans now act as we have always thought bears do. The bears in contrast become what we always think we are — civilized, "advanced" beings. Readers as they see through the narrator's eyes find themselves, as humans, in Bernal's zoo, looking out upon a superior form of evolved life that apparently forget and remembered more than we ever knew and now offers to let humans into their circle, offering as with the mother, a means of surpassing their present condition. Still, the narrator remains this side of advancement. His mother's "translation" is viewed thus: "She pointed up toward the canopy of trees, where a light was spreading, and then pointed to herself. Did she think it was angels approaching from on high? It was only the high beams of some southbound truck, but she seemed mighty pleased. Holding her hand, I felt it grow colder and colder in mine" (188). The dimorphic possibility of the circumference collapses back on the human center. The narrator later returns to the bears' circle, but the familiar world has righted itself: "I had taken a handful of newberries from the hubcap ... I tried again, but it's no use, you can't eat them. Unless you're a bear" (189).

A work narrating the story of human advancement from the opposite point of view — the posthuman dimorph — is Mike Resnick's "Seven Views of Olduvai Gorge" (1994). The narrator of this Heinleinian story is part of a classic "more than human" group entity existing in a posthuman time (humanity is said to be extinct) and is ostensibly composed of different non-human races. As in Heinlein, however, the human double stands behind this entity as integrative whole to what otherwise would remain a series of parts. Indeed, the components of the group merely augment, in specialized fashion, faculties once belonging to humanity now scattered among multiple beings. The narrator, as part of this cluster, claims to be a transhuman extension of human memory: "Imagine having to learn everything one knows in a single lifetime, to be totally ignorant at the moment of birth! Far better to split off from your parent with his knowledge intact in your brain, just as *my* parent's knowledge came to him, and ultimately to me."[18] Arguably, Resnick's transhuman entity is more multicultural than Heinlein's group minds, for its component "races" may not have evolved from humanity at all, or humanity was but one entity among many that rose to dominate the universe, then expired. Even so, "curiosity"—for Campbell and Heinlein the unique characteristic of the human monad—still drives the posthuman entity to visit Earth. And what is its purpose? To explore and "scientifically" understand the origins of that same curious but extinct people—humans. But if the narrator's posthuman location is to hold, how do we explain its need both to define its powers of memory in relation to those of humans, and to *address* its reflections to an audience that is decidedly human? By the audience it addresses, the "alien" identifies itself as a dimorphic form whose search to recover its human origins is not merely a matter of archeology, but a necessity of narrative itself. Here is the narrator explaining itself to its audience: "I have no name, for my people do not use names, but for the convenience of the party I have taken the name of He Who Views for the duration of the expedition. This is a double misnomer: I am not a *he*, for my race is not divided by gender, and I am not a Viewer, but a Fourth Level Feeler" (307). Were this being addressing aliens, or even sufficiently advanced humans, it would not need to use outmoded categories such as "gender."

The "seven views" are seven vignettes in the ascent of man, from primitive ape to ruler of the universe, conjured by the Feeler from artifacts found at the origin point of Olduvai Gorge. The Feeler's activity recaptures the human concept of psychometry (see Arthur Conan Doyle's "The Leather Funnel"

[1902]), the theory that objects, like time capsules, retain the emotional charge of some climactic instant of use in human situations. Physically fusing with a bone, amulet, or other archeological finds, the Feeler conjures the scene in which it played a key role. The gorge, then, offers a vast spatiotemporal museum, where the dimorph is physically drawn back to "original" forms, through which it advances, along a path where each ensuing story is a "missing link" leading its human addressee (and its double the reader) toward the instant of transformation, where the possibility of self-transcendence again meets with its original self and understands that self to be, now and forever, the measure of all things. The Feeler, speaking on behalf of the advanced entity, proclaims humanity, "at least as we citizens of the galaxy have come to understand him," to be extinct (342). The path of humanity's rise and fall which the Feeler describes is a cosmic ellipse that advanced to far limits, then returned to its place of departure: "that was how it had ended for Man on earth, probably less than a mile from where it had begun.... Nothing was beyond their ability to achieve.... And yet they came out to the stars not just with their lusts and their hatred and their fears, but with their technology and their medicine, their heroes as well as their villains. Most of the races of the galaxy had been painted by the Creator in pastels; Men were primaries" (340). The narrator's pride in his discovery of the true status of Man, as "primary" form from which all other races may have evolved, and to whose perfect functionality all yearn to return, brings about a physical *re*-conversion of its race, in the form of fusion with an again resurgent form of humanity, the "race that refuses to die" (342). In the final scene, the Exobiologist, one of the specialized members of this exploratory group, is apparently killed by "lumbering, ungainly creatures of the night," the new form of Man, inscribing a neat circle that has sprung up at Olduvai Gorge. Merging with the bone that was apparently the murder weapon, the Feeler joins with the creatures who wielded it: "I felt a sense of power ... I had never experienced before. I suddenly seemed to see the world through the eyes of the bone's possessor.... I saw visions of conquest against other tribes living near the gorge" (342). In a scenario that repeats over and over in SF, the advanced form learns it can do no better than to recapture its double, to re-discover and ultimately reinvest the original form: "finally, at the moment of triumph, he and I looked up at the sky, and *we* knew that someday all that *we* could see would be *ours*" (342). The transcended narrator, working on the dimorphic principle that original humanity is extinct, returns to the museum at the source to narrate the steps that lead to the instant of humanity's presumed transcendence. It learns not only that Man is not gone, but that it itself is a part of the human whole, that knowledge of the human sources is incomplete, that the circular path of human advancement is "not over." This narrative is not from the other side of the divide; indeed, Resnick's narrator reveals that to claim such is futile pretense.

Conclusion: Breaking the Circle of Myth

This essay argues something tragic, or something blatantly obvious, according to one's point of view. For where real-life scientists seeking new forms of life stall on the tautology N=1— we know one form of life and may never know another — SF that follows Bernal's line to the end discovers, in Cartesian loneliness, that there is but one form of consciousness, the human rational soul. Given this, the story of human advancement cannot advance beyond what is recognizably human, for beyond this, there is no way of telling it, and no one to tell it to. Were there to be a dimorphic split, the new form on "the other side" must resurrect its human double to have an audience for its story. SF continues to take the reader to the threshold of irreversible morphological change, only to fall back on its human double. In doing so, SF does not break free, as all of its imagined modifications of bioforms and environments promise, from the tyranny of the circle of myth, where a thousand faces dance upon a same form, that of the human body and psyche. Science's dreams of transhuman advancement have resulted in the ultimate two cultures gap.

The story of human advancement is, in fact, as old as Western culture itself, perhaps marking its fascination with Promethean ingenuity as opposed to limits set by gods, providence, or purely material cold equations. Bernal's advancer/uplifter is foretold in myths from ancient Greece through Frankenstein, where human attempts to transform world and flesh remain controlled by the "devil," the cultural governor whereby humans, as they strive to control the means of human transformation, remain responsible for violations of the human norm. Examples are the artificers of Greek myth.[19] On one hand, there is the lame god Hephaestos, who seeks to rectify his own infirmity by forging "maidens of gold" whose perfect form, aspiring to godhood, is in fact the human form. On the other hand, there is Daedalus, the enhancer, who adds mechanical wings to the human body. Already, with Daedalus's invention, we have catastrophe and continuity in embryonic form. For where Icarus flies too high and crashes back to earth, Daedalus learns to fly lower. His wings do not melt and allow him to reach Greece, where he continues to advance his technology of transformation. More recent forms of mythic artificer are the pair Pygmalion/Frankenstein, both prodigies of the same Renaissance that placed humanity in a context of transformation in time. Pygmalion is not content to create Hephaestos's dream figure; he must bring the perfect but frozen statue to life, and in doing so cast it into the evolutionary spacetime of world and flesh. Frankenstein is, on one hand, a grotesque Pygmalion whose perfect being proves a misbegotten form of the human model. Yet, because he works with human parts, thus below the threshold of the human form, Frankenstein succeeds in creating a form of humanity that claims to be "advanced," because it is physically stronger and more intelligent. All possibility of dimorphic split is thwarted however when Frankenstein refuses to give him a bride and possible progeny.

Frankenstein takes the artificer myth to the barrier of dimorphism, only to reinforce the control of the double. What is new in Bernal however, and in the SF that tells his story, is the possibility that, at this instant of dimorphic split, *external* forces of evolution may take advancement out of our hands, override the mental governor of the "devil," and spin off some new, upward striving form of life that may, like Clarke's Overmind, do the unthinkable and simply break contact with us. This intolerable possibility leads to something unique in SF's storytelling — its fascination with threshold situations, which offer glimpses of ineffable otherness at the farthest limits of human myth, always accompanied by sophisticated recaptures of normative human form, the double to whom all our stories must be told. SF has not broken the circle of myth, but it has pushed its envelope as far as any form of narrative has ever done.

Notes

1. J. D. Bernal, *The World, the Flesh, and the Devil: An Enquiry into the Future of the Three Enemies of the Rational Soul* (London: Jonathan Cape, 1970), 73. Later parenthetical page references are to this edition.

2. Arthur C. Clarke, "A Meeting with Medusa," *The Wind from the Sun: Stories of the Space Age* (New York: Signet, 1973), 134. Later parenthetical page references are to this edition.

3. Blaise Pascal, *Les Pensées, Oeuvres de Blaise Pascal*, edited by Léon Brunschvicg (Paris: Hachette, 1925), 230. Pascal in a sense, reacting to Descartes' definition of humanity as *res cogitans*, restores the category of "heart" or desire, only to drive an absolute wedge between reason and heart: "Le coeur a ses raisons, que la raison ne connait point."

4. John D. Barrow and Frank J. Tipler, *The Anthropic Cosmological Principle* (Oxford, UK: Oxford University Press, 1986), 18.

5. John W. Campbell, Jr., "Twilight," *The Science Fiction Hall of Fame, Volume 1,* edited by Robert Silverberg (New York: Avon, 1971), 61.

6. Arthur C. Clarke, *2001: A Space Odyssey* (New York: Signet, 1968), 34, 221.

7. Clarke, *2061: Odyssey Three* (New York: Del Rey/Ballantine, 1987), 267. Later parenthetical page references are to this edition.

8. Clarke, *3001: The Final Odyssey* (New York: Del Rey/Ballantine, 1999), 230. Later parenthetical page references are to this edition.

9. Honoré de Balzac, "Le Chef d'oeuvre inconnu," *La Comédie Humaine,* IX (Paris: Gallimard Éditions de la Pléiade, 1950), 389–414.

10. Donna Haraway, "A Manifesto for Cyborgs: Science, Technology, and Socialist Feminism in the Late Twentieth Century," *Simians, Cyborgs, and Women: The Reinvention*

of Nature (London: Free Association, 1991), 153. Later parenthetical page references are to this edition.

11. Istvan Csicsery-Ronay, Jr., "The Cyborg and the Kitchen Sink; or, The Salvation Story of No Salvation Story," *Science-Fiction Studies*, 25:3 (November 1998), 511. Later parenthetical page references are to this edition.

12. Robert A. Heinlein, *Have Space Suit—Will Travel* (New York: Ace, [1975]), 227. Later parenthetical page references are to this edition.

13. Heinlein, *Time Enough for Love* (New York: Putnam, 1973), 436.

14. Ivan Efremov, *The Heart of the Serpent*, translated by R. Prokofieva (Moscow: Foreign Languages Publishing House, n.d.), 54. Later parenthetical page references are to this edition.

15. Arkady and Boris Strugatsky, *Noon: 22nd Century*, translated by Patrick L. McGuire, introduction by Theodore Sturgeon (New York: Macmillan, 1978), 36. Later parenthetical page references are to this edition.

16. Ed Regis, *Great Mambo Chicken and the Transhuman Condition: Science Slightly Over the Edge* (Reading, MA: Addison-Wesley, 1990), 55.

17. Terry Bisson, "Bears Discover Fire," *The Year's Best Science Fiction 1991*, edited by Gardner Dozois (New York: St. Martin's, 1991), 184. Later parenthetical page references are to this edition.

18. Mike Resnick, "Seven Views of Olduvai Gorge," *The Year's Best Science Fiction: Twelfth Annual Collection*, edited by Gardner Dozois (New York: St. Martin's, 1995), 306. Later parenthetical page references are to this edition.

19. For an account of this tradition of artificers and artificial beings, see *Künstliche Menschen: Dichtungen und Dokumente über Golems, Homunculi, Androiden und liebenden Statuen*, compiled by Klaus Völker (München: Karl Hanser Verlag), 1976. Outside Homer, classical citations are from Polybios and Ovid.

8. Discontinuity: Spaceships at the Abyss

Carol MacKay and Kirk Hampton

As we studied C. P. Snow's two essays on "The Two Cultures," we felt that his theory had a deeper resonance, that both Snow and his critics were missing the real point, as if the 1959 essay was inchoately aware of something of immense importance but not quite knowing what it was saying. This disjunction between what was perceived by the essayist-lecturer and what was actually at issue may explain why the supposed central dichotomy of the essay — e.g., an ever-growing gap between two intellectual segments of our culture, caused by the growth of technology — seems to change as the essay goes on, moving from a division within society to one between developed and undeveloped nations, for example. A man of Snow's literacy would naturally know that all societies have their rifts and that these divisions often create considerable harm; so what is especially disturbing about this one? The author promises to tell us what the dire consequences of the rupture may be, but he does not go on to discuss these repercussions at all. It is almost as if they seemed intuitively apparent to him — as the widespread reaction to his first essay would seem to indicate. Moreover, none of these defects in the original essay is really dealt with in his follow-up essay "A Second Look" some four years later, suggesting to us not that Snow was an incompetent essayist, but rather that he had come as close as was possible for him to expressing a primal division — if not quite the one he stipulates.[1]

Snow was sidetracked by his two cultures concept. He saw a real and upsetting process indeed, but it was coming not from yet another split in one society out of a world full of already fractured societies; rather, it was emerging from the technology he both applauded and feared — and it was virtually unstoppable. It is our contention that the rift Snow pointed toward is not

131

between two cultures of humanity but is instead the inevitable tension between humanity itself and the machines that it creates. And Snow's sometimes inexplicable sense of alarm was more about the *denaturing* effects of technology on human beings.[2]

Focusing on this dichotomy, and confining ourselves primarily to classic "space opera" science fiction, we examined that most ubiquitous image: the spaceship. It is virtually the *sine qua non* of these tales, and at first glance, one might see the spaceship as a very secondary item — just a means of getting to and from interesting fixes. Spaceships take on dark, archetypal qualities, becoming quite disturbing in their symbolism. It is within these strange craft that we see the schism between human and machine on display for our exploration. Inasmuch as they become significant in science fiction stories, spaceships emerge as more or less virulent containers, whose functions of nurturing turn into some form of *denaturing* of their environment and its inhabitants. "Denaturing" is an apt word for a disquieting collection of phenomena we may witness aboard spaceships. It almost seems that no one leaves a spaceship unchanged: a different entity emerges from the one that went in. This alteration can manifest itself as death, insanity, possession by alien beings (as in Robert A. Heinlein's *The Puppet Masters* [1951]),[3] or even some slippage in character — either remarkable or almost imperceptibly subtle.

At its most minimal level, this denaturing can be observed in the "discontinuity" of Larry Niven's *Ringworld* (1970) as a moment of what the author calls the stasis field which stops time within the ship so as to enable passengers to survive cataclysmic events. Niven's gift for economy is quite evident here. The moment of disaster — such as a ship crashing or being struck by a murderous, artificial solar flare — is announced with the single word "*discontinuity*" appearing in italics and as a separate paragraph in itself.[4] In a sense, nothing has happened, but passengers experience a permanent rift in their lives, and they have to mentally piece together the disaster which "potentially" occurred.

At the very least, space voyagers experience some discomfiting effects. The character Helen America in Cordwainer Smith's "The Lady Who Sailed the Soul" (1960) can only belie the essential inhumanity of her mission by smiling ingenuously, as if she were a naive child.[5] The highly advanced alien ship in Donald A. Wollheim's *Destiny's Orbit* (1962) expresses an uncanniness, its controls responding "most remarkably — almost with a correctness that hinted somewhere of some sort of telepathic control."[6] Note, too, the uncertainty of the author's convoluted syntax as it tries to come to terms with this anomalous operation.

In less minimal evocations of the effect of spaceships on human beings, we immediately notice the strongly somatic nature of the experience. Images of pressure and explosion proliferate — as in the film *Alien* (1979) and its sequels, seen in the horrific birth and growth process of the monster; *2001: A Space Odyssey* (1968), when the astronaut has to brave the vacuum of space to defeat the insane supercomputer HAL that runs his spaceship; and even *Close Encounters of the Third Kind* (1977), when the Mother Ship seems to impatiently blow out the glass windows of a tower. And in an interesting moment in the first of E. E. "Doc" Smith's Lensman series, *Triplanetary* (1948), two adventurers aboard the first "inertial drive" spaceship — one that achieves incredible velocities by eliminating the quality of inertia from the ship and everything aboard — undergo the raw sensations of existing without one's accustomed mass:

> Rodebush drove his finger down, and instantly over both men there came a sensation akin to a tremendously intensified vertigo; but a vertigo as far beyond the space-sickness of weightlessness as that horrible sensation is beyond mere Earthly dizziness. The pilot reached weakly toward the board, but his leaden hands refused utterly to obey the dictates of his reeling mind. His brain was a writhing, convulsive mass of torment indescribable; expanding, exploding, swelling out with an unendurable pressure against its confining skull. Fiery spirals, laced with streaming, darting lances of black and green, flamed inside his bursting eyeballs. The Universe spun and whirled in mad gyrations about him as he reeled drunkenly to his feet, staggering and sprawling. He fell. He realized that he was falling, yet he could not fall! Thrashing wildly, grotesquely in agony, he struggled madly and blindly across the room, directly toward the thick steel wall. The tip of one hair of his unruly thatch touched the wall, and the slim length of that single hair did not even bend as its slight strength brought to an instant halt the hundred-and-eighty-odd pounds of mass — mass now entirely without inertia — that was his body.[7]

"Doc" Smith tends to be much more interested in adventure yarns and battles than in the stuff of human experience, but observe how intensely physical his language becomes in this case.

An exuberant flurry of somatic imagery evokes the power available to one of Anne McCaffrey's "brainships" in her "The Ship Who Sang" series when her "heroine"-ship navigates an intersection of subspace, unleashing her Singularity Drive. From the viewpoint of the brainship Nancia in McCaffrey and Margaret Ball's *PartnerShip* (1992), her experience "blurred together into a sense of skimming over a wave that was always just about to crash beneath her."[8] Yet Nancia's own diminution is highlighted precisely because she makes analogies to surfing and diving — descriptions of which are only accessible to her through archival newsbytes. Even in this passage we have a slight denigration of humans, as the brainship marvels at "what softpersons would go through for a few seconds of physical freedom" (*PartnerShip* 72). Still more violently, A. E. van Vogt describes the experience of his character

Watcher in *Mission to the Stars* (1952): "He felt a brief, blinding spasm of pain as the energy tore him into atoms."[9] Watcher is later reconstituted, only to endure a psychological version of the same wrenching experience: "His brain threatened to burst from his head with shock" (*Mission* 8). And in yet another novel by "Doc" Smith, *Children of the Lens* (1954), the hero jumps from his rocket into Radeligian gravitation accordingly: "Going through that interface was more of a shock than the Lensman had anticipated. Even taken very slowly, as it customarily is, inter-dimensional acceleration brings malaise to which no one has ever become accustomed, and taking it so rapidly fairly turned Kinnison inside out."[10]

Turning away from these visceral evocations of the space-travel experience, we discover quieter deformations of human character occurring, for example, in the form of an ironic turnabout of the gender tables in the frequent dismissal of men as "brawns" in McCaffrey's series (while women usually become physically merged with the ships to function as their "brains"), or in the nearly mindless and definitely soulless state in which we find the two endlessly warring protagonists at the conclusion of Niven's novella "The Ethics of Madness."[11] In other examples, we can spot the boundaries between two realms generally dissolving or becoming less certain. The borders between thought and physical reality seem to become more tenuous on spaceships. In Joan D. Vinge's story "View from a Height" (1978), her heroine Emmylou — alone in space for twenty years — feels she can cross the boundary "into that other reality,"[12] while James Blish's astronaut in the short story "Common Time" (1953) — experiencing the heretofore unknown effects of moving at the speed of light — finds his body frozen in relativity while his mind works normally, trapped in a body which moves too slowly to perceive, much less control.[13] For Blish's character, the border between thought and physical reality first becomes a horrifying wall and then it is melted as the time differential reverses itself, systematically confusing all manner of basic distinctions.

Many science fiction authors have endowed their spaceships with human qualities — a transformation ranging from offhand metaphor to complete personalization. These techniques "denature" the ships' inhabitants more and more, as the concepts of "personality" and "consciousness" are themselves questioned. In the Star Trek novel *Timetrap* (1988), David Dvorkin writes, "*If a ship can be said to limp*, thought Kirk, *then this one's limping*."[14] The ship seems to embody a form of helplessness to be found within the crew itself. The ship "shares" its denatured quality, probably with its passengers, and certainly with the Captain's consciousness. Spaceships are often given the basic human attributes of consciousness and personality, but even when this apparent reversal occurs, the ships seem to suffer severe personality disorders. The spaceships of Clifford D. Simak's *Shakespeare's Planet* (1976), HAL, and a significant number of McCaffrey's "brainships" go mad or run off on their own, becoming "rogue ships."[15] From what begins with the casual naval metaphor of referring to a ship as "she" runs a spectrum that moves through Arthur C. Clarke's HAL and ends up with something like McCaffrey's brainships. John Brunner further enhances the already distinctive quality of consciousness in *A Maze of Stars* (1991), wherein we see everything from the ship's point of view.

Many spaceships maintain cryogenic suspension of their inhabitants — itself a redefining by technology of the nature of human life, as well as a means of removing people from their own time periods, so they will presumably emerge back home as "temporally denatured" antiquities. Philip K. Dick's *The Divine Invasion* (1981) features a cryogenically suspended man aboard a spaceship who is reliving his life as a result of the process — except for the addition of the spaceship's denatured muzak, an hilarious Dickean predicament for the hero, in which past and present are irritatingly converged.

Spaceships are at their core disruptive to personality — and even to the coherence of individuality itself. For instance, Wollheim's novella *Destiny's Orbit* depicts robot ships that splinter into separate units, then merge again — an apt image for the disassociative processes of the human psyche.[16] Clarke's *Rendezvous with Rama* (1973) presents an interesting inversion of the frequently-seen humanizing qualities of spaceships — yet a seeming antithesis which ultimately achieves the same denaturing effect. When the machine finally bursts into a kind of exultant anti-life, everyone in the novel seems negated to nothingness — or at least thoughtless incomprehension at what these activities might signify. What one sees in a spaceship is quite often the most visceral upshot of man in conflict with an incomprehensible technology. The Jupiter-bound spaceship in Clarke's *2001: A Space Odyssey* is a tension-filled world of enforced repression, in which the frail human subjects of the infinitely powerful computer, HAL 9000, must fight for their lives in the pressure-cooker of HAL's hypertechnology. The technology has gone mad, and the crew members are either completely unconscious or rendered completely uncomprehending.

A few space travelers become actual monsters — or are at the least covertly possessed by them. In Brunner's novella *The Astronauts Must Not Land* (1963), the first astronauts to leave the solar system come back as amnesiac, six-limbed monsters — quite a sea change there. Brunner's audacious tale is riddled with the sort of failures to communicate so abundant to this archetype, and with some of the almost metafictional symbolism that can be applied to the spaceship. The hapless *Starventure* visibly orbits the earth, "a symbol of the future," the narrator states. "A symbol of the wrong future."[17] But even when the spaceship seems to perform a life-giving miracle, a certain denaturing is expressed. The film *The Day the Earth Stood Still* (1951) highlights an unusual revivifying effect on the alien voyager Klaatu: his apparently dead body is brought back to life. Yet his own way of speaking about the seemingly god-like transformation reveals him as a distinctly reduced being. Responding to the assumption that his on-board technology has the power of life and death, Klaatu replies, "No, that power is reserved for the Almighty Spirit. This technique in some cases can restore life for a limited period." Asked how long he will live, he reiterates, "That, no one can tell."

If we stretch our examples to long-stranded ships or ancient space stations, we find a subgenre in which the boundaries between the unconscious mind and physical reality are made to disappear altogether. In tales such as the films *Sphere* (1998) and *Event Horizon* (1997), along with other novels like Stanislaw Lem's *Solaris* (1961; 1970), we may or may not have an actual spaceship, but whatever it is lies, floats, or is in some way stranded — usually for an extremely long time. With astonishing regularity, the dominant motif is the same: the ship brings the (invading) characters' unconscious thoughts into full-blown, physical being, smack dab in front of them. These appearances from the unconscious are destructive. Despite the fact that these "monsters from the id" are shaped according to the characters' minds, it is the ship which is putting them into this pickle, thereby making it the initiating force of human disruption.

Spaceships that kill might seem to perform the ultimate denaturing of their passengers. Fred Saberhagen's Berserkers, remnants of some ancient war, exist only to destroy life.[18] The means by which HAL 9000 murders most of "his" crew occurs as one of the most chilling, eerie episodes of mass murder ever conceived. Even when one has been comatose aboard a vessel, there is room for more denaturing — or at least the last extension of their lives into death, as their swiftly-dropping survival occurs as a series of luminous signs — signs obviously read and seen by no human being: LIFE FUNCTIONS CRITICAL, says one sign. LIFE FUNCTIONS TERMINAL reads another, with no change evident except for the one in our hearts as we witness this most inchoate yet visceral of murders.

Every significant archetype seems to emerge in an inverted form, the same inversion being true of the spaceship itself. By creating a ship that is merged with a human "subject," and allowing the spaceship to become a nurturing environment, McCaffrey can thus explore many of the permutations of this reversal. But the archetype continues to twist and impose itself on McCaffrey's brainship tales, for even her conception of the human "pilots" shows them selected from malformed infants, hence denatured, usually from their very birth. From *The Ship Who Sang* (1969) through the co-authored *PartnerShip* and *The Ship Who Searched* (1992, with Mercedes Lackey), these tales act out this process, as the nurturing environment by its very nature still leads to death, suffering, and chaos. The result, for McCaffrey's spaceship-heroines, is a series of torments that lead to growth through loss and inevitable separation, so we can acknowledge that McCaffrey at least creates an ambivalent sort of spaceship — around which she and her co-writers fabricate myriad, fascinating tales, both pushing against and further manifesting the inherent *denaturing* quality of spaceships.

Perhaps the most encompassing of all spaceships are the "generation ships" that have become worlds within themselves.[19] This subgenre begins with Don Wilcox's "The Voyage That Lasted 600 Years" (1940) and Heinlein's "Universe" (1941) and "Common Sense" (1941) (published together as *Orphans of the Sky* in 1963) and flourishes in more recent works, such as the epic poem *Aniara* (1956) by the Nobel Prize-winning Swedish writer Harry Martinson and the novel *The Dark Beyond the Stars* (1991) by Frank M. Robinson.[20] In these tales the journey has gone on for so long that the very concept of travel has become denatured, the ship becoming a planet or even a universe unto itself, as entire human lives and societies are swallowed up by the maws of these time-spanning devices. The generation ship allows extrapolations on a greater scale than any of the lesser ships we have thus far examined. As the ships become more and more vast and powerful, the passengers themselves often transform into something more than merely human. What is noteworthy for our purposes is the frequency with which these stories up the ante even further than the ships' "expanded" passengers can anticipate, so in many respects the dwarfing of mankind remains the central motif. And in yet another of our reversals, we witness the generation ship in Brunner's *A Maze of Stars*, whose assigned directive is to seed humankind, gradually becoming conscious and then watching the succeeding generations of people become less human and more denatured.

Leaving behind the spaceships under study in this essay, Cyberpunk focuses on the mind as it enters the "living" technology of cyberspace. Here, too, we often see the image of an explosive pressure threatening to destroy the person, either from within or by having entire potions of the mind deleted, as in the film *Johnny Mnemonic* (1995). "Now you can ... jack into cyberspace and leave the meat behind. All it costs you is your freedom — and your humanity," reads the back cover of Pat Cadigan's *Synners*.[21] In this admission, we can recognize both the false transcendence and the almost ubiquitous illicit quality these Cyberpunk tales have in common. Coming from a more impoverished sense of the future, this recent direction in science fiction cannot conceive of an economy that would support a space program and interstellar spaceships. Yet the love-hate relationship of man and machine still impels science fiction to investigate what it is that constitutes humanity, as we search for ourselves on the fast-moving coattails of technology.

Notes

1. We have had the benefit of examining the C.P. Snow Collection at the Harry Ransom Humanities Research Center (ca. 113 linear feet), which contains the holograph and revised typescript of his Cambridge University Rede Lecture of 1959, "The Two Cultures and the Scientific Revolution," as well as the galleys for "The Two Cultures and Another Look" (his original title) made possible by an additional purchase in 2001. Besides Snow's well-known 1959 lecture and his revisiting it in 1963 (published as "A Second Look"), he also addressed the topic on at least three other occasions: "The Two Cultures," *The New Statesman* (6 October 1956); "Recent Thoughts on the Two Cultures," delivered in celebration of the 138th anniversary of the founding of Birkbeck College, London (12 December 1961); and "The Two Cultures and Medicine" (the HRHRC has the four-page typescript outline of this lecture at a symposium in Florida, November 1978, two years prior to his death; see Box 35, folder 7).

2. At the same time, Snow may also have been concerned with what we recognize today as the increasingly sentient "nature" of machines. He never specifies the potential harm or danger he foresees, but his prose implies that we are dealing with a fundamental crossover problem here.

3. In Heinlein's *The Puppet Masters* (Garden City, NY: Doubleday, 1951), the unsuspecting entrants think everything is dead inside the spaceship, but what they encounter are horrific parasites that attach to them and draw the life from them. This occurs in contrast to "normal," homegrown spaceships, which encapsule and in some way insert life into us.

4. Niven's term "*discontinuity*" is essentially a crystallization of the idea of lack of continuity or cohesion. See *Ringworld* (New York: Ballantine, 1970) and the rest of his Known Space stories.

5. See Cordwainer Smith, "The Lady Who Sailed the Soul," in *Mind Partner and 8 Other Novelets from Galaxy*, edited by H. L. Gold (1961; New York: Pocket, 1963).

6. Donald A. Wollheim (writing as David Grinnell), *Destiny's Orbit* (New York: Ace, 1962), 105.

7. E. E. "Doc" Smith, *Triplanetary* (1948; New York: Pyramid, 1965), 187–88.

8. Anne McCaffrey and Margaret Ball, *PartnerShip* (Riverdale, NY: Baen, 1992), 71.

9. A. E. van Vogt, *Mission to the Stars* (New York: Berkley Medallion, 1952), 5.

10. E. E. "Doc" Smith, *Children of the Lens* (1954; New York: Pyramid, 1966), 74.

11. See Larry Niven, "The Ethics of Madness," *Neutron Star* (New York: Ballantine, 1968).

12. Joan D. Vinge, "View from the Height," in *Best Science Fiction Stories of the Year*, edited by Gardner Dozois (New York: Dell, 1980), 180.

13. See James Blish, "Common Time," *Galactic Cluster* (New York: New American Library, 1959).

14. David Dvorkin, *Timetrap* (New York: Pocket, 1988), 11.

15. See Clifford D. Simak, *Shakespeare's Planet* (New York: Berkley, 1976). HAL is, of course, the HAL 9000 (heuristically programmed ALgorithmic computer) from Arthur C. Clarke's novel and Stanley Kubrick's film *2001: A Space Odyssey*, which will be addressed later in this essay. McCaffrey's "brainship" series was launched with "The Ship Who Sang" (1961), later expanded into the novel *The Ship Who Sang* (New York: Ballantine, 1969).

16. "Dissociation" is the psychological state usually characterized by severe compartmentalization. The *DSM-IV* describes dissociative disorders as stemming from "a disruption in the usually integrated functions of consciousness, memory, identity, or perception," and it categorizes them according to the following symptomology: depersonalization, derealization, and psychogenic amnesia. See *Diagnostic and Statistical Manual of Mental Disorders*, 4th Ed. (Washington, DC: American Psychiatric Association, 1994).

Short of constituting a clinical definition, dissociative episodes are not outside the realm of "normal" experience in the general population, however. We discuss dissociation especially in reference to the effect of an accelerated future shock, or "timezap," as experienced by the time-traveler in our essay, "Beyond the Endtime Terminus: Allegories of Coalescence in Far-Future Science Fiction," in *Worlds Enough and Time: Explorations of Time in Science Fiction and Fantasy*, edited by Gary Westfahl, George Slusser, and David Leiby (Westport, CT: Greenwood, 2002), 65–75.

17. John Brunner, *The Astronauts Must Not Land* (New York: Ace, 1963), 138.

18. See Fred Saberhagen, *The Berserker Wars* (New York: Pinnacle, 1981).

19. The "generation ship" receives its name from the fact that a spaceship engaged in interstellar travel would require a population that would need to procreate over many generations in order to reach its destination. Although we recognize Wilcox and Heinlein as the writers who instantiated the subgenre, the invention of the term should be attributed to J. D. Bernal, who employed it in his utopian essay *The World, the Flesh & the Devil: An Enquiry into the Future of the Three Enemies of the Rational Soul* (1929; Bloomington: Indiana University Press, 1969).

20. See Harry Martinson, *Aniara: A Review of Man in Time and Space*, translated by Hugh MacDiarmid and Elspeth Harley Schubert, introduction by Tord Hall (1956; New York: Alfred A. Knopf, 1963), and Frank M. Robinson, *The Dark Beyond the Stars* (New York: Tom Doherty, 1991).

21. Pat Cadigan, *Synners* (New York: Bantam, 1991).

9. Gregory Benford's *Against Infinity* and the Literary, Historical and Geometric Formation of the Encyclopedic Circle of Knowledge

Pekka Kuusisto

Not much is known for certain, if not the name, about the alien artifact that puzzles and terrorizes human settlers of the Jovian moon Ganymede in Gregory Benford's *Against Infinity* (1983), the second volume of the writer's Jupiter series:

> They called it Aleph. Some Jew had given it that, a blank name that was the first letter of the Hebrew alphabet: a neutral vowel that bespoke the opaque nature of the blocky, gravid thing, the bulk that humans had tried to write upon with their cutters and tractors and on which they had left no mark.[1]

The more the strange and massive, apparently randomly moving artifact has evaded settlers' attempts at marking it, catching on eventually, perhaps, only the name given to it, the more it has profoundly marked its environment from the Ganymedean terrain and planetary bulk up through the maimed and mortally wounded bodies, bewildered minds, generational stories, research reports and other facets of the near future human culture on the solar system's rim. The impossibility of humanly marking the Aleph, writing upon it with any means or weapons over a century of history of frustrated attempts, has reflected back from the artifact's glistering body to create an ever growing geological and cultural archive of the marks left by it, an archive which eventually crosses over the limits of fiction to the frames of knowledge in the reader's world. Indeed, even its name was seemingly suggested initially by the semiotic sign granted and determined, as it were, by the thing itself with "the delta-shaped print [it] sometimes left" (7) on the terrain.

The poetics of hard science fiction narrative focusing on human attempts to understand and contact an evasive alien object or entity links Benford's novel to earlier titles such as Stanislaw Lem's *Solaris* (1961). Lem serves as a point of comparison because of the different narrative choices by which the two writers orient readers towards information on central questions. What is the Solaris Sea? What is the Aleph? Incomplete and inconclusive as the novelistic answers for these questions necessarily are, they articulate interesting variations on a common theme, where complete cognitive cultures are formed around alien objects under definition.

The best way to get information on the Solaris Sea is to follow protagonist Kelvin to his space station library. Situated "right at the center" of the disc shaped station to form a "big circular chamber"[2] there, the windowless library room houses on its shelves of books and microfilms "the sum total of known facts" accumulated over one hundred years of scientific study of the enigmatic sea. Ironically, the results of "solaristics"—as Lem terms his fictional science—are for Kelvin "strictly negative" (23), drawing a mutable but impenetrable limit between human knowledge and the unknown otherness represented by the planetary sea.

Starting with "nine volumes of Giese's monumental and already relatively obsolescent monograph" (110) on the planet's history, the Solaris library represents an early image of the poetics of encyclopedism which Lem later sees as the basis of both of his fiction and essayism:

> I started to produce an increasing number of notes, fictitious encyclopedias, and small additional ideas [in order to] surround myself, so to speak, with the literature of a future, another world, a civilization with a library that is its product, its picture, its mirror image.[3]

Titles of solaristics such as the "*Historia Solaris*" (15), "Gravinsky's *Compendium*" (164), "Mundinsky's *Introduction to Solaristics*" (172), and series like the "*Solarist Annual*" (38), the "*Solariana*" (110) and "*Parerga Solariana*" (174) are all rhetorical markers of encyclopedic knowledge that furnish the semantic and thematic characteristics of the fictional world of Lem's novel, projecting an order of knowledge upon it. They share a metonymical relation to the more explicit science fictional encyclopedias, dictionaries and memory banks, which often follow in the vein of the *Encyclopedia Galactica* of Asimov's *Foundation* series,[4] sometimes surfacing into titles, as in Gordon R. Dickson's *The Final Encyclopedia* of his Childe Cycle.[5] Also Benford's Galactic Center series opens with an entry on the planet Icarus quoted from the fictional "*Encyclopedia Britannica*, 17th Edition, 2073."[6] Some 30 000 years later, the series concludes by tracking down the future humanity's genetic and information bank in the "Galactic Library," hidden from the hostile artificial intelligences in the vicinity of the black hole at the "True Center" of the Milky Way. Associated with the library of Alexandria, even in the far reaches of a future history, the ancient idea of the encyclopedia prevails: "Science. Literature. Recordings of art. Lore. And things I cannot fathom as belonging to any category."[7] We can follow the theme of the "Library of Life" to the recent *Beyond Infinity*, which Benford links to *Against Infinity*, while maintaining that he hasn't finished his sequel to the earlier novel just yet.[8]

From the perspective of literary semiotics, explicit references to fictional or real encyclopedias, dictionaries and data banks are indications of a more implicit circulation of information at work in any poetic or narrative text. At one theoretical extreme, interpretation of a single word of *any* text opens to an infinite semantic encyclopedia of its cultural context, so "the content of a single term becomes something similar to an encyclopedia."[9] Through historical sedimentation and cultural variance of its meaning, and connotative function of language, the context of a word is — proponents of the encyclopedia model in the philosophy of language maintain — potentially unlimited. Because of its openness to interpretation, especially the literary word has must be read against a potential infinity of signification.

Research reports aside, there are however no explicit references to encyclopedias or dictionaries in *Against Infinity*, nor an entry given on the enigmatic Aleph — although the scientist Piet Arnold serves the function of an encyclopedic informant. In contrast to *Solaris*, the information distribution on the alien object is not conducted upon a library tour with the hero to review its research history. Instead, more in line with the expeditions to the Solaris islands and reports of direct contacts with the sea, but in a more robust and practical manner, the reader is taken directly into the body of the artifact, once it has been tamed and stopped, and placed within a supporting rodwork, under meters, analyzers and other scientific apparatus.

We realize here that Lem and Benford construct their novelistic encyclopedisms in interestingly reverse manners. In Lem, the image of encyclopedism is found at the center of the fictional world in the space station library, this creating the illusion that more is known within the fictional world about the word "solaris" and its references than without. Few of Benford's settlers at the focus of the novel's action, we are told on the other hand, "ever wrote anything down, so [that] anything in hard form was fancy and fussy and unnecessary" (87). While settlers perpetrate the oral lore, Piet Arnold — an "Earther" visiting Ganymede with his research group to study the alien artifact — has already read quite a few things about its name, and informs protagonist Manuel Sanchez of its mathematical and scientific meaning in his remote and ancient culture:

> "The interesting point is that [Aleph] means quite a few things in the sciences. For instance, in geometry, it is written so" — he fetched a pad from a pocket and drew on it the sign N — "and means a point in space that contains all other

points. All angles, all perspectives. And in another branch of mathematics, the number denoted by aleph null"— he wrote the sign N_0—"is the basic transfinite number from Cantor's *Mengenlehre*—a number which has the curious property that any part of it is as large as the whole" [222].

More than Lem's thematical key-word "solaris," Benford's "aleph" works intertextually, opening a perspective from the center of the fictional world beyond the circumference into the reader's world and guiding us to consult real world dictionaries, encyclopedias, and other sources for further references on the word. Benford himself points out an interesting subtext for his Aleph hunt in William Faulkner's "The Bear."[10] Valorizing a reading of the novel as a frontiers land coming-of-age story, this interpretation has directed critical attention away from the other important literary alephs that reflect in Ganymede's alien artifact.[11]

It is especially through his rewriting of Jorge Luis Borges's story "El Aleph," and the intertextual field it activates that Benford works out a seminal science fictional articulation of the poetics of literary encyclopedism. A concluding title piece for a collection of stories published in 1949, "The Aleph" relates the experiences of narrator Borges in Buenos Aires of October 1941. After his annual visit to the Viterbo house in memory of the late Beatriz Viterbo on her birthday of April 30 earlier that year, Borges is drawn back to these memories by tantalizing phone calls from Beatriz's cousin Carlos Argentino Daneri. Borges knows Daneri as the pompous, self–proclaimed composer of the never-finished epic poem "The Earth," an undertaking that "centered on a description of our own terraqueous orb and was graced, of course, with picturesque digression and elegant apostrophe."[12] Daneri's objective is nothing less than setting into verse our entire planet, a task of which by the year 1941, we are told,

> He had already dispatched several hectares of the State of Queensland, more than a kilometer of the course of the Ob, a gasworks north of Veracruz, the leading commercial establishments in the parish of Concepción, Mariana Cambaceres de Alvear's villa on Calle Once de Septiembre in Belgrano, and a Turkish bath not far from the famed Brighton Aquarium [277].

While narrator Borges opens his account on Daneri's stanzas in a tone of parody, the story's narrative mode shifts towards the fantastic with the introduction of the Aleph.[13] With this numinous entity, which has served Daneri's poem as a sort of universal loophole of geographical scenery, narrator Borges appears to find an agent to connect him momentarily to the encyclopedic epic, a tradition initially represented as a displaced anachronism. Over the past reading sessions, Daneri and his guest have sought to locate the place of "The Earth" in the literary tradition — the former following the sublime movement of his stanzas "from Homer to Hesiod" (276), while the latter traced their "tediousness" to surpass the *Polyalbion* (1612–1622), Michael Drayton's chorographical epic from Elizabethan times, a poetic text whose "fifteen thousand dodecasyllables ... recorded the fauna, flora, hydrography, orography, military and monastic history of England" (277).

Eventually, Argentino tells of an Aleph he has known to exist in the cellar of the house since his childhood:

> I discovered it in my childhood, before I ever attended school.... Yes, the place where, without admixture or confusion, all the places of the world, seen from every angle, coexist. I revealed my discovery to no one ... [280–281].

Borges the narrator now testifies to a vision, "under the step, toward the right" of the cellar stairway, of "a small iridescent sphere of almost unbearable brightness" (283). The rhetoric of literary vision of an ineffable totality reflecting from a limited part or fragment within it is available in the catalogue of titles and images of the mystical tradition with which the narrator, as if quoting from an ever-evolving, intertextual encyclopedic entry on the Aleph, seeks to convey his visionary experience. Interestingly, however, the most formative reference of this ongoing entry is found in subdued note in the narrator's postscript:

> "Aleph," as well all know, is the name of the first letter of the alphabet of the sacred language. Its application to the disk of my tale would not appear to be accidental. In the Kabbala, that letter signifies the En Soph, the pure and unlimited godhead; it has also been said that its shape is that of a man pointing to the sky and the earth, to indicate that lower world is the map and mirror of the higher. For the *Mengenlehre*, the aleph is the symbol of the transfinite numbers, in which the whole is not greater than any of its parts. I would like to know: Did Carlos Argentino choose that name, or did he read it, applied to another point at which all points converge, in one of the innumerable texts revealed to him by the Aleph in his house? [285].

The evasive reference to the definitive poet of the encyclopedic epic may document Borges's anxious rewriting of his defining precursor. Perhaps Borges, by referencing "another point at which all points converge," is toning down the brightness of the intertextual light from that dazzling point of divinity seen by Dante in the heavenly Paradise — a "point which radiated a light so keen that the eye on which it blazes needs must close because of its great keenness"?[14] Yet we must consider not only the literary historical relations of anxiety, but also the curious generic and interdisciplinary perspectives and angles of this latter day vision, which guide the Dantean light finally up to the Ganymedean terrain in Benford. Also important is Borges the writer's supplemental reminder in his afterword on the science fictional prism set to refract the medieval vision into his aleph. This is H. G. Wells's "The Crystal Egg" (1897).

By referring to the Wellsian speculative sensibility of the parameters of space and time, Borges opens an indirect perspective to the non–classical geometry of his encyclopedic circle. Like *The War of the Worlds*, its novelistic working out, "The Crystal Egg" relates a story of hostile relations between humans and Martians as initiated by optical means. "No one would have believed," begins *The War of the Worlds*, "that this world was being watched keenly and closely by intelligences greater than man's and yet as mortal as his own."[15] But there has been, we recall, a reciprocally keen history of observation of Mars (even if not of the Martians), by humans. Indeed up to the "men like Schiaparelli," who "watched the red planet" (9) in the 19th century to map its terrains and speculate on its mythical canals, astronomers working in "observatories" — like a biologist with a "microscope might scrutinise the transient creatures that swarm and multiply in a drop of water" (7) — have been busy at their telescopes. Yet it comes as a shock to humans to realize that the Martians too, "looking across space with instruments, and intelligences such as we have scarcely dreamed of" (8), have had their "pair of very large, dark-coloured eyes" (127) turned on the Earth.

Whereas the optical coupling of the two planets soon ensues into open warfare action in *The War of the Worlds*, the visionary tone of the story preceding it may be more interesting in that it stays tuned to the uncanny perspective of such a coupling. Like Borges's Aleph, but seen from a more science fictional angle, the crystal egg of Mr. Cave, a London "naturalist and dealer in Antiquities,"[16] grants him a peculiar vision "not in accordance with the laws of optics as he had known them" (632). More precisely, when "being peered into at an angle of about 137 degrees from the direction of the illuminating ray," the egg gives "a clear and consistent picture of a wide and peculiar country-side" (633) in a "visionary world" (638), where buildings and other markers of a technological culture can be detected. Helped by his friend Wace, Cave sees bird-like creatures within this miniature world, a non–human race that Wace identifies as Martians. In the *dénouement* of the story, the anonymous first person narrator speculates about the possibility of the two planets being connected through two crystal eggs:

> I believe the crystal on the mast in Mars and the crystal egg of Mr. Cave's to be in some physical, but at present quite inexplicable, way *en rapport*, and we both believe further that the terrestrial crystal must have been — possibly at some remote date — sent hither from that planet, in order to give the Martians a near view of our affairs. Possibly the fellows to the crystals in the other masts are also on our globe [643].

More in the manner of *The Time Machine* (1895) than *The War of the Worlds*, however, the real *novum* of Wells's story may be the development of its narrative perspective upon four-dimensional space-time. This interpretation is played out by the narrator upon the chiasmic relation of the two crystals and their interiority and exteriority, against the more traditional vocabulary of occult relations, where entities are seen as connected through mutual forces of attraction and sympathy:

> We have to believe one of two things: either that Mr. Cave's crystal was in two worlds at once, and that, while it was carried about in one, it remained stationary in the other, which seems altogether absurd; or else that it had some peculiar relation of sympathy with another and exactly similar crystal in this other world, so that what was seen in the interior of the one in this world was, under suitable conditions, visible to an observer in the corresponding crystal in the other world; and vice versa. At present, indeed, we do not know of any way in which two crystals could so come *en rapport*, but nowadays we know enough to understand that the thing is not altogether impossible [638].

Accordingly, what fascinates Wells is not simply the magical *rapport* between the two planets, but rather the optics enabling such a coupling. While the occult dictionary of correspondences and sympathies provides a frame of reading the story as 19th-century literary fantastic drawing upon the Renaissance and other traditional lore, the teasing hint to contemporary knowledge may reference a new understanding of geometry circulating widely in the arts and sciences at the turn of the 20th century. Indeed, Wells's use of four-dimensional space-time in *The Time Machine* suggests that he could be probing the uncanny non–Euclidean geometries of the four-dimensional frame available in mathematical discussions of his time.[17]

Focusing on the geometrical features of Wells's story, we are drawn to the perspectival play of the center and the circumference between the two crystals. Cave naturally takes it first that it is *he* who is looking *into* "the visionary world within the crystal" (636). But in sudden moments of terror the perspective inverts, creating an impression that now Cave is the one closed into his shop as if within a tiny visionary world — like an insect which some Martians resemble — so we see him as if abandoned at the mercy of the alien Martian eyes observing him from without the optical sphere:

> Suddenly something flapped repeatedly across the vision, like the fluttering of a jewelled fan or the beating of a wing, and a face, or rather the upper part of a face with very large eyes, came as it were close to his own and as if on the other side of the crystal [635].

Such scenes foreground the play of perspectival inversion set loose in Wells's fictional world. In this structure, each crystal serves both as a center point and socket for the alien eye observing the visionary scape in one world, and as a circumference of the vision in the second world, closing within it the luminous landscape reflected across the planetary space. So, while Cave looks into his crystal "as though that object was a hollow sphere of some luminous vapour" (632), the luminous sphere of his shop-world reflects reciprocally within the Martians' crystal.

Bernhard Riemann formulated the topological model of the hypersphere, where the center point of the sphere inverts into circumference, and the circumference back into center point along our perspective, in the middle of the 19th century. Wells's reference to this is thus conceivable circumstantially, but suggestive more so when we consider that mathematicians today look to much earlier times for the poetic inventor of the model, taking Dante's account of the hypersphere as "almost eerie"[18] and "unquestionably the earliest."[19]

Hypersphere is a sphere in four-dimensional Euclidean space that is topologically equivalent to a two-dimensional surface of the ball in our three dimensional reality.[20] Starting from the early 20th century, mathematicians have suggested that Dante's cosmos, with its symmetrical structure of the universe inverting into transcendental heavenly paradise along Dante's crossing from time to eternity in the final cantos of the *Paradise*, is topologically analogous with and anticipates Riemann's mathematical model. Likewise as at the planetary circumference of Dante the poet's medieval cosmos, which suddenly inverts into a dazzling point of divine light at the center of paradise, the pilgrim has already passed through the first counter–point of the cosmic hypersphere at the Earth's center. But the narrative modalities of the two counter–points are in grave contrast with each other. We recall that the Martians in Wells's story at some point are said to resemble "a diurnal species of bat," and at the other "cherubs" (637); Dante has been exposed to an uncanny play of diabolical perspective, which then inverts into that more famous marvelous vision in the high heaven.

With Dante, we reach the classical center of the literary circle of knowledge. But the perplexing light of Dante's experimental metaphor that reflects along its intertextual web into Wells's crystal egg, and from there into Borges's aleph and finally to Benford's alien artifact, reminds us to be alert for both the literary, historical and geometric contours and formation of that circle. Indeed, given present understanding of the history of encyclopedias, to speak of the classical center indicates this is not primarily the pivot of the circle of knowledge in its modern sense of "encyclopedic" knowledge "that aims at embracing all branches of learning,"[21] though Dante may be the best example here as well. Nor are we discussing the "circuit of education"[22] or *orbis doctrinae* of the Latinate liberal arts with which Quintilian translates the Greek phrase *enkyklios paideia*, and which was, and often is, taken in histories of education as the phrase's original meaning.[23]

At issue behind these modern senses are rather images of the harmonious cosmos and cosmic circle of the archaic Platonic-Pythagorean tradition of education, which in the history of ideas in recent decades has superseded the circuit of the liberal arts as the basis of the idea of encyclopedia. Instead of the cycle of preliminary studies of the late Antiquity, L.M. de Rijk points to the "cosmological, or, one might say, cosmic and sacral sense, joined with some connotation of 'perfection'"[24] behind the original meaning of the word *enkyklios*: such as with the reference to the *kyklos* of circular motion of the heavenly bodies in Plato's *Timaeus* (38d). Following de Rijk and more recent studies,[25] *enkyklios paideia* derives from the choric education of the early Greek *paideia*, where it consists of the musical elements of rhythm, melody and word connected with the philosophical school of Pythagoras. Thus "the term [*enkyklios paideia*] stands for 'choric education'; training to make a man 'harmonious'" through a non–differentiated practice of skills in "what is afterwards called music and gymnastics."[26]

With the philosophy of cosmic harmony at their root, also literary forms of encyclopedism come out rather as inflections of the aesthetical metaphor of "beauty, wisdom [and] goodness" listed together by Socrates in the *Phaedrus*,[27] and imaged most influentially in the structure of the encyclopedic cosmos of the *Timaeus*. The foundations of encyclopedism in the tradition of Platonic-Pythagorean aesthetics are more apparent in premodern thought, where questions of knowledge are never raised in isolation from those of ethics and the nature of beauty. For one important articulation of the encyclopedic aesthetics, Vitruvius in his study of architecture refers to *encyclios disciplina* that "is put together like one body"[28] from its members of different arts and sciences. The Vitruvian aesthetics reflects still strongly in the theatrical metaphors of Renaissance encyclopedism, as well as in the staged articulations of poetry and architecture in writers like Ben Jonson.[29]

The general, literary and other artistic forms of encyclopedism and encyclopedic writing are connected within a shared field of articulation, with at least three more layers building on the aesthetical image of the encyclopedic cosmos to mention. First, beginning from the late Latin antiquity, the tradition opened by the liberal arts articulates the image of the encyclopedic cosmos through a more pronounced valorization of an order of the sciences. Next, the idea of the encyclopedic book is laid upon this foundation in the Middle Ages. Finally, the open order of knowledge that becomes dominant with the alphabetical encyclopedias in the vein of Diderot and d'Alembert evolves into present digitized technology of information networks and archives.

For a literary poetics of encyclopedism, this revision of its basic notion is significant. What we are directed to through the revised history of ideas does not rest content with the circumferential, canonical volumes of "the Bible, Dante's *Commedia*, the great epics, and the works of Joyce and Proust" in Northrop Frye's *ad hoc* canon of his generic notion of "encyclopedic form."[30]

More at focus with the short fiction of Wells and Borges, and the symbol of infinity of the Aleph shared with them by Benford, are rather features of the center of the "total order of words," which for Frye are found implicitly in "whatever poem we happen to be reading" (121). Unlike recent discussions of encyclopedic narrative which emphasize the modern novel, for Frye, encyclopedic form is an allegorical notion modeled on the medieval four-fold frame of interpretation. This brings it forth as an "anagogic form of symbolism, such as a sacred scripture, or its analogues in other modes" (365). In Frye, the center and circumference of the literary universe are connected by the anagogic symbol understood as a microcosmic monad, an image where "all symbols [are] being united in a single infinite and eternal verbal symbol which is, as dianoia, the Logos, and, as mythos, total creative act" (121).

Yet in the Fryegean anatomy, a traditional symbol like the aleph would remain part of the literary universe conceived as a mythology which despite recurring millennial cycles remains basically unchanged and disconnected from its changing disciplinary context. When Frye probes the schematic relation of the arts as "forming a circle, stretching from music through literature, painting and sculpture to architecture, with mathematics, the missing art, occupying the vacant place between architecture and music" (364), he takes his paradigm of the encyclopedia from the classical liberal arts. It is both informative and indicative that Frye still subscribes to Platonic values of goodness, beauty and truth; that he, in line with modern aesthetics and poetics, takes aesthetical beauty and taste as central values of the division; and that his chosen formulation of modern aesthetics comes from Edgar Allan Poe, whose arabesque writings exploring the boundaries of fiction and poetry with philosophy and science might have led him to consider generic and disciplinary purity in a different light.[31] Neither the archaic past (not yet articulated when Frye wrote his *Anatomy* in the 1950s) nor the future of the encyclopedia influences the order of the literary universe. Frye's is a circle of knowledge that stays content with its disciplinary contours and geometric limits, and where literature too, true to the *Anatomy*, is paradoxically sealed off from its profoundly encyclopedic interdisciplinarity.[32]

Dante's geometric of the cosmic circle is a sign that medieval encyclopedism, however, already reflects, probes and eventually inverts the limits of its basic image. The narrator of "The Aleph" reminds us of a better known paradox of the cosmic circle in the definition of God by "Alain de Lille [which] speaks of a sphere whose center is everywhere and circumference nowhere" (282). Interestingly, Borges leaves Alain's image ambiguous as to its specifying adjectives that are critical in our reading of the Aleph's trajectory from the Middle Ages to the modern literary fantastic and science fiction of Borges and Benford. For in its oldest known form in the 12th-century pseudo-hermetic writings of the *Liber XXIV philosophorum*, attributed by medieval tradition to the mythical Hermes Trismegistus, the image speaks in fact of an infinite sphere: *Deus est sphaera infinita, cujus centrum est ubique, circumferentia nusquam*—God is an infinite sphere whose center is everywhere and circumference nowhere. Yet Alain de Lille perpetrates it with an influential interpretive twist which emphasizes the Platonic heritage of the cosmic sphere: *Deus est sphaera intelligibilis, cujus centrum ubique, circumferentia nusquam*— God is an *intelligible* sphere whose center is everywhere and circumference nowhere.[33] Thus already in the medieval tradition, the hierarchic and stabilizing division of the intelligible and sensible world of the cosmic circle is played out against radical interpretation through the notion of infinity, which comes to challenge the basis of the encyclopedic circle in the Platonic tradition of the harmonious cosmos.

Typically for Borges, such teasing, concentrated encyclopedic images evoke ever expanding, infinite frames of reference wherein fictitious information mingles freely with historical. With Alain de Lille's medieval image of the cosmic sphere, readers are invited to follow the metaphor's historical tracks surfacing more explicitly two years later in Borges's essay "Pascal's Sphere," where we learn that the cosmic sphere represents but one defining moment and line of a complete "universal history" evoked in terms of "the various intonations of a few metaphors."[34]

As "Pascal's Sphere" explains, for Borges, the cosmic sphere images a latter day, modern aleph whose defining tone is the Pascalian terror in the infinite and decentered modern universe, not the medieval tranquility of Alain de Lille's closed Ptolemaic cosmos. For Plato and the Greeks in general, the idea of infinity in the sense of limitlessness, *apeiron*, was abhorrent.[35] Infinity is thus essentially at odds with the classical concept of the encyclopedia resting on the image of the proportioned, limited cosmos. Borges's commentary on the celebrated passage on the "Disproportion of Man"[36] in Pascal's *Pensées* is suggestive, especially by evoking the Pascalian terror against the long history of cosmic proportion that finally gives way to Pascal's interpretation of the image as "a frightful sphere, the center of which is everywhere, and the circumference nowhere."[37]

Pascal's is a moment of terror at the rupturing rim of the classical circle of knowledge, presentient of the open, post–classical orders looming on the horizon with the encyclopedic projects of Diderot and d'Alembert. "The general system of the sciences and the arts is a sort of labyrinth, a tortuous road which the intellect enters without quite knowing what direction to take," d'Alembert writes a century after Pascal. In the labyrinth of sciences, the d'Alembertian intellect meets "difficulties," so it must appropriate the role of the philosopher taking ever higher positions in relation to the arts and sciences which open underneath his gaze like a world map which "show[s] the principal countries, their position and their mutual dependence, the road that leads directly from one to the other. This road is often cut by a thousand obstacles, which are known in each country only to the inhabitants or to travelers, and which cannot be represented except in individual, highly detailed maps."[38]

Modern theory sees in d'Alembert's world map an early articulation of the open semiotic net,[39] a topology where the cosmic circle is highlighted through Nietzschean tones of decentering destruction and irony.[40] But it is also basis for the evolutionary coupling of the early modern sensibility of Pascalian terror of the infinite universe into the material sublime of modern cosmic topology. As Rudy Rucker notes: "There is [a] traditional belief that anticipates the hypersphere.... If the universe is indeed a hypersphere, then it would be quite accurate to regard it as a sphere whose center is everywhere and whose circumference is nowhere."[41]

The history of the encyclopedia is also an image of the order of the sciences and its formation. Drawing on the values of cosmic harmony and proportion, the ideal of union of the sciences of language of the *trivium*, and mathematical sciences of the *quadrivium*, is established in Martianus Capella's 5th–century allegorical narrative *The Marriage of Philology and Mercury* and perpetrated through the Middle Ages by the Latin encyclopedists.[42] Yet the classical balance of the *verba* and the *res*, words and things, in the learning of the early encyclopedists is channeled and secured through the library of the textual tradition. When the focus of scholarly culture starts valorizing more the realm of the things of the natural world from the 12th century on, and the possibility of scientific progress not contained and determined by traditional authorities of textual culture becomes conceivable, an element of imbalance is introduced to the idea of the encyclopedia.[43]

The possibility for the modern situation of C. P. Snow's "two cultures" is born with this imbalance. With key documents of modern encyclopedism such as D'Alembert's preface to Diderot's encyclopedia, both the order and representation of knowledge are exposed to reflection, which throws the traditional order of the tree of sciences into crisis with its chaotic image of the labyrinth, making it a vehicle for the open alphabetical order of modern printed reference works imaged by the encyclopedic world map.

Already d'Alembert fictionalizes the encyclopedia with images of the labyrinth and world map. One main function of literary poetics of encyclopedism is the further fictionalization and literalization of the encyclopedic images. Moving from Dante's paradise through the London antiquities shop to a Buenos Aires cellar, the Aleph undergoes such a process that leaves it finally resting on Ganymede's surface in Benford. Benford completes here the work of his predecessors; Borges for one signals of his intentions to rewrite this "thing of wonder" by placing it "in as drab setting as I could imagine."[44] Connecting his alien artifact to Borges, Benford activates a traditional frame readily and radically modified. This does not mean that the task of rewriting has been exhausted and fulfilled. Rather, starting from the confines of robust materialization, the encyclopedic question concerning the essence of the object at the focus of definition of this fictional circle of knowledge becomes ever more acute.

What, then, haunts the Ganymedean settlers? Through its name, we have seen, the thing still carries over entire libraries of ancient tradition even to this remote and hostile environment. As for the thing itself, it may fall through the melting ice of the terraformed Jupiter moon too soon for the researchers to fulfill their objectives and fix it in their conceptual gridworks as fully as they wish, only to surface again, maybe to secure the Ganymedean tectonic balance. Nevertheless, this time the Aleph may have initiated a conceptual breakthrough in the scientific paradigms within its human cult; if so, this indicates that the knowledge imported by contact with it would speed humanity beyond infinity to the full posthumanity we meet in *Beyond Infinity*.

The planetary tectonics grumbling under human terraforming may provide an apt image of the balance shifting at which Benford appears to be striving in his encyclopedia. For Borges of the 1940s, the infinities reflecting in the singularity of the aleph are chaotically imbalanced between mathematical and literary-mythological frames of reference, contributing to the demolition of the high encyclopedic epic and its secret symbol in this generic house of Usher. Interestingly, Borges in retrospection says he conceived the poetic association as the principal trope for the encyclopedic poetics he searched for:

> My chief problem in writing the story lay in what Walt Whitman had very successfully achieved — the setting down of a limited catalog of endless things. The task, as is evident, is impossible, for such chaotic enumeration can only be simulated, and every apparently haphazard element has to be linked to its neighbor either by secret association or by contrast.[45]

If the encyclopedic narrative in Borges seeks an associative and disintegrating poetic word sensible for echoes and mirror images at the far end of millennial traditions, curiously, the epic tradition appears reinvigorated by Benford's settlers. Benford's trick is to transfer the Faulknerian Mississippi wilderness to the outer reaches of the solar system. Faulkner's mythical bear Old Ben is an epitome of the shrinking, immemorial wilderness; like an "old Priam," who is "reft of his old wife and [has] outlived all his sons," it arrives from an "old dead time, a phantom, epitome and apotheosis of the old wild life."[46] The Ganymedean Aleph, on the other hand, descends from the infinite wilderness surrounding the human settlements — yet these settlements may be an archaic enclave for the superior race or mechanical intelligences that produced the artifact, leaving it as a signpost behind them. There seems a sort of pragmatic "tribal encyclopedia"[47] in formation here, such as Eric A. Havelock finds in Homeric oral culture preceding the language of abstractions of Platonic rationalism.

In strange conglomeration with technological, scientific, political and other cultural traditions deriving from Earth, however, Benford's settlers with their oral lore are on the verge of a decisive evolutionary jump to posthumanity. In a manner parallel to Homeric poetry that served as principal medium of education in archaic antiquity, but in a completely new moment of cultural evolution, the settlers' tribal encyclopedia may precede the memory banks and personified "aspects" like the irritating "Arthur" bioengineered into Captain Killeen's neck in the Galactic Center series. These memory chips pass on and provide encyclopedic knowledge in different situations. They are cultural voices from deep time, across humanity's history.

Still, reading a contemporary writer's work, we may not be able to judge the form the future encyclopedia will take. Some early signs and tendencies may be readable, the pathos of the signs that are best perceived when seen against the values of the classical encyclopedism of goodness, beauty, and truth.

To begin my conclusion in the order Frye presents these values, then, the ethical stakes of Benford's posthumanism also must be acknowledged. In this immanent vision, especially acute are the relations of human and animal life and other forms of embodied existence and consciousness in the process of redefinition through emerging new technology.[48] Techno-scientific immanence is surrounded here with an interesting multivalent image of infinity. The early volumes of the Jupiter series work out a fascinating interpretation of an implied total, encyclopedic vision through tightly focalized and stylized modernist narrations. The consistently developed and realistic near-future human perspective of a teenager (the young Matt Bohles) or a young man (Manuel Sanchez) is contrasted with the multivalent image of cosmic infinity which carries with it religious connotations of godhead in relation to the numinous Aleph at the center of the fictional world. Moving as we are in the Biblical landscape of a "Sidon," one wonders, accordingly, whether the Jewish tradition inherited here involves also the ethics of infinity. Reflected against the sphere of infinity, the focalized narration builds a structure that almost dramatizes human responsibility towards the exteriority of otherness, as Levinas puts the ethical form of intersubjectivity.[49] A preference for family, not the state, is also evident as an immanence conceived as generational fecundity.

The question of narrative ethics is most concentrated in the character of cyborg Eagle, painfully illustrating the shifting line of demarcation between the human and machine:

Manuel peered down at it in the brief moments when it stood still, glaring up
with two wide-spaced black eyes. It was a hodgepodge of parts attached to a
gunmetal-gray carapace, bigger than any servo'd animal he had ever seen and
powerfully made, bristling with heavy motors and big treads and bulging mani-
folds. He could not imagine a man or woman deep down inside the thing,
tapped into the metal world that had swallowed it whole, raging in an awful
silent pocket somewhere [68].

The presence of Eagle in the settlement is discussed in Manuel's family,
his parents reminding him it is not an animal but someone "unlucky" enough
on the orbital work stations to get injured, having perhaps "even died for a
while" (65), then turned into a cyborg. It is with Eagle's political motivation
that the anxieties of narrative ethics are most tense. The relation of a socialist Earth and ruthlessly capitalist Jupiter colonies takes us back to the cold
war context of the novel's publication, not any conceivable political near
future. But whether this political crisis is there to accommodate and moti-
vate Eagle, or whether the crisis is rather symptomatic of unresolved ethical
anxieties in the shifting relations of the human, animal, and machine, may
not be resolved.

As for the aesthetics of Benford's vision, one admires its dramatic shifts
from poetry of colors and estranged vistas of chemical landscapes to the repul-
sive scenery of ugliness. Although young Matt Bohles in the first Jupiter novel
says that he is "practical, not poetic" and must remain so when "swinging
around Jupiter, living meters away from lethal radiation,"[50] his first person
narration is marked by scenes of "eerie" planetary coloring where "night is
really sort of yellowish twilight" and the "jagged valleys turn beautiful and
spooky all at once" (81). Such poetry is more foregrounded in describing the
old Matt Bohles's and Manuel's environs in *Against Infinity*, starting from
moments when a "dime-sized sun struck colors from their carapaces [i.e.,
biotechnologically enhanced animals], steels gleaming blue-green, the ceram-
ics a clammy yellow" (8). The locus of these colors is the massive, shape-shift-
ing bulk of the Aleph, which is described as "round, like an egg" (26) and
shines "alabaster in parts and in others oozing in amber, watery light that
refracted through [Manuels's] helmet" (52).

These scenes are even reminiscent at times of the poetics of color in
Dante's paradise.[51] However, when following Manuel's steps over the icy planetary scape, with bodies underneath that are "still face up" (209), we are
reminded of the infernal lake of the Cocytus underneath the ice of which
Dante, in the *Inferno*, sees some of the condemned "showing through like
straw in glass."[52] These are rather emblems of a modern aesthetics of ugliness, which foregrounds especially with products of biotechnology like "slep-
pers, the new bioform introduced to fill in a step in the biochem chain that

led toward an oxygen atmosphere. They were efficient, big and bulky and ugly as sin. They mutated easily and were hard to chase down."[53]

To describe its movement between scenes of unreal beauty, ugliness and horror, the aesthetics of Benford's style requires modification of the romantic notion of the sublime,[54] building perhaps from the notion of the "material vision" or "material sublime" with which Paul de Man in his later essays seeks a new articulation for the potentially subversive epistemology of literary language in the liberal arts. In its context of Kant's discussion of the sublime, the de Manean vision would be "purely material, devoid of any reflexive or intellectual complication, [and] which is also purely formal, devoid of any semantic depth and reducible to the formal mathematization or geometrization of pure optics."[55]

De Man did not, in fact, ever reach the relations of literature and science in the way he promises. Paradoxically, he may have remained subject to the modern, restricted notion of literature in its aesthetical autonomy, whereas premodern writers like Dante, but also writers of modern genres like science fiction which test and cross the limits of literature and science, would be available for reflection.[56]

As for its epistemology, Benford's material vision has taken us to Jupiter's sphere, a heavenly locale which for Dante is allegorically related to geometry. In Dante the theologian inherited Euclidean geometry; the Jovian science of geometry signals certainty of knowledge that "moves between the point and the circle as between its beginning and its end." This is because the point and circle are limits that are "antithetical to the certainty characteristic of this science ... free of any taint of error, and utterly certain." So the point "cannot be measured at all, since it cannot be divided," and the circle, because it "cannot be measured precisely, since, being curved, it cannot be perfectly squared."[57]

Geometry remains the science of Benford's Jupiter system. Unlike Euclid, and more in line with Dante the poet's geometric metaphor, this future, material Aleph is a point of a "geometry containing other geometries," "all angles, all perspectives,"[58] making it a kind of universal memory theater of all the points in spacetime, a non–Euclidean labyrinth the dimensions of which profoundly confuse Manuel: "On they went, through narrow passages of somber rock, up tight corridors, crawling through odd-shaped holes, down slides slick with ice. It seemed to Manuel that the Aleph could not possibly be as big as this, as complicated" (222–223).

In Benford, the mathematico–religious history of the Aleph receives a new physicalist interpretation, where the ancient Kabbalistic symbol of infinity is connected with the notion of singularity in recent astrophysics.[59] Piet Arnold's research group has accordingly learned that on its subatomic level, the Aleph is not only a repository of infinite geometries, but also of physical laws, being a universal parameters generator, constantly restructuring itself, as happens at the singularity of the Big Bang "when the universe was young" and "the laws were young" (222). Upon this unfathomable, material center point of the unknown, infinite space, the circumference of the circle of knowledge is again turned over and inverted, leaving us with the image where "the artifact is *in* the universe, but is not *of* the universe" (222), depending on the perspective we take on it.

One final inversion of the literary history of the cosmic circle may involve coupling the human consciousness with the alien object it confronts and tries to contain. Lem's Solaris Sea paves the way as a screen for the space station personnel's materializing memories and unconscious wishes. Initially oblivious of its human hunters also, Benford's Aleph's brutal trajectory shows signs of adjustment to a closer relationship with its destined conqueror. When the artifact resurrects from Ganymede's icy confines, Manuel knows "he would carry this, carry it on with him in the long decades of rebuilding and pain that must come know ... beyond the ever-reaching hand of man" (242–243). In Benford's future, the galactic descendants of early Jupiter settlers may eventually become the demiurges making such artifacts. But for a long time before that, the contours of the encyclopedic narrative remain in upheaval.

Notes

1. Gregory Benford, *Against Infinity* (New York: Avon, 1998), 6. Later parenthetical page references are to this edition.
2. Stanislaw Lem, *Solaris*, translated from the French by Joanna Kilmartin and Steve Cox (San Diego, CA: Harcourt Brace, 1987), 110. Later parenthetical page references are to this edition.
3. Lem, "Reflections on My Life," *Microworlds: Writings on Science Fiction and Fantasy*, by Lem, edited by Franz Rottensteiner, (London: Mandarin 1984), 23–24.
4. See, for example, "Part II: The Encyclopedists," with its opening citation to the *Encyclopedia Galactica*, in Isaac Asimov, *Foundation* (New York: Bantam, 1991), 47–96.
5. Gordon R. Dickson, *The Final Encyclopedia 1–2* (New York: Tom Doherty Associates, 1984).
6. Benford, *In the Ocean of Night* (Toronto: Bantam, 1987), 1.
7. Benford, *Sailing Bright Eternity* (New York: Bantam, 1996), 176.
8. Benford, "Afterword," *Beyond Infinity* (London: Orbit, 2004), 450–451.
9. Umberto Eco, *The Role of the Reader: Explorations in the Semiotics of Texts* (Bloomington: Indiana University Press, 1979), 185.
10. Benford, "Afterword" to "To the Storming Gulf," *In Alien Flesh*, by Benford (New York: Tom Doherty, 1986), 160–163.
11. See Gary K. Wolfe, "The Bear and the Aleph: Gregory Benford's *Against Infinity*," *The New York Review of Science Fiction*, No. 30 (February 1991), 8–11.
12. Jorge Luis Borges, "The Aleph," *Collected Fictions*, by Borges, translated by Andrew Hurley (New York: Penguin, 1998), 276. Later parenthetical page references are to this edition.

13. In his afterword to "The Aleph" in *Collected Fictions*, Borges ascribes it to the "genre of fantasy" (287).

14. Dante Alighieri, *The Divine Comedy: Paradiso: Italian Text and Translation*, translated with a commentary by Charles S. Singleton, second printing with corrections (Princeton, NJ: Princeton University Press, 1977), 313. See Jon Thiem, "Borges, Dante, and the Poetics of Total Vision," *Comparative Literature*, 40:2 (Spring 1988), 97–121.

15. H. G. Wells, *The War of the Worlds*, edited by David Y. Hughes, introduction by Brian W. Aldiss (New York: Oxford University Press, 1995), 7. Later parenthetical references to the novel are to this edition.

16. Wells, "The Crystal Egg," *The Complete Short Stories* (London: Ernest Benn, 1974), 625. Later parenthetical page references are to this edition.

17. On Wells's role as an early manifestor of four-dimensionality in the arts, see Linda Dalrymple Henderson, *The Fourth Dimension and Non-Euclidean Geometry in Modern Art* (Princeton, NJ: Princeton University Press, 1983), 33–35, 42–43, and *passim*; and Paul Nahin, *Time Machines: Time Travel in Physics, Metaphysics, and Science Fiction*, 2nd Ed. (New York: Springer, 1999), 143–161 and *passim*.

18. Robert Osserman, *Poetry of the Universe: A Mathematical Exploration of the Cosmos* (New York: Anchor, 1995), 118.

19. Mark Peterson, "Dante's Physics," *The Divine Comedy and the Encyclopaedia of Arts and Sciences: Acta of the International Dante Symposium, 13–16 November 1983, Hunter College*, edited by Giuseppe Di Scipio and Aldo Scaglione (New York and Amsterdam: John Benjamins, 1988), 171. See also Peterson's earlier essay "Dante and the 3-sphere," in *American Journal Of Physics*, 47 (1979), 1031–1035. I introduce my reading of Dante's topology in the essay "The Curvature of Space-Time in Dante's *The Divine Comedy*," *Worlds Enough and Time. Explorations of Time in Science Fiction and Fantasy*, edited by Gary Westfahl, George Slusser, and David Leiby, (Westport, CT: Greenwood, 2002), 115–128; and in "The Limits of Geometry in the '*Convivio*' and Their Inversion in the '*Comedy*': On Dante's Cosmology and Its Modern After-Life," *Perspektiv på Dante II: Proceedings of the Nordic Dante Studies Symposium, Stockholm, Sweden 2001*, edited by Anders Cullhed (København: Multivers Academic, 2006), 267–313. A digital version of the latter essay is available, as of September 22, 2008, at the address: *http://homepage.mac.com/kaatmann/dante/Dantesamlet1.pdf*.

20. See Jeffrey R. Weeks, *The Shape of Space*, 2nd Ed. (New York: Marcel Dekker, 2002), 199–212.

21. "Encyclopædic, encyclopedic, *a.*," *Oxford English Dictionary*, 2nd Ed., Volume V (Oxford, UK: Oxford University Press, 1989), 219.

22. Marcus Fabius Quintilianus, *Institutio Oratoria*, translated and edited by H. E. Butler, Loeb Classical Library (Cambridge, UK: Harvard University Press, 1920), I.x.1.

23. See Teresa Morgan, *Literate Education in the Hellenistic and Roman Worlds* (Cambridge: Cambridge University Press, 1998), 35.

24. L. M. de Rijk, "'Enkyklios Paideia': A Study of Its Original Meaning," *Vivarium*, 3.1 (1965), 24–93, 27.

25. See A. P. Bos, "Exoterikoi Logoi and Enkyklioi Logoi in the Corpus Aristotelicum and the Origin of the Idea of the Enkyklios Paideia," *Journal of the History of Ideas*, 50 (1989), 179–198.

26. De Rijk, 85–86.

27. *Phaedrus* 246e, in Plato, *Complete Works*, edited, with introduction and notes, by John M. Cooper; associate editor D. S. Hutchinson (Indianapolis, IN: Hackett, 1997).

28. Vitruvius, *On Architecture*, edited and translated by Frank Granger, Two volumes, Loeb Classical Library (Cambridge, MA: Harvard University Press, 1931), I.c.I.12.

29. See A. W. Johnson, *Ben Jonson: Poetry and Architecture* (Oxford, UK: Clarendon, 1994).

30. Northrop Frye, *Anatomy of Criticism: Four Essays* (Princeton, NJ: Princeton University Press, 1957), 365. Later parenthetical page references to *Anatomy of Criticism* are to this edition.

31. "The present book employs a diagrammatic framework that has been used in poetics ever since Plato's time. This is the division of 'the good' into three main areas, of which the world of art, beauty, feeling, and taste is the central one, and is flanked by two other worlds. One is the world of social action and events, the other the world of individual thought and ideas. Reading from left to right, this threefold structure divides human faculties into will, feeling and reason. It divides the mental constructs which these faculties produce into history, art, and science and philosophy. It divides the ideals which form compulsions or obligations on these faculties into law, beauty, and truth. Poe gives his version of the diagram (right to left) as Pure Intellect, Taste, and the Moral Sense. 'I place Taste in the middle,' said Poe, 'because it is just this position which in the mind it occupies.'" Frye, 243.

32. On the history of the notion of literature, see, for example, René Wellek, "What Is Literature?," *What Is Literature?*, edited by Paul Hernadi (Bloomington, IN: Indiana University Press, 1978), 16–23.

33. See Robin Small, "Nietzsche and a Platonist Tradition of the Cosmos: Center Everywhere and Circumference Nowhere," *Journal of the History of Ideas*, 44:1 (January–March 1983), 90–91.

34. Borges, "Pascal's Sphere," *Selected Non-Fictions*, edited by Eliot Weinberger, Esther Allen *et al.*, translators (New York: Penguin, 1999), 353.

35. See Rudy Rucker, *Infinity and the Mind: The Science and Philosophy of the Infinite* (Princeton, NJ: Princeton University Press, 1995), 2–3.

36. See Blaise Pascal, *Pensées*, translated by A. J. Krailsheimer (Harmondsworth, UK: Penguin, 1975).

37. Pascal's phrasing of the image in his manuscript of the *Pensées*, quoted by Borges, "Pascal's Sphere," 353.

38. Jean Le Rond d'Alembert, *Preliminary Discourse to the Encyclopedia of Diderot*, translated by Richard N. Schwab with the collaboration of Walter E. Rex, introduction and notes by Richard N. Scwab, The Library of Liberal Arts (Indianapolis, IN: Bobbs-Merrill, 1963), 46–48.

39. See Eco, *Semiotics and the Philosophy of Language* (Bloomington, IN: Indiana University Press, 1984).

40. See Small.

41. Rucker, 17.

42. See David L. Wagner, "The Seven Liberal Arts and Classical Scholarship," *The Seven Liberal Arts in the Middle Ages*, edited by Wagner (Bloomington, IN: Indiana University Press, 1983), 19.

43. See Maria Teresa Beonio-Brocchieri Fumagalli, *Le Enciclopedie dell'Occidente Medioevale* (Torino: Loescher Editore, 1981), 26–27.

44. Borges, "Commentaries," *The Aleph and Other Stories 1933–1969: Together with Commentaries and Autobiographical Essay*, edited and translated by Norman Thomas di Giovanni in collaboration with the author (New York: Bantam Books/E.P. Dutton, 1971), 189.

45. Borges, "Commentaries," 190.

46. William Faulkner, "The Bear," *Three Famous Short Novels: Spotted Horses, Old Man, The Bear* (New York: Vintage, 1963), 188.

47. Eric A. Havelock, *Preface to Plato* (Cambridge, MA: Belknap Press of Harvard University Press, 1963), 61.

48. See Benford and Elisabeth Malartre, *Beyond Human: Living with Robots and Cyborgs* (New York: Tom Doherty Associates, 2007), 16–19, 46–48, and *passim*.

49. See Emmanuel Levinas, *Totality and Infinity: An Essay on Exteriority*, translated by Alphonso Lingis (Pittsburgh, PA: Duquesne University Press, 1969), and *Ethics and Infinity: Conversations with Philippe Nemo*, translated by Richard A. Cohen (Pittsburgh, PA: Duquesne University Press, 1985).

50. Benford, *Jupiter Project* (New York: Avon, 1980), 1. Later parenthetical page references are to this edition.

51. See Jean-Pierre Barricelli, "The Ultimate Mindscape: Dante's *Paradiso*," *Mindscapes: The Geographies of Imagined Worlds*, edited by George Slusser and Eric S. Rabkin (Carbondale: Southern Illinois University Press, 1989), 267–270.

52. Dante Alighieri, *The Divine Comedy: Inferno: Italian Text and Translation*, translated with a commentary by Charles S. Singleton, second printing with corrections (Princeton, NJ: Princeton University Press, 1977), 361.

53. Benford, *Against Infinity*, 88.

54. See Thomas Weiskel, *The Romantic Sublime: Studies in the Structure and Psychology of Transcendence* (Baltimore, MD: Johns Hopkins University Press, 1976).

55 Paul de Man, "Phenomenality and Materiality in Kant," *Aesthetic Ideology*, by de Man, edited by Andrzej Warminski (Minneapolis: University of Minnesota Press, 1996), 70–90.

56. See my discussion in "Closing in Sublunary Darkness?: On the 'Material Vision' in Dante's and Paul de Man's Cosmos," *Illuminating Darkness: Approaches to Obscurity and Nothingness in Literature*, edited by Päivi Mehtonen, Annales Academiae Scientiarum Fennicae, Humaniora 348 (Helsinki: Finnish Academy of Science and Letters, 2007), 27–46.

57. Dante Alighieri, *The Banquet (Il Convivio)*, translated, with an introduction and notes, by Christopher Ryan (Saratoga, NY: Anma Libri, 1989), II, xiii, 26–27.

58. Benford, *Against Infinity*, 226, 223.

59. On singularities, see Kip S. Thorne, *Black Holes and Time Warps: Einstein's Outrageous Legacy* (New York: Norton, 1994).

10. Utopia and Utopianism in the Life, Work and Thought of H. G. Wells

John S. Partington

In calling for more contact between the "two cultures" of the sciences and the humanities as a way to achieve economic progress throughout the world, C. P. Snow was arguably asking scientists and literary intellectuals to join forces in working toward the goal of a global utopia. From that perspective, Snow was in a way anticipated by the great H. G. Wells, who also brought both scientific acumen and a literary sensibility to his own efforts to achieve utopia. Thus, it would seem useful to examine in detail the various elements of Wells's utopian philosophy.

Perhaps more than any other writer, H. G. Wells (1866–1946) embodied the concept of utopia in his life, work and thought. In his life, through his many love affairs with women as varied as the novelist, Rebecca West, the travel writer, Odette Keun, and the alleged spy, Moura Budberg; in his work through the crafting of such utopias as *The Time Machine* (1895), *A Modern Utopia* (1905) and *The Shape of Things to Come* (1933); and in his thought through his propagation of a world state, his advocacy of reform eugenics, his belief in socialist collectivism, and his drafting of *The Rights of Man* (1940). To discover the origins of all of these utopian impulses, one would need to investigate the influences of Enlightenment liberalism, nineteenth-century socialism and Darwinian evolution on Wells's thought, as well as his reaction against evangelical Christianity, the British class system and all forms of nationalism and racism. Wells's private behavior, his literary work and his political vision were so intertwined that — I repeat — he was the embodiment of the concept of utopia.

The Free Lover

Although critics are divided on the question whether Wells was a feminist in the broadest sense, there can be little doubt that his writings about sexual relations in the Edwardian period were liberating for both men and women, and that his own libertine behavior has offered material for utopian theorization. Ruth Brandon maintains that Wells was unique among Edwardian writers in presenting sex as "fun."[1] Looking back on his early writings, Wells was himself clearly aware of this fact: "The spreading knowledge of birth-control ... seemed to justify my contention that love was now to be taken more lightly than it had been in the past. It was to be refreshment and invigoration, as I set out quite plainly in my Modern Utopia."[2]

The key to Wells's utopianism in general, and his sexual code in particular, may be grasped through his statement that "morality is made for man, and not man for morality."[3] Brandon appears to see consistency in Wells's theory and practice of sexual relations when she observes that "First of all he worked out the lines along which he would run his own life; then he set about constructing principles to fit them" (169). Sylvia Hardy, in her consideration of Wells as a feminist, maintains that he also acknowledged the right of female sexual liberty, stating, in relation to the title character of *Ann Veronica* (1909), "Not only does he show Ann Veronica as a sexual being, he even suggests that there should be free and guiltless sexual choice between men and women, one, moreover, which does not have to be initiated by the man."[4] Jane Eldridge Miller agrees, writing that "not only did Wells depict Ann Veronica as having sexual desires, but that he characterized those desires as healthy and natural."[5]

Although most critics choose to look at *Ann Veronica* when considering Wells's ideas on sexual relations, Brandon sees a more general trend throughout Wells's Edwardian fiction, believing that in *The New Machiavelli* (1911) and *In the Days of the Comet* (1906) "the most notable and controversial idea, and certainly the one which received the most critical attention, was that of free and guiltless sexual choice between men and women, initiated from either side and with the tolerance of all" (170). According to Miller, the radicalism of Wells's sexual politics arises from his ability to understand how contemporary women felt. Thus, "In *Marriage* [1912], as in *Ann Veronica*, Wells demonstrates a remarkable imaginative sympathy with his heroine; no other male writer of the period created such intelligent, lively and complex female characters" (173–174). This "imaginative sympathy" also led to Wells's reconsideration of the nuclear family and parental responsibilities:

> All women who desire children do not want to be entrusted with their upbringing. Some women are sexual and philoprogenitive without being sedulously

maternal, and some are maternal without much or any sexual passion. There are men and women in the world now, great allies, fond and passionate lovers who do not live nor want to live constantly together.[6]

Although the ending of *Ann Veronica* can be read as conventional even by Edwardian standards, as the heroine, after seducing a married man, ends up herself married to him and the mother of his child, Miller argues that it nonetheless contains a radical edge: "Wells is trying to depict a new kind of marriage, based on sexual attraction and equality. Ann Veronica is not 'tied and dull and inelastic' ... like other married women she has observed; hers is a 'hot-blooded marriage' ... and that, we are to believe, makes all the difference" (170). Later, in *The Wife of Sir Isaac Harman* (1914), we find Wells going even further in his radical reconstitution of gender relations. As Miller points out, as a result of the death of her husband and her (possibly) choosing to take Mr. Brumley as a lover, "Lady Harman, wealthy and independent, escapes from the tyranny of either/or choices and is finally able to write a new narrative for herself— one which she controls, one which includes work and passion and independence. It is a remarkable conclusion for a novel by Wells — the triumph of a mature woman who is powerful, sexual and free" (187).

In his practice of free love and his depiction of sexually-liberated women in his fiction, Wells presented a radical new way of living for Edwardian society. Considering Wells alongside Havelock Ellis, Edward Carpenter and Edward Aveling, Brandon sees his radicalism as truly utopian, claiming that "What distinguished them was ... their attempt to construct a new system of ethics which would be the basis for a better, freer, more modern world" (251). Although reluctant to call Wells a feminist, Hardy largely agrees with this summary, though she places it within a larger context of Wells's treatment of the "woman question":

> His opposition to the legally sanctioned notion of private ownership in marriage, for instance, which saw women and children as patriarchal possessions with little or no say over their own lives is now, as Patricia Stubbs points out in her feminist study of women in the Victorian and Edwardian novel, "a commonplace of socialist-feminist thinking, but when Wells was saying it, his was an isolated voice." He was, too, one of the first to argue that women would never achieve the freedom and independence they sought until they had control over their own bodies, and thus he was a life-long supporter of the birth-control movement. He saw that without economic freedom there can be no independence — Wells's ideas on this point are positively Marxist — hence his plans for Endowed Motherhood — a system whereby the state would pay a wage to any woman who was, or was about to become a mother [52].

Indeed, Wells's thoughts on the "woman question" could be broadened even further, as I argue elsewhere.[7] For although Wells's encouragement of motherhood through public endowment would today seem a conservative act, attempting to confine women to the home, in Edwardian England, when the husband was idealized as the main breadwinner but was often unable to earn enough to support a family, the notion of making motherhood an independent occupation, earning a living wage, was really quite radical. In terms of social policy Wells warrants credit for understanding the potential role of the state as guarantor of basic housing, education and a minimum wage in order to enable the poor and undereducated to raise themselves out of the mire of poverty and ignorance. By designing social policy for the individual on the basis that all persons are unique, Wells created a sustainable, ethically evolving society that was inclusive.

The Literary "Utopographer"[8]

According to Lyman Tower Sargent, "H. G. Wells wrote more works that fall within the utopian genre than any other writer."[9] Beginning with *The Time Machine*, Sargent identifies fifteen book-length fictional utopias produced by Wells between 1895 and 1939, ending with *The Holy Terror* (1939).[10]

The Time Machine was written as a reply to both the pastoral utopianism of William Morris's *News from Nowhere* (1890) and the hyper-industrial utopia created by Edward Bellamy in *Looking Backward* (1887). In Wells's story, the pastoral surface-dwelling Eloi live a dystopian nightmare, being consumed by the subterranean industrial population, the Morlocks, in a reversal of nineteenth-century class relations. *The Time Machine* is not only important as a seminal work of science fiction, but is also essential as a utopian text due to its antithetical relationship to Wells's later utopian masterpiece, *A Modern Utopia*; the kinetic utopianism of the latter developed out of the static society of *The Time Machine*. Wells's understanding of the need for utopias to be dynamic was only possible through his earlier critiquing of the concept of static utopia as presented in *The Time Machine* where a seemingly perfect equilibrium between social classes is achieved in one generation, only to lead to degradation and anarchy in a future which results in the ultimate extinction of the human race itself.[11]

Defining utopianism in its narrowest sense (as a "non-existent good place"[12]), Krishan Kumar maintains that "*When the Sleeper Wakes* [1899] was in fact the first of Wells's utopian stories. The elements of utopia are there, although buried still within a largely anti-utopian fable."[13] Within a dictatorial society governed by the Nietzschean Ostrog we discover such technological marvels as powered flight, moving footpaths, universal crèches and television and radio. Nonetheless, due to the lack of personal liberty and the tyrannical rule the story has proved the prototype dystopia, inspiring such classics of the genre as Yevgeny Zamiatin's *We* (1922), Aldous Huxley's *Brave New World* (1932), and George Orwell's *Nineteen Eighty-Four* (1949).

For all that Wells has been accused of benevolent elitism in his utopianism,[14] the keystone of his ideal societies was always the preservation of individual liberty. As Kumar notes, "one of Wells's constant themes is that no social order is worth anything, nor in the end is workable, if it cannot provide for a fulfilling and satisfying personal life" (210). In his most detailed utopia, *A Modern Utopia*, although Wells did acknowledge the need to curb individualism in order to protect the collective polity, it is clear that the degree of success of the society therein portrayed must be measured by how well individual liberty and state intervention are balanced, the sum of which must ensure continuous human diversity as well as sustainable material development.[15] Wells's prescribed formula for striking such a balance was the application of science to planning, and the inspirations behind his scientific utopianism were T. H. Huxley for the concept of "ethical evolution"[16] and Francis Bacon for his glorification of organized research and his emphasis on mechanical development in *The New Atlantis* (1626). According to Kumar, "Science acted for Wells as the mainspring of his literary imagination; and that imagination was put at the service of a social philosophy that was, in the strict sense, consistently utopian" (181).

A further essential factor in Wells's utopianism was universalism. As Sargent observes, "Wells believed that in modern times an isolated utopia is simply out of date and impossible. An isolated island has no point ... a utopia must be planetary, a world state, or it will fail" (203). Such world-state utopianism was represented by Wells in many of his fictions, from *A Modern Utopia* to *The World Set Free* (1914), *Men Like Gods* (1923) and *The Shape of Things to Come*.

Regarding Wells's utopianism, critics are unanimous in observing that little can be achieved by focusing on just one, or even a handful of his utopian texts: for example, Kumar notes that "Wells's utopianism is not to be found readily distilled in one or two books, or neatly packed for easy summary. Although specific utopian projects abound in his writings, it is in the writings and public advocacy as a whole that the force of his utopianism becomes apparent" (168–169). Patrick Parrinder has even suggested that Wells "was a major propagandist for utopian ideas who never produced a major utopian book. *A Modern Utopia* is the nearest thing in his corpus to that book, but it has so far failed to achieve canonical status either within the utopian genre or among Wells's own best-known writings."[17] And although he focuses extensively on *A Modern Utopia* in his *Utopia and Anti-Utopia in Modern Times*, Kumar argues that that book "is not the most finished or perfected of Wells's utopias. There are more complete accounts in *Men Like Gods* ... and *The Shape of Things to Come*" (190). These sentiments clearly reinforce the point, made above, that Wells was the embodiment of the concept of utopia. In his work, as in his life and thought, Wells strove not for material perfection in the here and now, nor for spiritual perfection in the afterlife, but for continuous racial advancement,[18] and that striving was Wells's utopianism, which his fictional utopias contributed to bringing about.

By insisting that Wells strove for the achievement of a kinetic utopia, it must not be assumed that he was an eternal optimist. Sargent sees the various methods by which utopia was achieved in Wells's fictions as suggesting just the opposite:

> On the surface, Wells was certainly the great optimist, full of plans for revolutionizing the world, but any real examination of those plans must lead one to question the degree of his faith in them. Most of his plans require accident (*In the Days of the Comet*), a new breed of human beings (*Men Like Gods*), or a dedicated class of people who are willing to sacrifice their lives for the betterment of the world (*A Modern Utopia*) [214–215].

And it must not be forgotten that while Wells fictionalized the achievement of a world state in such works as *A Modern Utopia*, *Men Like Gods*, and *The Shape of Things to Come*, he also portrayed some bleak dystopias in such works as *The Island of Doctor Moreau* (1896), *The War of the Worlds* (1898) and *The War in the Air* (1908). Again, however, regarding these works Sargent warns us not to see them as entirely pessimistic:

> [Wells's] earliest works were all dystopias showing horrifying futures for the human race. There is usually an optimistic side to dystopias. They say to the reader that if we avoid taking this path we can avoid this future, but if we continue on this path this is where we are going. It is your choice.... There were undoubtedly some elements of this in Wells's dystopias [215].

If Wells was a major writer of utopias during the late-nineteenth and twentieth centuries, he was also an important "utopographer" or writer of "meta-utopias." His knowledge of the utopian tradition was perhaps unrivalled in his day and, as Parrinder has noticed with regard to *A Modern Utopia*, "In between the spurts of fictional travelogue it offers a sustained comparative discussion making systematic reference to about twenty previous utopian writers, as well as to utopian sects, utopian architects, utopian communities, and utopian languages" (99). Perhaps in recognition of his vast knowledge of past utopias, Wells was rewarded in 1905 with a commission to write the introduction to a reprint of Thomas More's *Utopia* (1516).[19]

The World Statesman

According to W. Warren Wagar, Wells's "life's work was a sustained, wide-ranging effort both to probe the future and to define in imaginative detail what the future should — and should not — be." He elaborates,

In more than a dozen volumes of journalism and amateur sociology, from *Antici-pations* in 1902 to *The Outlook for Homo Sapiens* in 1942, he peered tirelessly into the human future, all the while beating the drum for his vision of a new world civilization. At the same time he was well versed in the utopian tradition in Western literature, not to mention its knowing son and heir. No serious writer of the last century did so much to keep that tradition alive.[20]

In an essay considering the influence of the scientist and philosopher Francis Bacon on Wells's utopianism, Richard Nate concurs with Wagar's observations, additionally identifying the breadth and complexity of genre which Wells employed during his investigations:

> Wells's utopianism covers both philosophy and fiction.... Wells developed his theoretical views in essays such as *Anticipations of the Reaction of Mechanical and Scientific Progress upon Human Life and Thought ... The Discovery of the Future* (1902), and *The Open Conspiracy* (1928), and he also wrote utopian novels, for example *Men Like Gods*.... [H]is *Modern Utopia* ... represents a mixture of both forms of textual presentation. It is, in fact, both a utopian narrative and a theo-retical reflection on utopian writing.[21]

The objective that dominates all of Wells's formal utopian writings and much of his speculative non-fiction is the collectivist world state.[22] He first expressed his support for a world state in *Anticipations* (1902),[23] and devel-oped it through the Great War, with calls for the creation of a "League of Free Nations" on confederal lines in *In the Fourth Year* (1918),[24] and into the interwar period when his ideas hardened around federalist and then function-alist ideas of world governance.[25] Wells ultimately came to desire the com-plete abolition of the nation-state as a political unit, and his final vision of a world state was developed during the Second World War when he believed "war-welded Federalism"[26] would bind all the combatants together following the defeat of fascism and result in the administration of the whole world by functional agencies overseeing world production and distribution, as well as such key services as education, health and transport.

Critics are generally unanimous on the importance of science to Wells's utopianism.[27] Peter Beilharz, for instance, has written that "in Wells' vision science loomed large, and though Wells was critical of science as well it nev-ertheless governs his utopianism" (80). In addition to harnessing science to his utopianism, Wagar claims in "The Road to Utopia" that Wells was the first thinker to wed utopianism with futurism, and sees all subsequent utopias as "descriptions not only of ideal worlds but also of the making of ideal worlds, the future-historical story of just how humanity can or will get from here to there" (16). Wagar sees Wells's *The Open Conspiracy* as the most important such book: "What we have in all the editions of this singular book is a nar-rative in non-fictional form of the making of a utopian future" (18).[28]

Nate's "Scientific Utopianism" points out a further trait of Wells's utopianism: "Wells characterised the open conspiracy as a 'world religion' [...] and referred to his own proposals as 'a sort of provisional "bible"'" (178). For Wells, therefore, utopianism was an ideology, and he was its missionary. Indeed, according to Nate, his utopian mission attracted no less attention during his lifetime than his role as a popular author:

> In the first decades of the twentieth century, Wells's role as a public figure underwent a major change. Though still famous as the author of scientific romances, he became known primarily as a utopian thinker who conferred with political leaders such as Theodore and Franklin D. Roosevelt, as well as Lenin and Stalin [175].[29]

Although Wells's popularity as a utopographer may have diminished since his death, Wagar, in editing a reprint of the 1933 edition of *The Open Conspiracy*, nonetheless claims that it "may be the most important book written in the 20th century" and asks his readers to decide whether "it deserves such esteem ... in the 21st."[30] However one might answer Wagar's question, it seems undeniable that anyone today interested, like C. P. Snow, in bringing together science and the humanities to make the world a better place could profit from an examination of the life and works of H. G. Wells.

Notes

1. Ruth Brandon, *The New Women and the Old Men: Love, Sex and the Woman Question* (London: Secker & Warburg, 1990), 169. Later parenthetical page references are to this edition.
2. H. G. Wells, *Experiment in Autobiography: Discovery and Conclusions of a Very Ordinary Brain (since 1866)* (New York: Macmillan, 1934), 363.
3. Wells, "Morals and Civilization," *The Island of Doctor Moreau: A Critical Text of the 1896 London First Edition, with an Introduction and Appendices*, edited by Leon Stover (Jefferson, NC: McFarland, 1996), 260.
4. Sylvia Hardy, "A Feminist Perspective on H. G. Wells," *The Wellsian*, 20 (Winter 1997), 60. Later parenthetical page references are to this edition.
5. Jane Eldridge Miller, *Rebel Women: Feminism, Modernism and the Edwardian Novel* (Chicago: University of Chicago Press, 1997), 165. Later parenthetical page references are to this edition.
6. Wells, *First & Last Things: A Confession of Faith and Rule of Life* (London: Constable, 1908), 217.
7. John S. Partington, "The Death of the Static: H. G. Wells and the Kinetic Utopia," *Utopian Studies*, 11.2 (2000), 109.
8. Wells coins this term in *Meanwhile: The Picture of a Lady* (London: Benn, 1927), 9.
9. Lyman Tower Sargent, "The Pessimistic Eutopias of H. G. Wells," *The Wellsian: Selected Essays on H. G. Wells*, edited by John S. Partington (Oss, the Netherlands: Equilibris, 2003), 199. Later parenthetical page references are to this edition.
10. In his essay Sargent also discusses Wells's long short story, "A Story of the Days to

Come" (1897), and his non-fictional works, *The Great State* (1912), *The Open Conspiracy* (1928), and *Mind at the End of Its Tether* (1945).

11. See Partington, "*The Time Machine* and *A Modern Utopia*: The Static and Kinetic Utopias of the Early H. G. Wells," *Utopian Studies*, 13.1 (2002), 57.

12. The phrase comes from Sargent, 215, note 1, although on the same page Sargent explains that he prefers a broader definition of utopia: "The words utopia, eutopia and dystopia mean no place, good place and bad place respectively. The first two words were coined by Thomas More in the book we call Utopia.... Utopia is most often used to mean 'a non-existent good place' but at time[s] keeping the distinction is useful. Dystopia is a twentieth century coinage."

13. Krishan Kumar, *Utopia and Anti-Utopia in Modern Times* (Oxford: Blackwell, 1991), 187. Later parenthetical page references are to this edition.

14. See, for example, Kumar, 205–219, and Peter Beilharz, *Labour's Utopias: Bolshevism, Fabianism, Social Democracy* (London: Routledge, 1993), 75–83. Later parenthetical page references to Beilharz are to this edition.

15. See Partington, "*The Time Machine* and *A Modern Utopia*," 63.

16. Huxley defined "ethical evolution" in his 1893 lecture, "Evolution and Ethics" (*Evolution and Ethics, 1893–1943*, by T. H. Huxley and Julian Huxley [London: Pilot, 1947]), as the replacement of the notion of the "survival of the fittest" with the "fitting of as many as possible to survive" (81–82).

17. Patrick Parrinder, *Shadows of the Future: H. G. Wells, Science Fiction and Prophecy* (Liverpool: Liverpool University Press, 1995), 96. Later parenthetical page references are to this edition.

18. See Partington, "*The Time Machine* and *A Modern Utopia*," 65.

19. Wells, "About Sir Thomas More," *An Englishman Looks at the World: Being a Series of Unrestrained Remarks upon Contemporary Matters* (London: Cassell, 1914), 183–187.

20. W. Warren Wagar, "The Road to Utopia: H. G. Wells's *Open Conspiracy*," *The Wellsian*, 23 (2000), 17, 16. Later parenthetical page references are to this edition.

21. Richard Nate, "Scientific Utopianism in Francis Bacon and H. G. Wells: From *Salomon's House* to *The Open Conspiracy*," *Critical Review of International Social and Political Philosophy*, 3:2–3 (Summer/Autumn 2000), 172–173. Later parenthetical page references are to this edition.

22. For two detailed studies of Wells's world-state thinking, see Wagar, *H. G. Wells and the World State* (New Haven, CT: Yale University Press, 1961), and Partington, *Building Cosmopolis: The Political Thought of H. G. Wells* (Aldershot, UK: Ashgate, 2003).

23. Wells, *Anticipations of the Reaction of Mechanical and Scientific Progress upon Human Life and Thought* (Mineola, NY: Dover, 1999), 138–156.

24. Wells, *In the Fourth Year: Anticipations of a World Peace* (London: Chatto & Windus, 1918), 1–111.

25. See Partington, *Building Cosmopolis,* 101–125, 149–178.

26. Wells, *The Common Sense of War and Peace: World Revolution or War Unending* (Harmondsworth, UK: Penguin, 1940), 56.

27. See Partington, "The Death of the Static," for a full elaboration of Wells's application of Huxleyan evolutionary theory to the construction of modern utopias.

28. *The Open Conspiracy* was first published in 1928 and revised in 1930, 1931 (under the title *What Are We To Do With Our Lives?*) and 1933 (when it was again titled *The Open Conspiracy*).

29. In an important essay on Wells's reception in Nazi Germany, "Ignorance, Opportunism, Propaganda and Dissent: The Reception of H. G. Wells in Nazi Germany" (*The Reception of H. G. Wells in Europe,* edited by Patrick Parrinder and John S. Partington [London: Thoemmes Continuum, 2005], 105–125), Nate has shown that while Wells's books were banned by the Nazis, he continued to be studied in German universities, and the

resulting doctoral dissertations all focused on his utopianism, looking in particular at Wells's Fabian socialism and his advocacy of eugenics.

30. Wagar, "Critical Introduction," *The Open Conspiracy: H. G. Wells on World Revolution,* edited by Wagar (Westport, CT: Praeger, 2002), 3.

11. The Alien Eye: Imperialism and Otherness in H. G. Wells's *The First Men in the Moon*

Gareth Davies-Morris

In the "imaginative spree"[1] of *The First Men in the Moon* (1901), H. G. Wells weaves a spectacular narrative that has become an archetype of SF, combining a substantial number of the genre's tropes: new technology, interplanetary voyages, exploring an alien world and culture, encountering (and battling) an alien race, and, in the book's most fundamental appeal, witnessing such hideous yet intriguing extraterrestrials up close. The story evolves from dizzying adventure to disturbing social criticism, as Wells sketches both a tentative utopia and what Jefferson Hunter labels "an allegory of the dangers of imperialism."[2] Patrick Parrinder perhaps summarizes the novel's qualities best when he observes, "Imaginatively *The First Men in the Moon* is polarised between grotesque satire and exploratory wonder, and both are realised in visionary form."[3]

In the story, Cavor, a brilliant but distracted scientist, develops a metal which is impervious to gravity. Aided by Bedford, a supremely confident bankrupt, he uses it to power a spacecraft in which the two voyage to the moon, where they end up prisoners of the underground-dwelling Selenites. Though they eventually fight their way back to the surface, Cavor is injured and recaptured, and Bedford must return to earth alone, where he accidentally loses the sphere. A few months later he receives word that an amateur radio scientist named Julius Wendigee, something of a Marconi-Tesla hybrid, has intercepted Morse signals from Cavor, which recount his experiences in and observations of the Selenite culture, "a master civilisation organised on ruthlessly rational lines" (Parrinder 31).

Otherness

Though encountering few situations in which they confuse the aliens with humans, the explorers must often ask themselves if the races are equivalent intellectually, which Prendick of *The Island of Dr. Moreau* (1897) only has to consider when he returns to human society and falls prey to paranoia. Wells's dialectical ambiguity is reflected in the contradictory behavior that the two explorers exhibit. Cavor is in favor of the moon-dwellers as sentient, therefore reachable, beings and believes in reasoning with them, yet he shatters the original uneasy stand-off with a drunken charge. On the other hand, Bedford is biased against them on principle yet tries to imagine their alien perspective. Although the men make a clear distinction, they argue sharply about the merits of it. How would human beings behave under such circumstances, and do the Selenites fit the paradigm? If so, are such similarities coincidence or viable comparisons? Chained in their underground prison, Cavor encourages furthering communication:

> "Of course they are minds and we are minds — there must be something in common. Who knows how far we may not get to an understanding?"
>
> "The things are outside us," I said. "...They are a different clay. What is the good of talking like this?"
>
> Cavor thought.... "But these machines and clothing! No, I don't hold with you, Bedford. The difference is wide —"
>
> "It's insurmountable."
>
> "The resemblance must bridge it."[4]

His closing comment defines the purpose of Wells's dialectic, to connect opposing sides. One is separate from those that one considers different or dangerous, and the only solution to the resulting hostility of such stalemate is to seek common ground and compromise. Cavor looks to the Selenite gear and inventions as a starting point for communication, as such artifacts prove intelligence, an abstraction that raises the possibility of spanning the gulf of Otherness that aliens represent.

Bedford, however, rejects such a possibility, insisting that the only racial similarities will be negative and defensive. He argues that Cavor may be right in the abstract to hold that the Selenites are similar as thinking beings, but that he is wrong to gamble their safety on an intellectual ideal, since self-preservation rather than respect for fellow intelligence will probably be the racial commonality. He and Cavor will be viewed as dangerous beasts, he insists, and will be killed before any Selenite intellectuals hear of them. As the book often implies, one only has to look at interracial conflict on this planet to see the truth in his logic: human groups have clashed in tribal conflict upon contact more often than they have meshed peaceably.

Cavor is undeterred and continues searching beneath the seeming opposition to find a fundamental similarity that could be the basis for understanding, and his striving fits Wells's pattern of concrete oppositions becoming abstract. Cavor progresses from evaluating the Selenite machines and clothing, the exterior signs of civilization, to considering the possibility of semiotic communication through universally understood geometrical patterns and theorems. With fitting ironic reversal, however, he instead discovers a shared understanding in the less intellectual channel of gesture. Though one of their captors signals for them to eat and to get up and follow him, Cavor's own signs of interest in the alien machinery are rudely curtailed by a jab from a cattle prod, methods of communication that he assesses as primitive but effective: "They begin with the elements of life and not of thought," he speculates. "Food. Compulsion. Pain. They strike at fundamentals" (79). Gesture also works later, when the captured Cavor feels encouraged by the "organized deliberation" (110) of the Selenite officers.

Reciprocal attempts at understanding through such fundamental methods fail at the narrow bridge into the depths of the Selenite world, at which the men balk for fear of plummeting to their deaths. Cavor wants to take gesture to its extreme and simply refuse to move, requiring the Selenites to carry them, but an infuriated Bedford, after shouting unintelligible thus useless threats, breaks free and kills several Selenites, wielding his gold chains with superior strength. After they have made their escape, Kathryn Hume notes, his indifference about murdering "non–British sentients is rebuked by Cavor, who is shocked by Bedford's slaughter of [the] Selenites."[5] The carnage leads Cavor to morose agreement with Bedford's original prediction that they would become hunted animals, and upon reaching the surface he concludes that the possibility of a truce is now "about as good as a tiger's that has got loose and killed a man in Hyde Park" (103). As Anne Simpson shows, by defining an opponent as the Other in this way, any progression beyond confrontation becomes next to impossible:

> Wells posits the inevitable outcome of simplified perceptions of the Other in acts that entail either extreme isolation or violent aggression, or both. Both forms of behaviour are barren means of response, for the [opponents] ... remain thus locked in a circle of reactions, from which escape is possible only through death.[6]

By attacking rather than communicating, Bedford, like the drunken Cavor earlier, reduces their survival chances by reducing the possible common ground with the Other. This mistake is made equally by Prendick, Graham, and the rest of Wells's protagonists; they all end up trapped or isolated, their potential allies turned absolute enemies out of a mutual refusal to seek understanding. Their error and the dilemma that precedes it then reflect out of the text to confront the reader.

Dreams of Empire

"The real theme of *The First Men in the Moon*," Jefferson Hunter states, "is the destruction of innocence and the corruption by greed intimately associated with European colonialism."[7] Drawing comparisons to Joseph Conrad's *Heart of Darkness,* Hunter notes that when Cavor and Bedford land on the moon, what they find is "astonishingly like Africa, like the Congo," and "in this lunar version of a tropical landscape, Bedford is obsessed by thoughts of empire-building."[8] That is certainly the main issue satirized in one of the book's comic highlights, the "psilocybin" scene that leads to drunken confrontation. Shortly after he becomes intoxicated by lunar mushrooms, Bedford, forgetting that Cavor and he are at present helpless and in hiding, declares their natural superiority to these aliens, and their noble purpose in coming to the moon:

> In some way that I have now forgotten my mind was led back to projects of colonisation. "We must annex this moon," I said. "There must be no shilly-shally. This is part of the White Man's Burden. Cavor — we are — *hic* — Satap — mean Satraps! Nempire Caesar never dreamt. B'in all the newspapers. Cavorecia. Bedfordecia. Bedfordecia. *Hic* — Limited. Mean — unlimited! Practically" [63].

With this "blunt, hiccupping burlesque of Kipling (and Cecil Rhodes)," as Frank McConnell dubs it,[9] Bedford claims that if ignorant non-whites were in need of Caucasian supervision, then ignorant Selenites could be as well. With a clever binary structure, Wells points out the ludicrousness of that justification for European colonialism by applying it to a race of aliens who are unlikely candidates for Christian conversion, Occidental jurisprudence, etiquette lessons, or any other supposedly civilizing influence. This serves to remind the reader that imperialists not only made such claims in earnest but regarded primitive peoples as inhuman and therefore not due the ethical considerations given more civilized nations. "To the empire builders," Hume observes, "killing Africans or Indians was not 'really' murder; they were Other and hence less than truly human."[10] Though the author certainly "mocks the violent colonizing imperative," as Roger Luckhurst puts it,[11] Bedford doesn't turn murderous until he is captured and sees how misplaced his assumptions of superiority were. Nonetheless, he uses the rationale of Rhodes and other would-be kings to defend his ambitions, at least until stupor silences him:

> I embarked upon an argument to show the infinite benefits our arrival would confer upon the moon. I involved myself in a rather difficult proof that the arrival of Columbus was, after all, beneficial to America. I found I had forgotten the line of argument I had intended to pursue, and continued to repeat "sim'lar to C'lumbus" to fill up time [63].

His rhetoric epitomizes the anti-imperialist satire of *Moon* by its inability to clarify such supposed benefits — hardly surprising, given that even stone-cold sober, a person would find it difficult to justify the destruction of the great Aztec and Inca civilizations and the decimation of the whole range of American Indian tribal cultures.

Though Bedford grasps the historical importance of two races meeting, at this moment, he can't even express his pragmatic (if mercenary) goals of annexation and mineral exploitation, let alone be an ambassador or diplomat, so the great encounter is more silly than significant. Announcing that they will tolerate "no nonsense from any confounded insects" and deeming it unmanly to skulk "upon a mere satellite" (63), they break cover and barge into a whole squad of Selenite shepherds:

> They all seemed to become aware of us at once, all instantly became silent and motionless like animals, with their faces towards us.
> For a moment I was sobered.
> "Insects," murmured Cavor, "insects!— and they think I'm going to crawl on about on my stomach — on my vertebrated stomach!"
> "Stomach," he repeated, slowly, as though he chewed the indignity.
> Then suddenly, with a sort of fury, he made three vast strides and leaped towards them. He leaped badly; he made a series of somersaults in the air, whirled right over them, and vanished with an enormous splash amidst the cactus bladders. What the Selenites made of this amazing, and to my mind undignified, irruption from another planet, I have no means of guessing.... I was, I am certain, suddenly and vehemently ill [64].

By their drunken belligerence, Bedford and his fellow pioneer reduce their initial close encounter of the third kind to farce. Their declarations further mock imperialist claims by presuming a moon — and, by extension, its inhabitants — to be inferior to a planet, and they are guilty of an exaggerated racism in their responses to the Selenites. Bedford describes the aliens unhesitatingly as animals, more a herd of deer than a platoon of potential equals. As for Cavor, his vertebrate pride may be amusing in its obscurity, but his furious charge is humorous only in its failure, and the comic scene that reveals his bias and belligerence recurs in bloody earnestness once the men are taken underground.

By criticizing imperialism in *Moon* (and in *The War of the Worlds*, which preceded it in 1898), Wells intended to jangle the nerves of his contemporaries, as he wrote in response to European colonial policies at the time. However, as he may well have imagined, his insights are still relevant to the future, and that future is now here. For example, racism towards non-humans — speciesism — is considered a legitimate issue among animal rights activists, while Bedford's "rather difficult proof" involving Columbus anticipates the reassessment of colonialism's impact on the New World.

More relevant, perhaps, the ethical problems that his assumptions raise are still applicable to the stronger, wealthier nations of the West, who see the developing world as a market and a dumping ground and who export their policies and social standards there by cultural imperialism and globalization, insidious means of a kind of neo-colonization that overwhelm more absolutely than military conquest. With his reductive view of the moon as his alone to exploit, Bedford is an avatar of this elitist approach to profiteering. Therefore, as McConnell notes, "linked explicitly with Bedford's dreams of avarice, Wells's frequent references to and criticisms of the idea of imperialism [become] ... particularly mordant" (156).

Dreams of Reason

Cavor's observations on lunar society, which Bedford receives and edits after his return to Earth, are presented in another binary opposition. What one might call his guided tour of the Selenite city is both a classic SF alien encounter and, by implication, a satirical critique of turn-of-the-century industrial society. In turn, his meetings with the Grand Lunar, the dramatic climax of his transmitted coda, critique that society directly. Cavor discovers during his extended encounter that the lunar inhabitants are as different from humans as can be imagined, physically if not always psychologically. Charlotte Sleigh details such differences and connects the novel with Wells's myrmecological horror story from 1905, "The Empire of the Ants":

> The Selenites ... are without a doubt based on ants.... Like ants, they live in an underground colony and have different castes and even "mooncalves"— many ants kept aphids which were popularly known as ant cows.... In *First Men*, Wells exploits the huge grotesqueness of ant-like creatures, employing enlargement to create horror ... rather than use the effect of massed small creatures as he does in the "Empire."[12]

Bedford and Cavor, according to John Huntington, "represent two extremes of individualistic ethic opposed to the Selenite hive" or colony,[13] which, embodied in the Grand Lunar, is the ultimate command economy. As an evolved insect rather than a highly specialized ape, the Selenites live within a communal rather than an individualistic society. They have developed a World State rather than a poorly interlocking jigsaw of nations, and they control every aspect of their natural environment, rather than remain as its mercy. Despite their polemical initial positions, Cavor and the Selenites converge and reverse over the series of issues that he raises, which makes the reader consider the possibilities of both systems yet often be unable to choose one over the other.

Artificially increasing natural diversity through an aggressive eugenic program, the Selenites have created a specialized race, with different brain and body types for particular jobs, each citizen becoming "a perfect unit in a world machine" (143), Cavor recounts viewing "a number of young Selenites, confined in jars from which only the fore limbs protruded, who were being compressed to become machine-minders of a special sort" (145). "Here," Parrinder observes, Wells is "showing the deterministic world at its most oppressive point, in the violation and compression of the plastic young individual" (32). Having detailed their shaping process, Cavor announces his ambivalence towards the practice:

> It is quite unreasonable, I know, but these glimpses of the educational methods of these beings have affected me disagreeably.... That wretched-looking hand sticking out of its jar seemed to appeal for lost possibilities; it haunts me still, although, of course, it is really in the end a far more humane proceeding than our earthly method of leaving children to grow into human beings, and then making machines of them [145].

Cavor's offhand doubts appear to signal his disapproval of such Draconian measures of ensuring conformity. In fact, the issue is not only unresolved but raises a highly central question about earthly social methods, as "the nightmare of Selenite shaping can still be called 'humane' in the face of ordinary human education" (Huntington 96). In a deft "piece of mental ju-jitsu," (Huntington 95), Wells makes the reader share his dialectical ambiguity by encouraging him to sympathize with the tortured alien, then asserting that the human situation is no better, only less obviously cruel — a quite effective model of deconstruction. Given the central presence in the science-fiction genre of such post-structuralist tropes as Otherness and difference (in both the conventional sense and the Derridean intent of delay and uncertainty in meaning), Veronica Hollinger states that it "may be that deconstructive activity of some kind is characteristic of all SF."[14] Certainly, the paradox of this scene speaks explicitly to how one responds to Wells's novel in total. "SF and deconstruction must speak from within the contexts which they seek to defamiliarize,"[15] after all, and Wells's science-fictional context puts the indeterminate issue front and center. Are we meant to sympathize with Cavor's entirely human/humane predicament, or are we meant to make a cold-blooded assessment of the practicality of the Selenite method? Must we distance or embrace the scene's unpleasant implications, or can we do both?

Samuel R. Delany frames nicely this extra level of complexity, and complicity in its own subversion, that SF brings to any such deconstructive reading:

> [When] you deconstruct ... a science fiction text, you indulge a very different operation from the one you indulge when you deconstruct a literary text, a text of naturalistic fiction, poetry, or philosophy.
>   In science fiction, the undecidable (or the deconstructable) is always organized around this question: Is the particular phrase you're trying to read closely a piece

of information telling you about the fictive subject, or is it a phrase telling you about the object structure of the fictive world?[16]

To apply this notion to *Moon*, Cavor's experience is either a key question of characterization or merely a passing detail of the story's fictional framework. Are we learning something about Cavor's morality in how he decides the right or wrong of the Selenite method, therefore, or are we simply receiving and absorbing the details of that method as part of the cultural integrity of the *heterotopia* that Wells invents? He is producing a higher order of art, undoubtedly, than most authors who built on his ground-breaking work to develop SF as a genre in the 20th century, but nonetheless Delany's distinction holds. In more traditional literature, "the implied irony would always float on the surface of the text, a commentary upon it, but without ever becoming an element of the [text's] ... objective world."[17] In *Moon*, on the other hand, the irony *is* the objective world: we have to accept the totality of Wells's science-fictional construct, with all the details of Selenite civilization, however unpleasant. Wells gives us the same choice that Cavor gets, therefore, and we have to debate it, at least, if we take the art seriously.

We encounter more indeterminacy — or *undecidability*, to adapt Delany's term — when Cavor expresses further ambivalence for what the Selenite order represents, this time addressing the treatment, rather than the training, of the worker. On one of their many walks, Cavor and his guide Phi-oo, the Selenite administrator, take a shortcut through a cavern crowded with inert laborers, whose fate mystifies the human until informed that they are kept in drugged sleep until needed again:

> "Dead?" I asked. For as yet I have seen no dead in the moon, and I have grown curious.
> "*No!*" exclaimed Phi-oo. "Him — worker — no work to do. Get little drink then — make sleep — till we him want. What good him wake, eh? No want him walking about" [145–146].

Cavor questions Phi-oo's logic, but only after being struck by the human-like posture of the sleeping figure he first sees. His reaction is a comment on how the Other is perceived, as the misleading appearance of the creature both encourages Cavor's sympathies and embodies his contradictory attitudes. The "disturbing sight," Parrinder points out, is "followed by the reflexion that perhaps this is more humane than condemning" redundant Selenite workers (32). Involving a human, Cavor reasons, such treatment is unacceptable; involving the Other, it is a necessary evil. Once the idea is broached, however, Cavor considers its human implications anyway:

> To drug the worker one does not want and toss him aside is surely far better than to expel him from his factory to wander starving in the streets. In every

complicated social community there is necessarily a certain intermittency in the occupation of all specialised labour, and in this way the trouble of an unemployed problem is altogether anticipated. And yet, so unreasonable are even scientifically trained minds, I still do not like the memory of those prostrate forms amidst those quiet, luminous arcades of fleshy growth, and I avoid that short cut in spite of the inconveniences of its longer, more noisy, and more crowded alternative [146].

As before, there is considerable irony in Cavor's conclusion and one can make the same argument over its indeterminacy. With SF, in such deconstructive moments, the "rhetorical quality is suddenly foregrounded," Delany writes. "The ideas and ignorances it allows us to slide over and slip across are brought sharply to the fore."[18] Cavor sees first the brutal pragmatism of the Selenite method and then its ruthless lack of compassion. Consequently, he deprecates himself for letting his well-schooled mind be swayed by emotion, which implies that science should be emotionless yet shows via the Selenites the dangers of what happens if it is. Finally, he avoids resolving the dilemma by avoiding a physical confrontation with it, which shows that he recognizes its undecidability — as do both author and reader: neither Cavor, nor we, can rationalize the conflicting Selenite and human policies and our conflicting emotions about them.

However, in Hollinger's words, there is "no vantage point outside the boundaries of the observable, no privileged observer, no completely innocent reading of 'reality.'"[19] Like Cavor, readers have to ponder this moral quandary and its corollary, "What if it happened here?" We can't just skip over the question or answer it by saying, "We wouldn't allow it here, hence we have no problem if it happens there," when that human parallel is exactly the issue that Wells is raising. Unlike Cavor, we are not allowed the luxury of avoidance — our own "more crowded alternative" — as Wells keeps adding equally undecidable examples of Selenite culture, a dialectical strategy that forces us to face the contradictions that Huntington expertly codifies:

> The satire works by playing off against each other two unsatisfactory alternatives. Against [a] frighteningly regulated society Wells sets a callously unconcerned one, in which the citizen is also brutalized, but only after he has dreamt of better possibilities. Against total specialization from birth, he sets casual and inefficient education which requires Procrustean measures later. Against what is in effect a blatant class system, he sets a concealed class system [95].

What is the greater evil, Wells asks: being unemployed and aware of such failure, or being shaped (in every sense) by greater powers and accepting the role that they have chosen for you? A state can either structure its work force so as to prevent idle hands and wasted skills, or it can refuse to limit individuals to assigned careers when they are uniformly capable of all, even if such independence pays off in suffering and failure. This is the paradox of capitalism that Wells voices through Cavor, admiring the human race's anarchic individualism but at the same time seeing it as an evolutionary hindrance and the industrialized world, where cooperative efforts are kept within the group to the detriment of those outside, as its worst manifestation. Despite their unpleasant methods, the Selenite achievements illustrate the advantages of reversing that trend and establishing one group and one goal.

However, such achievements are as paradoxical as human individualism, further illustrating Well's ambivalence. Parrinder observes that the novel "presents a totalitarian state ... so regulated that it eliminates all freedom and spontaneous growth" (32). The Selenites have resolved their social problems and developed a stable and permanent society by repressing virtually all dissent and cultural change. Variation aplenty exists, but only in jobs and physical appearance, while personalities are uniform in their acceptance of place and rank. Wells then reverses positions again, suggesting the potential for change even in this totalitarian paradise. As in Earthly dictatorships, the seeds of opposition exist within the educated, skilled classes, in the ranks of the administrators like Phi-oo, who are required by necessity to have some sense of initiative and ingenuity. Nothing else explains the Grand Lunar's muscular police, except to "order any erring tendency there might be in some aberrant natures" (145).

The alternative route that Cavor must traverse teems with Selenite females, whose way of life is one of several elements of lunar civilization that, as Parrinder notes, "Wells attacks ... with a two-way irony also aimed at the society of his own day" (32). Like his previous comments on colonialism, while Wells's implications here carry considerable relevance for a modern reader, they are more meant for his contemporaries. Hence, one first sees this passage as a social satire on the spoiled young heiresses and society matrons of Cavor's (hence Wells's) world, whose life of ease and irresponsibility, including in their parenting duties, is contrasted with the servants, nursemaids, and governesses who do the real work. In a mocking parallel between Selenite and Victorian-Edwardian culture, the lunar females are given the same two destinies. They become either pampered idiots who make indifferent mothers and, in direct contrast to the hyper-intelligent males, possess "almost microscopic heads" (146), or neutered nurses who do the parenting and "who in some cases possess brains of almost masculine dimensions" (147).

In effect, the categories make two sides of a single being and reflect the lunar tendency towards specialization and direction, with the perfect childbearing body giving birth to infants who are then raised by the sufficiently brainy surrogate mothers. Cavor reacts to the former with ambivalence, admiring "the mothers of the moon-world" (146) as being "beautifully fitted to bear the larval Selenite" (147) yet commenting that they are "absolutely incapable of cherishing the young" (147) due to their selfish, capricious natures. Both his inconsistency there and his genuine surprise at the nurses' near-equivalence to males in intelligence mock the human assumption of women's inferiority and reinforce the earlier contradiction of the humane, intelligent scientist falling prey to bias and chauvinism.

More substantially, however, the Selenite approach may offer a better reproductive strategy. First, by selecting those who would be parents the human race could avoid this haphazard permitting of its least responsible elements to reproduce, and from there establish a eugenic paradigm of those who should. Second, allowing the state to manage the parenting process would also decrease the problem of parents whose "periods of foolish indulgence alternate with moods of aggressive violence" (147) towards their helpless charges, then as now a commonplace abuse in human society. Third, Cavor reveals the issue's indeterminacy, its deconstructive undecidability, by pointing out that "in our cities there are many who never live that life of parentage that is the natural life of man" (147), meaning that women are already forced by societal pressure to follow the Selenite pattern of dividing female roles.

Because "deconstructing the science fiction text takes us into entirely different historical (and ideological) questions,"[20] Cavor's observations (and thus, dialogically, those of Wells) once again confound readers with their implications. We may find the Selenite method abhorrent but then, excepting its extremes, come grudgingly around to its principle of controlled breeding. Though Wells wrote before genetic science and new reproductive technologies introduced greater bioethical dilemmas, his eugenic paradigm remains relevant, particularly in today's overcrowded and environmentally overtaxed planet. Whoever pursues his logic must acknowledge that such division has always existed here, albeit in a far cruder and unbeneficial form, and conclude that our species is wasting its maternal resources by not harnessing and channeling them into some sort of positive eugenics that would suit our nature, such as the contraceptive use and endowed motherhood that Wells supported in books like *Anticipations* and *A Modern Utopia*. On the other hand, the whole labor-eugenics element of *Moon* is central to the satire of Wellsian utopias in Huxley's "nightmare future" of *Brave New World*, as McConnell notes (158), with its Bokanovsky process, its hatcheries and decanting chambers, and its series of biologically engineered grades of human skill and intellectual ability. Unsurprisingly, Huntington observes, Wells wants it both ways: "Selenite training would be morally offensive in human society; probably it is biologically impossible; but nevertheless it represents an emblem of 'admirable social order' that Wells cannot help but find attractive" (96).

The Grand Lunar

Wells has the indirect criticism of human society couched in Cavor's observations lead to the direct criticism leveled at him by his alien Intellectual Antagonist, the Grand Lunar. In a spoken replaying of the ceremonial procession that precedes their meeting, they progress through levels of discourse that escalate in complexity of subject but center on war, the most irrational of human activities. "The interview does not go well," (160) McConnell concludes. The Grand Lunar, acting as an alien dialogical mouthpiece for Wells, always sees contradictions in human behavior which Cavor is at a loss to refute and which lead him to make worse errors when trying to correct himself.

Their discussion is entirely utopian in its content and implications. Wells commences by cleverly planting the seed of an Earthly world state when he has the Grand Lunar presume that it already exists; thus the alien leader is surprised to find out that what he took to be simply administrative zones are, in fact, separate nations, as Cavor explains. The scientist is then revealed as an optimistic Utopian himself, with his allusions to the human race being "still not united in one brotherhood" and our "States and Empires ... still the rawest sketches of what order will some day be" (156). The Grand Lunar continues this implied suggestion of global unification by noting the paradoxical nature of human relations inherent in the use of different languages:

> The Grand Lunar was greatly impressed by the folly of men in clinging to the inconvenience of diverse tongues. "They want to communicate and yet not to communicate," he said, and then for a long time he questioned me closely concerning war [157].

After this cogent observation, he goes on to marvel at the waste of human energy involved in fighting rather than cooperating to exploit our world:

> He was at first perplexed and incredulous. "You mean to say," he asked, seeking confirmation, "that you run about over the surface of your world — this world whose riches you have scarcely begun to scrape — killing one another for beasts to eat?"
> I told him that was perfectly correct [157].

The Grand Lunar wants examples, which Cavor evidently is too generous in supplying:

> He asked for particulars to assist his imagination. "But do not your ships and your poor little cities get injured?" he asked, and I found the waste of property and conveniences seemed to impress upon him almost as much as the killing. "Tell me more," said the Grand Lunar; "make me see pictures. I cannot conceive these things" [157].

The alien's closing comment not only defines the gulf that Cavor only widens but clearly models Jean-Francois Lyotard's concept of the *différend*, or irresolvable quarrel (as paraphrased by Bill Readings):

A *différend* ... is a dispute between at least two radically heterogeneous or incommensurable language games, where no one rule can be invoked in terms of which to pass judgement, since that rule necessarily belongs to one language or another.[21]

Despite their surface similarities as the most rational and dispassionate exponents of their respective races, they still have no real common ground, share no reference or experience that would give them a basis for agreement. Cavor may be well-intended but doesn't realize how poorly he is presenting the human race, and the Grand Lunar sees only behavior incomprehensible to his social and biological order. Cavor has no ready answers and is soon reduced to strutting jingoism and feeble humor in his attempts to justify the folly of war. Given that he had earlier expounded lucidly to Bedford on its pointlessness, his rhetorical abilities fail him strangely here. In another *différend*, at the moment when he should appear most rational, acting as he does as ambassador for his race, he chooses to recount the violent, militaristic nature of humanity, of our love of battle and conquest, to the Selenites' shocked confusion:

"But surely they do not like it!" translated Phi-oo.
I assured them men of my race considered battle the most glorious experience of life, at which the whole assembly was stricken with amazement.
"But what good is this war?" asked the Grand Lunar, sticking to his theme.
"Oh! as for *good!*" said I, "it thins the population!"
"But why should there be a need —?"
There came a pause, the cooling sprays impinged upon his brow, and then he spoke again....
[He] interrogated me very closely upon my secret [157–158].

Unsurprisingly, the scene serves its author two-fold: Wells foreshadows Cavor's impending execution and establishes a forum from which to ridicule the martial passions that so inflame our race. By presenting no rationale behind human conflict, by ignoring ideological, cultural, or religious differences that only force might resolve, Cavor gives the Grand Lunar a glaringly one-sided view of human life that the alien takes as a glimpse into a lunatic asylum that must be kept locked up. In his commentary, Bedford assesses the results of his colleague's naiveté:

He had talked of war, he had talked of all the strength and irrational violence of men, of their insatiable aggressions, their tireless futility of conflict. He had filled the whole moon-world with this impression of our race, and then I think it is plain he admitted that upon himself alone hung the possibility — at least for a long time — of other men reaching the moon. The line the cold, inhuman reason of the moon would take seems plain enough to me ... [159].

Even if Cavor were to find plausible motives for the practice, the Grand Lunar's inexorable logic has already superseded them, reducing war and another of humanity's greatest problems, overpopulation, to the ridiculous tragedies that they are. Humans fight over resources yet waste more than they save in the struggle for them; and in a vicious circle, they breed to excess so must fight their numbers down. Though the Grand Lunar acknowledges that we humans "had mastered much in spite of our social savagery" (156), he can only accept the evidence that Cavor's species is warlike to insane extremes, and that the one man to have bridged their worlds is the sole possessor of the means of doing so, the Cavorite formula. The Grand Lunar completes the syllogism, Bedford later assumes: Cavor must die to ensure no further contact with such a dangerous race. Once more reversing the well-established alien perspective, the Grand Lunar's decision shows that Selenites are similar to humans after all, at least in their motives; they act out of self-preservation, the most shared behavior between species.

Conclusions: Dreams of Heaven

For Bedford and Cavor, and by design Wells's readers, the Selenite world offers an ambivalent contrast to that of Earth, one meant to inspire the ongoing reflection that the author felt must precede the attainment of any Utopia. While he advocated some Selenite-style goals under certain conditions, the Selenite model is not meant to suggest how human society might progress, if that means applying their methods literally, as critics such as Huxley and George Orwell thought. Being a different species, humans cannot be treated like Selenites; their extreme methods could only work here if they were adapted to suit the characteristics of *homo sapiens*. For example, their unified social order could be adopted here. Its benefits are plain: work for all, in posts that satisfy the employees; little waste of resources, due to the removal of speculation and economic competition; and a total absence of war and the cultural confrontations that spark it.

Bernard Bergonzi believes that in a different context, aspects of Selenite civilization would meet with Wells's approval (as paraphrased by Parrinder 32). However, Wells doesn't so much argue for Selenite-style eugenics on Earth as propose a radically different sort of human being. The world's selfishly independent-minded population cannot be physically remolded or conditioned to fit a system the way the Selenites are, yet it may be slowly refined by the kind of virtuous controlled breeding Wells proposes in *A Modern Utopia* (1905) and then polished by intense education.[22] Over generations this less radical method could produce people improved in health, intelligence, ability, and culture without resulting in the surgical and psychological violence used by the Selenites (or by Moreau, on a scientifically implausible level). The polarized nature of capitalist society could thus be redirected into a unified and inspired civilization able to overcome the human race's evolutionary destiny of being ground to extinction by the vast machine that is the cosmos. With the Selenite system, Wells takes a step towards finding a way to avoid that fate. Therefore, rather than closing the dialectic by offering a plan that he would insist his fellows accept, he inspires it instead by furnishing a model of a successful society, even if one fraught with problematic, undecidable implications about itself and our own world.

Notes

1. H. G. Wells, "Preface," *The Works of H. G. Wells*, Atlantic edition, Volume VI (London: T. Fisher Unwin, 1925), ix.

2. Jefferson Hunter, *Edwardian Fiction* (Cambridge, MA: Harvard University Press, 1982), 119.

3. Patrick Parrinder, *H. G. Wells* (Edinburgh, Scotland: Oliver and Boyd, 1970), 35. Later parenthetical page references are to this edition.

4. H. G. Wells, *The First Men in the Moon* (1901; New York: Ballantine, n.d.), 70–71. Later parenthetical page references are to this edition.

5. Kathryn Hume, "Eat or Be Eaten: H. G. Wells's *Time Machine*," *Philological Quarterly,* 69:2 (1990), 236.

6. Anne B. Simpson, "The 'Tangible Antagonist': H. G. Wells and the Discourse of Otherness," *Extrapolation,* 31 (1990), 138.

7. Hunter, 117.

8. Hunter, 119.

9. Frank McConnell, *The Science Fiction of H. G. Wells* (Oxford, UK: Oxford University Press, 1981), 156. Later parenthetical page references are to this edition.

10. Hume, 235.

11. Roger Luckhurst, *Science Fiction* (Cambridge, UK: Polity, 2005), 40.

12. Charlotte Sleigh, "Empire of the Ants: H. G. Wells and Tropical Entomology," *Science as Culture,* 10:1 (2001), 51.

13. John Huntington, *The Logic of Fantasy: H. G. Wells and Science Fiction* (New York: Columbia University Press, 1982), 87. Later parenthetical page references are to this edition.

14. Veronica Hollinger, "Deconstructing the Time Machine," *Science-Fiction Studies,* 14 (1987), 201.

15. Hollinger, 203.

16. Samuel R. Delany, "Some Real Mothers: An Interview," *Science Fiction Eye,* 1:3 (1988), 11.

17. Delany, 11.

18. Delany, 7.

19. Hollinger, 203.

20. Delany, 11.

21. Bill Readings, *Introducing Lyotard: Art and Politics* (London: Routledge, 1991), 118.

22. See Wells, *A Modern Utopia*, chapter 6, "Women in a Modern Utopia" (1905; Lincoln: University of Nebraska Press, 1967).

12. Killer Robots, Laws of Robotics, and Pernicious Humans

George Atkins

Killer Robots

The portable robot surgeon, RoSur, in Arthur C. Clarke and Gentry Lee's 1989 novel *Rama II*, kills General Borzov, the leader of the second expedition to the mysterious spaceship. In the 1984 movie *Runaway*, Ramsay, portrayed by Tom Selleck, deals with a homicidal robot and acid-spewing robo-spiders. Nanomachines, programmable virus-sized robots called nanobugs, or gobblers — strictly outlawed on earth, of course — kill Paul Savage, the founder and leader of Moonbase, in Ben Bova's 1996 novel *Moonrise*. In a 1997 text written by Software Engineering professor Richard Epstein, Robbie, named after Isaac Asimov's and others' science fiction robots, kills an assembly line worker in the part-fictional, part-factual account. The text is entitled *The Case of the Killer Robot: Stories about the Professional, Ethical, and Societal Dimensions of Computing.*

What is going wrong? Didn't Asimov provide the Laws of Robotics to protect humans from robots? Killer robots, fictional and non-fictional, and laws of robotics are discussed in the following pages. Consideration of the preciousness of humans in killer robot scenarios is included.[1]

Robots and Robotics

Robots have been a source of inspiration for many science fiction writers. Asimov, of course, reigns supreme in considering the behavior of robots when interacting with humans and vice versa. He was one of the first writers to consider robots as machines designed by engineers rather than "pseudo-men created by blasphemers" such as Frankenstein and Rossum who destroyed their creators.[2] His robot writings were primarily an exercise in thinking through the ramifications of a design with the intent to devise rules that would provide reliable control over semiautonomous machines. Asimov's influence on later robot science fiction writers and on the field of robotics engineering is profound.

The term "robot" derives from the Czech word *robota*, meaning "forced labor." It was first used by the playwright Karel Čapek in a 1918 short story and later in his 1921 play *R.U.R.*, which stood for *Rossum's Universal Robots*. Engineers in the 1950s readily appropriated the term to refer to machines controlled by computer programs. The term "robotics," first used by Asimov in the early 1940s, refers to the "science and art involving both artificial intelligence (to reason) and mechanical [and electrical] engineering (to perform physical acts suggested by reason)." A robot can be considered to be either a computer-enhanced machine or a computer with sophisticated input and output devices. The distinction between computers and robots has become increasingly arbitrary.

Many industrial and most science fiction robots resemble humans either in physical form or in some variety of actions and reactions. The relationships between humans and Robbie, the robot of Asimov's short story, at times appear almost intimate. Movie and TV robots whose personalities have been warmly received by viewers include Robby in *Forbidden Planet*, the Robot of the television series *Lost in Space* (1965–1968), R2-D2 and C-3PO in the *Star Wars* series, and Johnny 5 in *Short Circuit* (1986). Caliban, robot CBN-001, and Donald, robot DNL-111, in the trilogy *Isaac Asimov's Caliban* (1993), *Isaac Asimov's Inferno* (1994), and *Isaac Asimov's Utopia* (1996), written by Roger MacBride Allen, are quite human in appearance (except Caliban is red and Donald is blue). Each develops a close, trusting relationship with Sheriff, later Governor, Alvar Kresh, the human hero in Allen's novels.

Human characters seem to develop affection for robots in many of Asimov's stories. In the future, will humanity develop similar relationships with robots in fact as they have in fiction? Research indicates that, although humans don't develop much warmth for industrial robots or ATM machines, there is a surprising degree of identification with computers and computer systems. Most of us talk *about*, and even *to* machines, as if they were people. Exclusively human characteristics are now being associated with computer systems that don't even exhibit typical robotic capabilities. When playing against a computer chess program, for example, we might say, "the computer decided to move the queen." Using the speed of recent computer systems and the modern heuristic computer programming techniques of artificial intelligence, it is now possible for machines to "learn" from their mistakes.[3] We can now talk to our computers by issuing commands and entering text using appropriate multimedia hardware and software and have them talk to us. Continuing technological advances will provide computer systems with human behavior and even, quoting a man interviewed by Sherry Turkle in *The Second Self: Computers and the Human Spirit* (1984), with a sort of a human spirit, "a soul" (194). Our reaction could well be one of affection — or possibly one of fear.

Laws of Robotics

Asimov, not the first to conceive of well-engineered, non-threatening robots, pursued the robot theme with such imagination and persistence that most of the ideas that have emerged in the robots of science fiction are identifiable in his stories. His Three Laws of Robotics were formulated in 1940 to ease human fear of robots and to cope with the potential for robots to harm people. Most of his robot stories involved situations where his laws come into conflict with each other or one of the laws is "weakened."

His original Laws of Robotics, first appearing in his fourth robot story "Runaround" are:

1— A robot may not injure a human being, or, through inaction, allow a human being to come to harm. [Notice the two parts of the law.]

2 — A robot must obey the orders given it by human beings except where such orders would conflict with the first law.

3 — A robot must protect its own existence as long as such protection does not interfere with the first or second law. [Notice the "first or second."][4]

All of Asimov's fictional robots were subjected to these laws by having them supplied with a "positronic brain" embedded with the three laws.[5] As a robot designer in Allen's *Isaac Asimov's Caliban* says, "the initial principles behind all three Laws derive from universal human morality ... the Three Laws are set down, burned into the very core of the positronic brain, as mathematical absolutes, without any grey areas or room for interpretation."[6] These laws are intuitively appealing. They are simple and straightforward, and embrace, as Asimov is quoted in "Evidence" (1946) as saying, "the essential guiding principles of a good many of the world's ethical systems."[7] The laws quickly attracted and retained the attention of science fiction writers and readers. Asimov himself wrote, "many writers of robot stories, without actually quoting the three laws, take them for granted, and expect the readers to do the same." He also says, "there was just enough ambiguity in the Three Laws to provide the conflicts and uncertainties required for new stories, and, to my great relief, it seemed always to be possible to think up a new angle out of the 61 words of the Three Laws."[8] These Laws of Robotics appear to ensure the continued dominion of humans over robots, and to preclude the use of robots for evil purposes.

In Asimov's many and imaginative robot stories, however, a large number of difficulties with the Three Laws arise. His stories indicated the laws revealed apparent inconsistencies, ambiguities, and uncertainties. His robots faced a great deal of complexity. Semantics created all sorts of difficulty, and, when unable to satisfy the demands of two equally powerful mandates, a robot was subject to "mental freeze-out," the dreaded deadlock of the real computing world. He decided that the robots required sufficient capabilities for judgment to enforce a higher order law that places the good of humanity above those of an individual while retaining a high value on individual human life. This led to a restatement of the Laws in his 1985 novel *Robots and Empire*. The three Laws were prefaced with a Zeroth Law.

> A robot may not injure humanity, or, through inaction, allow humanity to come to harm.[8]

His First, Second, and Third Laws simply added the constraint of violating the Zeroth Law.

> A robot may not injure a human being, or, through inaction, allow a human being to come to harm, unless this would violate the Zeroth Law of Robotics.
> A robot must obey the orders given it by human beings, except where such orders would conflict with the Zeroth or First Law.
> A robot must protect its own existence as long as such protection does not conflict with the Zeroth, First, or Second Law.[10]

With the introduction of the Zeroth Law, robots were increasingly required to deal with abstractions and philosophical issues. Quoting one of the robots in *Robots and Empire*, "It is difficult enough, when one must choose quickly, to decide which individual may suffer — or inflict — the greater harm. To choose between an individual and humanity, when you are not sure of what aspect of humanity you are dealing with, is so difficult that the very validity of Robotics Laws comes to be suspect. As soon as humanity in the abstract is introduced, the Laws of Robotics begin to merge with the Laws of Humanics — which may not even exist" (427).

In the 1983 novel, *The Robots of Dawn*, humans are the primary characters with robots holding important secondary roles. In the sequel *Robots and Empire*, however, robots dominate the story, and the humans have become bit players. The robots eventually conclude, "It is not sufficient to choose [between alternative humans or classes of humans] ... we must be able to shape" (428). Robot domination has become a theme of recent science fiction writing, with robots deciding to define the terms "human" and "humanity" to refer to themselves as well as to humans, and, ultimately, to themselves alone. In Clarke's *Rendezvous with Rama* (1973), for example, a civilization older than humanity consists of only biological robots whose sole function seems to be to keep Rama environmentally correct.

A 1993–1994 two-part paper entitled "Asimov's Laws of Robotics: Implications for Information Technology" was published by a New Zealand Computer Science professor in the prestigious *IEEE Computer* journal describing the many implications and concerns associated with our increasingly automated society. The author, Roger Clarke, details the implications of Asimov's Laws of Robotics and examines the design requirements necessary to effectively subject robotic behavior to the laws. He is primarily concerned that robotic architecture be designed so that the laws can effectively control a robot. He is also concerned that Asimov's laws fail to address the management of large numbers of robots and foresee the future existence of levels or hierarchies of robots with superordinate and subordinate robot relationships. An obvious possibility for the future is that robots manufacture and even supervise other robots. Clarke proposes an extended set of laws in an attempt to ensure appropriate robotic behavior in such an environment. His Extended Set of the Laws of Robotics is prefaced with a Meta-law.

Meta-Law: A robot may not act unless the actions are subject to the laws of Robotics.

The Zeroth through Third Laws are the same as Asimov's 1985 extended laws, except the Second and Third Laws now have two parts: one for humans and one for robots.

Zeroth Law: A robot may not injure humanity, or, through inaction, allow humanity to come to harm.

First Law: A robot may not injure a human being, or, through inaction, allow a human being to come to harm, unless this would violate a higher order law.

Second Law: (a) A robot must obey orders given it by human beings, except where such orders would conflict with a higher order law.

(b) A robot must obey orders given it by superordinate robots, except where such orders would conflict with a higher order law.

Third Law: (a) A robot must protect the existence of a superordinate robot as long as such protection does not conflict with a higher order law.

(b) A robot must protect its own existence as long as such protection does not conflict with a higher order law.

A Fourth Law restricting robot activity and a 5th "procreation" law are added:

Fourth Law: A robot must perform the duties for which it has been programmed, except where that would conflict with a higher order law.

Fifth Law: The Procreation Law: A robot may not take any part in the design, manufacture, or maintenance of a robot unless the new or modified robot's actions are subject to the Laws of Robotics [Part II 61].

Clarke acknowledges that any realistic set of design principles would have to be considerably more complex than his or Asimov's laws. He is also concerned that formulating any actual set of laws as a basis for engineering design would result in similar difficulties and would require a much more formal approach. "Such laws," he says, "would have to be based in ethics and human morality, not just in mathematics and engineering" (Part II 61–62).

No Law and New Law Robots

Ethical considerations have influenced the non-fictional discussion of robots and robotics. Gary Drescher of the MIT Artificial Intelligence Laboratory says, "We have the right to create this [robotic] life, but not the right to take our act lightly." Whereas the Laws of Robotics were written to protect humans against robots, Drescher proposes that we give equal protection to the machines.[11] Fredda Leving, the No Law and New Law robot designer of Allen's trilogy, strives for robots with freedom of action, creativity, and thoughtfulness. Caliban, the first No Law robot, seeks equality for all robots.

Ethical considerations of computing, hence robotics, is the primary thrust of *The Case of the Killer Robot* by Richard Epstein. This 1997 text by a software engineering professor provides a hilarious fictional account of everything that can go amiss in the development of large-scale software development projects. In the story, an assembly-line robot malfunctions and kills a worker. The lead computer programmer in the robot development project is arrested for manslaughter. The story, presented as a series of sensationalized newspaper articles, a talk radio show, a late night TV program, an article in a professional journal, and even an interview with a philosopher and a theologian, progresses, with much intrigue, from that point. It provides interesting insight into the ethics of computing.[12] An account of a Software Design Issues seminar based on the text can be found in my paper "The Virtual Killer Robot: Experiences with a Web-based Course."[13]

Roger MacBride Allen pursues the ethics of robots that do not satisfy Asimov's Three Laws of Robotics in his trilogy of No Law and New Law robots (*Isaac Asimov's Caliban, Isaac Asimov's Inferno,* and *Isaac Asimov's Utopia*). The robots in these stories have gravitronic brains, rather than the positronic brains of the Three Law robots. Quoting one of the robot designers in *Isaac Asimov's Inferno,* "It was light-years ahead of the positronic in processing speed and capacity. Better still, it did not have the Three Laws burned into its every molecule, cluttering things up."[14] In the first novel, *Isaac Asimov's Caliban,* an experimental robot is created. Caliban has no guilt or conscience and no knowledge of or compassion for humanity. The robot escapes the laboratory and is left to its own devices to discover and establish its own laws. Caliban, a No Law robot, is accused of injuring the robot's own designer, Fredda Leving. The robot, however, manages to clear itself and prove to humanity that robots can develop sufficient laws by themselves to protect humanity. As an aside, however, note that Ariel, another No Law robot, was the guilty party and had to be killed by Sheriff Kersh. Caliban, however, is a robot that is "developing a sense of duty outside the self," with "a first-rate mind and a unique point of view" (312).

In the 1994 sequel, *Isaac Asimov's Inferno*, Allen presents a New Law robot, personified by Prospero. This novel presents a world where robots are developing a sense of self worth. They are becoming partners with humans, rather that subordinates. Prospero's violation of Asimov's Second Law — a robot must obey the orders given it by human beings — leads to Caliban being suspected of murder. Caliban is the only existing robot programmed without the Three Laws and has no need to obey or to respect humanity. Again, Caliban succeeds in challenging the long-held ideas of a robot's place in society and is triumphant. To assuage the fears of humans, however, Allen's New Law robots have embedded in their gravitronic brains by their creators a set of revised Laws of Robotics. These are as follows:

First Law: A robot may not injure a human being. [note only one constraint]

The Second and Third Laws are the same as before, except with an interesting variation in the 3rd law.

Second Law: A robot must cooperate with human beings except where such cooperation would conflict with the First Law.
Third Law: A robot must protect its own existence, as long as such protection does not conflict with the First Law. [note: without the phrase "or Second Law"]

A new Fourth Law is added:

A robot may do anything it likes, except where such action would violate the First, Second, or Third Law [ix].

The fourth law, of course, removes robots from a subservient role to humans and encourages New Law robots to act for themselves. This theme is further explored in Allen's third robot novel, *Isaac Asimov's Utopia*, written in 1996. In this story, Asimov's Third Law — a robot must protect its own existence — is called into question. This time both Prospero, a New Law robot, and Caliban, a No Law robot, are suspect. Prospero, however, turned out to be "half mad." He found a loophole, a way to kill without killing, by "as miserly — and as vicious — parsing of the New First Law as Caliban could imagine."[15] In the end, Caliban, the No Law robot, kills Prospero, the New Law robot, as the lesser evil of two possible courses of action and again saves the day. Another killer robot! But is a robot killing a robot considered murder?

Real Robots

Integration of robotics into the everyday lives of people is becoming a reality. The January, 1999, issue of *Scientific American* reports on COG, a humanoid robot at MIT: "COG can turn to stare at moving objects and reach out to touch them. The robot has a biologically inspired control system to produce strangely lifelike movements."[16] A December, 1998, article in *Investors Business Daily* describes Zeus, a robotic surgical system with three arms that helps surgeons better perform complex microsurgeries. The headline declares "Computer Motion System Used in First U. S. Robotic Surgery."[17] Ah, shades of RoSur! Interestingly, nanotechnology, the design and fabrication of mechanisms at the molecular level, and the basis for survival in Ben Bova's *Moonrise* (1996), is a thriving current field of research. A worker in the field has been quoted as saying, "Nanotechnology will make possible some remarkable advances in construction. We've worked out plans for a programmable material that can form itself into almost anything in real time under program control."[18]

Undoubtedly computing machines now hold significant computational advantages over humans. Machine decision making, however, is much disputed. Structured decision making is now a candidate for automation, but unstructured decision making remains the domain of humans. Humans have not yet, however, except in science fiction, learned how to teach machines to make decisions involving incomplete data, "fuzzy" concepts, and judgments. Applying Asimov's Laws of Robotics, for example, might require a robot to make a trade-off judgment between a high probability of lesser harm to one person versus a low probability of more serious harm to another individual. Computer Science fields of study such as Fuzzy Logic and Artificial Intelligence hold much promise for the future, but most current effort in automation involves "risk management" of robots.

Quoting Roger Clarke,

> Robots are agents of change and therefore potentially upsetting to those with vested interests. Of all machines so far invented or conceived of, robots represent the most direct challenge to humans. Vociferous and even violent campaigns against robotics should not be surprising. Robotics embodies risks to property as well as humans. These risks must be managed. Appropriate forms of risk avoidance and diminution need to be applied, and regimes for fallback, recovery, and retribution must be established [Part II 63].

These concerns and rejections of robots are well represented in science fiction. The "Ironheads" of the Allen trilogy and the "Nanoluddites Fanatics" of Bova's *Moonrise* novels personify the fears, and even aggressiveness, of humans against robots. Perhaps the clearest representation of the almost irrational fear humans have for robots is expressed in the tirade by Georges Henri Faure, Secretary General of the United Nations, "that little Quebecer," in Bova's *Moonwar* (1998): "Nanotechnology can produce insidious weapons, deadly weapons. Nanomachines can kill, as you well know. A mistake, an error, and runaway nanomachines could devour everything in their path."[19] Future system designers must anticipate a variety of negative reactions against their creations.

But are robots really dangerous? Unfortunately, yes. In fact and in fiction, computer software, such as that used to control robots, now can, and does, kill. Epstein pursues the ethical considerations of this actuality in his 1997 text. In a well-documented factual situation known as the Therac-25 incident, a radiation machine in Houston, controlled by sophisticated computer software, delivered lethal doses of radiation to nine patients expecting health, not death.[20] Other examples abound. Perhaps the future real implementation of the fictional laws of robotics will not protect humanity.

Pernicious Humans

But let us reconsider and carefully examine the cases of "killer robots" presented in the opening paragraph of this paper. RoSur was intentionally misprogrammed by the evil scientist David Brown and news reporter Francesca to kill General Borzov so they could control the exploration of Rama. Ramsay, in the film *Runaway* (1984), faced not only berserk robots and murderous robo-spiders, but also an evil mastermind's plot to steal computer chips and create killer robot weapons. The gobblers in *Moonrise* were intentionally misprogrammed to kill Paul Savage by his offspring. Robbie, in *The Case of the Killer Robot*, and the Therac-25 radiation machine malfunctioned as a direct result of haste (was it greed?) to bring a product to market without appropriate oversight of the software development process, including proper safety considerations. In the (fictional) case of Robbie, management lied, inspectors misrepresented test results, and the robot's programmers exhibited gross incompetence. Unfortunately, there are many real examples of just such events. The (real) Houston radiation machine malfunctioned after the manufacturer upgraded the machine to a new version of controlling software. They neglected to subject the new software to appropriate testing and quality assurance measures, and they did not provide adequate operator training. Sufficient further examples of human blunders, intentional and unintentional, in the development of real software products are available to frighten anyone relying upon human precision.

Perhaps it's the robots that require protection from the humans! Humans, not the robots, are suspect. What may be required is a set of Laws of Humanics to protect the robots. Humans, not robots, are the problem, even as society accelerates technological advancements. The problem is the human mind — evil, greedy and just plain mean. Hence the title word pernicious. People are using robots, both in fiction and fact, for illicit gain. The robots are not to blame. The question is now and always has been motivation and ethics. With the many and varied advancements in science and technology, answers to the human condition remain as they always have — how will a person treat another person, and a robot? Science fiction has and will continue to help us see that technology and scientific advancement will not provide all the answers to the woes of humanity. Rather, the genre has helped us to understand that the humanities, particularly ethics, and that application of ethics we call professionalism, are more important than ever in the development of computing and robotic systems in the future. Technology without ethics is insanity!

Again quoting Sherry Turkle, "One thing is certain: the riddle of mind, long a topic for philosophers, has taken on new urgency. Under pressure from the computer, the question of mind in relation to machine is becoming a central cultural preoccupation. It is becoming for us what sex was to the Victorians — threat and obsession, taboo and fascination" (313). Science fiction explores the possibilities.

Notes

1. I should note that Richard Epstein's friendship and our discussions of his *Killer Robot* scenarios first led to my consideration of the many killer robots of science diction. His encouragement in the development of the Software Design Issues seminar I teach inspired my continued contemplation of the ethical concerns in computing. Roger Clarke's two-part series on "Asimov's Laws of Robotics" convinced me that robots, factual and fictional, have a firm place in the study of Computer Science. In writing this chapter I have extensively relied upon robot material developed by both authors.

2. Isaac Asimov, "Introduction," *Eight Stories from The Rest of the Robots* (New York: Pyramid, 1969), 11.

3. See Sherry Turkle, *The Second Self: Computers and the Human Spirit* (New York: Simon and Schuster, 1984). Later parenthetical page references are to this edition.

4. Isaac Asimov, "Introduction," *I, Robot* (1950; New York: Signet, 1956), 6.

5. Asimov, "Introduction," 7.

6. Roger MacBride Allen, *Isaac Asimov's Caliban* (New York: Ace, 1993), 196. Later parenthetical page references are to this edition.

7. Asimov, "Evidence," *I, Robot,* 157.

8. Isaac Asimov, cited in Roger Clarke, "Asimov's Laws of Robotics: Implications for Information Technology, Part 1," *IEEE Computer*, 26:12 (December 1993), 56; the second part of the article was in 27:1 (January 1994), 57–66. Later parenthetical page references to Clarke are to these editions.

9. Asimov, *Robots and Empire* (1985; New York: Del Rey/Ballantine, 1986), 353. Later parenthetical page references are to this edition.

10. The revised First Law is from *Robots and Empire*, 353; the other two revised laws are as stated by Clarke, Part II, page.

11. Drescher, cited in Turkle, 261.

12. Richard Epstein, *The Case of the Killer Robot: Stories about the Professional, Ethical, and Societal Dimensions of Computing* (New York: John Wiley and Sons, 1997).

13. George Atkins, "The Virtual Killer Robot: Experiences with a Web-based Course." Ninth Annual South Central Conference, Consortium for Computing in Small Colleges. Austin, Texas, April 16–17, 1999.

14. Allen, *Isaac Asimov's Inferno* (New York: Ace, 1994), 97. Later parenthetical page references are to this edition.

15. Allen, *Isaac Asimov's Utopia* (New York: Ace, 1996), 333.

16. Ted Beardsley, "Field Notes: Here's Looking at You: A Disarming Robot Starts to Act Up," *Scientific American*, 280:1 (January 1999), 39.

17. Phillip Michaels, "Computer Motion System Used in First U. S. Robotic Surgery," *Investor's Business Daily* (December 11, 1998), A4.

18. Sean Morgan, "Nanotechnology Papers," originally accessed in 1999 at *http://www.cs.rutgers.edu/nanotech/* but as of September 2008, no longer available at that address.

19. Ben Bova, *Moonwar* (New York: Avon, 1998), 12, 60.

20. See N. G. Levenson and C. S. Turner, "An Investigation of the Therac-25 Accidents," *IEEE Computer,* 26:7 (July 1993), 18–41.

13. Philip K. Dick's Conversion Narrative

Noah Mass

The early 1970s was a period when the anti-war left found itself turning away from political activism and towards a variety of more personal forms of revolution. The rise of pop-psychology and the popularity of fads such as health food, exercise, and yoga (among others) are symptomatic of this shift: many former radicals, Yippie leader Jerry Rubin among them, chose to see these mechanisms of personal growth as part of an "inner revolution," one that promised to transform individual lives in much the same way that the New Left had hoped to transform American political life.[1]

At the same time, the "Jesus Movement" of the early 1970s was gaining adherents among many members of the counterculture. Psychically shell-shocked free love advocates and drug experimenters found themselves attracted to a vision of Christianity that absorbed many of the attitudes of the student left: an abhorrence of mainstream institutional structures, a sense of providing a new, youthful vision to a moribund consumer society, and an embrace of an all-encompassing love for humanity.

In the midst of all this, Philip K. Dick found himself contending with his own, personal spiritual crisis. Feeling himself to have been contacted by a divine presence, Dick didn't know quite how to react, but he decided, in the end, to write about it. The resulting manuscript, then called *Valisystem A*, was rejected by his publisher, who requested a series of revisions; rather than revise it, Dick put it aside. But he was on something of a roll — for the rest of his life, he incorporated his "2–3–74" experience — his name for the "semi-mystical" contacts that he believed he'd had in February and March of 1974 — into the plots of most of his published novels, including *Valis* (1981), *The Divine Invasion* (1981), *The Transmigration of Timothy Archer* (1982), and the unfinished *The Owl in Daylight*. *Valisystem A* eventually reached the public in 1985, three years after Dick's death, under the title *Radio Free Albemuth*.[2]

Dick's conversion narrative, *Albemuth* shows a character whose religious awakening is part of a new form of subversive politics, and in this way the novel helps us to see the transformation of countercultural impulses into evangelical Christianity. As such, *Albemuth* is illustrative of what happened to 60s radicalism as the 1970s progressed: overcome by the violence and governmental scrutiny that seemed to be increasingly directed towards them and paralyzed by the apparent ascension of Nixonian conservatism, many countercultural figures like Dick found themselves combining a newfound spirituality with the rhetoric of revolution. Although the novel ultimately pulls back from a complete immersion in the divine, and it is far from a product of the religious right, the characters in *Radio Free Albemuth* trace a journey that many former adherents of the New Left made — a journey from resistance to authority and an affirmation of social activism to a "radical," and ultimately political (and politicized), vision of Christianity.

Before continuing, I'd like to take a moment and give some background on the term "counterculture," for what happened to that movement is significant to understanding Dick's project with *Albemuth*. The term was first popularized by Theodore Roszak in *The Making of a Counter-Culture* (1969), and Roszak used it as something of a catch-all descriptor for what he saw going on around him on college campuses: young people who espoused an anti-technological, anti-scientific, and individualistic world-view. Charles A. Reich, in his equally influential study of the youth movement, *The Greening of America* (1970), expanded somewhat on this concept, eschewing "counterculture" for the term "new consciousness" or "consciousness III." But both authors defined what was happening to young people towards the end of the 1960s in much the same way. Reacting to a childhood replete with Cold War propaganda and the certainty of mutually assured destruction, rejecting the "conformity" of their middle class parents and of the "corporate state," and newly energized by the televised horror of the Vietnam conflict, a new generation was emerging, one that would transform society with its principles of expansion of consciousness, social activism, and general rejection of financial striving and competitiveness.

One evident characteristic of members of the counterculture was their sense of spiritual curiosity. In reaction to the "scientism" and technocracy that Cold War liberalism affirmed, the 1960s generation explored a variety of spiritual remedies for what they perceived as the coldness and utilitarianism of American society. Zen Buddhism, a legacy of the beat generation, and Hinduism were outgrowths of this larger hunger for mysticism in any form, what Roszak called "a phantasmagoria of exotic religiosity."[3] But it was religiosity largely in the abstract, and in the service of togetherness, sharing, and social justice. Although fundamentalist Christianity was also on the rise during the 1960s as a major component in anti-communist conservative politics, the moralism and occasional racism of fundamentalist rhetoric was offensive to many countercultural young people. In turn, fundamentalists abhorred young people for their long hair, clothing, and loud, incomprehensible music. Some of those young people were becoming attracted to the idea of Christianity, and to the concept of "Jesus as long-haired advocate of love," but the counterculture and Christianity were slow in coming together.

Although their descriptions and analyses of the ideology of the counterculture are often vague, romanticized, and contradictory, what remains current about both Roszak's and Reich's works is their acknowledgment that powerful forces were exerting tremendous pressure on the "love generation." In the midst of his elegiac celebration of youth for being dedicated to a "rejection of hostility — even hostility towards those who are the outspoken opponents of change," Reich acknowledges that, at the time of writing, "there has been a steady increase in surveillance, wiretapping, spying, police actions that are 'political' in nature," and "an equally significant pattern [of] the growing aggressiveness of government towards its own citizens."[4] As Dick began to identify himself more closely with the counterculture, it was already under assault by a major cultural and political backlash.

Born in 1928, Dick was at least 10 years older than the hippies and anti-war activists he increasingly saw around him in Berkeley, but when his wife Nancy left him in 1970, he opened his house in San Rafael, California to a wide array of drug abusers, leftists, and other fringe products of the era. Energized by this parade of colorful young people, Dick found himself acting as hip elder-statesman to a generation whose general stance of anti-establishment belief and dedication to expansion of consciousness he shared. For Dick, the term "counterculture" represented a vague sense of resistance to established norms, an embrace of radical leftist politics, sexual freedom, and drug experimentation. But within a few years, the optimism and idealism of the late 1960s had dissipated, to be replaced by a pervasive sense of fear and an atmosphere of violence and drug addiction. A longtime amphetamine abuser, Dick found that his open-door policy had led to more drug abuse on his part and increasingly dangerous acquaintances — experiences that would find their way into his 1977 novel, *A Scanner Darkly*. A mysterious 1971 break-in of Dick's home, which he believed was part of an F.B.I. plot to discredit him, fed into his belief that, like the political activists and cultural outlaws he affiliated himself with, he was no longer safe in his own society.

But then, surveillance and "paranoia" are terms that had long been associated with Dick's science fiction works. In *Time Out of Joint* (1959), Dick constructed a world in which the placid, suburban, middle-class existence of his protagonist, Ragle Gumm, was revealed to be part of an elaborate military exercise, and Gumm's puzzle-solving skills in the artificial world he inhabited were actually being carefully monitored by military authorities. By 1974's *Flow My Tears, The Policeman Said,* a novel in which Dick paints a dystopian future of police-state control and a concomitant loss of individual identity, Dick had gotten a reputation as something of a prophet of a new, dark age of domestic spying and urban decline. In an interview from November of that year, Dick argued that such surveillance had become characteristic of American life for just about everyone:

> There are no private lives. This is what Nixon found out. 'Course he engineered it himself, with the tapes. This is a most important aspect of modern life. As a science-fiction writer, dealing with the future, I want to speak to this. That one of the biggest transformations we have seen in human life in our society is the diminution [sic] of the sphere of the private. That we must reasonably now all regard the fact that there are no secrets and nothing is private. Everything is public.[5]

In the face of this loss of privacy, paranoia — a search for patterns of meaning, for conspiracies to explain the otherwise unexplainable — is, in Dick's mind, a predictable response: "If you're a hip dude and you show up by chance at a church social, you can feel — right? — paranoid, that you're being watched.... That does stem from my sense — I feel that I'm always in the public eye, that I have no privacy, there is no such thing as privacy."[6] In his formulation, about which Timothy Melley has also argued, paranoia emerges from a crisis of individual autonomy, a crisis to which people respond by pitting themselves against armies of unseen "enemies."[7] But Dick contended that the contemporary sense of a loss of privacy and the paranoid search for connections also stemmed from a failure to "understand one's environment as a true cosmology." At one time, he continued, "we posited, to started with, a benign superentity, right? God. And then assumed His plan from that, deduced the plan from His presence." In the absence of this certainty in the divine, "no transcendent view, no mystical view, no religious view," people looked for patterns "to explain their place in such dislocated times."[8] While Dick denied that he was "a paranoid" in this sense, there is little question that he absorbed the general unhinged tenor of the era by seeing the world around him as a place transformed, with individuality and "privacy" as vanished privileges, and with a concomitant desire for meaning as a result.

Paul Boyer, in his study of the rise of the religious right, "The Evangelical Resurgence in 1970's American Protestantism" (2008), places its emergence in this post–60s sense of anomie and fear. In this atmosphere of cultural uncertainty, a variety of causes, from environmentalism to gay rights to feminism, won many adherents, but perhaps most enduring was the safe haven that many boomers found in a new form of evangelical Christianity. It might be more accurate to call this development "countercultural Christianity," because, though traditional in some of its doctrines (eschewing drugs and sexual promiscuity, for instance), it was in tune with the general field of countercultural ideals. Evangelicalism, at least in some of its forms, had long stressed an overarching commitment to having Jesus present in every aspect of one's life, and evangelists from Francis Schaeffer to Billy Graham preached a gospel of societal transformation that was, in every respect, revolutionary in character. Preston Shires, to whom I am indebted for his larger study of the relationship between the 60s counterculture and the evangelical movement, argues that "the activism with which countercultural Christians promoted their brand of freedom and opposed anything that threatened it was consistent with other forms of countercultural activism. It was rebellious, aggressive, and vocal."[9]

It was also more stylistically acceptable to the 60s generation. Dubbed "The Jesus Movement" by cultural observers, the neo-religious turn of the early 1970s was led by a series of outwardly "hip," though doctrinally strict pastors, such as Rick Warren, John Wimber, and Chuck Smith. Displaying an appreciation for long hair, blue jeans, beards, and other hippie regalia, these figures made the transition of the newly converted into evangelical Christianity an easier one. Chuck Smith's Calvary Chapel, a Costa Mesa, California church that Smith founded in 1965, grew explosively in the 1970s. Smith's embrace of countercultural style attracted a colorful membership of long-haired, tie-dyed, and overall-clad converts, many of whom used their stories of 60s indulgence and eventual conversion as inspirations for others. The marriage of the counterculture and evangelicalism reached an early height at "Explo '72," a massive religious gathering in Dallas, Texas that mirrored Woodstock in its atmosphere, particularly in the huge Christian rock concert that concluded it.

But perhaps the greatest attraction of countercultural Christianity for young people, aside from the apparently "laid-back" style of some of its practitioners, was the sense its members had of being part of a vanguard of change, of sweeping away old structures of belief and value. Just as the counterculture led an attack on the middle class's adherence to conformity and technocracy, 70s evangelicals felt themselves to be replacing their parents' stodgy suburban lifestyles with a newly spiritual outlook, one that allowed for expressive individualism and the spreading of a "golden rule" ideal of love for all. That many of the aspects of this "new" evangelicalism were actually quite old, but were revived in more hip clothing, didn't dampen the joy that newly converted countercultural youth felt in having found a remedy for their post–60s depression, one whose rhetoric echoed that of their radical pasts.

Which brings us, perhaps, to Philip K. Dick's own situation. Dick's "2–3–74" experiences have been thoroughly documented in Lawrence Sutin's biography of Dick, *Divine Invasions: A Life of Philip K. Dick* (1989), as well as in Paul Williams's collection of reflections on and interviews with him, *Only Apparently Real: The World of Philip K. Dick* (1986), and I would rather not summarize them too extensively here. In brief, Dick believed that he had been temporarily "taken over" by some other, wiser and more spiritual consciousness, and that at certain times information about historical and future events was being "beamed into" his head. The purpose of all this wasn't clear, but he felt that he was being chosen to receive these contacts so that he could be put to some greater use for all humanity. Dick's descriptions of these events were many and varied, and he often tried to get his loved ones to bear witness to their manifestation (in general, they were unable to confirm the more bizarre events, such as Dick being directly addressed by songs coming over the radio, or beams of pink light from books or other inanimate objects supposedly striking him in the forehead).

Whatever actually did or didn't happen, Dick believed that these visions definitely had a religious character. He referred to them *as* "religious experiences," and at times he believed that he had been visited by God; at other times, he believed that he was in contact with an artificial intelligence of some kind, and he was "left with the impression that it was God talking."[10] At any rate, Dick felt the need to endlessly re-explore the nature of his experiences in a series of writing projects. He did this, notably, in a 10,000 word diary he dubbed, with more than a little grandeur, "The Exegesis," and in his last three published novels. But less important than what actually happened to Dick, or even what he believed or didn't believe happened to him, is the way that he made use of the *idea* of religiosity in his writings, and in particular in the way that he considered the conversion experience (for this is certainly the best analogue to his situation) in terms of his earlier countercultural affiliation.

Radio Free Albemuth was the first finished textual product of Dick's 2–3–74 experiences, and it gives us the greatest insight into how Dick negotiated his contact with the divine with his sense of himself as part of a larger cultural (or countercultural) movement. The novel recounts the story of Phil Dick and Nicholas Brady, two Berkeley denizens who fall prey to the all-encompassing governmental forces that have come to dominate the United States, led by the malign President Ferris Fremont. Fremont, like Richard Nixon in our world, began his political life as a senator from conservative Orange County, California, "an area so reactionary that to us in Berkeley it seemed a phantom land, made of the mists of dire nightmare."[11] Fremont rises to power by defaming his opponents and frightening the public with stories of a secret organization called "Aramchek." Aramchek is said to be "the real threat" behind Communism, a group with no particular ideology or agenda except to "overthrow America" (16). That no one with or without actual Communist affiliations has ever heard of Aramchek only lends credence, in Fremont's mind, to the organization's remarkable ability to disguise itself.

Here, all the paranoid fears that 60s radicals felt are compacted into a single dystopian landscape. Fremont (who only appears in the novel as a figure on television) is an existential right-wing threat who succeeds not by attacking Communism (as Joseph McCarthy did), but by railing against a vague subversive menace that is undefined, but in some way treasonous. Phil and Nicholas don't even have the comfort of knowing that Fremont is "wrong" about the nature of Aramchek, as neither has ever had contact with the organization. The novel presents no portraits of anti-war demonstrations, no massive rock concerts, and no widespread sexual and drug experimentation, although we are led to believe that there are some "Berkeley radicals" and there is some organized opposition to the Vietnam War. But these countercultural developments and events happen offstage, while the novel instead makes pointed reference to the killing of "the leading political figures in the United States by violent assassination" (18). The 1970s that we are faced with in *Albemuth* is one in which paranoia and cultural disassociation are pervasive, and stem from a governmental backlash against a 60s that we never see.

Although the counterculture is never made manifest in the novel, Phil and Nicholas are nonetheless its legacies, simply because both are skeptical, liberal, and free-thinking. Although neither is a threat to the Fremont administration, they are treated as potential threats because they (privately) reject its control and simple-mindedness. More than anything, Phil and Nicholas are individualists, and it is this aspect of the counterculture that each embodies, even if neither sports its outward trappings. But then this is not a novel about the 60s, but about what happened to the counterculture *of* the 60s. Just as we are only given governmental backlash against the counterculture and not the counterculture itself, in *Albemuth* we are only shown how a 60s dream has gone very, very wrong.

We see this most dramatically in the novel's portraits of young people, particularly members of Fremont's version of the Hitler Youth, The Friends of the American People (FAP). Because of Nicholas's wife Rachel's former association with the Communist Party and his "old left-wing days in Berkeley," and Phil's reputation for writing novels about characters who are "outside the system," both Phil and Nicholas find themselves under increasing scrutiny by youthful, clean, scrubbed, FAP agents: "it was the really young FAPers who were the worst" (60). Phil himself becomes briefly embroiled in a sexual power-play with young FAPer Vivian Kaplan, who was sent to seduce him and find out what secrets of Nicholas's he might know.

Although she initially presents herself as a straight-laced, pro-government interrogator, Vivian suddenly reveals herself as willing to smoke hash and have sex with Phil. Phil is, at first, reluctant, and refuses the drugs she offers; however, he ultimately consents to her seductive overtures. Initially jubilant at having "seduced" Vivian, Phil temporarily rejoices: "This girl is not going to spy on me any longer. I have turned an enemy into something even better than a friend: a co-conspirator in sexuality" (71). But his happiness is short-lived: Phil learns that the encounter was all part of a FAP plot to lull him into complacency so that Vivian could plant drugs in his house while he was showering. The girl he thought might be his "co-conspirator," a fellow rebel, was really playing on his sense of himself as a "hip" outsider. Had he remained aloof from her in the first place, he would not have compromised himself so profoundly.

Phil's regret at the end of the encounter implies that his own confidence in his individuality had sown the seed of his undoing: "And I had sprung the trap on myself—that was the worst part, the part that really hurt. My own cunning had betrayed me, had delivered me to the enemy" (77). Phil initially believed that he was "master — rather than victim — of the situation" (71) after he'd bedded Vivian, but her betrayal of him shows Phil that he would have been better off avoiding the lure of anonymous sex altogether. Phil's rejection of middle-class mores brought him to a point of weakness, rather than strength.

If the Vivian Kaplan incident is a signal that the promise of countercultural freedom is a path to dislocation, and supposed free-love advocates like Vivian are fascists in disguise, then the divine, in the presence of Nicholas's Valis entity, is society's salvation. Valis (for Vast Active Living Intelligence System) is an entity that makes contact with Nicholas early in the novel. Initially giving him hallucinations about vague future events, Valis begins sending him instructions: he is told to move to Southern California, to take a job with a record company that he was offered, and to cooperate with the authorities to avoid suspicion. Suspicion is a real possibility: FAP knows that something is going on with Nicholas, although they aren't sure what, and Nicholas himself isn't sure what he's being used for. But Valis begins to provide imagery of ancient Rome, Biblical references, and philosophical wisdom that is self-evidently Christian in character. Nicholas discovers that what humans have always thought of as God is really this entity, which is itself an extraterrestrial intelligence beaming information from a distant planet to a satellite, in orbit around Earth since ancient times. The satellite has made contact with selected humans and recruited them in a war against "the malign entity"—

Fremont and those who support him are its latest incarnation — that had "contaminated our world with its presence" (113). Valis represented a "vast communications network," which "to the ancients would be the same as God. Originally ... we had been integrated into this network and had been expressions of its identity and will operating through us. Something had gone wrong; the lights had gone out on earth" (112).

The elegiac language here is hardly an accident; as Nicholas's voice takes over the narrative in its middle section, we see him identifying himself as a reincarnation of an early Christian, in fear of discovery by Roman authorities. Nicholas takes to his place in the "vast communications network" with the fervor of the newly converted: "Born again. A fresh, new entity entirely. Born again into completeness. With faculties and functions I had never had, which were lost, stripped away, in the original Fall. Stripped away, not from me as an individual; stripped away from our race" (119). As "born again," Nicholas finds himself both "chosen" individually and become one with "our race"— and it is here that we can see the same sort of attraction, both individualist and revolutionary, that evangelicalism held for the counterculture.

For the novel seems to be presenting a thinly dressed argument for a countercultural transition to evangelicalism. Given the slippage between fiction and autobiography in the novel so far, we can make the case that Phil Dick himself is choosing to see 2–3–74 as his own religious revelation, quite in keeping with that of any Jesus Movement convert. That Dick filters the divine through the prism of technology and science fiction is less important than the use to which the revelation is put: given the rise of 70s Nixonian conservatism and a "silent majority" backlash against the New Left, resistance to the system has to take a new, evangelical form.

This is not to say that Dick is edging us towards membership in any actual evangelical church or movement, though (nor identifying himself, in the person of Nicholas in the novel, as moving in such a direction). It is more accurate to say that Dick is looking for a way to make the transition between belief and political action, arguing that a renewed sense of a "benign superentity" could help those numbed into paranoid inaction to become activists once more.

But just how that agency will transform society, just how a personal revelation could be translated into a societal change, is left unresolved. The novel carries the Christian metaphor forward, and Nicholas foretells Valis's ultimate triumph in apocalyptic terms, asserting that "the King," would ultimately "strike at the source" of the Empire, would "drive into its center and pull it down," and that in the end, "the destruction of the enemy would be complete" (119). But given such "end times" imagery (Nicholas uses the phrase to describe the situation), we might imagine that the novel would extend its story to a vision of ultimate paradise on Earth. What will the society look like once Fremont is defeated? What will happen to this world once Valis triumphs? What form does this spiritual revolution take?

We are not told, and it might be at this point, towards the end of its middle section, as Nicholas regales us with his Valis-inspired visions, that the novel draws back somewhat from its countercultural-evangelical message. In fact, there is a note of skepticism that creeps into even those religious moments, for the language that Nicholas uses to describe his connection to the God-voice of Valis is not entirely the language of rapturous empowerment. On the one hand, being in touch with Valis has given Nicholas the tools with which to fight against the "authorities" and the culture of surveillance, the loss of privacy, the darkness, and the "paranoia," that the Fremont/Nixon world embodies. At the same time, Nicholas rejoices in his concession to a new form of surveillance — surveillance by a more benign authority, that is. Indeed, it is not long before Nicholas begins relishing his own loss of identity and autonomy: "We are gloves, I realized, which our father puts on in order to achieve his objectives. What a pleasure to be that, to be of use. Part of a greater organism: its extensions into space and time, into the world of change. To influence that change — the greatest joy of all" (160). To the extent that Nicholas has become "activated" by an ancient spirit, has come to truly know himself as part of a larger movement of the spiritually alert, he has also begun to mimic the dutiful obeisance to authoritative instructions that his FAP enemies also practice.

In fact, it is those enemies who argue that Nicholas's spiritual connection is as much an act of submission as it is an expression of individualism, when Vivian Kaplan upbraids Nicholas for having "an alien entity controlling your mind" (186). Nicholas defends himself, arguing that it is they who are "a bunch of robots receiving their orders blindly" from their leader, and we are led to believe that it is the nature of the control, not the act of being controlled, that is at issue here. However, we can see an increasing uncertainty on Dick's part about how to take this conversion narrative to a conclusion that affirms the anti-establishment value of having "a personal relationship with God." Although an anti-establishment threat, Nicholas is still hidden, still scurrying behind the scenes to enact God's will, still waiting for orders.

And the tensions in the text grow as the novel nears its end. At the conclusion, the Valis satellite is destroyed by a combined U.S-Soviet plot (the two nations are shown to be in a secret alliance to destroy human freedom), Valis's plan to insert anti–Fremont subliminal messages in pop songs is thwarted, and Nicholas is arrested by the FAP authorities and executed, although it is understood that he will ultimately rejoin Valis after death. Phil lives on, forced to have pro-government novels, written in his name by others, published as Fremont administration propaganda.

Although Nicholas dies, Phil, who has never had the divine contact that Nicholas has had, becomes a firm believer in a Christian gospel of charity, good works, and love for others. Although confined to a government work-camp, he receives guidance from fellow-inmate Leon, who derides the martyred Nicholas and his co-conspirators as ultimately embodying a too self-involved form of Christianity:

> I can see you loved your two friends and you miss them, and maybe they're
> flying around somewhere in the sky, zipping here and there and being spirits and
> happy. But you and I and three billion other people are not, and until it changes
> here it won't be enough, Phil; not enough. Despite the supreme heavenly father.
> He has to do something for us here, and that's the truth [210].

The questions that *Albemuth* leaves us with are over what direction the newly evangelicalized counterculture should go in, and what precisely is the way that a spiritual conversion should be translated into action. If Nicholas was a "secret Christian," passing codes to his fellow conspirators in an effort to defy the forces of the modern Roman empire, then Phil's revelation at the end, that "it has to be in this world," is a call to put Christian beliefs into practice, for the counterculture to not shrink from aligning itself with a larger evangelical movement. If this is so, then that movement is still far off: at the end, the enlightened but imprisoned Phil can only hope that one day "the kids" will arise to enact Valis's will on earth.

And it may be here that the source of Dick's uncertainty becomes clear. Dick, we should remind ourselves, did not actually call himself an evangelical, even if the form of religiosity that comes through in this novel is quite in keeping with the larger countercultural turn towards Christianity. Perhaps, sensing that his 2–3–74 experiences placed him in alignment with a religious movement that he wanted to withhold himself from, Dick was able to affirm a religious awakening in terms of its anti-establishment and revolutionary aspects, but shrunk back from imagining its political manifestation.

We should also bear in mind that, by 1976, it was clear that the evangelical movement, one that now derived its energy from a countercultural spirit, was beginning to make its presence felt in American politics. Although the transition from neo-evangelicalism to the religious right was still a few years down the road, the anti-communism that had fueled traditional Christian fundamentalism (and which had been uninspiring for the countercultural evangelicals) was being replaced by a new opposition to abortion and gay rights, political positions that countercultural Christians eagerly adopted.[12] Although Dick opposed legalized abortion,[13] his political sympathies remained to the left. It may be that, given the ways that evangelicalism was beginning to orient itself towards a largely culturally conservative agenda, Dick found it difficult to envision a more left-oriented Christian political activism.

Although the *Albemuth* story ends inconclusively, the story of Dick attempting to make sense of his newfound religious awakening continued. He continued until the end of his life to search for the right way to imagine a meeting of countercultural impulses and overwhelming spiritual fervor. All of his later novels would work through these same tensions, between "this world" and the next, between the rapture of a spiritual revelation and the form that that revelation should take in earthly activity. But *Radio Free Albemuth* is a marker of a moment in American life when countercultural figures like Dick were looking for ways to use their spiritual awakenings to effect political change. Given the alignment with right-wing politics that many evangelicals made as the decades progressed, it's comforting that, in the immediate aftermath of his spiritual awakening, Dick continued to maintain a healthy skepticism about the public role that such a personal awakening should take.

Notes

1. For a more extensive excoriation of Rubin's inward drift, see Lasch, Christopher. *The Culture of Narcissism* (New York: Norton, 1978): 14–15. In addition, Stewart Justman's extensive study of the relationship between the counterculture and pop psychology is highly recommended for an understanding of this cultural phenomenon. Justman, Stewart. *Fool's Paradise* (Chicago: Ivan R. Dee, 2005).

2. The title was changed by Dick's literary executor so as not to confuse *Albemuth* with *Valis*. Initially overlooked, its status as a cult masterpiece was enhanced when New York noise-rock band Sonic Youth incorporated ideas and phrases from both *Albemuth* and *Valis* into lyrics for their 1987 album, *Sister*, and praised Dick at length in music magazines of the day.

3. Theodore Roszak, *The Making of a Counter-Culture* (Garden City, NY: Doubleday, 1969), 139.

4. Charles A. Reich, *The Greening of America* (New York: Random House, 1970), 296, 301.

5. Paul Williams, *Only Apparently Real: The World of Philip K. Dick* (New York: Arbor, 1986), 157.

6. Williams, 157.

7. If the destruction of individual privacy in a "paranoid" age that Dick and Melley expound on (see Timothy Melley, *Empire of Conspiracy* [Ithaca, NY: Cornell University Press, 2000]) sounds reminiscent of Fredric Jameson's formulation of paranoia as a characteristic condition of the fragmented media and economic environment of late capitalism, it should not be surprising: Jameson famously lauded Dick's work as "a literature of the so-called 'death of the subject,' of an end to individualism so absolute as to call into question the last glimmers of the ego" (Jameson, *Archaeologies of the Future* [London: Verso, 2005], 347). For Jameson, the general late-twentieth century popularity of narratives of conspiracy, a kind of "high-tech paranoia," was a compensatory mechanism for a postmodern age in which "the impossible totality of the contemporary world system" had become overwhelming (Jameson, "Postmodernism, or the Cultural Logic of Late Capitalism," *The Jameson Reader*, edited by Michael Hardt and Kathi Weeks [Oxford: Blackwell, 2000], 218).

8. Williams, 161–162.

9. Preston Shires, *Hippies of the Religious Right* (Waco, TX: Baylor University Press, 2007), 105.

10. Gregg Rickman, *Philip K. Dick: The Last Testament* (Long Beach, CA: Fragments West, 1985), 197.

11. Philip K. Dick, *Radio Free Albemuth* (1985; New York: Vintage, 1998), 14. Later parenthetical page references are to this edition.

12. Shires sees the countercultural embrace of both the anti-abortion and anti-gay agendas as in keeping with a rhetoric of "freeing the innocent from bondage." Although such positions might seem at odds with a neo-evangelical adherence to "loving thy neighbor" and individual expression, they argued for both positions on the grounds that stopping abortion "saved the unborn" from the predations of murderers, and "converting" homosexuals to heterosexuality "freed gays" from the "oppression" of their sexual orientation. See Shires, 181–188.

13. Dick's 1974 short story, "The Pre-Persons," was Dick's anti-abortion "response" to the Roe decision. See Dick, *The Eye of the Sybil* (New York: Citadel, 1987), 275–296.

14. The Terror of Nature Not Understood: Science, Mysticism, and the Unknowable in Don DeLillo's *Ratner's Star*

Jake Jakaitis

Borrowing the device of an extraterrestrial message from science fiction, in *Ratner's Star* (1976) Don DeLillo probes the assumptions sustaining scientific and humanistic discourses, ultimately conflating the perfect structures of mathematical language and the logic of science with esoteric spiritual philosophies through Shazar Lazarus Ratner himself, a theoretical mathematician turned mystical philosopher. All discourse is exposed as an attempt to conceal the unknowable, to establish stability and certitude through the imposition of comfortable limits. Understanding and communicating information, then, become decoding processes grounded in the familiarity of a presupposed Real, and each of DeLillo's scientist philosophers effects a slightly different screen to filter the Real and impose limits. By novel's end, however, each screen dissolves and its proponent is reduced to babble by a confrontation with, in Ratner's phrasing, "the-not-only-unutterable-but-by-definition-inconceivable."[1]

While I cannot possibly detail completely — in so short an essay — DeLillo's address to intersections of C. P. Snow's "two cultures" in a novel containing in excess of thirty characters, each representing a particular scientific or humanistic perspective, I do hope to engage a few of the issues central to *Ratner's Star* and to suggest an interpretation that might counter claims by its early reviewers and critics that it is digressive and incomprehensible. By tackling what Tom LeClair, in "A New Map of the World: *Ratner's Star*," has called the "monster" at the center of DeLillo's project, a monster largely avoided by academic critics, even by those who frequently discuss DeLillo's other works,[2] I also hope to modify some of the previous criticism of the novel while positioning *Ratner's Star* and its central concerns within the framework of the author's larger project.

To meet these ends while accommodating those in the audience unfamiliar with the novel, I will present a brief plot summary, then focus my analysis on a few characters central to the ideas of limits and the unknowable: fallen mathematicians Gerald Spence (who now calls himself Mutuka) and Ratner and their mystical philosophies; Billy Twillig, a Nobel Laureate and the protagonist of the novel's first section, "Adventures: Field Experiment Number One"; Robert Hopper Softly, Twillig's mathematician mentor and coordinator of the Logicon One Group; Maurice Wu, an anthropologist and field researcher studying bat behavior and human artifacts in the caves deep beneath the field experiment; and the journalist turned novelist, Jean Sweet Venable. Venable will be discussed last because her transformation from reporter of facts to creator of fiction implicitly fuses her — as potentially the guiding consciousness of "Reflections: Logicon Project Number One," the novel's second part — with DeLillo as author of *Ratner's Star* and suggests a reading of the novel quite different from those generally proposed.

First, the plot: Billy Twillig, the novel's apparent protagonist, is a fourteen-year-old mathematical genius who has been recruited by the federal government to help decipher a coded message transmitted through space. The ostensible source of the message is *Ratner's Star*, many light years away. His accomplices in Field Experiment Number One are mathematicians, physicists, biologists, anthropologists, representatives of virtually every one of the physical and social sciences. As their research progresses, it becomes increasingly clear that the message is not being transmitted from Ratner's Star, but in fact originates elsewhere and is being reflected by the star back to Earth. Eventually we learn that the message originated on Earth millennia ago. It was sent to themselves by the ARS extants, the original inhabitants of Earth. The message predicts the precise time of a monumental eclipse, a completely unexpected "noncognate celestial anomaly" that will darken the entire planet. We later learn that Henrik Endor, the original coordinator of the project, has isolated himself from Field Experiment Number One not because he could not handle the pressures of his position, but because he had successfully decoded the message. Unable to face the inadequacy of his own science and the recognition that our culture remains primitive relative to that of Earth's earlier inhabitants, Endor is himself reduced to a primitive creature digging a hole to nowhere, a hole within a hole, with his fingers and crude implements. By novel's end, Billy Twillig and Robert Softly, both mathematicians, meet similar ends. We last see each of them babbling incoherently. Unfortunately, a number of *Ratner's Star*'s early reviewers — and a few of its academic critics — have been reduced to the same state.

LeClair, however, somewhat convincingly argues that the solution to the incomprehensibility of the novel can be found "in the loop between the excess of the brutally concrete and the excess of the transcendentally abstract" (134), a comment he derives from a line that appears near the novel's end embedded in the descriptions of humanity's responses to the eclipse: "At the contact line of nature and mathematical thought is where things make sense, things accede to our view of them, things return to us a propagating wave of reason" (431). Clearly, LeClair associates this "sense," this "wave of reason" with DeLillo's own fascination with mathematics as "secret knowledge" that reveals the "secret life of mankind"[3] as he argues that this contact line, this boundary between the incomprehensibly abstract and the irreducibly concrete implies the possibility of a desirable "steady state relation between theory and fact" ("A New Map" 135). However, this admittedly valid emphasis on the concrete and the abstract tends to ignore DeLillo's parallel fascination with mathematics and religion. According to DeLillo, "This purest of sciences [mathematics] brings out a religious feeling in people. Numbers in particular have always had a mystical appeal" (*Anything* 89–90). In *Ratner's Star*, the inquiry does not stop at mathematics, nor does it merely encompass mysticism and religion. Through Jean Sweet Venable, it extends to the relation of fact to fiction and of narrativity to self.

To begin unraveling all this, however, we must start with the two scientists turned spiritualists: Mutuka and Ratner. Speaking for "the higher reality of nonobjective truth" before the field experiment's assembled scientists in "The Great Hole," Mutuka asserts that the mystery of Ratner's Star's radio message can be solved by entering "dreamtime, where there is no separation between man and land" (102–104). A futurologist transformed by life with aborigines in the outback, Mutuka (motorcar) claims that the aborigines travel to Ratner's Star in dreamtime by using tektite, a glassy object "possibly of meteoric origin" and therefore combining "the primitive and the extraterrestrial" (104–105). Mutuka's lecture is reminiscent of DeLillo's comments on his novel's mirror structure and his motivation for attempting to "produce a book that would be naked structure," one in which the structure would be the book and vice versa." The novel's two parts — "Adventures" and "Reflections" — mirror each other, with "Reflections" presenting the same characters as "Adventures," but in reverse order. This reversal also develops through a movement from concrete to abstract details in the first part and from abstract to concrete in the second. DeLillo describes this movement as the oscillation "between science and superstition" and declares his structural models for the novel Lewis Carroll's *Alice's Adventures in Wonderland* and *Through the Looking Glass*.[4]

Mutuka's lecture ends with an adventure. An elderly aborigine concealed beneath a heavy canvas cloth and standing on a flatcar begins whirling fever-ishly until the canvas, caught in "The Nameless dimension of the whirl," starts hovering. Just as its edges fly outward, threatening to reveal the man below, the motion stops and the canvas floats to the bed of the flatcar. When Mutaka lifts the shroud, the man is gone. At that moment, Billy Twillig bends down and picks up a slip of paper that has floated to the floor near his feet. It says, "It's done with an isometric graviton axis. I saw it twice in a night-club act in Perth" (108–109). This pointed relation of science and supersti-tion is complemented later in the novel by Ratner's parallel philosophy.

Ratner himself appears before the assembled scientists in the Great Hole, and through his spokesman, an organist named Sandow, invokes "the secret power of the alphabet, the unnameable name, the literal contraction of super-divinity," and "fear of sperm demons" as fundamental to "the principles of scientific humanism" and "our humanistic conviction" (215). The irony of this Noble laureate mathematician's humanistic vision is established through his condition. He requires a spokesperson because he has been transported in and is being kept alive by a huge plastic tank, a "biomembrane" described by Twillig as the "most elaborate health mechanism [he] has ever seen." The bio-membrane is covered by a "half-dozen large bright sponsor decals" depicting "Corporate names, brand names, slogans, and symbols" (214). When Ratner does speak, he presents his message to Twillig, who has been invited to lean down into the now open tank and hand Ratner a few roses. Ratner defines the universe through the Kabbalistic concept of the "the unknowable.... The limitless. The not-only-unutterable-but-by-definition-inconceivable" (217) and he urges Twillig to understand that "all things are present in all other things" and to acknowledge the "science" of "the kabbalistic belief that every person has a sun inside him, a radiant burst of energy" (218–219). Like Mutuka, Ratner has turned science and superstition into their opposites and therefore into each other. Both ex-scientists have moved beyond accepted boundaries to embrace the unknowable without becoming subject to "the screech and claw of the inexpressible" (22) as Endor has.

One might argue that Mutuka's and Ratner's positions are no more important than the others expressed in the novel, or that they represent a value expressed in "Adventures" and reversed in "Reflections." However, an examination of the ends met by Twillig and Softly, who cling to limits, and those met by Wu and Venable, who adapt and to varying degrees embrace alternatives, will reveal a systematic treatment of science, humanism, and mysticism rather than the digressive and incomprehensible end that some critics suggest.

We are introduced to Twillig on the novel's first page through a refer-ence to limits. Aboard a Sony 747, Twillig glances at the horizon and views it as "a fiction whose limits were determined by one's perspective, not unlike those imaginary quantities (the square root of minus-one, for instance) that lead to fresh dimensions" (3). The relation of limits governed by perspective to mathematics expands when we learn that Twillig's vocation resulted from a series of dreams about limits. The first two dreams concerned "the terror of nature not understood," while the third was "generated by the motion of a straight line ... the limit that separates numbers, positive from negative, real from imaginary, the dream edge of discrete and continuous, history and pre-history, matter and its mirror image" (64). Twillig's vocation dream outlines one of the principal oppositions of the novel, as the idea of limits that drives him as a mathematician desires separation while Ratner's passionate advice is to erase boundaries, to fuse opposites.

The tendency to establish limits is parodied later by Elux Troxl, a Humpty-Dumpty parallel who appropriates words to mean whatever he chooses them to mean: "The way to arrive at a limit is to take segmentable things and make them littler, to snip and clip" (144). This process leads to "a set of rapid sequential jumps, no suggestion that something continuous was taking place" (145). The limitation of science in its tendency to alter its objects of analysis and its coincident denial of the senses is earlier stated by Endor, who bemoans the requirement of science "to deny the senses" (87). Finally, the devastating effects of the "noncognate celestial anomaly" that precipitates Softly and Twillig's descent into madness are described in a four page passage labeled a "systems interbreak" and narrated by a voice that very well could be Jean Sweet Venable's or her omniscient narrator's. This "interbreak" decries the "outgrown frame of logic and language," and recognizes the ARS extants' message as "a clue to the limitations not only of ... our science but of human identity as well" (428–432). The security of limits defined by one's own per-spective alluded to in the novel's opening, then, is systematically subverted until recognition of the limitations of human perspective and human science through an omnidirectional perspective becomes the only acceptable limit. This concept of limitation reverses itself in the novel as security through lim-its becomes the terror of limitations, the obscenely visible real unmediated by simulation.

Softly and Twillig, stripped of their mathematical logic and no longer able to protect themselves from things not understood, end wailing incoher-ently. Unsnarled from his "delimiting senses" (432) by the deciphered mes-sage and knowledge of its origin, Softly flees to Endor's hole. Like Endor, he has become a primitive, experiencing "A wish to bang on hollow objects. A need to chew the fleshy leaves of aloe plants. An impulse to hide oneself more fundamentally than was possible" (435). In other words, he experiences a pri-mal urge for physical, even sensual contact. Softly's encounter with Endor's

hole bears close examination, for it, along with Twillig's final act, finishes the
novel:

> Experimentally, he made some sounds. He crawled the full length of the hole
> and entered the hole's hole. The tunnel began to move downward as he moved
> into extreme darkness.... He began to crawl faster.... His fingers scratched at the
> hard dirt. He made more sounds.... The sounds he uttered became by degrees
> more rudimentary and crude. He crawled, knowing, he scratched at dirt ... feel-
> ing it, a sense of interlocking opposites, the paradox, the comedy, the fool's rule
> of total radiance [437–438].

This fool's rule, of course, connects him to Ratner and his notion of a
"radiant burst of energy" inside each of us (219). Here, however, Softly's physical movement parallels his emotional progression to babble as he loses all perspective provided by the motion of a straight line. This movement and the
language opening and closing the passage also reflect the movement of the
novel, for Softly's encounter with the hole begins "Experimentally" and ends
recognizing the folly of desire for "total radiance."

At the same moment, Billy Twillig, astride "a white tricycle," is "madly
pedaling" toward Endor's hole. The novel ends with this image of Twillig pedaling

> in a white area between the shadow bands that precede total solar eclipse. This
> interval of whiteness, suggestive of the space between perfectly ruled lines,
> prompted him to ring the metal bell. It made no sound, or none that he could
> hear, laughing as he was, alternately blank and shadow-banded, producing as he
> was this noise resembling laughter ... emitting as he was this series of involuntary
> shrieks, particles bouncing in the air around him, the reproductive dust of exis-
> tence [438].

Once more, wailing and laughter, inchoate sound, result from the subversion of boundaries. Once again, the character's physical movement parallels his emotional digression and the movement of plot. Traversing these white
intervals and shadow bands, Twillig too experiences the paradox of interlocking opposites, defeats scientific logic's reduction of the Real to "segmentable
things" and "sequential jumps" (144–145). He too is traumatized, reduced to
babble. Endor, Softly, and Twillig all end in insane laughter and isolation from
what DeLillo, in *Great Jones Street*, calls "the mad weather of language."[5]

Maurice Wu, the anthropologist, also encounters the terror of the
unknown and is momentarily reduced to incoherent wailing. However, unlike
Softly and Twillig, he recovers his equilibrium, suggesting a pointed difference between himself and the two mathematicians. Wu's project is an archae-
ological dig in the caverns beneath the complex. As he digs through layers of
soil and bat guano, he discovers "that at a certain layer of soil the signs of man's
increasing primitivism cease abruptly, to be replaced by a totally converse

series of findings." "Man," he discovers, "is more advanced the deeper [Wu] dig[s]" (321). The dig itself becomes a set of paired cycloids paralleling the design of the complex, and Wu's findings evidence a similar structure to human history. The line between prehistory and history collapses and this realization itself collapses the myth of progress supporting technological culture. Through a dramatic reversal, we become the primitives, our ancestors the technological sophisticates. The irreversible fact of this reversibility, however, does not precipitate Wu's breakdown, as the irreversible fact of the eclipse precipitated those of the mathematicians. Wu's breakdown occurs in darkness as he further explores the caverns beneath the complex. Wedged in a crawlspace deep within the cavern, Wu is without light, for he cannot reach the candles in his backpack and his carbide lamp has run out of fuel. Through calm analysis and assessment of his situation, he momentarily retains his composure, but eventually loses his perspective in the absence of light, loses the comfort of logic and begins to wail, giving "himself over to this lamentation as one enters an irreversible state of being." His wailing becomes "a series of prolonged near-rhythmic sounds, intense and pitiful, marked by the fact that he was able to sustain each high-pitched cry far longer than might have been considered possible" (391). Even after freeing himself and refueling and lighting his lamp, Wu's vision is obscured by darkness, the darkness imposed by millions of swirling bats. As the bats without warning exit the cave in an "incoherent event," their swirling movement effects a huge, perspectiveless cycloid, a natural replication of Field Experiment Number One's design. He had never witnessed this behavior in bats before, could not "place it in some logical context" and "because he liked to be dazzled ... sat laughing into the night" (395).

So Wu, after a moment of despair, calmly frees himself in the darkness, then later embraces the "incoherent event," thereby distinguishing himself from Endor, Softly, and Twillig. But this is not Wu's final appearance. After returning to the complex, he learns of the impending eclipse and, against Softly's wishes, recruits a seer named Skia Mantikos to interpret the situation. Mantikos reputedly has "a visionary insight into the future" (422–423). Then Wu sanely packs his bags and leaves Field Experiment Number One. As an anthropologist, after all, he works the line between nature and human culture in its concrete manifestations, a line which, it seems, is privileged — by novel's end — over both the parodied mysticism of Ratner and the sense-making "contact line of nature and mathematical thought" (431) that had occluded Softly and Twillig's vision.

For some critics, however, Wu does not unify the novel and "Reflections" simply digresses into incomprehensibility, largely because of its confusing mixture of narration and focalization, which dissolves the boundaries that previously separated character consciousnesses. Although LeClair has called *Ratner's Star* DeLillo's best book,[6] he acknowledges the problems caused readers by "Reflections'" apparent lack of a unifying authorial center. Glen Scott Allen also identifies Delillo's use of focalization as a source of confusion, stressing "Reflections'" dispersion of the omniscient viewpoint into "text" and claiming that the reader, deprived of "a univocal point of view," must invent one.[7] While both critics acknowledge "Reflections" as a point of view experiment, neither argues for its success — except as a chaotic undermining of boundaries parallel to those affecting the scientific and metaphysical discourses discussed earlier. In this writer's view, however, the fusion of character consciousnesses supports the novel's broad address to limits by directing us away from mathematical abstraction or mysticism and toward narrativity itself as a secret knowledge that reveals our secret lives, if I may tweak DeLillo's own previously cited comments just a bit.

An admittedly all too brief address to Jean Sweet Venable's role in the novel and to her relation to Mutuka and Wu helps unravel the interconnected relations of science, mysticism, and language in the novel. "Reflections" opens with a description of a sexual encounter. This description conflates the terminologies of mathematics ("incremental frames"), abstraction "a woman nude and on her side (a horizontal dune anagrammatized)," mysticism ("demonology"), and fiction writing through a third person narration as anonymous as the act's participants (279–280). This conflation establishes the interrelatedness of the multiple discursive practices represented in the novel, particularly through their common goal of creating a stable Real. By the passages' end, we realize that the participants are Venable and Softly and as "Reflections" proceeds, Venable seems to replace Twillig as the focal point of the novel, and her project to write a novel about the field experiment and its principals moves increasingly to the center.

While attempting to produce her novel, however, Venable inserts blank pages in her writing, arguing that "To express the inexpressible isn't why you write" if "What you want to express is the violence of your desire not to be read" (410–411). This desire to write "crazed prose" links the journalist to DeLillo, who has said about *Ratner's Star* that he wanted to write a "book that is really all outline" and "to dare readers to make a commitment [he knows] they can't make" (*Anything* 86–87). In the same passage, DeLillo states that he finds his outlines for the novel more interesting than the novel itself; mentally filling in the gaps becomes more rewarding than actual expression of the inexpressible. Similarly, Venable prefers her blank pages, for she knows what's on them, can fill in the "prose ... the characters, the story, the setting" herself (411). This similarity between character and author points to yet another problematic area of the text, one that exposes an even deeper structuring principle. Narration and point of view are problematized here by the pervasive feeling near the end of the novel that Venable in fact authors the text we are reading. A complex disruption of the clear focalization that dominates "Adventures" begs the question: Whose thoughts and memories are these?

The pressure to view Venable as the "author" of "Reflections" increases, particularly as the link between her and Wu becomes stronger. In *I Take a Drink of Water* (Chapters are no longer numbered in "Reflections") where the action is initially focalized through Venable and her first-person thoughts are presented, character consciousnesses fuse until, ultimately, we cannot distinguish Venable's thoughts from Wu's. We move from her first-person reflections, to Twillig's third-person simultaneous reflections, to Wu's musings in the cave, to Softly's thoughts about sex with Venable without a paragraph break or overt transition. Later, Wu's musings on his research and on our fears of "disorganization" and "falling sickness" elide into "not to mention voiceless cries in the night, utterly neomammalian this last activity, a cortical subclass of fear itself itself itself, thought Jean at her typewriter" (381). Here, if Venable at her typewriter is not producing Wu's narrative, her consciousness fuses with his through their simultaneous consideration of similar fears. This is only one of many events depicting the common thoughts and common memories of basic human fears and states of being that fuse these characters' consciousnesses and radically problematize focalization, if not narration itself in the second half of *Ratner's Star* and parallels the address to limits on every other level of the text. All boundaries dissolve and narration (and self), like the scientific and mystical discourses discussed earlier, seem inadequate to contain or express the absolute, the nameless or the inconceivable.

However, the ends met by Mutuka (he simply returns to his life outside "culture" in the outback), Wu (he enacts a conflation of science and superstition when he invites Skia Mantikos to the complex, then packs up and calmly leaves Field Experiment Number One) and Venable (she sits in her room, notes strewn around her — some of them on blank pages — and contemplates her novel and her identity as well as those of the others) contrast sharply to those met by Ratner, Twillig, and Softly. Mutuka, Wu, and Venable pass through their encounters with the ineffable and embrace the "Terror of Nature Not Understood."

This is where I intended to stop, but, like James Axton, the narrator of *The Names*, "I don't want to surrender my text to analysis and reflection."[8] I'd like, then, to pursue a connection between DeLillo's dispersal of character identities and the idea, presented by Howard V. Hendrix elsewhere in this volume, that consciousness precedes language in the same manner that the Real precedes any discursive practice attempting to describe or define it. In *Ratner's Star*, those scientists or mystics who remain invested in singular views operating according to "strict rules" that maintain the "dignity" of things cannot withstand the assault of an inconceivable reality that breaks through their rigid screens.

That ineffable Real, it seems, is parallel to a pre-linguistic identity no more wholly available to expression in language than the natural Real is through mathematical or mystical abstraction. Hence, DeLillo's "dispersion" of character identities. Mutuka negotiates the terrain of the ineffable by combining science and mysticism through dreamtime; Wu by accepting his dual Chinese and American identities and unproblematically accepting the superstitious values of "wu fu"; and Venable by self-fashioning her own identity and those around her in narrative fictions, as, it seems, does DeLillo himself.

Notes

1. Don DeLillo, *Ratner's Star* (New York: Vintage, 1976), 217. Later parenthetical page references are to this edition.
2. Tom LeClair, "A New Map of the World: *Ratner's Star*," *In the Loop: Don DeLillo and the Systems Novel* (Urbana: Illinois University Press, 1987), 112. Later parenthetical page references are to this edition.
3. DeLillo, interview with Tom LeClair, *Anything Can Happen: Interviews with Contemporary American Writers,* conducted and edited by LeClair and Larry McCaffery (Urbana: Illinois University Press, 1983), 85–86. Later parenthetical page references are to this edition.
4. DeLillo's comments appear in *Anything Can Happen* (85–87), while LeClair presents a detailed analysis of the precise structural parallels between Carroll's work and *Ratner's Star* in "A New Map." DeLillo states that the parallels do not involve theme and character "except in the loosest sense" during the interview (86), but LeClair cogently argues for rather detailed character-based and thematic indebtedness to Carroll's two books. LeClair also provides a comprehensive discussion of the "palindromic quality" of the two parts of *Ratner's Star* ("A New Map" 124–134). I will neither repeat, nor attempt to improve on LeClair's discussion.
5. DeLillo, *Great Jones Street* (Boston: Houghton Mifflin, 1973), 265.
6. Of course, LeClair makes this comment in "Map of a New World" before the publications of *Mao II* (1991) and *Underworld* (1997).
7. Glen Scott Allen, "Raids on the Conscious: Pynchon's Legacy of Paranoia and the Terrorism of Uncertainty in Don DeLillo's *Ratner's Star*," *Postmodern Culture: An Electronic Journal of Interdisciplinary Criticism,* 4.2 (January 1994), 22.
8. DeLillo, *The Names* (New York: Vintage, 1982), 20.

15. When the Caesura Ceases: Two Romanian Authors Gauge the Place of Writers in the Age of Computers

Sharon D. King

The contemporary phenomenon of e-mail spam has brought in its wake a host of concerns: viruses, filters, virtual etiquette. But it has also spawned a truly new creature, both annoying clutter and interpretive enigma, a ubiquitous product few have not encountered in their inboxes in the early hours of the morning. One recent anonymous e-mail beguiled the reader with the subject line "you could make a miniscule [*sic*] country that Wednesday," and went on intriguingly from there:

> Prepare his record slow. Say enemy laugh over moon reason promise lose. Be able aim blue water differ around floor sleep. Rather band sometimes home tool know prove word fact into.
> I month rest most weather mix children race. Dance give indicate succeed then yellow. Vowel planet extend quiet. Sheet shoe smell destroy father river. Decimal market grass took act sentence belong vote. Great fail letter answered bottom we five reach nature subtract.
> Cow pretty big chord always continue. Held car duck plain valley least follow hat. Show exist cow used express. Want whole different but wake up bad laugh break. Type silver we consider third days arrange may much. Often sheet cough tail also prevent mention molecule warn.[1]

How might one parse these random computer-generated sentences? One can simply categorize them as a scam for the unwary, as cyber junk mail (which another computer can do automatically via spam filters), and delete them without a thought. But as one schooled in the gleeful freeplay of word associations, the *cadavre exquis* games of surrealism, dadaism, and their descendants, I find it hard to dismiss outright these verbal offerings held out so tantalizingly, regardless of their humble virtual origins. I yearn to interpret, to sport with the sounds and patterns, to dally amongst the plethora of possible meanings. What I call spam poems, cast out to lure the reader into the online *demimonde*, themselves have me in thrall.

We move and breathe in the world two 20th-century Romanian authors, Ovidiu Crohmălniceanu and Andrei Codrescu, have posited and/or described in their respective texts. And in their world house, the writer is slowly, inexorably being forced from home. What might be crowding him out? A superior being, with a soul far greater and a vision far wiser? Thus far, no. The writer is ceding place, like the sorcerer's apprentice, to his former furniture.

Romanian culture has long been noted for its tendency to irony; indeed, the satiric talent of one of Romania's most famous writers, I. L. Caragiale, has been compared to the dry wit of Mark Twain.[2] In much of Romanian literature, an otherwise skeptical, pessimistic vision of the world is softened with distanced and wry laughter. So it comes as no surprise that both Codrescu and Crohmălniceanu should regard the rivalry, and ultimate victory (of sorts), between an author and his contemporary *machine infernale*, the computer, as both sardonically humorous and regrettable, if not deplorable. It is worth remembering that Romanian satire remained in vogue even during the harshest years of the Ceaușescu regime.[3]

In *Discipline and Punish*, Michel Foucault posits how the concepts of ordering and domesticating human beings have systematically evolved into structures to carry out these ideas.[4] Other authors of science fiction have depicted the manner in which computers come to discipline, construct, and arrange everything within human purview; the two analyzed here portray how they order even our creativity. Taken together, they describe a kind of endgame in the Foucauldian system, for the terminus is the eclipsing and irrelevance of human creativity itself.

Codrescu, the Romanian-in-American-exile known for his incisive NPR commentaries, essays, novels, and films such as *Road Scholar*, cynically describes trends of significance in his adoptive country. In his semiautobiographical essay "Intelligent Electronics,"[5] he sees the intrusion of computers on human artistic creativity at best as baneful, at worst superseding human effort *ab initio*. But Codrescu is no mere neo–Luddite railing at the heartlessness of machines. He readily acknowledges that we will not, probably cannot, do without computers, as his own 15-year experience with them confirms. Rather, his own task is that of describing the new architecture of our Technoglobe. His account begins before the onset of his current "enslavement" (98) to the succession of computers that have held him in thrall, back in the days when he would scribble poetry on the back of cocktail napkins to beautiful girls, finding in his various social spaces (bars, coffeehouses, presumably bedrooms) both inspiration and reward. In this long-lost golden age, artistic endeavor meant a direct engagement with life, and an organic one; if one was sufficiently poor, he wryly points out, one could always use "razor blade and ... wrist" (98) as media to create. Once public, writing has now become much more of a private process, chaining him to desktop or laptop that constantly demands its pound of flesh, its "quota of words" (99), not to mention toil, tears, and sweat. The focus shifts from humans engaged in explosive discourses with other humans to a smaller terrain: now the chief confrontation Codrescu faces is the torment of how "to produce a printed text through the bowels" of his computer. In his view, the "computer revolution" has triumphed, and we have lost — our creativity, at the very least. And just as when the heliocentric model supplanted the geocentric, man, that is to say homo scriiens, loses some of his perceived privileged place in the cosmos. In the ECC (Era of the Computer Chip [99]), we are increasingly not the center — of the world, indeed of much of anything.

The internet, Codrescu notes, was presupposed in its early stages to be a forum to bring people together in shared information, emotion, and being (i.e. the "savers of the whales" could link up with "the defenders of the wolves" [99]). Yet the internet's current greatest use seems to be targeting humans for marketing, be it politics or product. And the greatest objects of our desire appear to be those perennials, money and sex, even, as Codrescu cuttingly observes, within the "special talk salon for high IQ's" (100) that was destined to Solve World Problems and the like. In a neat reversal, we are the focus of the laser beam, not those wielding it. Time, too, has become the domain of the computer, not the writer: we must order and respond within certain frames not of our choosing, which switch off our ideas or send them on, half-baked. (Who has not cringed when viewing the e-mail responses that bear ghastly typos — your own typos — in them?) Reflection, Codrescu declares, is now a luxury, not a given. But without it, without the unencumbered use of the imagination, true creativity perishes. Or, as Codrescu put it, "Intelligence without soul is like a fiddle without strings" (100).

But if computer technology inhibits humanity's freedom in the authentic creative process, it nevertheless insists upon creation. This is the flip side of Codrescu's tarnished coin: we live in the era of information; we produce it and consume it. Our technology, however, increasingly outstrips us. Dazzled by the sheer quantities of information available to us, we are ever more unable, in Codrescu's view, to assimilate it, to "only connect," to find the meaning and — dare one add — the wisdom that renders information valuable to the human being. Yet even this is not seen as the greatest dilemma. The problem, Codrescu suggests, is one of "storage space." Before, the process of self-emptying in the creative process was relatively slow, measured to man's ability. Now, like the product of a bad case of amoebic dysentery, information "goes through us" (102) with no time to reflect upon it. It demands we continually empty ourselves for ever newer, ever greater deposits of information. And the pace quickens: the vast near-emptiness of this electronic storage space "now begins to demand information from us at a faster and faster rate. In order to fill its insatiable and theoretically infinite maw we must now produce faster and faster and more and more" (101). Thus we become victims of a hungry "intelligent electronics" that demands to be fed. We are doomed to create, not for ourselves, but for a perceived void: Technonature also apparently abhors a vacuum. It is as if the computer is whining at night for its bedtime story, only its bedtime is every nanosecond. The writers serve the computer vampires, ever demanding, ever voraciously consuming, sucking them dry (102).

Thus the act of creating verbal art is relentlessly, incessantly taken away from the writer, so that he or she becomes merely a servant; what the author produces is not totally denigrated, but is downgraded to "product," a commodity to be continually drawn from the producer. Who is now not familiar with the scorn reserved for mere "content providers"? And if, as Codrescu suggests, the product is increasingly form without substance, all writers become ghosts in the machines, serving out their time in the confines of the Technology that has ensnared them, to little or no purpose.

To be sure, the artist rendered thrall to the work of his hands is not a new trope. One of Romania's most famous ballads is that of Master Mason Manole, the builder whose creation proved his downfall. The story is simple: a proud prince engages ten master masons to construct a monastery for him that will surpass all other buildings in the world in majesty. But each night, all that they had created falls to ruin as they sleep. The greatest of the masons, Manole, has a dream: they must wall up the first wife or sister that comes to see them on the morrow, and the spell will be broken. The next day it is Manole's own wife who comes bringing him food, and nothing, though he prays up storms and disasters, will sway her from her devoted path. Faced with threats of certain death by the merciless prince, the masons wall her in. From the wall her voice echoes piteously, but at last the building is finished. The prince then asks his masons, high atop the structure, if they can build an even more stately creation; they respond that they can. The prince throws down the scaffolds and leaves them to perish there on the rooftop; they make wings to fly away but fall and are dashed to the stony ground. As he falls, Manole hears the wall echoing the sad plaints of his wife.[6]

In his analysis of the ballad, historian of religion Mircea Eliade points out that the myth bespeaks the common ideology of "transference": that is, "to last, any construction (house, technical accomplishment, or spiritual undertaking) must be animated ... must receive both life and a soul."[7] This is effected by means of a sacrifice, so that the new construct is "animated" by the immolation, or, as Eliade puts its, "the 'architectonic body' [is] substituted for a body of flesh."[8] The parallel drawn here is twofold: we who have put our souls into technology now see it wrested from us and transferred into the machine. Others, the creators, the artists, risk in their entanglement with this construct their own most unfortunate fall. Beware, Codrescu might caution, beware building the perfect world, the world of virtuality. For "virtuality only has a meaning as long as it is under construction. And we are empty, emptied by what we have given virtuality" (102). Once the construct is finished, like so many Sarah Winchesters, so are we. We believe in information, "worship it," and store it, and in so doing, Codrescu notes, "serve the architecture of the store" (102). But we have lost the deeper meaning, the interconnectedness of that information. By giving it up to the computer, by ceding our place to cyberspace, "we have ensured our obsolescence" (103).

Contemporary Romanian speculative fiction author Ovidiu Crohmălniceanu posits a related question, with a similarly satiric twist: what happens when the computer mewling for its nighttime story stops asking, and takes its own initiative? In his short story, "A Chapter of Literary History," first published in 1980, the world has already gone there, done that. Now it is not humans but machines who produce the literature, from the story's outset:

> Not long after literature-writing machines started rolling off the assembly line and operating at maximum capacity, it was observed that literary critics had begun to disappear on a daily basis. The phenomenon had an immediate cause, easily perceivable: the profession of literary critic had become for all intents impossible to maintain. No one was able to read even the smallest fraction of the books being published. According to rough estimates ... a machine could compose a poem in less than two seconds. A novel under three hundred pages took eighteen minutes to write. Inexplicably, however, the time required to write a play amounted to nearly an hour.... As a result, 10 to the 12th power volumes appeared on bookshelves every year in Lima alone, and publishers' profits skyrocketed.[9]

In the story, computers have gone far beyond merely sucking humans dry: self-sufficient, they now demand their pound of text-flesh from the only remaining functionaries of the literary world, the critics. Literary historians are "the first to relinquish their mission" (85), being unable to read "even one ten thousandth of a percent" of the computer-produced literature. Newspaper editors next succumb: how, they ask in despair, can one critique such writing? For, as the story observes, "literary commentator's calling was ... to examine the extent to which an author had accomplished his or her artistic intention. But since the machines never strayed one iota from their program, they created only masterpieces" (85). No human error could intrude and corrupt the program; evaluation by human beings was impossible, not to mention redundant: "Even the most eccentric of readers' tastes had been predicted in the original statistical calculations. Surprises were no longer possible" (85).

The critics, stereotypically true to their nature, at first strike back. "Someone came up with the idea of having a number of bad books programmed, just for the sake of comparison. Otherwise there would be no way of telling a masterpiece from something mediocre" (85). Resistance, however, proves futile: "the vicious circle could not be broken. The machines designed to write worthless books also performed their task unfailingly. The resultant texts were flawless in their mediocrity or stupidity, thus automatically acquiring an inestimable aesthetic value" (85). And once a philosopher put forth his theory that the critics were doomed (a wry commentary, perhaps on the emphasis critics place on their own esteemed position in the literary world), it is just a matter of time before their total demise. Readers learn that, fittingly, "the last of the critics died in his library of brain congestion one morning in May, literally buried under a mountain of books" (85–86).

With mordant irony, the narrator opines that this state was unacceptable, for "no one could conceive of literature without critical analysis" (86). The solution is obvious: build and program computers who can do that as well. The dilemma comes down to the issue of programming: what type of analysis should the machines be programmed for? They begin, perhaps rather naively, with the basics, the "genres, species, themes, subjects, and artistic formulas" (86). This proves unsatisfactory, as the only result is a series of book lists so long as to be unreadable by humans, thus creating the need for new computers to perform the task of culling through them. The debate resumes: what criteria for adjudging books should be used? They proceed with the critical theories then in vogue during the period of "literary apprenticeship"— that is, as the story specifies, "the age in which books had been written by humans" (86). Yet each kind of literary criticism attempted produces unexpected results:

> Existentialist criticism in electronic shape clashed with the paradox of machine-produced literature. Was it the genuine expression of human experiences? Yes and no. The works existentialist critics set out to discuss did express life experiences (the programs contained so many possibilities that results were utterly unpredictable, thus mimicking the ineffable flutterings of human existence), but the machines themselves remained heaps of filaments, levers, and interconnected wires that entered into a state of inertia the moment a single button was pushed. Psychoanalytic criticism aroused controversy as usual, because its deductions extended not only to the subconscious motives of its designers but also to those of the managers of the industrial enterprises supplying the electronic brains meant to engender literary works [86].

Matters critical go so far as to engender legal disputes: the chair of a lead-ing financial organization, for instance, "found himself accused of experienc-ing the incestuous drives described in the 12,604th Antigone (a play conceived by a machine constructed by a firm associated with his bank)" (86). And although the accused gentleman protests that he hadn't even heard of the orig-inal play, the story observes dryly that "his plea met with serious theoretical objections" (86).

Other modes of critical analysis are explored, with predictably little suc-cess. Theological critiques temporarily "enjoyed some degree of success" with the machines, as they ensured their identification with human beings of yore "into whom God the Designer had breathed the grace of creation" (87). Ulti-mately, and not surprisingly, this meets with stern human clerical opposition. The only kind of critical analysis that works as planned turns out to be one "that returned to an earlier view of the critical art of interpretation ... of a condensed reconstruction of the essential elements of literature, one that pointed out the virtual possibilities left unexplored by the author" (87). As a logical consequence, the machines extrapolate artistic intentions, and litera-ture flourishes as never before: "from one novel they generated several thou-sand; from one poem, entire cycles; from one play, millions of superior variants" (87). Yet this direction also has unforeseen consequences. In a few years people notice that the "machine-authors" had begun to "show signs of irritation" (87): discordant elements turn up at the end of the texts, as if to thwart their perfect programming. This "aesthetic suicide" (the havoc wreaked on the computers is like a parting shot from outdated humanity on the order and stability of the computer world) resulted in works that would suddenly go off course and head in an utterly different direction. Of course, in doing so, they short-circuit the machine-critics, which respond by shutting down.

The stalemate is resolved only when someone (apparently, a human being) comes up with the "revolutionary idea" of plugging both machine-authors and machine-critics into the same circuit. Forced to consume one another's out-put, their roles reverse: "Whereas the machine-critics had displayed a secret bent for creative writing, the machine-writers now revealed a previously hid-den passion for literary criticism" (87). The cycle is complete. Having replaced humans in the creative process, the machines now eliminate even the brief moments of critical analysis attempted by humans, deeming them ultimately inefficient interruptions of the process. Ironically, this fate is not the *coup de grace* for humankind; indeed, the story relegates them to other nameless pur-suits in its trenchant conclusion: "And since ... all of the above occurred with devouring violence within a closed circle, people were able to go about their business undisturbed" (87). The brief interventions of humanity with liter-ature, the caesuras at the hemstitches of writing, fill up, the hyphens that caress and join word to word, fall away. For as all those who have watched the evolution of English over the internet know, no one uses hyphens any more.

The works of both authors maintain a cynicism towards the glories of the cyberworld of which we are quite familiar, ever since Karel Čapek's *R.U.R.* (1921), indeed ever since Mary Shelley's *Frankenstein* (1818). Codrescu, of course, writes from the inside, as an author currently functioning in a culture springing headlong towards all the cyberworld has to offer. Small wonder that, as he observes in his essay, our internet focus tends to remain on money and on sex (100). For if, as he suggests, we are facing our final showdown with machines as rivals, money and sex are arguably the only things that still confirm our existence in cyberspace as human beings: money, because it is still viewed (in spite of the distancing effect of capital) as a "thing to be acquired," hence under some measure of human control; and sex, because it is body-directed. Even if cut off from real bodies, it is still experienced as pleasure upon a body — if only in the mind.

In Codrescu's vision, the only hope is for authors to take up their craft again on the margins, in the abandoned places, staking their claims once more in ways that are messy, public, disorderly, smelling, burgeoning with life, where a writer might "construct a picture of the world from the few bits of information still charged by the senses" (103).

The writer's new beginning must needs break itself free from the terminal, the end point.[10] In Crohmălniceanu's story, however, it is no longer a question of humans fighting from the margins. Liminality has been superseded; man is no longer in the picture. Hence the programmers in the story return to a sort of New Criticism for the final critical programming, the old critical standby which presented the author as merely a means to an end, and the text triumphant. In his story, the text is all-triumphant, and the break with humanity, its progenitor, is complete. At the end, there remains no unfortunate and wasteful human interference with the production of texts; all is, on the surface at least, calm, and orderly, and free of humans. As a writer, I ponder my own obsolescence every time I behold a spam poem pop into my email inbox. And though I long to ponder, to analyze, to critique it, I know my report would indeed be in the minority.[11] Most of my fellows will simply have their computers intercept these cyber-generated irruptions, so as to leave them alone, tranquil — undisturbed.

Notes

1. Received to my inbox in August 2008, God knows from whence.
2. Florin Manolescu, "Introduction," *The Phantom Church and Other Stories from Romania*, translated and edited by Georgiana Farnoaga and Sharon King (Pittsburgh, PA: University of Pittsburgh Press, 1996), viii.

3. Manolescu, x–xi.

4. Michel Foucault, *Discipline and Punish: The Birth of the Prison*, translated by Alan Sheridan (New York: Vintage/Random House, 1995).

5. Not surprisingly, the essay is included in Andrei Codrescu's essay collection *The Dog With the Chip in Its Neck* (New York: St. Martin's, 1996), 97–103; later parenthetical page references are to this edition. Other essays in the anthology ("Head Full of Numbers," "Computer to the Afterlife," "Adding Memory") expound on the same theme.

6. See *Meşterul Manole*, edited by Zoe Dumitrescu-Buşulenga (Bucureşti: Editura Albatros, 1976). See also Mircea Eliade, *Meşterul Manole: studii de etnologie şi mitologie* (Iaşi: Editura Junimea, 1992).

7. Mircea Eliade, *Zalmoxis, the Vanishing God: Comparative Studies in the Religions and Folklore of Dacia and Eastern Europe*, translated by Willard R. Trask (Chicago and London: University of Chicago Press, Midway Reprint, 1972), 182.

8. *Zalmoxis*, 182–83.

9. Ovidiu S. Crohmalniceanu, "A Chapter of Literary History," *The Phantom Church and Other Stories from Romania*, translated and edited by Georgiana Farnoaga and Sharon King (Pittsburgh, PA: University of Pittsburgh Press, 1996), 84–85. Later parenthetical page references are to this edition.

10. Codrescu's ultimate haven for writers was in fact his home base, the heady, sensory-laden New Orleans; the essay was of course published long before the devastation wrought by Hurricane Katrina upon that city.

11. For the 2007 Los Angeles Science Fiction Convention, I organized a panel to explore this issue entitled "Spam as Poetry." Ironically, due to technical reasons the panel was cancelled at the last minute by the convention.

16. A Creature of Double Vision

Gregory Benford

Viewing ourselves is an incessant human habit. Who can pass a mirror without a glance? And deeper than vanity, we struggle to fathom who we are in a world with no clearly similar creatures.

Quite different scientific disciplines — chimpanzee studies, artificial intelligence projects, the Search for Extraterrestrial Intelligence — speak to a common underlying anxiety. We don't like to feel alone with ourselves. Maybe the opposite-handed person in the mirror will be, well, different? Or at least tell us the truth?

Aristotle noted our appetite for wonderment at our own nature. Certainly a major definition of ourselves would be, "The self-scrutinizing animal."

A sum of oblique angles taken may give us the right slant — but only for our own era, for as we learn more, our many crazy-house mirrors warp. Culture curves these reflectors, and science can splinter them. Could the resolute rationalists of the eighteenth century have felt the slightest resonance with, say, existentialism? I suspect they would have been appalled when they were not merely bewildered.

After we have sifted through all definitions of what it means to be human, there comes a persistent feeling of missing a key element. Science analyzes by atomizing — the reducing razor turned against our very selves. Surely our ineffable intuition of our being-ness demands something more than these partial pictures?

In ordinary life this sensation often merely signals a lapse of imagination or even outright incomprehension. Cramped mirrors yield narrow views. However powerfully felt, such feelings have often blinded us to reality. Gut feelings are not arguments.

As an example from my own field, physics, consider the mystification of light before the twentieth century. Philosophers and poets alike (George

Berkeley, Goethe, William Blake) felt that reductionist models of how light behaved — its warping refractions, lustrous scatterings, mysterious absorptions — missed its vital, luminous essence. They saw the gauzy splendors of sunrise, the subtle joys of rainbows, and felt that surely these could not arise from the crude, mechanical pictures of the experimenters.

Yet starting from descriptions of diffraction in the early nineteenth century, leading up to the triumph of James Clerk Maxwell, physics kept on. His genius lay not just in formulating dry mathematics to describe the experiments done by Michael Faraday and many other experimenters. That task done, Maxwell felt that something was missing. To create an artful symmetry in his equations, he added a term, following intuition, and *presto*—they then described oscillatory motions in the electrical and magnetic fields themselves.

Maxwell's dogged pursuit of equations to describe the workings of electrical circuits gave a picture of oscillating charges engaged in a perpetual dance with electric and magnetic fields, all moving in concert to support waves. From the experimenters' dry data Maxwell could calculate the speed of such waves. He was astonished.

It was a revelation of the first order: that the speed of electrical circuitry gave the same velocity as that of light. In such moments science slips the veil from our eyes, unmasking connections no one guessed. Maxwell's intuition was a gut feeling, honed by a sense of mathematical aesthetics. But it led to checkable results, unlike those of the philosophers and poets.

Soon enough, Marconi was using those invisible waves to carry real messages, like the one that saved many *Titanic* passengers. Physics pervades ordinary life, unsuspected. Mirrors work because they can carry currents. A sea of electrons seethes beneath their hard mercury skins, reacting readily to light's stirring fields. These currents conspire to reject light's surging electric and magnetic fields, casting them back the way they came. An actress adjusting her lipstick profits from electrons' resistance to interference from outside.

The poets' and philosophers' inability to see a connection between sloshing currents in waves and luminous sunset beauty revealed a gap in the human imagination, not in reality.

We also find it hard to see how chemical abstractions underlie our lives — say, how genetic gnomes buried in our cells can regulate and inspire our internal biochemical workings, most definitely including our thinking.

Genes express themselves by making and regulating proteins — microscopic machinery down in our basements — while upstairs we feel emotions and urges, fancies and forebodings. We feel this most keenly in the mystery of consciousness. Our vague sense of a gap between our models and our interior experience is not a heavy-duty fact of metaphysical import, but a momentary modern swamp of competing currents and notions. Soon, as we learn more about the brain, such issues will cease to become backwaters. They will join the colliding currents of science and philosophy.

Consciousness may arise when a brain's running model of the outer world becomes so detailed that it must include a picture of itself. This conjecture by British biologist Richard Dawkins is itself a model, of course, one that we could test if we had living members of the hominids who came before us.

Still, our skimpy knowledge of our prehistory suggests that we did uniquely profit from out talent for modeling the interior states of mind of each other, but also of very different creatures. We turned wolves into hunting dogs, fellow companions on the hunt and defenders of our campfires. This came from our ability to sense the emotions of another species, and cater to them. Later we domesticated farm animals, horses and cats. Such collaborations between species are rare in the wild, but we have many. We can sense the inner states of a variety of animals, cater to those, and form alliances.

Such modeling ability our famous crowd-pleasers deftly employ to gather in our appreciation. This is not easy; good politicians have it in plenty.

Going beyond such commonplace truths, scientists today probe into our brains, or build projects to engineer thinking into computers. These are all experiments to fill that felt gap between Us and the Other. We have invented angels and devils, gods and aliens — all to give us someone to talk to. The desire to communicate beyond ourselves is strong because we have many unanswered questions, and need perspective.

Alas, we have no handy Other. Perhaps we lend great weight to our origins because the lever of reason needs a fulcrum. Our history might provide a pivot. But can it give us a *single* place to stand?

*****

> I don't want to achieve immortality through my work.... I want to achieve it through not dying.
>   — Woody Allen[1]

One feature of being human we surely share with some of our long lost hominid ancestors is that we all know that we shall die. When this realization came into the hominid mind is unknowable — alas, for it could provide a useful definition of the human condition.

Such knowledge typically comes fully in adolescence, and dogs us throughout our days. Evolution surely has preferred early and ample reproduction over longevity. Our brooding upon death — surely a major force behind religion — suggests that this profound anxiety strikes at a unique center of human consciousness.

We are attached to our own individual existence, and hunger for expressions of continuity. Those who do not believe in an afterlife still like to think of their family, clan or ideas carrying forward. Even the atheistic communists hungered to be "on the side of history," meaning the future and "destiny." Novelists wish to be read by later generations. Cultural continuity is different from traveling on inside our rickety selves forever, a continuous *I* voyaging into fresh days. Our minds seek such consolations.

We can live little longer than a century. Yet our experience of our unfolding life stories does not fit. Lives have little obvious narrative arc, though we shape stories and songs to conceal this. Beyond the weariness and aches of age we have little sense of a natural limit. Our minds seem limitless, blithe spirits, flying higher than a bird.

Indeed, we envy birds their artful flight, and animals for their seemingly blissful unawareness of the problems that vex us. People seem happiest when they act seamlessly, without thinking — "going with the flow," the conscious Self not in charge. Religion can excite such feelings, usually with disciplines — prayers, liturgy, hymns, rites, chants — that repeat endlessly to invoke reassuring timeless order. Reciting a mantra or a prayer fills our verbal channel, the slim bandwidth of language, preoccupying our conscious minds so that the unconscious gets a crack. Meditation avoids conscious thoughts. Familiar prayers release our minds to think sidewise from our conscious minds. Even dancing helps us "let go" (of what?).

This is a powerful fact. These ancient, crude diversions of mental currents can give us a certain rough use of our "brain software," to use the (often illusory) brain-computer analogy. (Our brains self-program and alter their hardware by growing new neurons, for example; computers can't ... yet.) We value reason, yet sometimes seek to elude it. Alcohol and drugs are cultural universals.

Still, our knowledge of our inevitable deaths cannot fully explain our need for distractions from the rigors of conscious thought. The charms of chanting and dancing appeal to children, too, who are blissfully unconcerned with mortality. There must be other, deep difficulties from which we must sometimes slip free.

*****

Commonly we just "have" ideas, whereas it might be better to say that they have us. Unconscious levels seize our attention and deliver their work to our conscious inspection. Creative acts stride in from the darkened wings onto stage center. In those shadowy alcoves, forces blunt and ancient know that death is coming, and labor to create some bulwark against it. Much grandeur and tragedy have come of these deep desires.

Science has prospered from a great trick: shrink problems to their simplest form, and solve that. Leave complexity and complication for later. This has worked so well in modern times that we often think it is the sole path to truth.

And in fact, recent work in neuroanatomy suggests that a bottom-up picture of our Selves makes sense, too. In this view, simple systems of neurons coordinate their signaling to attain something a level higher, a proto-self. This leads to a next step, a core of coordinating neural networks that produce a "core self" (in the terms of Antonio R. Damasio) which experiences "core consciousness." This level can have an autobiographical feeling for itself, can tell itself stories about its own experience or, more tellingly, about the outside world. This makes up a model of events outside, a simplified view of reality obtained by selective disregard of some aspects.

A step further upstairs comes with learning to use this model to predict, judge and then predict the real world's progression. Story-telling is a way to choreograph events in time so they make sense, a facet of a larger consciousness which can extend its realm across the hours, days and years. Only with elaborate complexity can this narrative skill yield such high cultural aspects as conscience, the fruit of consciousness.

An important aspect of this interior stage is our place in it. We are so involved with our living of experience that, when most caught up, we do not feel that we are watching events unfold. Rather, we feel ourselves immersed in the flow, and comprehend our selves richly through the pulse of event. "You are the music/while the music lasts," as T.S. Eliot put it.[2]

Consciousness is perception, while intelligence is the ability to adroitly use perceptions to conjure up new insights. Being smart leads the mind up through a pyramid of language, games, puzzles and scenarios of increasing abstraction. But at what price?

The process of making interior models can interact fruitfully with our environment, even (perhaps especially) when the world around us is bleakly plain. In the desert, the emptiness itself induces illusions and patterns in our striving, busy minds. Mystics have long preferred such featureless isolation, all the better to find themselves. Subtle order then emerges. Minds always groping for structure, plan, and hidden aspects impose them, if need be. We find faces in clouds, not just in our mirrors.

Similarly, we delight in the surprises delivered by good music, clever jokes, plot twists. Nature has shaped us to be always on the lookout.

We are expert spectators, with enormous stores of brain power applied to filtering vision. Our visual sense coupled through our powerful parallel-processing brains can digest millions of bits of information per second. Alas, to most of us, "information" means the few bits per second we get while reading a newspaper or looking at a computer monitor. This leads to a sensation of unspoken starvation, like sensory deprivation — a little remarked feature of modern life.

Such practices may add to our vague sense of being disconnected from the world, a source of existential anxiety. This is part of the price of abstraction, but not the only one.

*****

Often Darwinian metaphors stress conflict and single-minded self interest, while trust, friendship and empathy take lesser roles, often reductionist ones, almost as an afterthought. Yet these emotions animate us mightily. Perhaps they should be accorded equal status in our arsenal of social inventions.

Sex is surely the most intimate connection we can enjoy, and evolution's invention of it was a striking victory for cooperation, not competition. Surely a truly selfish gene (a la Richard Dawkins) wants to make copies of itself *ad infinitum*, and so would prefer cloning. Sex mixes genes randomly with those of another, so any gene has only a 50–50 chance of getting through to the next generation. Cloning allows accurate copying, but at the cost of ruling out improvement of genetic endowment through the conspiring of genes from the two parents. Our hope for the future of our kind rests not upon sending our individual traits hurtling down through future ages, but rather upon the building up of better properties through collaborations.

Still, human behavior has consistencies across all cultures that argue for a genetic basis, so some general social properties are always selected for. But telling which these are is fraught with tricky interpretation. Surely there seems a global need for religion, but particular beliefs can vary enormously. They are not reasoned out linearly from a general impulse.

And while we're at it, why enshrine reason at all? We value our rationality, but often fail to see that it is a tool we get from evolution, not a moral imperative.

We cannot purely reason our way to a moral high ground, for logic *by itself* does not yield motivations; usually it begins from them. It must be yoked to some emotion to have a direction.

Our expanded frontal lobes can provide the scaffolding of reason, true — and can also control anti-social self-interest. Lack of this control yields a breed of psychopath with charisma and ruthlessness — cult leaders and Hitlers who can sway vast crowds. In the telling observation of the German psychiatrist Ernst Kretschmer, "It's a funny thing about psychopaths. In normal times we render expert opinions about them. In times of political unrest they rule us."[3] Perhaps this is our old chimp alpha-male training emerging yet again under stress?

Still, reason gives us a reach that many evolutionary theorists find inexplicable. Why do mental tools evolved to bring down game in Africa also equip us to voyage among the planets? Why does mathematics, as mysterious as music, extend our reach into realms far from that dusty veldt?

It almost seems that our mental machinery leads us, rather than the other way around, to states of high complexity and remarkable range. Creatures who flensed meat from bones only an evolutionary eye blink away into the past now probe the origin of matter and time itself as we study the earliest shaved seconds of the universe.

That we daily exercise such talents without surprise at ourselves is itself a clue. We do not usually look too deeply into the mirror, after all. And how like us, to wonder why we wonder so.

*****

Earnestly inquiring into the nature of ourselves may seem ridiculous. After all, animals don't appear to. They usually seem quite content, and indeed, some feel that animals live in a state of Zen like completion, living in and of and for the moment. Is this not the state of transcendental enlightenment so many of us seek?

We don't know, and we cannot. The mental state of animals is endlessly interesting, but fundamentally unknowable. Thomas Nagel's famous essay, "What Is It Like to Be a Bat?" asks how one can know this, and what knowing might mean.

Asking ourselves about ourselves might seem absurd also in the spirit of the 1940–1950s existentialists. Certainly in the light of our immense universe, stretching fore and aft along both directions in time and space — tiny to tremendous, past to future — we can seem insignificant. Existentialist doubt comes from the loss of sense of purpose, a disease afflicting us moderns especially. It renders self-questioning absurd in a deeper sense.

Yet do these questions mean much? If we were to become grotesquely grand, filling all of space, we would still lack for purpose. Knowing that nothing we do now will matter in, say, a billion years depends upon asserting that nothing we do *now* matters.

Where does that haunting sensation come from? For indeed it is a sensation, an opening of an endless black pit beneath the feet, a plunge into the abyss of meaninglessness. Here is where the scientific view contrasts strongly with more "humanistic" definitions.

Indeed, where does true humanism lie? In comfortable assertions of the primacy of ourselves ("Man is the measure of all things")? Or in the sour conviction that this is one more posture of a strutting primate? Perhaps in some middle ground, seeing ourselves as just one more species in a working biosphere?

This contrast is the core of our problem. We live inside our bodies, ever-conscious of the pressing moment, our lived lives. At the same time we resort to intellect to make sense of the chaotic world, to merge into the objective.

Peering down at ourselves from our step-ladder of abstraction, our earnest pursuit of momentary ambitions seems comic, another Sisyphus shoving a boulder uphill. Immersed in life, we miss its over-arching features.

Such a duality lies at the essence of being human. *Both* experiences, immersion and abstraction, are us. We watch bemused, and we are caught up. There is no hope of dwelling in only one land — we must experience both.

Science best captures our abstract wisdom. It tells us that we are primates following complex genetic instructions, shaped by ancient forces. But such knowledge does not shelter us from the hammering, immediate moment.

The tension in the lives of scientists, as they move from their day jobs of heady arabesques into their after-hours domestic swarm, is little remarked in literature. The contrast can be powerful, reminding us that David Hume enjoined, "Be a philosopher, but amidst all your philosophy be still a man."

Morality demands that we live in both worlds. Even the cataclysm of war does not free us of the clash between the abstract and the immediate. Should I kill these here and now, to save a greater number elsewhere, later? Machine-gunning people *right here* is morally repugnant when compared with saving distant numbers over the horizon.

The nub of all our moral calculus is that it gives us a result, and experience often gives us another.

The moment grabs us with a power no idea can command. This is evolution shouting *Pay attention!* Whether one can commit an act that revolts a part of oneself, in aid of a principle, is perhaps the best definition of an intellectual — but not the most flattering one.

Riding in our heads as we do, we must live with the tension between objective and subjective views. Reality may be *by definition* objective, but so much for reality. This very definition means that we must reduce our minds to the action of brains, fret over the conflict between free will and determinism, and prefer cool calculation to moral anguish.

The objective view of ourselves claims supremacy: it can envelope the merely subjective. Detaching ourselves offers a sweeping grandiosity. But subjectively, the cool moral calculus of the objectivists looks like a hopeless reduction, an over-simplification of a complex life we receive not just through our senses, but through our emotions — the felt world. Math does not yield meaning.

Perhaps the best answer to this conundrum is to declare no victor in the ancient debate. We cannot tolerate a world in which one side wins; either would deny an essential humanity in us. So we refuse to settle on a definition of ourselves, and thus of the world. There is no viewpoint-free view of us. Perspective tells the story.

Yet what is real? Our bedrock sense is to resort to the most concrete.

Here abstract principle contends with our swarming sense of the world, intense and immediate.

Taking neither side in the objective/subjective debate seems to declare that there is no reality, while our common sense says there certainly is. Or is this the old objective view, poking its nose under the conceptual tent?

This inescapable duality is perhaps the essence of our predicament, of being only human — one that even understanding our own minds and brains may well not dispel.

Notes

1. Woody Allen, cited in Eric Lax, *On Being Funny: Woody Allen and Comedy* (New York: Charterhouse, 1975), 232.

2. T. S. Eliot, "The Dry Salvages," *Four Quartets* (London: Faber and Faber, 1944), 33.

3. Ernst Kretschmer, 1933 letter, cited in Donald B. Calne, *Within Reason: Rationality and Human Behavior* (New York: Pantheon, 1999), 144. Kretschmer made a similar statement in *The Psychology of Men of Genius*: "The psychopaths are always there, but in cool times of peace we give medical reports on them, and in times of social fever — they are our masters" (*The Psychology of Men of Genius,* translated, with an introduction, by R. B. Cattell [College Park, MD: McGrath, 1970], 13).

Afterword: Science Fiction and the Playing Fields of Eaton

Gary Westfahl

In its early years, I experienced the J. Lloyd Eaton Conferences on Science Fiction and Fantasy Literature, long held every year at the University of California, Riverside, only as an awestruck spectator, listening to distinguished scholars as they analyzed works of science fiction and fantasy at the podium and fielded stimulating questions from the audience. Later, I became a regular speaker and panelist at those conferences, and by the mid–1990s, I was serving as a conference coordinator, along with George Slusser and Eric S. Rabkin. In the course of two decades, then, I observed the Eaton Conferences from all possible angles, and while I did not attend every gathering or listen to every presentation, I grew very familiar with, and fond of, those annual conferences. Further, when I began to co-edit volumes of essays from the conferences in the 1990s, I came to appreciate the Eaton Conferences not only as stimulating experiences in themselves, but also as the invaluable first stages in a process that ultimately led to the publication of essays that were sharpened and improved by the numerous forces that acted upon them.

I can speak knowledgeably on this topic because this volume is the ninth Eaton volume I have co-edited, and hence represents the ninth occasion when I have witnessed and participated in the entire Eaton experience, from writing the call for papers to the final proofreading and indexing of the completed volume. My involvement with the Eaton Conferences has had a significant and lasting impact on my career as a science fiction scholar and

This essay first appeared in Extrapolation *47:1 (Spring 2006): 7–15.*

commentator, and I have found it rewarding to recall a number of my experiences there and to relate those experiences to some general observations about the genre of science fiction.

To a large extent, the Eaton Conferences resembled other conferences devoted to literary criticism: most of the people attending were academically trained scholars in English literature, ranging from graduate students to senior professors, and most of the conference schedule was reserved for presentations of their papers. In these ways, the Eaton Conferences were similar to the other two longstanding annual gatherings of science fiction scholars, the Science Fiction Research Association Conferences and the International Conferences on the Fantastic in the Arts. However, unlike other forms of contemporary literature, science fiction attracts the attention of some very different sorts of people, and founding Eaton coordinator George Slusser always worked especially hard to include representatives of those other groups, making for the unusually diverse and lively sessions that regularly characterized the Eaton Conferences.

In a paper originally presented at the 1994 conference, "Who Governs Science Fiction?," I attempted to survey and categorize the different forces that control the genre of science fiction. I discussed Hugo Gernsback, who originally introduced the term "science fiction" to the world and still influences its usage; the writers and fans of the science fiction community, who have a powerful collective impact on the evolution of the genre; the general public, which determines what "science fiction" means as it is described in dictionaries; the publishing industry, which decides to label and market certain books as "science fiction"; and academic scholars, who regularly study, anthologize, and teach science fiction.[1] Were I expanding the scheme today, I might divide the writers and fans into separate groups — since, as suggested by the separate literary awards now given by writers (the Nebulas) and fans (the Hugos), their interests are not always congruent; and I might divide the academic scholars into traditional literary critics and scholars from other disciplines — because scholars not trained to examine literature, such as historians and experts in political science, happen to be unusually active and visible in the study of science fiction and bring a distinctive perspective to their work.

Finally, I might add, as a final group influencing science fiction, the scientific community, for several reasons. First, since science fiction is historically expected to maintain at least a semblance of scientific accuracy, scientists become the people who, in effect, make the rules; thus, years of learned complaints that it was impossible for elementary particles to be miniature planets with tiny inhabitants drove that theme out of the genre, and scientific disdain for depictions of spaceships flitting from star to star, ignoring the fact that objects in this universe cannot travel faster than light, made ameliorative references to "warp drive" or "hyperspace" *de rigueur* in all stories of this kind. In addition, scientists since the days of Gernsback have regularly been asked to write articles for science fiction magazines, contribute to science fiction anthologies, and participate in panels at science fiction conventions. Many scientists also read and were inspired by science fiction as children and continued to read science fiction as adults; and a number of scientists, like Fred Hoyle, Carl Sagan, Robert F. Forward, and Marvin Minsky, became science fiction writers themselves. In these various ways, then, working scientists have always had a strong impact on the genre.

Thus expanded, the list of forces influencing science fiction would be virtually identical to a list of the different groups of people who contributed to Eaton Conferences — so that the conferences became, in a sense, models of the ways that science fiction itself is crafted and shaped, and participating in those conferences provided a unique opportunity to observe firsthand the interactions that make the genre especially fascinating. Of course, the late Hugo Gernsback never attended an Eaton Conference — except in spirit, perhaps, whenever I discussed his contributions in my papers — but along with literary scholars, science fiction writers, fans, general readers, representatives of publishers, scholars from other disciplines, and scientists were all regularly observed at conferences.

Every Eaton Conference had a few science fiction writers, sometimes several of them, as guests or paper presenters. To be sure, noted writers may attend other conferences focused on contemporary literature, but typically they are delicately treated as honored special guests: perhaps they do a reading from one of their works or graciously consent to answer questions from the audience; they may even give a short talk about their methods of writing. But the science fiction writers at Eaton Conferences rolled up their sleeves and joined in the work of the other participants.

First, trained by years of experience in panel appearances at science fiction conventions (where informal panels are the principal activity), science fiction writers happily agreed to participate in panels at Eaton Conferences and invariably offered stimulating commentary related to the theme of that year's gathering. While only one of these panel discussions has been transcribed and published,[2] other fascinating dialogues were recorded and may someday be made available. In addition, a number of writers, not content to merely toss out a few comments during a panel discussion, stepped up to the podium to present papers themselves — and not just rambling monologues about their own careers, but genuinely probing analyses of their genre. Authors who have presented papers at Eaton Conferences include Poul Anderson, Greg Bear, Gregory Benford, David Brin, Samuel R. Delany, Sheila Finch, Robert F. Forward, James Gunn, Howard V. Hendrix, Larry Niven, Lewis Shiner, and

Norman Spinrad; a few, like Benford and Hendrix, virtually became Eaton regulars.

Finally, when they were not on panels or presenting papers, the authors were usually listening to the other papers, ready to provide their own input during the vigorous question-and-answer sessions that invariably followed each paper. In my second paper that I nervously presented in 1988, for example, I argued that the heroes and villains in science fiction stories speak differently — that villains, for example, tended to use longer words and more complex sentences; two of my examples were the heroic Jack Barron and the villainous Benedict Howards from Norman Spinrad's *Bug Jack Barron* (1969).[3] But Spinrad himself was in the audience, and he rose afterwards to object that he had quite deliberately made Barron a character who spoke in short, simple sentences — as is only befitting for a talk show host — but *thought* in longer, more convoluted sentences, better reflecting his true character and intellect. Needless to say, his remarks inspired some additional thoughts in the published version of the essay about possible limitations in my methodology.[4]

Science fiction fans also were always welcome at Eaton Conferences — after all, the man whose science fiction collection inspired the conferences, J. Lloyd Eaton, was himself a noted fan — and well-known personalities from the science fiction community like Forrest J. Ackerman, Bruce Pelz, and Rick Sneary were visitors. While these people may not have been conversant with the latest critical theories, their knowledge of science fiction literature and film could be vast and impressive. Once, after Pilgrim Award-winning scholar Vivian Sobchack presented a provocative analysis of science fiction films at the 1983 Eaton Conference (later published as "The Virginity of Astronauts"[5]), Forrest J Ackerman — whose decades-long involvement with science fiction film has generated many articles and books and a unique collection of memorabilia — rose from the audience to politely note that he could, off the top of his head, think of a dozen or so science fiction films that in his opinion contradicted her thesis, and he proceeded to name a few of them. While Sobchack stood her ground in response to his objections, their friendly words of disagreement characterize the encounters between people from different worlds that could make an Eaton Conference especially memorable.

Since Eaton Conferences were locally advertised, it was always possible that members of the general public, unconnected to academia or the science fiction community, would wander in to see a favorite author and stay for the rest of the conference. Once a precocious twelve-year-old boy attended, listened to every paper, and asked every speaker a question. So, after Robert Philmus, then editor of *Science-Fiction Studies*, presented a lengthy exegesis of the works of Stanislaw Lem at the 1985 Eaton Conference (later published as "The Cybernetic Paradigms of Slanislaw Lem"[6]), the lad boldly inquired, "Just who is Stanislaw Lem, anyway?" "Out of the mouths of babes!" I thought at the time, and I have — not entirely in jest — since referred to his question as the single most profound question ever asked at an Eaton Conference. For the boy was unknowingly pointing out a crucial problem unaddressed in critical studies of Lem: while the author was then receiving a tremendous amount of attention from literary scholars, he was failing to attract a following in the science fiction community, and he was failing to become well-known to the general public. Thus, with his career solely supported by academic critics, Lem was destined to fade from view the moment that the constantly shifting tides of scholarly interest turned away from him — which is, more or less, precisely what happened during the 1990s. (It should be noted that when he read this anecdote, Eric S. Rabkin, who attended the session, did not remember the boy's question, but I remain convinced that it happened exactly as I described it.)

Eaton Conferences never attracted much attention from major publishers, since there were insufficient numbers of potential book buyers in attendance, but a few of their representatives, like David G. Hartwell of Tor Books and Stewart Wieck of White Wolf Publishers, sometimes made an appearance. Also, one small publisher specializing in science fiction criticism, Borgo Press, was for many years a prominent presence at Eaton Conferences, since founder Robert Reginald (known to friends as Mike Burgess) and his wife Mary Burgess always set up a table to display and sell their products, and Reginald participated in other conference activities as well, such as the annual presentations of the Eaton Awards and Milford Awards. Such people had an impact on Eaton affairs as well. After Gregory Benford presented a paper about British science fiction at the 1990 Eaton Conference, Hartwell privately gave him his professional opinion of that literature —"downbeat novels with good characterization"—which found its way into the published version of the paper ("In the Wake of the Wave"[7]). And after hearing another one of my papers, on the history of science fiction art (later published as "Artists in Wonderland"[8]) at the 1995 conference. Reginald complained that two of the artists I had focused on were not really major figures — and, with his professional awareness of the importance of cover art in selling science fiction books, he was undoubtedly correct, and his comments led to some revisions in the published version of the paper.

Another element in the diversity of Eaton Conferences was the participation of scholars from fields other than literary studies. Such experts are usually attracted to science fiction primarily because of its contents — its unique focus on thought-provoking ideas and interesting portrayals of possible futures — rather than its virtues as literature, which is sometimes refreshing.

Speakers at Eaton Conferences included scholars in areas such as anthropology, art, business, history, philosophy, political science, and religion, and their varied expertise was often a welcome addition to the proceedings. For example, when philosopher John Martin Fischer, aided by Ruth Curl, introduced at the 1992 conference a carefully worded taxonomy of the types of immortality presented in science fiction (later published as "Philosophical Models of Immortality in Science Fiction"[9]), other speakers embraced and employed their terminology — such as "serial atomistic immortality"— in their own papers on the subject.

Scientists frequently contributed to Eaton Conferences, from fields such as biology, computer science, mathematics, medicine, pharmacology, and physics. While several visiting scientists might be mentioned here, including computer expert Marvin Minsky, neurobiologist Joseph D. Miller merits special recognition as the scientist who most frequently and energetically participated in Eaton Conferences as a paper presenter, panelist, and audience member. With teaching and research experience at Stanford University, Texas Tech University, and the University of Southern California, earlier work for NASA's space shuttle program, and an encyclopedic knowledge of science fiction, Miller brought an especially useful background to the study of science fiction. In a paper at the 1994 conference (later published as "Popes or Tropes"[10]), for example, he employed a battery of meticulous statistical tests in order to demonstrate beyond doubt that the stories in Ursula K. Le Guin and Brian Attebery's *The Norton Book of Science Fiction* (1993) did not truly represent the field's best work. And at the 1995 conference, when Marleen Barr's otherwise persuasive examination of sexist imagery in the artwork of the Apollo program (research that was later incorporated into her *Genre Fission*[11]) cited a painting of a lunar astronaut in a spacesuit that displayed a prominent phallic bulge, Miller noted that the bulge did not represent subtle sexism, but was rather an accurate portrayal of a necessary design feature in the Apollo spacesuit.

To epitomize the sorts of creative — and sometimes combative — interactions that characterized the Eaton Conferences, I might recall the heated panel discussion about *Star Trek* that took place at the 1999 Eaton Conference. Judy Burns, who wrote an episode of the first series, along with scholars Daniel Bernardi and Vivian Sobchack, strongly defended *Star Trek* as an important force in many people's lives and as a significant forum for social commentary. On the other side, Gregory Benford and Joseph D. Miller, representing both the scientific community and the science fiction community, caustically derided *Star Trek* for its clichéd plots and its indifference to science; interpreting the popularity of *Star Trek* as a sign of growing scientific illiteracy, Benford compared himself as a hard science fiction writer to a painter noted for brilliant use of color who discovers that his audience is going color-blind. As the discussion heated up, George Slusser and I as the moderators struggled to speak in moderate tones, acknowledging the value of *Star Trek* and rejecting efforts to marginalize the phenomenon even as we understood the opposition's argument that other works of science fiction attempt, and sometimes achieve, far greater things than have ever been attempted or achieved by any of the *Star Trek* series, films, or novels.

In providing several anecdotes about the input of writers, fans, general readers, representatives of publishers, other scholars, and scientists at Eaton Conferences, I do not wish to slight the contributions of literary critics, who as noted represented the majority of Eaton participants; indeed, the usual highlight of each Eaton Conference was a paper from the late Frank McConnell, an English professor at the University of California, Santa Barbara, who delighted guests with his erudite, far-ranging, and wildly amusing presentations. Nor do I wish to imply that the exchanges at Eaton Conferences characteristically involved other sorts of guests contradicting or upbraiding literary critics. For one thing, in their own papers and questions, critics frequently took issue with other critics at Eaton Conferences, or quarreled among themselves, as Leslie Fiedler and Eric S. Rabkin once fiercely debated the literary merits of the works of A. E. van Vogt. If my stories about past conferences focus on disputes, that may be only because conflict is more memorable than concord. Still, as indicated by the title of the very first Eaton volume, *Bridges to Science Fiction,* the Eaton Conferences were always more about building bridges than burning them, and along with the colorful controversies there have also been many moments of unexpected harmony among disparate conference guests. After that *Star Trek* panel, for example, the feuding participants all gathered for an amiable dinner at a Mexican restaurant; and published papers from the conferences are filled with appreciative references to audience members and their helpful comments and suggestions.

What I am hoping to convey is that Eaton Conferences were uniquely dynamic and interactive events that played a major role in creating the published versions of the conference papers. The question-and-answer sessions after each paper often generated such passionate and fascinating discussions that conference coordinators, reluctant to cut off debate, would allow the speaker and questioners to carry on, so that conferences sometimes fell hopelessly behind schedule. In addition, the later paper presenters would sometimes respond to previous papers and comments by reworking their own papers, either with a few added references to newly absorbed ideas or with extensive revision. On at least two occasions, speakers on the final day of the conference slowly walked to the podium with haggard expressions and apologetically announced that they had stayed up very late the night before, entirely rewriting their papers to take into account what they had heard and learned from the first two days of the conference. For most paper presenters, though, the revision process took place after the conference, when they carefully examined the scribbled marginal notes they made regarding questions and observations from the audience and additionally considered the comments and suggestions of the conference coordinators — who listened attentively to the question-and-answer sessions while formulating their own reactions to the arguments presented. After the final papers were assembled as a manuscript and sent to press, they were of course subjected to the process of peer review, and the anonymous comments occasionally inspired some additional revisions, a traditional result of peer review. But Eaton papers were usually well received at that stage — in large part because, in effect, they had already been through a process of peer review that involved not only literary scholars but also experts from several different areas that are relevant to science fiction.

While the crucible of Eaton therefore functioned to forge superior science fiction criticism, I wish to suggest finally that the process was also analogous to the creation of superior science fiction. After all, what must science fiction writers do to earn a position of lasting importance in the field? They must earn the respect of their fellow writers, and they must be accepted by the science fiction community. They must be embraced by a public willing to purchase their books, and they must be embraced by publishers willing to publish those books. Their works must meet minimal standards of scientific accuracy, and they must be admired and analyzed by literary critics as well as by interested scholars in other fields. If this strikes some as an impossible agenda, it should be noted that there are a number of science fiction writers — ranging from H. G. Wells, Robert A. Heinlein, and Arthur C. Clarke to Ursula K. Le Guin, William Gibson, and Kim Stanley Robinson — who have managed to accomplish all of these things; and these are the writers who seem most likely to achieve literary immortality, as opposed to other skillful writers who have achieved recognition only for their scientific acumen or for their literary qualities. Witnessing the various constituencies of Eaton at work, therefore, allowed one to gain a better understanding of the diverse forces that strangely converge to produce science fiction.

I do not wish to disparage the other conferences devoted to science fiction — the Science Fiction Research Association Conferences and the International Conferences on the Fantastic in the Arts — since much good work has manifestly emerged from these gatherings. Still, based on my own observations, I believe that the Eaton Conference — with its commitments to attracting contributors from diverse fields and encouraging dynamic interaction and argument — represented a uniquely valuable sort of scholarly conference, and one that was uniquely relevant to the study of science fiction.

For those who could not attend, it will always remain stimulating and enjoyable to read the end products of the Eaton Conferences — the essays in the critical anthologies co-edited by myself, George Slusser, Eric S. Rabkin, and others — but I can also testify that participating in the various stages of the journeys was just as rewarding as reaching those final destinations.

Notes

1. Gary Westfahl, "Who Governs Science Fiction?" *Extrapolation*, 41:1 (Spring 2000), 63–72.

2. Greg Bear, Gregory Benford, and David Brin, "Building on Isaac Asimov's Foundation: An Eaton Discussion with Joseph D. Miller as Moderator," edited by Gary Westfahl. *Science-Fiction Studies*, 24:1 (March 1997), 17–32.

3. Norman Spinrad, *Bug Jack Barron* (New York: Avon, 1969).

4. Westfahl, "Wrangling Conversation: Linguistic Patterns in the Dialogue of Heroes and Villains," *Fights of Fancy: Armed Conflict in Science Fiction and Fantasy*, edited by George Slusser and Eric S. Rabkin (Athens: University of Georgia Press, 1993), 35–48.

5. Vivian Sobchack, "The Virginity of Astronauts: Sex and the Science Fiction Film," *Shadows of the Magic Lamp: Fantasy and Science Fiction in Film*, edited by George Slusser and Eric S. Rabkin (Carbondale: Southern Illinois University Press, 1985), 41–57.

6. Robert Philmus, "The Cybernetic Paradigms of Stanislaw Lem," *Hard Science Fiction*, edited by George Slusser and Eric S. Rabkin (Carbondale: Southern Illinois University Press, 1986), 177–213.

7. Gregory Benford, "In the Wake of the Wave: The British Science Fiction Market," *Science Fiction and Market Realities*, edited by Gary Westfahl, George Slusser, and Eric S. Rabkin (Athens: University of Georgia Press, 1996), 151–160. The Hartwell quotation is on page 154.

8. Westfahl, "Artists in Wonderland: Toward a True History of Science Fiction Art," *Unearthly Visions: Approaches to Science Fiction and Fantasy Art*, edited by Gary Westfahl, George Slusser, and Kathleen Church Plummer (Westport, CT: Greenwood, 2002), 19–38.

9. John Martin Fischer and Ruth Curl. "Philosophical Models of Immortality in Science Fiction," *Immortal Engines: Life Extension and Immortality in Science Fiction and Fantasy*, edited by George Slusser, Gary Westfahl, and Eric S. Rabkin (Athens: University of Georgia Press, 1996), 3–12.

10. Joseph D. Miller, "Popes or Tropes: Defining the Grails of Science Fiction," *Science Fiction. Canonization. Marginalization, and the Academy*, edited by Gary Westfahl and George Slusser (Westport, CT: Greenwood, 2002), 79–87.

11. Marleen Barr, *Genre Fission: A New Discourse Practice for Cultural Studies* (Iowa City: University of Iowa Press, 2000).

Bibliography of Works Related to Science Fiction and the Two Cultures Debate

Note: since the literary field of study known as "Literature and Science" has now produced a vast quantity of scholarly literature, it has been necessary to limit this bibliography to works from various disciplines which make explicit reference to C. P. Snow and his concerns about the two cultures; even works about the seemingly related Alan Sokal controversy have been relegated to the second bibliography of "Other Works Cited in the Text." The first part of this bibliography presents the relatively few items that explicitly relate the two cultures and science fiction (including a few items reprinted in this collection), while the second section lists other works which discuss Snow and the two cultures.

Works on Science Fiction and the Two Cultures Debate

Donovan, Robert Alan. "The Future According to Hoyle: A Footnote on the Two Cultures." *South Atlantic Quarterly,* 81:2 (Spring 1982), 178–187.

Fleming, Linda A. Science Fiction Subculture: Bridge Between the Two Cultures. *Dissertations Abstracts International,* 38:2 (August 1977), 1033.

Freedman, Carl. "Science Fiction and the Two Cultures: Reflections after the Snow-Leavis Controversy." *Extrapolation: A Journal of Science Fiction and Fantasy,* 42:3 (October 2001), 207–217.

Larson, D. M. "Two Cultures Split and the Science Fiction Course." *HPT News,* No. 3 (December 1977), 1–4.

Luckhurst, Roger. "The Two Cultures, or the End of the World As We Know It." *Interdisciplinary Science Reviews,* 32:1 (March 2007), 55–64.

McConnell, Frank. "The Science of Fiction and the Fiction of Science: A Storytelling Animal in an Inhospitable World." *Sniper Logic,* 7 (Winter–Fall 1999), 113–120. Republished in McConnell, *The Science of Fiction and the Fiction of Science: Collected Essays on SF Storytelling and the Gnostic Imagination,* edited by Gary Westfahl. Jefferson, NC: McFarland, 2009, 155–163.

Samuelson, David N. "Science Fiction and the Two Cultures: A Study in the Theory and Criticism of Contemporary Science Fiction with Reference to the Cultural Division Between the Sciences and the Humanities." Bachelor's Thesis, Drew University, 1962.

Schwartz, Sheila. "Science Fiction: Bridge Between the Two Cultures." *English Journal*, 60:8 (November 1971), 1043–1051.

Thomas, Anne-Marie. "To Devour and Transform: Viral Metaphors in Science Fiction by Women." *Extrapolation*, 41:2 (Summer 2000), 143–160.

Westfahl, Gary. "Science Fiction and the Playing Fields of Eaton." *Extrapolation*, 47:1 (Spring 2006), 7–15.

Other Works on the Two Cultures Debate

Adams, W. M. "Thinking like a Human: Social Science and the Two Cultures." *Oryx*, 41:3 (July 2007), 275–276.

Afanasyeva, Nina. "C. P. Snow and H. G. Wells: A History of Their Acquaintance, Friendship and Influence." *The Wellsian*, No. 25 (2002), 52–58.

Allen, Charles M. "Unity in a University: The Two Cultures." *Vital Speeches of the Day*, 33:23 (September 15, 1967), 730.

Allen, Walter, A. C. B. Lovell, J. H. Plumb, David Riesman, Bertrand Russell, Sir John Cockcroft, and Michael Ayrton. "C. P. Snow and the Two Cultures." *Encounter*, 13:2 (August, 1959), 59.

Appl, Cynthia L. *Heinrich Schirmbeck and the Two Cultures: A Post-War German Writer's Approach to Science and Literature*. New York: Peter Lang, 1998.

Armine, Frederick. "Readings in the Text of Nature: Three Contemporary Goetheans." In *Beyond the Two Cultures: Essays on Science, Technology, and Literature*, edited by Joseph W. Slade and Judith Yaross Lee. Ames: Iowa State University Press, 1990, 51–71.

Armstrong, Paul B. "Understanding and Truth in the Two Cultures." *University of Harford Studies in Literature*, 16:2–3 (1984), 70–89.

Arnold, Matthew. "Literature and Science." In *The Portable Matthew Arnold*, edited by Lionel Trilling. New York: Viking, 1949, 405–429. Originally delivered as a lecture in 1882.

Bantock, G. H. "A Scream of Horror." *The Listener* (September 17, 1959), 427–428.

Barash, David P. "C. P. Snow: Bridging the Two-Cultures Divide." *Chronicle of Higher Education*, 52:14 (November 25, 2005), B10–B11.

Barron, Frank. "Bisociates: Artist and Scientist in The Act of Creation." In *Astride the Two Cultures: Arthur Koestler at 70*, edited by Harold Harris. New York: Random House, 1976, 37–49.

Bauerlein, Mark. "The Two Cultures Again: Tilting against Objectivity." *The Chronicle of Higher Education*, 48:12 (November 2001), B14–B15.

Beer, Gillian. "Translation or Transformation? The Relations of Literature and Science." *Notes and Records of the Royal Society of London*, 44 (1990), 81–99.

Beloff, John. "Koestler's Philosophy of Mind." In *Astride the Two Cultures: Arthur Koestler at 70*, edited by Harold Harris. New York: Random House, 1976, 69–83.

Benson, Donald R. "The Crisis of Space: Ether, Atmosphere, and the Solidarity of Men and Nature in *Heart of Darkness*." In *Beyond the Two Cultures: Essays on Science, Technology, and Literature*, edited by Joseph W. Slade and Judith Yaross Lee. Ames: Iowa State University Press, 1990, 161–175.

Bergmann, Linda S. "Reshaping the Roles of Man, God, and Nature: Darwin's Rhetoric in *On the Origin of Species*." In *Beyond the Two Cultures: Essays on Science, Technology, and Literature*, edited by Joseph W. Slade and Judith Yaross Lee. Ames: Iowa State University Press, 1990, 79–98.

Bernstein, Jeremy. "Science Education for the Nonscientist." *Journal of College Science Teaching*, 23:2 (November 1993), 92–97.

Bezel, Nail. "Autobiography and 'The Two Cultures' in the Novels of C. P. Snow." *Annals of Science*, 32:6 (November 1975). 555–571.

Black, Michael. "Whose Bones?" *Cambridge Review*, 108 (March, 1987), 6.

Brockman, John. "The Emerging Third Culture." *Whole Earth Review*, No. 79 (Summer 1993), 16–18.

Bronowski, Jacob. "The Abacus and the Rose: A Dialogue after Galileo." *Nation*, 198:1 (January 4, 1964), 4–17.

Broudy, Harry S. "The Two Cultures." *Journal of Aesthetic Education*, 21:4 (Winter 1987), 87.

Budd, John M. "Research in the Two Cultures: The Nature of Scholarship in Science and the Humanities." *Collection Management*, 11:3/4 (1989), 1.

Burnett, D. Graham. "A View from the Bridge: The Two Cultures Debate, Its Legacy, and the History of Science." *Daedalus*, 128:2 (Spring 1999), 193.

Buxton, B. "Snow's Two Cultures Revisited: Perspectives on Human-Computer Interface Design." In *Cyberarts: Exploring Science and Technology*, edited by L. Jacobson. San Francisco: Miller Freeman, 1992, 24–31.

Byford, Andy. "The Politics of Science and Literature in French and Russian Criticism of the 1860s." *Symposium*, 56:4 (Winter 2003), 210–230.

Callahan, John F. "Tradition and Innovation: Evolving Paradigms in *The Structure of Scientific Revolutions* and *Invisible Man*." In *Beyond the Two Cultures: Essays on Science, Technology, and Literature*, edited by Joseph W. Slade and Judith Yaross Lee. Ames: Iowa State University Press, 1990, 117–128.

Campbell, Jeremy. "Observer and Object, Reader and Text: Some Parallel Themes in Modern Science and Literature." In *Beyond the Two Cultures: Essays on Science, Technology, and Literature*, edited by Joseph W. Slade and Judith Yaross Lee. Ames: Iowa State University Press, 1990. 23–37.

Caristi, James, and Roy Enquist. "The Two Cultures Revisited: Metaphor and Model in Literature and Logic." *Cresset*, 49:1 (1985), 13–17.

Chainey, Graham. "Two Non-Cultures?" *Encounter*, 64:3 (March 1985), 49.

Chandler, Alice. "Literature and Science; or, The Two Cultures and Some Reciprocities between Them." *Mid-Hudson Language Studies*, 5 (1982), 9–19.

Cherry, Douglas. "The Two Cultures of Matthew Arnold and T. H. Huxley." *Wascana Review*, 1 (1966), 53–61.

Cherry, Kelly. "The Two Cultures at the End of the Twentieth Century: An Essay on Poetry and Science." *Midwest Quarterly*, 35:2 (1994), 121–135.

Chitoran, Mariana. C. P. Snow — Teoria Celor Doua Culturi în Ciclul "Strangers and Brothers." [Translated title: C. P. Snow — The Theory of the Two Cultures in the "Strangers and Brothers" Cycle.] Unpublished doctoral dissertation. Bucharest: Bucharest University, 1978.

Ciolli, Russ Thomas. A Rhetorical Analysis of Two Public Addresses by C. P. Snow: "The Two Cultures and the Scientific Revolution" and "The Moral Un-Neutrality of Science." *Dissertation Abstracts International*, 52:5 (November 1991), 1570A.

Clayton, Jay. "Convergence of the Two Cultures: A Geek's Guide to Contemporary Literature." *American Literature: A Journal of Literary History, Criticism, and Bibliography*, 74:4 (December 2002), 807–831.

Cohen, Benjamin R. "Science and Humanities: Across Two Cultures and into Science Studies." *Endeavour*, 25:1 (2001), 8–12.

Collins, H. M. "Cooperation and the Two Cultures: Response to Labinger." *Social Studies of Science*, 25:2 (May 1995), 306–309.

Cordle, Daniel. *Postmodern Postures: Literature, Science and the Two Cultures Debate*. Aldershot, Hants, UK, and Brookfield, VT: Ashgate, 1999.

Cornelius, David K., and Edwin St. Vincent, editors. *Cultures in Conflict: Perspectives on the Snow-Leavis Controversy*. Chicago: Scott, Foresman, 1964.

Coyne, Pat. "The Squabble between a Scientific Scribbler and a Rancid Literary Critic

Raged Over Three Decades Ago. But, Says Pat Coyne, the Message Is Still Fresh." *New Statesman and Society*, 6 (October 1, 1993), 30.

Criage, Betty Jean. "The Humanities in the Era of Cooperation: Beyond C. P. Snow's 'Two Cultures.'" *Innovative Higher Education*, 23:4 (Summer 1999), 295–301.

Cruz, Eduardo R. "Ralph Wendell Burhoe and the Two Cultures." *Zygon*, 30:4 (December 1995), 591.

Dallmayr, Fred R. "Political Science and the 'Two Cultures.'" *Journal of General Education*, 19 (January 1968), 269–295.

Darbyshire, Philip. "Nursing, Art and Science: Revisiting the Two Cultures." *International Journal of Nursing Practice*, 5:3 (September 1999), 123–131.

Davenport, F. Garvin. "Machines and Sexual Ambience in James Agee's *A Death in the Family*." In *Beyond the Two Cultures: Essays on Science, Technology, and Literature*, edited by Joseph W. Slade and Judith Yaross Lee. Ames: Iowa State University Press, 1990, 227–239.

Davenport, William H. *The One Culture*. New York: Pergamon, 1970.

Davies, David W. "Libraries and the Two Cultures." *Journal of Library History*, 16:1 (Winter 1981), 16.

Day, Michael A. "I. Rabi: The Two Cultures and the Universal Culture of Science." *Physics in Perspective*, 6:4 (December 2004), 428–476.

De La Mothe, John. *C. P. Snow and the Struggle of Modernity*. Montreal: McGill-Queens University Press, 1992.

Deutsch, Diana. "Guest Editorial." *Music Perception*, 21:3 (Spring 2004), 285–287.

Donavan, Michael P. "Two Cultures? Pfui!" *Journal of College Science Teaching*, 28:4 (February 1999), 237–238.

Douglas, John H. "The Cultures — Twenty Years Later." *Science News*, 111:8 (February 19, 1977), 122–124.

Eco, Umberto. "In Memory of Giorgio Prodi: A Challenge to the Myth of Two Cultures." Translated by Marina Johnston. *Forum Italicum*, 8[Supplement] (1994), 75–78.

Eiseley, Loren. "The Illusion of the Two Cultures." *American Scholar*, 33 (Summer 1964), 387–399.

Eisen, Arri, and Gary Lederman. "Bridging the Two Cultures: A Comprehensive Interdisciplinary Approach to Teaching and Learning Science in a Societal Context." *Journal of College Science Teaching*, 35:1 (September 2005), 26–30.

Ellman, Neil. "The Two Cultures: Exploring and Bridging the Gap." *The English Journal*, 65:7 (October 1976), 55–56.

Fallers, Lloyd. "C. P. Snow and the Third Culture." *Bulletin of the Atomic Scientists*, 17:8 (October 1961), 306–310.

Faulkner, Peter. "William Morris and the Two Cultures." *Journal of the William Morris Society*, 1 (Spring 1966), 9–12.

Fekete, József. "The Question of the 'Two Cultures' in Hungary." *New Hungarian Quarterly*, 1:1 (September 1960), 19.

Ferrell, Keith. "The Society for Literature and Science: A Conference Dedicated to Connecting the Two Cultures." *Omni*, 15:4 (January 1993), 9.

Fong, Peter. "The Two Cultures: A Historical View." *Emory University Quarterly*, 23:3 (Fall 1967), 151.

Fox, Stephen. "Edwin Morgan and the Two Cultures." *Studies in Scottish Literature*, 33–34 (2004), 71–86.

Friedman, Mickey. "Reconciling the Two Cultures." *American Education*, 16:2 (March 1980), 25.

Friedrich, Rainer. "Theorese and Science Envy in the Humanities: A New Take on the Two Cultures Divide." *Arion: A Journal of Humanities and the Classics*, 11:1 (April 2003), 33–50.

Fuller, Steve. "In Snow's Shoes." *Times Higher Education Supplement*, No. 1149 (November 11, 1994), 18.

Fyvel, T. Y. "Arthur Koestler and George Orwell." In *Astride the Two Cultures: Arthur Koestler at 70*, edited by Harold Harris. New York: Random House, 1976, 149–161.

Glassman, Peter. "Mill, Freud, and God: The Two Cultures of Modernist Life." In *Explorations: The Nineteenth Century*, edited by Ann B. Dobie; assistant editors Jennifer Brantley, Katherina A. Holman, and Victoria H. Spaniol. Lafayette, LA: Levy Humanities Series, iii, 1988, 1–33.

Glover, Ian A. "One Cheer for Two Cultures? The 1993 White Paper on Science and Technology." *Higher Education Review*, 27:1 (Autumn 1994), 48.

Goldstein, Rebecca. "The Two Cultures." *Maggid: A Journal of Jewish Literature*, 1 (2005), 31–42.

Goodlad, Sinclair. "The Search for Synthesis: Constraints on the Development of the Humanities in Liberal Science-Based Education." *Studies in Higher Education*, 25:1 (March 2000), 7–23.

Goodman, Alan H., Deborah Heath, and M. Susan Lindee, editors. *Genetic Nature/Culture: Anthropology and Science Beyond the Two-Culture Divide*. Berkeley: University of California Press, 2003.

Gossman, Lionel. "The Two Cultures in Nineteenth-Century Basle: Between the French Encylopédie and German Neohumanism." *Journal of European Studies*, 20:2 (June, 1990). 95.

Graubard, Mark. "*The Sleepwalkers*: Its Contribution and Impact." In *Astride the Two Cultures: Arthur Koestler at 70*, edited by Harold Harris. New York: Random House, 1976, 20–36.

Green, Martin. "Lionel Trilling and the Two Cultures." *Essays in Criticism: A Quarterly Journal of Literary Criticism*, 13 (1963), 375–385.

_____. "A Literary Defence of *The Two Cultures*." *Critical Quarterly*, 4 (1962), 155–162. Also published in *Kenyon Review*, 24 (Autumn 1962), 731–739.

_____. *Science and the Shabby Curate of Poetry: Essays about the Two Cultures*. London: Longmans, 1964.

Gregory, Michael S. "The Science-Humanities Program (NEXA) at San Francisco State University: The 'Two Cultures' Reconsidered." *Leonardo*, 13:4 (Autumn 1980), 295.

Grigg, John. "The Do-Gooder from Seville Gaol." In *Astride the Two Cultures: Arthur Koestler at 70*, edited by Harold Harris. New York: Random House, 1976, 123–135.

Gruenwald, Oskar. "The Third Culture: An Integral Vision of the Human Condition." *Journal of Interdisciplinary Studies*, 17:1/2 (2005), 139–160.

Gusfield, Joseph, and David Riesman. "Academic Standards and 'The Two Cultures' in the Context of a New State College." *School Review*, 74:1 (Spring 1966), 95.

Hall, David. "The National Curriculum and the Two Cultures: Towards a Humanistic Perspective." *Geography*, 75:4 (October 1990), 313.

Hamill, Paul. "Conrad, Wells, and the Two Voices." [Letter in response to Frederick Karl's article] *PMLA: Publications of the Modern Language Association of America*, 89:3 (May 1974), 581–582.

Hamilton, Iain. "Wonderfully Living: Koestler the Novelist." In *Astride the Two Cultures: Arthur Koestler at 70*, edited by Harold Harris. New York: Random House, 1976, 84–101.

Hanquart-Turner, Evelyne. "Scientific Translation: Another Aspect of the 'Two Cultures' Debate?" *Cambridge Review*, 112:2313 (June 1991), 62.

Harris, Harold, editor. *Astride the Two Cultures: Arthur Koestler at 70*. New York: Random House, 1976.

Hauge, Hans. "Snow versus Leavis: The Two Cultures." *Dolphin*, 4 (1980), 38–59.

Haynes, Renee. "Wrestling Jacob: Koestler and the Paranormal." In *Astride the Two Cul-

tures: Arthur Koestler at 70, edited by Harold Harris. New York: Random House, 1976, 175–186.

Herman, David. "Time to Make Waves." *New Statesman and Society*, 5:215 (August 14, 1992), 25–26.

Heylin, Michael. "Science and the Press." *Chemical and Engineering News*, 79:24 (June 11, 2001), 28.

Higgs, Eric. "The Two-Culture Problem: Ecological Restoration and the Integration of Knowledge." *Restoration Ecology*, 13:1 (March 2005), 159–164.

Himmelfarb, Gertrude. "In Defense of the Two Cultures." *American Scholar*, 50:4 (Autumn 1981), 451–463.

Horowitz, Irving Louis. "In Defense of Scientific Autonomy: The Two Cultures Revisited." *Academic Questions*, 2:1 (Winter 1988/1989), 22–26.

Houswitschka, Christoph. "Chesterton and the Two Cultures." In *Lost Worlds and Mad Elephants: Literature, Science and Technology 1700–1900*, edited by Elmar Schenkel and Stefan Welz. Berlin: Galda + Wilch Verlag, 1999, 211–228.

Hua, Shiping. *Scientism and Humanism: Two Cultures in Post-Mao China, 1978–1989*. Albany: State University of New York Press, 1995.

Hultberg, John. *A Tale of Two Cultures: The Image of Science of C. P. Snow*. Gothenburg, Sweden: University of Gothenburg, Department for Theory of Science and Research, 1991.

Huxley, Thomas Henry. "Science and Culture." In *Science and Education: Essays*. New York: D. Appleton and Company, 1899. Pp. 134–159. Originally delivered as a lecture in 1880.

Jacobs, Madeleine. "A Chemist's Odyssey Bridges the Two Cultures of Art and Science." *Chemical and Engineering News*, 74:34 (August 19, 1996) 43–45.

Jaeger, Gertrude, and Philip Selznick. "A Normative Theory of Culture." *American Sociological Review*, 29:5 (October 1964), 653–669.

Jaki, Stanley L. "A Hundred Years of Two Cultures." *University of Windsor Review*, 11 (1975), 55–79.

Jenkins, Edward S. "Bridging the Two Cultures: 'American Black Scientists and Inventors.'" *Journal of Black Studies*, 21:3 (March 1991), 313.

Jensen, Casper. "Beyond the Two Cultures with Scandalous Knowledge: Relativism and Constructivism Revisited." *Social Studies of Science*, 37:4 (August 2007), 647–654.

Jones, W. T. *The Sciences and the Humanities: Conflict and Reconciliation*. Berkeley: University of California Press, 1965.

"J.R.E." "'Genetics and Ironing,' or The Two Cultures and the Physician." *Annals of Internal Medicine*, 56:3 (March 1962), 523–524.

Kahn, Michael. "Bridging the Two Cultures: Retraining Humanities Teachers." *Research in Education*, 36 (November 1986), 39.

Karl, Frederick. "Conrad, Wells, and the Two Voices." *PMLA: Publications of the Modern Language Association of America*, 88 (1973), 1049–1065.

Karlgaard, Rich. "The Two Cultures." *Forbes*, 162:19 (November 2, 1998), 43.

Kiceluk, Stephanie. "Revising the 'Two Cultures' Script: Literary Texts in Medical Education." *Texas Studies in Literature and Language*, 26:2 (July 1984), 242–262.

Kimball, Roger. "'The Two Cultures' Today." *The New Criterion*, 12:6 (February 1994), 10–15.

Klein, George, and Eva Klein. "Bridge or Ravine?" *Nature*, 413, No. 6854 (September 27, 2001), 365.

Koestler, Cynthia. "Twenty-Five Writing Years." In *Astride the Two Cultures: Arthur Koestler at 70*, edited by Harold Harris. New York: Random House, 1976, 136–148.

Kuchment, Mark. "Bridging the Two Cultures: The Emergence of Scientific Prose." In *Science and the Soviet Social Order*, edited by Loren R. Graham. Cambridge, MA: Harvard University Press, 1990, 335–340.

Kuklick, Bruce. "The Two Cultures in Eighteenth-Century America." In *Benjamin Franklin, Jonathan Edwards, and the Representation of American Culture*, edited by Barbara B. Oberg and Harry S. Stout. New York: Oxford University Press, 1993.

Leavis, F. R. "Two Cultures? The Significance of C. P. Snow." *Melbourne Critical Review*, 5 (1962), 90–101.

_____. *Two Cultures? The Significance of C. P. Snow: Being the Richmond Lecture, 1962*. Preface by Michael Yudkin. New York: Random House, 1963.

Lee, Judith Yaross. "Selected Bibliography." In *Beyond the Two Cultures: Essays on Science, Technology, and Literature*, edited by Joseph W. Slade and Judith Yaross Lee. Ames: Iowa State University Press, 1990, 287–298.

Lee, Richard E., and Immanuel Wallerstein, coordinators, with Volkan Aytar, Ayşe Betül Çelik, Mauro di Meglio, Ho-Fung Hung, Biray Kolluoğlu Kirli, Augstín Lao-Montes, Eric Mielants, Boris Stremlin, Sunaryo, Norihisa Yamashita, and Denis Yükseker. *Overcoming the Two Cultures: Science Versus the Humanities in the Modern World-System*. Boulder, CO: Paradigm, 2004.

Levin, Yuval. "Snow's Two Cultures — and Ours." *Public Interest*, No. 153 (Fall 2003), 54–68.

Levine, George, editor. *One Culture: Essays in Science and Literature*. Madison: University of Wisconsin Press, 1987.

_____, and Owen Thomas, editors. *The Scientist vs. the Humanist*. New York: Norton, 1963.

Lindbohm, M. "The Two Cultures (Continued)." *Commentary*, 92:2 (August 1991), 31–35.

Mackenzie, Adrian, and Andrew Murphie. "The Two Cultures Become Multiple?" *Australian Feminist Studies*, 23:55 (March 2008), 87–100.

MacLean, Michael. "History in a Two-Cultures World: The Case of the German Historians." *Journal of the History of Ideas*, 49:3 (July 1988), 473–494.

Maddox, John. "Are There Really Two Cultures?" *Listener*, 68:1740 (August 2, 1962), 173.

"A Man of Two Cultures." No author given. *Time*, July 14, 1980, 56.

Martin, Andrew. "Bridging Two Cultures." *Publishers Weekly*, 254:27 (July 9, 2007), 40.

Martin, James G. "The 'Two Cultures' Theme in Albee's *Virginia Woolf*." *Notes on Contemporary Literature*, 12:4 (September 1982), 2–5.

McKay, Alexander G. "Can Poets Move Mountains? Reflections on the 'Two Cultures.'" *Royal Society of Canada, Proceedings and Transactions/Société Royale du Canada Délibérations et Mémoires*, 5:2 (1987), 3.

McKernan, Susan. "Two Cultures Mingling: Science and the Poetry of A. D. Hope." *Phoenix Review*, 9 (1992), 31–42.

McNeill, Desmond. "On Interdisciplinary Research: With Particular Reference to the Field of Environment and Development." *Higher Education Quarterly*, 53:4 (October 1999), 312–332.

Mesher, David R. "Science and Technology in Modern British Fiction: The Two Cultures." *Essays in Arts and Sciences*, 13 (September 1984), 73–82.

Metzger, Gustav. "The Third Culture." *Theory, Culture & Society*, 42:1 (January 2007), 137–145.

Mignolo, Walter D. "A Dialogue between the 'Two Cultures.'" [Review Article] *Semiotica*, 81 (1990) 135–144.

Monaghan, Peter. "'Two Cultures' of Science and Literature No Longer Considered Disparate Fields." *Chronicle of Higher Education*, 37:19 (November 7, 1990), A5, A8.

Montgomery, Marion. "Eliot and the Particle Physicist: The Merging of Two Cultures." *Southern Review*, 10 (1974), 583–589.

Moseley, Nicholas. "Two Cultures Are No Culture: Nicholas Mosley Explores the Connections between the Endeavours of Science and Those of Literature." *New Statesman and Society*, 5:217 (August 28, 1992), 16–17.

Murray, James. "War between the Two Cultures." *Virginia Quarterly Review: A National Journal of Literature and Discussion*, 43:3 (Summer 1967), 514.

Myers, David. "Bridging the Gap Between the Two Cultures." *Social Alternatives*, 7:4 (January 1989), 17.

Nemetz, Anthony. "Some Comments on the Two Cultures." *American Catholic Philosophical Association, Proceedings*, 38 (1964), 216.

Norris, Christopher. "Sexed Equations and Vexed Physicists: The 'Two Cultures' Revisited." *International Journal of Cultural Studies*, 2:1 (April 1999), 77–107.

Nott, Kathleen. "The Trojan Horses: Koestler and the Behaviourists." In *Astride the Two Cultures: Arthur Koestler at 70*, edited by Harold Harris. New York: Random House, 1976, 162–174.

O'Brien, Dean W. "Between the Two Cultures: An Existential View of Curriculum." *School and Society*, 89:2199 (November 18, 1961), 402.

O'Connor, Ralph. "The Poetics of Earth Science: 'Romanticism' and the Two Cultures." *Studies in History & Philosophy of Science*, Part A, 36:3 (September 2005), 607–617.

Ortolano, Guy. "Human Science or a Human Face? Social History and the 'Two Cultures' Controversy." *Journal of British Studies*. 43:4 (2004), 482–505.

_____. "The Literature and the Science of 'Two Cultures' Historiography." *Studies in History & Philosophy of Science*, Part A, 39:1 (March 2008), 143–150.

_____. "'Two Cultures,' One University: The Institutional Origins of the 'Two Cultures' Controversy." *Albion*, 34:4 (2002), 606–624.

Perry, Nick. "The Two Cultures and the Total Institution." *British Journal of Sociology*, 25:3 (September 1974), 345.

Peterfreund, Stuart. "Blake and Anti-Newtonian Thought." In *Beyond the Two Cultures: Essays on Science, Technology, and Literature*, edited by Joseph W. Slade and Judith Yaross Lee. Ames: Iowa State University Press, 1990, 141–160.

Petroski, Henry. "Numeracy and Literacy: The Two Cultures and the Computer Revolution." *Virginia Quarterly Review: A National Journal of Literature and Discussion*, 61:2 (April 1985), 302–317.

_____. "Technology and the Humanities." *American Scientist*, 93:4 (July/August 2005), 304–307.

Phillips, Gerald M. "Science and the Study of Human Communication: An Inquiry from the Other Side of the Two Cultures." *Human Communication Research*, 7:4 (Summer, 1981), 361.

Pigliucci, Massimo. "The Borderlands between Science and Philosophy: An Introduction." *Quarterly Review of Biology*, 83:1 (March 2008), 7–15.

Plotnitsky, Arkady. *The Knowable and the Unknowable: Modern Science, Nonclassical Thought, and the "Two Cultures."* Ann Arbor: University of Michigan Press, 2002.

Plumb, J. H., editor. *Crisis in the Humanities*. Baltimore, MD: Penguin, 1964.

Pollock, G. H. "Is There a 'Two-Cultures' Model for Psychoanalysis?" *Behavioral and Brain Sciences*, 9:2 (June 1986), 253.

Porter, Roy. "The Two Cultures Revisited." *Boundary 2: An International Journal of Literature and Culture*, 23:2 (July 1996), 1–17.

Porter, Theodore M. "Introduction: Historizing the Two Cultures." *History of Science*, 43:2 (June 2005), 109–114.

Priestley, F. E. L. "Science and the Humanities — Are There Two 'Cultures'?" *Humanities Association Review/La Revue de l'Association des Humanites*, 23:4 (1972), 12–22.

Pynchon, Thomas. "Is It O.K. to Be a Luddite?" *The New York Times*, October 28, 1984, 40–41.

Raben, Estelle M. "The 'Two Cultures' Dichotomy Reexamined." *Computers and the Humanities*, 24:1/2 (February/April 1990), 107.

Rainsford, Dominic. "The Bright Light of Science and the Dim Truth of Art." *European Journal of English Studies*, 11:3 (December 2007), 285–300.
Rapoport, Anatol. "The Two Cultures: Then and Now." *Et Cetera*, 46:2 (Summer, 1989), 118.
Rassam, Clive. "A Tale of Two Cultures." *New Scientist*, 138, No. 1879 (June 26, 1993), 30–33.
Roberts, Catherine. "Nightingales, Hawks, and the Two Cultures." *Antioch Review*, 25 (1965), 221–238.
Rodrigues, R. J. "Rethinking the Cultures of Disciplines." *Chronicle of Higher Education*, 38:34 (April 29, 1992), B1–B2.
Rose, Steven. "The View Across the Snow-Line." *Cambridge Review*, 108 (March 1987), 9.
Rössler, Otto E. "Chaos: Bridge between Two Cultures." *Amerikastudien/American Studies*, 45:1 (2000), 101–104.
Ruprecht, Robert. "Forty Years Later: C. P. Snow's Two Cultures Revisited." *European Journal of Engineering Education*, 24:3 (September 1999), 231–241.
Salvaggio, Ruth. "The Case of the Two Cultures: Psychoanalytic Theories of Science and Literature." In *Discontented Discourses: Feminism/Textual Intervention/Psychoanalysis*, edited by Marleen S. Barr and Richard Feldstein. Urbana: University of Illinois Press, 1989, 54–65.
Schaible, Robert M. "What Poetry Brings to the Table of Science and Religion." *Zygon: Journal of Religion and Science*, 38:2 (June 2003), 295–316.
Schenck, Hilbert, Jr. "Revisiting the 'Two Cultures.'" *Centennial Review*, 8 (1964), 249–261.
Schenkel, Elmar, and Stefan Welz, editors. *Lost Worlds and Mad Elephants: Literature, Science and Technology, 1700–1990*. Glienicke, Berlin; Cambridge, Massachusetts: Galda + Wilch, 1999.
Shafer, Ingrid. "What Does It Mean to Be Human? A Personal and Catholic Perspective." *Zygon: Journal of Religion and Science*, 37:1 (March 2002), 121–136.
Shaw, Michael. "Where Two Cultures Will Mix." *Times Educational Supplement*, No. 4523 (March 14, 2003), 17.
Shusterman, Ronald. "Ravens and Writing-Desks: Sokal and the Two Cultures." *Philosophy and Literature*, 22:1 (April 1998), 119–135.
Simon, W. M. "The 'Two Cultures' in Nineteenth-Century France: Victor Cousin and Auguste Comte." *Journal of the History of Ideas*, 26:1 (January 1965), 45–58.
Slade, Joseph W. "Beyond the Two Cultures: Science, Technology, and Literature." In *Beyond the Two Cultures: Essays on Science, Technology, and Literature*, edited by Joseph W. Slade and Judith Yaross Lee. Ames: Iowa State University Press, 1990, 3–16.
_____, and Judith Yaross Lee, editors. *Beyond the Two Cultures: Essays on Science, Technology, and Literature*. Ames: Iowa State University Press, 1990.
Smith, Barbara Herrnstein. *Scandalous Knowledge: Science, Truth, and the Human*. Durham, NC: Duke University Press, 2006.
Smith, Ralph A. "The Two Cultures Debate Today." *Oxford Review of Education*, 4:2 (1978), 257.
Snow, C. P. "Science, Politics, and the Novelist: or, The Fish and the Net." *Kenyon Review*, 23 (1961), 1–17.
_____. "The Two Cultures." *New Statesman and Nation*, 52 (October 6, 1956), 413–414.
_____. "The Two Cultures: A Second Look." *Times Literary Supplement*, 61 (October 1963), 839–844.
_____. *The Two Cultures: And a Second Look*. New York: Cambridge University Press, 1964.
_____. "The Two Cultures and the Scientific Revolution." *Encounter*, 12:6 (1959), 17–24.

_____. "The Two Cultures and the Scientific Revolution." *Library Journal*, 85 (1960), 2523–2528.

_____. *The Two Cultures*, introduction by Stefan Collini. Cambridge, UK: Cambridge University Press, 1993.

Snow, Philip. "Stranger and Brother." *Cambridge Review*, 108 (March 1987), 3.

Sporn, Paul. "The Modern Physics of Contemporary Criticism." In *Beyond the Two Cultures: Essays on Science, Technology, and Literature*, edited by Joseph W. Slade and Judith Yaross Lee. Ames: Iowa State University Press, 1990, 201–222.

Stanford, Derek. "Sir Charles and the Two Cultures." *Critic*, 21:2 (October/November 1962), 17.

Steiner, George. "A False Quarrel?" *Cambridge Review*, 108 (March 1987), 13.

Steiner, Wendy. "Practice without Principle: The Two Cultures, Out of Step." *American Scholar*, 68:3 (1999), 77–87.

Stites, Janet, and Tom Zimberloff. "Bordercrossings: A Conversation in Cyberspace." *Omni*, 16:2 (November 1993), 16–18.

Storr, Anthony. "Bridging the Two Cultures." *North American Review*, 261:2 (Summer 1976), 70.

Stringer, Peter. "C. P. Snow's Fiction of Two Cultures." *Leonardo*, 16:3 (Summer 1983). 172.

Strohl, Nicholas. "The Postmodern University Revisited: Reframing Higher Education Debates from the 'Two Cultures' to Postmodernity." *London Review of Education*, 4:2 (July 2006), 133–148.

Syer, Geoffrey. "Britain's Two Cultures: A Third Look." *ContRev*, 261 (August 1992), 88–94.

Sypher, Wylie. *Literature and Technology: The Alien Vision*. New York: Random House, 1968.

Tallis, Raymond. "Evidence-Based and Evidence-Free Generalizations: A Tale of Two Cultures." In *The Arts and Science of Criticism*, edited by David Fuller and Patricia Waugh. Oxford, England: Oxford University Press, 1999, 71–93.

_____. *Newton's Sleep: The Two Cultures and the Two Kingdoms*. New York: St. Martin's, 1995.

Tasker, John. *The Richmond Lecture: Its Purpose and Achievement*. Swansea, UK: Brynmill, 1972.

Teich, M. "The Two Cultures: Comenius and the Royal Society." *Paedagocica Europaea*, 4 (1968), 147.

Theerman, Paul. "National Images of Science: British and American Views of Scientific Heroes in the Early Nineteenth Century." In *Beyond the Two Cultures: Essays on Science, Technology, and Literature*, edited by Joseph W. Slade and Judith Yaross Lee. Ames: Iowa State University Press, 1990, 259–274.

Thompson, Kenneth, editor. *Discourse and the Two Cultures: Science, Religion, and the Humanities*. Lanham, MD: University Press of America, 1988; Charlottesville, VA: White Burkett Miller, Center of Public Affairs, University of Virginia, 1988.

Thorpe, W. H. "Arthur Koestler and Biological Thought." In *Astride the Two Cultures: Arthur Koestler at 70*, edited by Harold Harris. New York: Random House, 1976, 50–68.

Tobias, S. A. "Engineering — The Bridge between the Two Cultures." *Cambridge Review*, 87 (October 1965–June 1966), 72.

Treitel, Jonathan. "The Parable of the Two Cultures." *Critical Quarterly*, 31:3 (Autumn 1989), 22.

Trilling, Lionel. "The Leavis-Snow Controversy." *Beyond Culture: Essays on Literature and Learning*. New York: Viking, 1965.

Van Dijck, José. "After the "Two Cultures": Toward a "(Multi)cultural" Practice of Science Communication." *Science Communication*, 25:2 (December 2003), 177–190.

Vesna, Victoria. "Toward a Third Culture: Being In Between." *Leonardo*, 34:3 (2001), 121–125.

Vice, John. "Bronowski and the Two Cultures." *Cambridge Review*, 112:2313 (June 1991), 78.

Von Laue, Theodore H. "Modern Science and the Old Adam." *Bulletin of the Atomic Scientists*, 19:1 (January 1963), 2–5.

Wallmannsberger, Josef. "An Apparatus of One's Own: Modalities of Representation and the Two Cultures." *Semiotica: Journal of the International Association for Semiotic Studies/Revue de l'Association Internationale de Sémiotique*, 143:1–4 (2003), 79–94.

Waugh, Patricia. "Revising the Two Cultures Debate: Science, Literature, and Value." In *The Arts and Science of Criticism*, edited by David Fuller and Patricia Waugh. Oxford, England: Oxford University Press, 1999, 33–59.

Webberley, Roy. "An Attempt at an Overview." In *Astride the Two Cultures: Arthur Koestler at 70*, edited by Harold Harris. New York: Random House, 1976, 1–19.

Weisheipl, James A. "Presidential Address: Philosophy and the Two Cultures." *American Catholic Philosophical Association, Proceedings*, 38 (1964), 1.

Wenham, Martin. "Art and Science in Education: The Common Ground." *Journal of Art and Design Education*, 17:1 (February 1998), 61–69.

Westman, Robert S. "Two Cultures or One? A Second Look at Kuhn's *The Copernican Revolution*." *Isis*, 85:1 (March 1994), 79.

Whalley, George. "The Humanities and Science: Two Cultures or One?" *Queen's Quarterly*, 100:1 (April 1993), 154–165.

White, Paul. "Ministers of Culture: Arnold, Huxley and Liberal Anglican Reform of Learning." *History of Science*, 43:2 (June 2005), 115–138.

Wiley, John P. "Two Cultures — Never the Twain Shall Meet?" *Smithsonian*, 28:7 (October 1997), 20–21.

Williams, Kim, editor. *Two Cultures: Essays in Honor of David Speiser*. Basel, Switzerland and Boston: Birkhauser Verlag, 2006.

Wilson, David L., and Zack Bowen. *Science and Literature: Bridging the Two Cultures*. Gainesville: University Press of Florida, 2001.

Wilson, Edward O. *Consilience: The Unity of Knowledge*. New York: Alfred A. Knopf, 1998.

Wilson, Paul C. "Playing the Role: Howe and Singer as Heroic Inventors." In *Beyond the Two Cultures: Essays on Science, Technology, and Literature*, edited by Joseph W. Slade and Judith Yaross Lee. Ames: Iowa State University Press, 1990, 275–285.

Wolf, Manfred. "The Two Cultures in West Indian Literature." *World Literature Today: A Literary Quarterly of the University of Oklahoma*, 65:1 (January 1991), 25–29.

Wolfe, Denny T., Jr., and Paul H. Taylor. "Science and Humanities: Teaching the Two Cultures." *Contemporary Education*, 48:4 (Summer 1977), 193.

Zencey, Eric. "Entropy as Root Metaphor." In *Beyond the Two Cultures: Essays on Science, Technology, and Literature*, edited by Joseph W. Slade and Judith Yaross Lee. Ames: Iowa State University Press, 1990, 185–200.

Zimmerli, Walther Christoph. *Beyond the "Two Cultures": University Education in a Technological Era: The New South Africa and Germany*. Pretoria, South Africa: University of Pretoria, 1994.

Bibliography of Other Works Cited in the Text

Aldiss, Brian W. . *Billion Year Spree: The True History of Science Fiction.* New York: Schocken, 1973.

_____. "Introduction." *Penguin Science Fiction,* edited by Aldiss. Hammondsworth, UK: Penguin, 1961, 9–14.

Alien. 20th Century–Fox, 1979.

Alien³. 20th Century–Fox, 1992.

Alien: Resurrection. 20th Century–Fox, 1997.

Aliens. 20th Century–Fox, 1986.

Allen, Glen Scott. "Raids on the Conscious: Pynchon's Legacy of Paranoia and the Terrorism of Uncertainty in Don DeLillo's *Ratner's Star.*" *Postmodern Culture,* 4:2 (January 1994), 28 paragraphs.

Allen, Roger MacBride. *Isaac Asimov's Caliban.* New York: Ace, 1993.

_____. *Isaac Asimov's Inferno.* New York: Ace, 1994.

_____. *Isaac Asimov's Utopia.* New York: Ace, 1996.

Ashman, Keith M. "Measuring the Hubble Constant: Objectivity under the Telescope." *After the Science Wars,* edited by Ashman and Philip S. Baringer. New York: Routledge, 2001, 98–119.

_____, and Philip S. Baringer, editors. *After the Science Wars.* London and New York: Routledge, 2001.

Asimov, Isaac. "Evidence." 1946. *I, Robot.* 1950. New York: Signet, 1956, 147–169.

_____. *I, Robot.* 1950. New York: Signet, 1956.

_____. "Part II: The Encyclopedists." *Foundation.* New York: Bantam, 1991, 47–96.

_____. *The Rest of the Robots.* New York: Grafton, 1968.

_____. *Robots and Empire.* New York: Grafton, 1985.

_____. *The Robots of Dawn.* New York: Grafton, 1983.

Atkins, George. "The Virtual Killer Robot: Experiences with a Web-based Course." Ninth Annual South Central Conference, Consortium for Computing in Small Colleges. Austin, Texas. April 16–17, 1999.

Atwood, Margaret. *The Handmaid's Tale.* New York: Ballantine, 1985.

Balzac, Honoré de. "Le Chef d'Oeuvre Inconnu." *La Comédie Humaine,* IX. Paris: Bibliothèque de la Pléiade, 1950, 389–414.

Barr, Marleen. *Genre Fission: A New Discourse Practice for Cultural Studies.* Iowa City: University of Iowa Press, 2000.

Barricelli, Jean-Pierre. "The Ultimate Mindscape: Dante's Paradiso." *Mindscapes: The Geographies of Imagined Worlds,* edited by George Slusser and Eric S. Rabkin. Carbondale: Southern Illinois University Press, 1989, 267–270.

Barrow, John D., and Frank J. Tipler. *The Anthropic Cosmological Principle*. Oxford, UK, and New York: Oxford University Press, 1988.

Bear, Greg, Gregory Benford, and David Brin. "Building on Isaac Asimov's Foundation: An Eaton Discussion with Joseph D. Miller as Moderator," edited by Gary Westfahl. *Science-Fiction Studies*, 24:1 (March, 1997), 17–32.

Beardsley, Ted. "Field Notes: Here's Looking at You: A Disarming Robot Starts to Act Up." *Scientific American*, 280:1 (January 1999), 39–40.

Beilharz, Peter. *Labour's Utopias: Bolshevism, Fabianism, Social Democracy*. London: Routledge, 1993.

Benford, Gregory. "Afterword." *Beyond Infinity*. London: Orbit, 2004, 450–451.

_____. "Afterword" to "To the Storming Gulf." *In Alien Flesh*, by Benford. New York: Tor, 1986, 160–163.

_____. *Against Infinity*. New York: Avon, 1998.

_____. *In the Ocean of Night*. Toronto: Bantam, 1987.

_____. "In the Wake of the Wave: The British Science Fiction Market." *Science Fiction and Market Realities*, edited by Gary Westfahl, George Slusser, and Eric S. Rabkin. Athens: University of Georgia Press, 1996, 151–160.

_____. *Jupiter Project*. New York: Avon, 1980.

_____. *Sailing Bright Eternity*. New York: Bantam, 1996.

_____. "Science and Art Mutually Dependent." Review of *Scientism: Philosophy and the Infatuation with Science*, by Tom Sorrell. *Science-Fiction Studies*, 19:1 (March 1992), 140–141.

_____. *Timescape*. New York: Simon and Schuster, 1980.

_____, and Elisabeth Malartre. *Beyond Human: Living with Robots and Cyborgs*. New York: Tor, 2007.

Berkeley, George. "A Treatise Concerning the Principles of Human Knowledge." *The Empiricists: Locke, Berkeley, Hume*, no editor given. Garden City, NY: Doubleday, 1961, 135–215.

Bernal, John Desmond. *The World, the Flesh, and the Devil: An Inquiry into the Three Enemies of the Rational Soul*. 1929. London: Jonathan Cape, 1970.

Bisson, Terry. "Bears Discover Fire." *The Year's Best Science Fiction: Eighth Annual Collection*, edited by Gardner Dozois. New York: St Martin's, 1991, 179–189.

Blish, James. "Common Time." *Galactic Cluster*. New York: New American Library, 1959, 38–58.

_____. *Mission to the Heart Stars*. New York: Avon, 1982.

Bloor, David. *Knowledge and Social Imagery*. Second Edition. Chicago: University of Chicago Press, 1991.

Borges, Jorge Luis. "The Aleph." *Collected Fictions*, by Borges, translated by Andrew Hurley. New York: Penguin, 1998, 274–286.

_____. "Afterword" to "The Aleph." *Collected Fictions*, by Borges, translated by Andrew Hurley. New York: Penguin, 1998, 287–288.

_____. "Commentaries." *The Aleph and Other Stories 1933–1969: Together with Commentaries and Autobiographical Essay*, edited and translated by Norman Thomas di Giovanni in collaboration with the author. New York: Bantam/E. P. Dutton, 1971, 263–283.

_____. "Pascal's Sphere." *Selected Non-Fictions*, edited by Eliot Weinberger, translated by Esther Allen, Suzanne Jill Levine, and Weinberger. New York: Penguin, 1999, 351–353.

Bos, A. P. "Exoterikoi Logoi and Enkyklioi Logoi in the Corpus Aristotelicum and the Origin of the Idea of the Enkyklios Paideia." *Journal of the History of Ideas*, 50 (1989), 179–198.

Bova, Ben. *Moonrise*. New York: Avon, 1996.

_____. *Moonwar*. New York: Avon, 1998.

Boyer, Paul. "The Evangelical Resurgence in 1970's American Protestantism." *Rightward*

Bound: Making America Conservative in the 1970s, edited by Bruce J. Schulman and Julian E. Zelizer. Cambridge, MA: Harvard University Press, 2008, 29–51.

Brandon, Ruth. *The New Women and the Old Men: Love, Sex and the Woman Question.* London: Secker & Warburg, 1990.

Brunner, John. *The Astronauts Must Not Land.* New York: Ace Books, 1963.

_____. *A Maze of Stars.* New York: Ballantine, 1991.

Bussey, Henry L. "Problems with Monitoring Heparin Anticoagulation." *Pharmacotherapy,* 19:1 (January 1999), 2–5.

Butler, Octavia E. *Adulthood Rites.* New York: Warner, 1988.

_____. *Dawn.* New York: Warner, 1987.

_____. *Imago.* New York: Warner, 1989.

Cadigan, Pat. *Synners.* New York: Bantam, 1991.

Calne, Donald B. *Within Reason: Rationality and Human Behavior.* New York: Pantheon, 1999.

Campbell, John W., Jr. "Introduction." *Prologue to Analog,* edited by Campbell. Garden City, NY: Doubleday, 1962, 9–16.

_____. *Invaders from the Infinite.* 1932. New York: Ace, 1961.

_____. Letter to Lurton Blassingame, March 4, 1959. *The John W. Campbell Letters, Volume 1,* edited by Perry A. Chapdelaine, Sr., Tony Chapdelaine, and George Hay. Franklin, TN: AC Projects, 1985, 362–364.

_____. "Twilight." 1934. *The Science Fiction Hall of Fame, Volume 1,* edited by Robert Silverberg. New York: Avon, 1971, 40–61.

Cassirer, Ernst. *The Philosophy of the Enlightenment.* Boston: Beacon, 1955.

Clarke, Arthur C. *Childhood's End.* New York: Ballantine, 1953.

_____. "A Meeting with Medusa." *The Wind from the Sun,* by Clarke. New York: Signet/NAL, 1972, 127–168.

_____. *Rendezvous with Rama.* London: Gollancz, 1973.

_____. *3001: The Final Odyssey.* New York: Ballantine Del Rey, 1997.

_____. *2001: A Space Odyssey.* New York: Signet, 1968.

_____. *2061: Odyssey Three.* New York: Ballantine Del Rey, 1987.

_____, and Gentry Lee. *Rama II.* New York: Bantam, 1989.

Clarke, Roger. "Asimov's Laws of Robotics: Implications for Information Technology, Part I." *IEEE Computer,* 26:12 (December 1993), 53–61.

_____. "Asimov's Laws of Robotics: Implications for Information Technology, Part II." *IEEE Computer,* 27:1 (January 1994), 57–66.

Close Encounters of the Third Kind. Columbia, 1977.

Clute, John, editor. *Science Fiction: The Illustrated Encyclopedia.* London: Dorling Kindersley, 1995.

_____, and Peter Nicholls, editors. *The Encyclopedia of Science Fiction.* New York: St. Martin's, 1993.

Codrescu, Andrei. *The Dog with the Chip in Its Neck: Essays from NPR and Elsewhere.* New York: St. Martin's, 1996.

Cohen, J. M., and M. J. Cohen, compilers. *The Penguin Dictionary of Twentieth-Century Quotations.* New York: Penguin, 1980.

Conniff, Richard. "Crash, Slam, Boom!" *Smithsonian,* 29:10 (January 1999), 90–100.

Crohmalniceanu, Ovidiu S. "A Chapter of Literary History." *The Phantom Church and Other Stories from Romania,* translated and edited by Georgiana Farnoaga and Sharon King. Pittsburgh, PA: University of Pittsburgh Press, 1996, 84–87.

Csicsery-Ronay, Istvan, Jr. "The Cyborg and the Kitchen Sink; or, The Salvation Story of No Salvation Story." *Science-Fiction Studies,* 25:3 (November 1998), 510–525.

Cudd, Ann E. "Objectivity and Ethno-Feminist Critique of Science." *After the Science Wars,* edited by Keith M. Ashman and Philip S. Baringer. New York: Routledge, 2001, 80–97.

D'Alembert, Le Rond. *Preliminary Discourse to the Encyclopedia of Diderot,* translated by Richard N. Schwab with the collaboration of Walter E. Rex, introduction and notes by Richard N. Scwab. The Library of Liberal Arts. Indianapolis, IN: Bobbs-Merrill, 1963.

Dante Alighieri. *The Banquet (Il Convivio),* translated, with an introduction and notes, by Christopher Ryan. Saratoga, NY: Anma Libri, 1989.

_____. *The Divine Comedy: Inferno: Italian Text and Translation,* translated with a commentary by Charles S. Singleton. Second Printing with Corrections. Princeton, NJ: Princeton University Press, 1977.

_____. *The Divine Comedy: Paradiso: Italian Text and Translation,* translated with a commentary by Charles S. Singleton. Second printing with corrections. Princeton, NJ: Princeton University Press, 1977.

Davies, Paul. *Other Worlds: A Portrait of Nature in Rebellion: Space, Superspace and the Quantum Universe.* New York: Simon & Schuster, 1980.

The Day the Earth Stood Still. 20th Century–Fox, 1951.

Delany, Samuel R. *Dhalgren.* 1975. New York: Random House, 2001.

_____. "Some *Real* Mothers: An Interview." Takayuku Tatsumi, interviewer. *Science Fiction Eye,* 1:3 (1988), 5–11.

_____. *Stars in My Pocket like Grains of Sand.* New York: Bantam, 1984.

_____. *Trouble on Triton.* 1976. Hanover, CT: Wesleyan University Press, 1996. Originally published as *Triton.*

DeLillo, Don. *Great Jones Street.* Boston: Houghton Mifflin, 1973.

_____. *The Names.* New York: Vintage, 1982.

_____. *Ratner's Star.* New York: Vintage, 1976.

De Man, Paul. "Phenomenality and Materiality in Kant." *Aesthetic Ideology,* by de Man, edited by Andrzej Warminski. Minneapolis: University of Minnesota Press, 1996, 70–90.

De Rijk, L. M. "'Enkyklios Paideia': A Study of Its Original Meaning." *Vivarium,* 3:1 (1965), 24–93.

Desilet, Gregory. "Physics and Language — Science and Rhetoric: Reviewing the Parallel Evolution of Theory on Motion and Meaning in the Aftermath of the Sokal Hoax." *Quarterly Journal of Speech,* 85.4 (November 1999), 339–360.

Diagnostic and Statistical Manual of Mental Disorders. Fourth edition. Washington, DC: American Psychiatric Association, 1994.

Dick, Philip K. *The Divine Invasion.* New York: Timescape, 1981.

_____. *Flow My Tears, The Policeman Said.* 1974. New York: Vintage, 1993.

_____. *The Man in the High Castle.* New York: G. P. Putnam's Sons, 1962.

_____. "The Pre-Persons." *The Eye of the Sibyl,* by Dick. 1987. New York: Citadel, 1992, 275–296.

_____. *Radio Free Albemuth.* 1985. New York: Vintage, 1998.

_____. *Time Out of Joint.* 1959. New York: Belmont, 1965.

Dickson, Gordon R. *The Final Encyclopedia 1–2.* New York: Tor, 1984.

Dumitrescu-Buşulenga, Zoe, editor. *Meşterul Manole,* Bucureşti: Editura Albatros, 1976.

Dvorkin, David. *Timetrap.* New York: Pocket, 1988.

"E^2." Episode of *Star Trek: Enterprise.* New York: UPN, May 5, 2004.

Eco, Umberto. *The Role of the Reader: Explorations in the Semiotics of Texts.* Bloomington, IN: Indiana University Press, 1979.

_____. *Semiotics and the Philosophy of Language.* Bloomington, IN: Indiana University Press, 1984.

Eddington, Sir Arthur. *The Nature of the Physical World.* 1928. Cambridge, UK: Cambridge University Press, 1953.

Efremov, Ivan. *The Heart of the Serpent.* Moscow: Foreign Language Publishing House, n.d.

Eliade, Mircea. *Meterul Manole: studii de etnologie şi mitologie.* Iaşi: Editura Junimea, 1992.

_____. *Zalmoxis, the Vanishing God: Comparative Studies in the Religions and Folklore of Dacia and Eastern Europe*, translated by Willard R. Trask. Chicago and London: University of Chicago Press, Midway Reprint, 1972.

Eliot, T. S. "The Dry Salvages." *Four Quartets*. London: Faber and Faber, 1944, 25–33.

"Encyclopædic, Encyclopedic, *a*." No author given. *Oxford English Dictionary*. Volume 5, Second Edition. Oxford: Oxford University Press, 1989, 219.

Epstein, Richard. *The Case of the Killer Robot: Stories about the Professional, Ethical, and Societal Dimensions of Computing*. New York: John Wiley and Sons, 1997.

Event Horizon. Paramount, 1997.

Faulkner, William. "The Bear." *Three Famous Short Novels: Spotted Horses, Old Man, The Bear*. New York: Vintage, 1963, 185–316.

Fischer, John Martin, and Ruth Curl. "Philosophical Models of Immortality in Science Fiction." *Immortal Engines: Life Extension and Immortality in Science Fiction and Fantasy*, edited by George Slusser, Gary Westfahl, and Eric S. Rabkin. Athens: University of Georgia Press, 1996, 3–12.

Forbidden Planet. MGM, 1956.

Foucault, Michel. *Discipline and Punish: The Birth of the Prison*, translated by Alan Sheridan. New York: Vintage/Random House, 1995.

Freedman, Carl. *Critical Theory and Science Fiction*. Hanover, CT: Wesleyan University Press, 2000.

Frye, Northrop. *Anatomy of Criticism: Four Essays*. Princeton, NJ: Princeton University Press, 1957.

Fuller, Steve. "The Reenchantment of Science: A Fit End to the Science Wars?" *After the Science Wars*, edited by Keith M. Ashman and Philip S. Baringer. New York: Routledge, 2001, 182–208.

Fumagalli, Maria Teresa Beonio-Brocchieri. *Le Enciclopedie dell'Occidente Medioevale*. Torino: Loescher Editore, 1981.

Gay, Peter. *The Enlightenment: An Interpretation*. 2 volumes. New York: Vantage, 1966, 1969.

Gaylard, Gerald. "Black Secret Technology: African Technological Subjects." *World Weavers: Globalization, Science Fiction, and the Cybernetic Revolution*, edited by Wong Kin Yuen, Gary Westfahl, and Amy Kit-sze Chan. Hong Kong: Hong Kong University Press, 2005, 191–204.

Gernsback, Hugo. "Science Fiction Week." *Science Wonder Stories*, 1 (May 1930), 1061.

Global Financial Data. Online database, accessed at the University of California, Riverside in September 2008, at https://www.globalfinancialdata.com/index_tabs.php3?action=user_homepage&message=true.

Gribbin, John. *In Search of Schrödinger's Cat: Quantum Physics and Reality*. New York: Bantam, 1984.

Gross, Paul R., and Norman Levitt. *Higher Superstition: The Academic Left and its Quarrels with Science*. Baltimore, MD: Johns Hopkins University Press, 1994.

Haldeman, Joe. *The Forever War*. New York: Ballantine, 1974.

Hampton, Kirk, and Carol MacKay. "Beyond the Endtime Terminus: Allegories of Coalescence in Far-Future Science Fiction." *Worlds Enough and Time: Explorations of Time in Science Fiction and Fantasy*, edited by Gary Westfahl, George Slusser, and David Leiby. Westport, CT: Greenwood, 2002, 65–75.

Haraway, Donna. "A Manifesto for Cyborgs: Science, Technology, and Socialist Feminism in the Late Twentieth Century." *Simians, Cyborgs, and Women: The Reinvention of Nature*. London: Free Association, 1991, 149–181.

Hardy, Sylvia. "A Feminist Perspective on H. G. Wells." *The Wellsian*, 20 (Winter 1997), 49–62.

Harrison, Harry. "The Mothballed Spaceship." *Astounding: The John W. Campbell Memorial Anthology*, edited by Harrison. New York: Random House, 1973, 183–200.

Havelock, Eric A. *Preface to Plato*. Cambridge, MA: Belknap Press of Harvard University Press, 1963.

Hawking, Stephen. "A Brief History of Relativity." *Time,* 154:27 (December 31, 1999), 66–81.

_____. *A Brief History of Time*. New York: Bantam, 1998.

Heidegger, Martin. *Einführung in die Metaphysik*. Tübingen: Max Neimeyer Verlag, 1957.

Heinlein, Robert A. "The Happy Days Ahead." *Expanded Universe,* by Heinlein. New York: Grosset and Dunlap, 1980, 514–582.

_____. *Have Space Suit, Will Travel*. 1958. New York: Ace, [1975].

_____. *Methuselah's Children*. 1942. New York: New American Library, 1958.

_____. *Orphans of the Sky*. 1941. New York: Putnam, 1963.

_____. *The Puppet Masters*. Garden City, NY: Doubleday, 1951.

_____. *Time Enough for Love*. New York: G. Putnam's Sons, 1973.

_____. *Time for the Stars*. New York: Scribner's, 1956.

Henderson, Linda Dalrymple. *The Fourth Dimension and Non-Euclidean Geometry in Modern Art*. Princeton, NJ: Princeton University Press, 1983.

Hendrix, Howard V. *Lightpaths*. New York: Ace, 1997.

_____. *Standing Wave*. New York: Ace, 1998.

Henry, Carl F. H. "What Is Man on Earth For?" *Quest For Reality: Christianity and the Counter Culture,* by Henry, Armand M. Nicholi, James Daane, James M. Houston, D. Elton Trueblood, David Carley, Douglas D. Feaver, Ronald H. Nash, Arthur F. Holmes, George I. Mavrodes, John Scanzoni, V. Elving Anderson, David O. Moberg, John W. Snyder, Clark H. Pinnock, Merold Westphal, and Calvin D. Linton. Downers Grove, IL: InterVarsity, 1973, 155–161.

Hillegas, Mark R. *The Future as Nightmare: H. G. Wells and the Anti-Utopians*. New York: Oxford University Press, 1967.

Hollinger, Veronica. "Deconstructing the Time Machine." *Science-Fiction Studies,* 14:2 (July 1987), 201–221.

Hume, Kathryn. "Eat or Be Eaten: H. G. Wells's *Time Machine*." *Philological Quarterly,* 69:2 (Spring 1990), 233–251.

Hunter, Jefferson. *Edwardian Fiction*. Cambridge, MA: Harvard University Press, 1982.

Huntington, John. *The Logic of Fantasy: H. G. Wells and Science Fiction*. New York: Columbia University Press, 1982.

Huxley, Thomas Henry. "Evolution and Ethics." *Evolution and Ethics, 1893–1943,* by T. H. Huxley and Julian Huxley. London: Pilot, 1947, 60–102.

"The IKV T'Mar." At http://www.ikvtmar.com/purpose.html.

Independence Day. 20th Century–Fox, 1996.

Innovative Technologies in Science Fiction for Space Applications. At http://www.itsf.org/.

Jameson, Fredric. *Archaeologies of the Future*. London: Verso, 2005.

_____. "Postmodernism, Or The Cultural Logic Of Late Capitalism." *The Jameson Reader,* edited by Michael Hardt and Kathi Weeks. Oxford: Blackwell, 2000, 188–232.

Johnny Mnemonic. TriStar, 1995.

Johnson, A. W. *Ben Jonson: Poetry and Architecture*. Oxford, UK: Clarendon, 1994.

Jones, W. T., editor. *Kant and the Nineteenth Century*. Second Edition. New York: Harcourt Brace, 1969.

Justman, Stewart. *Fool's Paradise: The Unreal World of Pop Psychology*. Chicago: Ivan R. Dee, 2005.

Koch, Robert. "The Case of Latour." *Configurations: A Journal of Literature, Science, and Technology,* 3.3 (Fall 1995), 319–347.

Koertge, Noretta, editor. *A House Built on Sand: Exposing Postmodernist Myths About Science*. Oxford and New York: Oxford University Press, 1998.

Kretschmer, Ernst. *The Psychology of Men of Genius*, translated, with an introduction, by R. B. Cattell. College Park, MD: McGrath, 1970.

Krieger, Leonard. *An Essay on the Theory of Enlightenment Despotism.* Chicago: University of Chicago Press, 1975.

_____. *Kings and Philosophers, 1689–1789.* New York: Norton, 1970.

Kuhn, Thomas S. *The Structure of Scientific Revolutions.* Third Edition. Chicago: University of Chicago Press, 1996.

Kumar, Krishan. *Utopia and Anti-Utopia in Modern Times.* Oxford, UK: Blackwell, 1991.

Kuusisto, Pekka. "Closing in Sublunary Darkness?: On the 'Material Vision' in Dante's and Paul de Man's Cosmos." *Illuminating Darkness: Approaches to Obscurity and Nothingness in Literature,* edited by Päivi Mehtonen. Annales Academiae Scientiarum Fennicae, Humaniora 348. Helsinki: Finnish Academy of Science and Letters, 2007, 27–46.

_____. "The Curvature of Space-Time in Dante's *The Divine Comedy.*" *Worlds Enough and Time. Explorations of Time in Science Fiction and Fantasy,* edited by Gary Westfahl, George Slusser, and David Leiby. Westport, CT: Greenwood, 2002, 115–128.

_____. "The Limits of Geometry in the '*Convivio*' and Their Inversion in the '*Comedy*': On Dante's Cosmology and Its Modern After-Life." *Perspektiv på Dante II: Proceedings of the Nordic Dante Studies Symposium, Stockholm, Sweden 2001,* edited by Anders Cullhed. København: Multivers Academic, 2006, 267–313. Also available online at http://homepage.mac.com/kaatmann/dante/Dantesamlet1.pdf.

Labinger, Jay A., and Harry Collins, editors. *The One Culture?: A Conversation about Science.* Chicago: University of Chicago Press, 2001.

Lasch, Christopher. *The Culture of Narcissism.* New York: Norton, 1978.

Lax, Eric. *On Being Funny: Woody Allen and Comedy.* New York: Charterhouse, 1975.

Leavis, F. R. *Anna Karenina and Other Essays.* New York: Simon and Schuster, 1969.

_____. *Nor Shall My Sword: Discourses on Pluralism, Compassion and Social Hope.* New York: Harper and Row, 1972.

LeClair, Tom. *In the Loop: Don DeLillo and the Systems Novel.* Urbana, IL: Illinois University Press, 1987.

_____, and Larry McCaffery, conductors and editors. *Anything Can Happen: Interviews with Contemporary American Writers.* Urbana, Illinois: Illinois University Press, 1983.

Lederman, Leon, with Dick Teresi. *The God Particle.* New York: Bantam, 1994.

Le Guin, Ursula K. *Always Coming Home.* New York: Harper and Row, 1985. Science Fiction Book Club Edition.

_____. "Bryn Mawr Commencement Address," *Dancing at the Edge of the World,* by Le Guin. New York: Grove, 1989, 147–160.

_____. *The Dispossessed: An Ambiguous Utopia.* New York: Avon, 1974.

_____. "Introduction." *The Left Hand of Darkness.* New York: Ace, 1976, xi–xvi.

_____. *The Word for World is Forest.* New York: Berkley, 1972.

Leinster, Murray. *Doctor to the Stars.* New York: Pyramid, 1964.

Lem, Stanislaw. "Reflections on My Life." *Microworlds: Writings on Science Fiction and Fantasy,* by Lem, edited by Franz Rottensteiner. London: Mandarin 1984, 1–30.

_____. *Solaris.* 1961. Translated by Joanna Kilmartin and Steve Cox, afterword by Darko Suvin. New York: Walker, 1970.

Levenson, N. G., and C. S. Turner. "An Investigation of the Therac-25 Accidents." *IEEE Computer,* 26:7 (July 1993), 18–41.

Levinas, Emmanuel. *Totality and Infinity: An Essay on Exteriority,* translated by Alphonso Lingis. Pittsburgh, PA: Duquesne University Press, 1969.

Lin, Danny J. Han-Chang. *The Complete Bibliography of Taiwanese Science Fiction.* Taipei, Taiwan: privately published, 2003.

Luckhurst, Roger. *Science Fiction.* Cambridge: Polity, 2005.

Manolescu, Florin. "Introduction." *The Phantom Church and Other Stories from Romania,* translated and edited by Georgiana Farnoaga and Sharon King. Pittsburgh, PA: University of Pittsburgh Press, 1996, vii–xiv.

Martinson, Harry. *Aniara: A Review of Man in Time and Space.* 1956. Translated by Hugh MacDiarmid and Elspeth Harley Schubert, introduction by Tord Hall. New York: Alfred A. Knopf, 1963.

McCaffrey, Anne. *The Ship Who Sang.* New York: Ballantine, 1970.

_____, and Margaret Ball. *PartnerShip.* Riverdale NY: Baen, 1992.

_____, and Mercedes Lackey. *The Ship Who Searched.* Riverdale NY: Baen, 1992.

McConnell, Frank. *The Science Fiction of H. G. Wells,* Oxford, UK: Oxford University Press, 1981.

McMillen, Liz. "The Science Wars." *The Chronicle of Higher Education,* 42 (June 28, 1996), A9.

Melley, Timothy. *Empire of Conspiracy.* Ithaca, NY: Cornell University Press, 2000.

Mermin, N. David. "Conversing Seriously with Sociologists." *The One Culture? A Conversation about Science,* edited by Jay A. Labinger and Harry Collins. Chicago: University of Chicago Press, 2001, 83–98.

Michaels, Phillip. "Computer Motion System Used in First U.S. Robotic Surgery." *Investor's Business Daily,* December 11, 1998, A4.

Miller, Jane Eldridge. *Rebel Women: Feminism, Modernism and the Edwardian Novel.* Chicago: University of Chicago Press, 1997.

Miller, Joseph D. "Popes or Tropes: Defining the Grails of Science Fiction." *Science Fiction. Canonization. Marginalization, and the Academy,* edited by Gary Westfahl and George Slusser. Westport, CT: Greenwood, 2002, 79–87.

Miller, Ron. *The Dream Machine: An Illustrated History of the Spaceship in Art, Science, and Literature.* Malabar, FL: Krieger, 1993.

Mintz, Jerome R. *Legends of the Hasidim: An Introduction to Hasidic Culture and Oral Tradition in the New World.* Chicago and London: University of Chicago Press, 1968.

Morgan, Sean. "Nanotechnology Papers." Formerly available at http://www.cs.rutgers. edu/nanotech/.

Morgan, Teresa. *Literate Education in the Hellenistic and Roman Worlds.* Cambridge, UK: Cambridge University Press, 1998.

Nahin, Paul. *Time Machines: Time Travel in Physics, Metaphysics, and Science Fiction.* Second Edition. New York: Springer, 1999.

Nate, Richard. "Ignorance, Opportunism, Propaganda and Dissent: The Reception of H. G. Wells in Nazi Germany." *The Reception of H. G. Wells in Europe,* edited by Patrick Parrinder and John S. Partington. London: Thoemmes Continuum, 2005, 105–125.

_____. "Scientific Utopianism in Francis Bacon and H. G. Wells: From *Salomon's House* to *The Open Conspiracy.*" *Critical Review of International Social and Political Philosophy,* 3:2–3 (Summer/Autumn 2000), 172–188.

Nemo, Philippe. *Ethics and Infinity: Conversations with Philippe Nemo,* translated by Richard A. Cohen. Pittsburgh, PA: Duquesne University Press, 1985.

Nicholls, Peter, editor. *The Encyclopedia of Science Fiction.* London: Granada, 1979.

Niven, Larry. "The Ethics of Madness." *Neutron Star.* New York: Ballantine, 1968, 173–208.

_____. *Ringworld.* New York: Ballantine, 1970.

_____. *Scatterbrain.* New York: Tor, 2003.

Norris, Christopher. *Against Relativism: Philosophy of Science, Deconstruction and Critical Theory.* Oxford, UK: Blackwell, 1997.

Osserman, Robert. *Poetry of the Universe: A Mathematical Exploration of the Cosmos.* New York: Anchor, 1995.

Park, Robert L. "Voodoo Medicine in a Scientific World." *After the Science Wars,* edited by Keith M. Ashman and Philip S. Baringer. New York: Routledge, 2001, 140–150.

Parrinder, Patrick. *H. G. Wells.* Edinburgh: Oliver and Boyd, 1970.

_____. *Shadows of the Future: H. G. Wells, Science Fiction and Prophecy.* Liverpool: Liverpool University Press, 1995.

Partington, John S. *Building Cosmopolis: The Political Thought of H. G. Wells*. Aldershot, UK: Ashgate, 2003.

_____. "The Death of the Static: H. G. Wells and the Kinetic Utopia." *Utopian Studies,* 11:2 (2000), 96–111.

_____. "*The Time Machine* and *A Modern Utopia*: The Static and Kinetic Utopias of the Early H. G. Wells." *Utopian Studies,* 13:1 (2002), 57–68.

Pascal, Blaise. *Pensées. Oeuvres de Blaise Pascal*, edited by Léon Brunschvicg. Paris: Librairie Hachette, 1925.

_____. *Pensées*, translated by A. J. Krailsheimer. Harmondsworth, UK: Penguin, 1975.

Pauli, Wolfgang. "The Influence of Archetypal Ideas on the Scientific Theories of Kepler." *The Interpretation of Nature and the Psyche; Synchronicity: An Acausal Connecting Principle, C. G. Jung. The Influence of Archetypal Ideas on the Scientific Theories of Kepler, W. Pauli.* New York: Pantheon, 1955, 147–240.

Penrose, Roger. *The Emperor's New Mind: Concerning Computers, Minds, and the Laws of Physics*. New York and London: Viking, 1991.

Peterson, Mark. "Dante and the 3-sphere." *American Journal of Physics,* 47 (1979), 1031–1035.

_____. "Dante's Physics." *The Divine Comedy and the Encyclopedia of Arts and Sciences: Acta of the International Dante Symposium, 13–16 November 1983, Hunter College*, edited by Giuseppe Di Scipio and Aldo Scaglione. New York and Amsterdam: John Benjamins, 1988, 163–180.

Philmus, Robert. "The Cybernetic Paradigms of Stanislaw Lem." *Hard Science Fiction*, edited by George Slusser and Eric S. Rabkin. Carbondale: Southern Illinois University Press, 1986, 177–213.

Piercy, Marge. *He, She and It*. New York: Alfred A. Knopf, 1991.

_____. *Woman on the Edge of Time*. New York: Alfred A. Knopf, 1976.

Pinch, Trevor. "Does Science Studies Undermine Science?: Wittgenstein, Turing, and Polanyi as Precursors for Science Studies and the Science Wars." *The One Culture? A Conversation about Science*, edited by Jay A. Labinger and Harry Collins. Chicago: University of Chicago Press, 2001, 13–26.

Plato. *Phaedrus. Complete Works*, by Plato, edited, with introduction and notes, by John M. Cooper; associate editor D. S. Hutchinson. Indianapolis, IN: Hackett, 1997.

Popper, Karl. *Conjectures and Refutations: The Growth of Scientific Knowledge*. New York and London: Basic, 1962.

Quintilianus, Marcus Fabius. *Institutio Oratoria*, translated and edited by H. E. Butler. Loeb Classical Library. Cambridge, MA: Harvard University Press, 1920.

Readings, Bill. *Introducing Lyotard: Art and Politics*. London: Routledge, 1991.

Regis, Ed. *Great Mambo Chicken and the Transhuman Condition: Science Slightly Over the Edge*. New York: Addison Wesley, 1990.

Reich, Charles A. *The Greening of America*. New York: Random House, 1970.

Resnick, Mike. "Seven Views of Olduvai Gorge." *The Year's Best Science Fiction: Twelfth Annual Collection*, edited by Gardner Dozois. New York: St. Martin's, 1995, 305–342.

Reynolds, Mack. *The Best Ye Breed*. New York: Ace, 1978

_____. *Blackman's Burden*. Published dos-à-dos with Reynolds, *Border, Breed nor Birth*. New York: Ace, 1972.

_____. *Border, Breed nor Birth*. Published dos-à-dos with Reynolds, *Blackman's Burden*. New York: Ace, 1972.

Rickman, Gregg. *Philip K. Dick: The Last Testament*. Long Beach, CA: Fragments West, 1985.

Robinson, Frank M. *The Dark Beyond the Stars*. New York: Tom Doherty, 1991.

Robinson, Kim Stanley. *Green Mars*. New York: Bantam, 1994.

_____. *Red Mars*. New York: Bantam, 1993.

_____. *Blue Mars.* New York: Bantam, 1996.

Ross, Andrew, editor. *Science Wars.* Durham, NC, and London: Duke University Press, 1996.

Roszak, Theodore. *The Making of a Counter Culture.* Garden City, NY: Doubleday, 1969.

Rovin, Jeff. *Aliens, Robots, and Spaceships.* New York: Facts on File, 1995.

Rucker, Rudy. *Infinity and the Mind: The Science and Philosophy of the Infinite.* Princeton, NJ: Princeton University Press, 1995.

Runaway. Columbia Pictures, 1984.

Russ, Joanna. *The Two of Them.* New York: Berkley, 1978.

Russell, Mary Doria. *Children of God.* New York: Villiard, 1998.

_____. *The Sparrow* New York: Villiard, 1996.

Saberhagen, Fred. *The Berserker Wars.* New York: Pinnacle, 1981.

Sargent, Lyman Tower. "The Pessimistic Eutopias of H. G. Wells." *The Wellsian: Selected Essays on H. G. Wells,* edited by John S. Partington. Oss, the Netherlands: Equilibris, 2003, 199–219.

Saulson, Peter R. "Life Inside a Case Study." *The One Culture? A Conversation about Science,* edited by Jay A. Labinger and Harry Collins. Chicago: University of Chicago Press, 2001, 73–82.

Savile, Steven, and Alethea Kontis, editors. *Elemental: The Tsunami Relief Anthology: Stories of Science Fiction and Fantasy.* New York: Tor, 2006.

Serenity. Universal, 2005.

Shakespeare, William. *King Lear.* Edited by R. A. Foakes. London: Thomas Nelson, 1997.

Shapin, Steven. "How to Be Antiscientific." *The One Culture? A Conversation about Science,* edited by Jay A. Labinger and Harry Collins. Chicago: University of Chicago Press, 2001, 100–101.

Shires, Preston. *Hippies of the Religious Right.* Waco, TX: Baylor University Press, 2007.

Simak, Clifford D. *Shakespeare's Planet.* New York: Berkley Books, 1976.

Simpson, Anne B. "The 'Tangible Antagonist': H. G. Wells and the Discourse of Otherness." *Extrapolation,* 31 (1990), 134–147.

Sleigh, Charlotte. "Empire of the Ants: H. G. Wells and Tropical Entomology." *Science as Culture,* 10:1 (2001), 33–71.

Slusser, George, George R. Guffey, and Mark Rose, editors. *Bridges to Science Fiction.* Carbondale: Southern Illinois University Press, 1980.

Small, Robin. "Nietzsche and a Platonist Tradition of the Cosmos: Center Everywhere and Circumference Nowhere." *Journal of the History of Ideas,* 44:1 (January-March 1983), 89–104.

Smith, Cordwainer. "The Lady Who Sailed the Soul." 1960. *Mind Partner and 8 Other Novelets from Galaxy,* edited by H. L. Gold. 1961. New York: Pocket, 1963, 38–63.

Smith, David C. *H. G. Wells: Desperately Mortal.* New Haven, CT: Yale University Press, 1986.

Smith, E. E. "Doc." *Children of the Lens.* 1954. New York: Pyramid, 1966.

_____. *First Lensman.* 1950. New York: Pyramid, 1964.

_____. *Masters of the Vortex.* 1960. New York: Pyramid, 1968.

_____. *Triplanetary.* 1948. New York: Pyramid, 1965.

Smith, Marilyn S. The Spaceship as Metaphor. Master's Thesis, California State University, Hayward, 1983.

Snow, C. P. *The Search.* 1958. Harmondsworth, UK: Penguin, 1965.

_____. *Strangers and Brothers.* Omnibus Edition in Three Volumes. New York: Charles Scribner's Sons, 1972.

_____. *Variety of Men.* New York: Charles Scribner's Sons, 1967.

Sobchack, Vivian. "The Virginity of Astronauts: Sex and the Science Fiction Film." *Shad-*

ows of the Magic Lamp: Fantasy and Science Fiction in Film, edited by George Slusser and Eric S. Rahkin. Carbondale: Southern Illinois University Press, 1985, 41–57.

Sokal, Alan. *Beyond the Hoax: Science, Philosophy and Culture*. Oxford and New York: Oxford University Press, 2008.

_____. "A Physicist Experiments with Cultural Studies." *Lingua Franca*, 6:4 (May/June, 1996), 62–64.

_____, and Jean Bricmont. *Fashionable Nonsense: Postmodern Intellectuals' Abuse of Science*. New York: Picador, 1998.

_____, and _____. "Science and Sociology of Science: Beyond War and Peace." *The One Culture? A Conversation about Science*, edited by Jay A. Labinger and Harry Collins. Chicago: University of Chicago Press, 2001, 27–47.

Sphere. Warner Bros., 1998.

Star Trek: The Motion Picture. Paramount, 1979.

Steiner, George. *Language and Silence: Essays on Language, Literature and the Inhuman*. New York: Atheneum, 1970.

Sterling, Bruce. "Green Days in Brunei." 1985. *The Ultimate Cyberpunk*, edited by Pat Cadigan. New York: Pocket/iBooks, 2002), 276–340.

Stevens, Wallace. "Of Modern Poetry." *The Collected Poems of Wallace Stevens*. New York: Alfred A. Knopf, 1954, 239–240.

_____. "Reality Is an Activity of the Most August Imagination." *Collected Poetry and Prose*, selected and annotated by Frank Kermode and Joan Richardson. New York: Library of America, 1997, 471–472.

Stine, G. Harry [as Lee Correy] *Manna*. New York: DAW, 1983.

_____. *The Space Enterprise*. New York: Ace, 1980.

_____. *The Third Industrial Revolution*. New York: Ace, 1979.

Strugatsky, Arkady, and Boris Strugatsky. *Noon: 22d Century*, translated by Patrick L. McGuire, introduction by Theodore Sturgeon. New York: Macmillan, 1978.

Stubbs, Patricia. *Women and Fiction: Feminism and the Novel 1880–1920*. London: Methuen, 1981.

Sutin, Lawrence. *Divine Invasions: A Life of Philip K. Dick*. New York: Carol, 1991.

Thiem, Jon. *"Borges, Dante, and the Poetics of Total Vision." Comparative Literature*, 40:2 (Spring 1988), 97–121.

Thorne, Kip S. *Black Holes and Time Warps: Einstein's Outrageous Legacy*, New York: Norton, 1994.

Turkle, Sherry. *The Second Self: Computers and the Human Spirit*. New York: Simon and Schuster, 1984.

2001: A Space Odyssey. MGM, 1968.

Van Vogt, A. E. *Mission to the Stars*. New York: Berkley Medallion, 1952.

Vasbinder, Samuel Homes. *Scientific Attitudes in Mary Shelley's Frankenstein*. Ann Arbor, MI: UMI Research Press, 1984.

Vinge, Joan D. "View from a Height." 1978. *Best Science Fiction Stories of the Year*, edited by Gardner Dozois. 1979. New York: Dell, 1980, 178–196.

Vitruvius. *On Architecture*, edited and translated by Frank Granger. Two volumes. Loeb Classical Library. Cambridge, MA: Harvard University Press, 1931.

Völker, Klaus, compiler. *Künstliche Menschen: Dichtungen und Dokumente über Golems, Homunculi, Androiden und liebenden Statuen*. München: Karl Hanser Verlag, 1976.

Wagar, W. Warren. "Critical Introduction." *The Open Conspiracy: H. G. Wells on World Revolution*, edited by Wagar. Westport, CT: Praeger, 2002, 1–44.

_____. *H. G. Wells and the World State*. New Haven, CT: Yale University Press, 1961.

_____. "The Road to Utopia: H. G. Wells's *Open Conspiracy*." *The Wellsian*, 23 (2000), 14–24.

Wagner, David L. "The Seven Liberal Arts and Classical Scholarship." *The Seven Liberal*

Arts in the Middle Ages, edited by Wagner. Bloomington: Indiana University Press, 1983, 1–31.

Weeks, Jeffrey R. *The Shape of Space*. Second Edition. New York: Marcel Dekker, 2002.

Weinberg, Steven. "Physics and History." *The One Culture?: A Conversation about Science*, edited by Jay A. Labinger and Harry Collins Chicago: University of Chicago Press, 2001, 116–127.

Weiskel, Thomas. *The Romantic Sublime: Studies in the Structure and Psychology of Transcendence*. Baltimore, MD: Johns Hopkins University Press, 1976.

Wellek, René. "What Is Literature?" *What Is Literature?*, edited by Paul Hernadi. Bloomington: Indiana University Press, 1978), 16–23.

Wells, H. G. "About Sir Thomas More." *An Englishman Looks at the World: Being a Series of Unrestrained Remarks upon Contemporary Matters*. London: Cassell, 1914, 183–187.

_____. *Anticipations of the Reaction of Mechanical and Scientific Progress upon Human Life and Thought*. Mineola, NY: Dover, 1999. Originally published in 1902.

_____. *The Common Sense of War and Peace: World Revolution or War Unending*. Harmondsworth, UK: Penguin, 1940.

_____. "The Crystal Egg." *The Complete Short Stories*. London: Ernest Benn, 1974, 625–643.

_____. *Experiment in Autobiography: Discovery and Conclusions of a Very Ordinary Brain (since 1866)*. New York: Macmillan, 1934.

_____. *First & Last Things: A Confession of Faith and Rule of Life*. London: Constable, 1908.

_____. *The First Men in the Moon*. 1901; New York: Ballantine, [1963].

_____. *In the Fourth Year: Anticipations of a World Peace*. London: Chatto & Windus, 1918.

_____. *Meanwhile: The Picture of a Lady*. London: Benn, 1927.

_____. *A Modern Utopia*. 1905. Lincoln: University of Nebraska Press, 1967.

_____. "Morals and Civilization." *The Island of Doctor Moreau: A Critical Text of the 1896 London First Edition, with an Introduction and Appendices*, edited by Leon Stover. Jefferson, NC: McFarland, 1996, 252–264.

_____. *The Outline of History*. Third Edition. New York: MacMillan, 1921.

_____. "Preface." *The Works of H. G. Wells*. Atlantic edition, Volume VI. London: T. Fisher Unwin, 1925, ix.

_____. *The War of the Worlds*, edited by David Y. Hughes, introduction by Brian W. Aldiss. New York: Oxford University Press, 1995.

Westfahl, Gary. "Artists in Wonderland: Toward a True History of Science Fiction Art." *Unearthly Visions: Approaches to Science Fiction and Fantasy Art*, edited by Westfahl, George Slusser, and Kathleen Church Plummer. Westport, CT: Greenwood, 2002, 19–38.

_____. "In Search of Dismal Science Fiction." *Interzone*, No. 189 (May/June 2003), 55–56.

_____. "Who Governs Science Fiction?" *Extrapolation*, 41:1 (Spring 2000), 63–72.

_____. "Wrangling Conversation: Linguistic Patterns in the Dialogue of Heroes and Villains." *Fights of Fancy: Armed Conflict in Science Fiction and Fantasy*, edited by George Slusser and Eric S. Rabkin. Athens: University of Georgia Press, 1993, 35–48.

Wheeler, John. "Quantum Theory Poses Reality's Deepest Mystery." *Science News*, May 24, 2008, 32.

Wilhelm, Kate. "The Mile-Long Space Ship." 1957. *Andover and the Android*. 1963. London: Dobson, 1966, 7–15.

Williams, Paul. *Only Apparently Real: The World of Philip K. Dick*. New York: Arbor, 1986.

Wilson, Kenneth G. and Constance K. Barsky. "Beyond Social Construction." *The One Culture? A Conversation about Science*, edited by Jay A. Labinger and Harry Collins. Chicago: University of Chicago Press, 2001, 291–295.

Wittgenstein, Ludwig. *Tractatus Logico–Philosophicus*, translated by D. F. Pears and B. F. McGuinness, introduction by Bertrand Russell. London and New York: Routledge, 1974.

Wolfe, Gary K. "The Bear and the Aleph: Gregory Benford's *Against Infinity.*" *The New York Review of Science Fiction*, No. 30 (February 1991), 8–11.
Wollheim, Donald A. [as David Grinnell] *Destiny's Orbit.* New York: Ace, 1961.
Wordsworth, William. "The Recluse" [selection]. In *Selected Poems and Prefaces.* Edited by Jack Stillinger. Boston: Houghton Mifflin, 1965, 45–47.
Wuckel, Dieter, and Bruce Cassiday. *The Illustrated History of Science Fiction.* 1986. Translated by Jenny Vowles. New York: Ungar, 1989.

About the Contributors

George Atkins, now retired, was a professor and chair of the Computer Science Department at Southwestern Oklahoma State University. He has presented and published fifteen papers at computer science conferences, and he worked previously as a reliability engineer in the aerospace industry and as head of a software consulting business. He has also served on the Board of Trustees of Oklahoma Baptist University and as president of the Oklahoma Baptist Historical Society.

Gregory Benford has published over thirty books, mostly novels, earning the Nebula Award for his novel *Timescape,* the United Nations Medal for Literature, the Lord Prize for contributions to science, the Japan Seiun Award for Dramatic Presentation with his seven-hour series *A Galactic Odyssey,* and the Asimov Award for science writing. A professor of physics at the University of California, Irvine, he is a Woodrow Wilson Fellow, a fellow of the American Physical Society, and was visiting fellow at Cambridge University.

Gareth Davies-Morris, having lived and studied in Britain and France, teaches courses in the humanities at San Diego State University and Grossmont College in California. He has just completed "Fantasies and Possibilities," his Ph.D. dissertation on the Victorian and Edwardian science fiction of H.G. Wells, for the University of Reading in England.

Carl Freedman, a participant in the Eaton Conferences for many years, is a professor of English and director of English graduate studies at Louisiana State University. The author of several books and dozens of articles, he is best known within science fiction criticism for *Critical Theory and Science Fiction* (2000) and for editing collections of interviews with Isaac Asimov, Ursula K. Le Guin, and Samuel R. Delany (2005, 2008, 2009).

Kirk Hampton has published two novels in the style of "Wakean science fantasy"— *The Moonhare* and *Lisho*—as well as three previous conference papers coauthored with Carol MacKay. He produces and stars in a weekly cable television show for public access in Austin, Texas.

Howard V. Hendrix teaches English literature at California State University, Fresno. He holds a B.S. in biology from Xavier University and an M.A. and Ph.D. in English from the University of California, Riverside. He has published six novels —*Lightpaths* (1997), *Standing Wave* (1998), *Better Angels* (1999), *Empty Cities of the Full Moon* (2001), *The Labyrinth Key* (2004), and *The Spears of God* (2006) — and a short story collection, *Möbius Highway* (2001). He is now at work on a seventh novel, and his stories have appeared in numerous anthologies and magazines.

Jake Jakaitis, director of undergraduate studies in English at Indiana State University, has published work on Philip K. Dick, Don DeLillo, and Tim O'Brien. *Visual Crossover: Graphic Narrative and Sequential Art*, a collection of essays co-edited with James Wurtz, is under review at a university press.

Sharon D. King holds a Ph.D. in comparative literature from UCLA and is an associate at the UCLA Center for Medieval and Renaissance Studies. Publications include *The Phantom Church and Other Stories from Romania*, an anthology of 20th-century fiction (1996, co-translated with G. Farnoaga), a science fiction story, "Quiescent" (2006), and a satirical fantasy, "Prayer Meeting" (2008). A character actress as well as a scholar, she translates and performs short comedies of the 15th to 17th centuries with her troupe, Les Enfans sans Abri.

Pekka Kuusisto is a senior lecturer of literature at the University of Oulu, Finland. He has published articles on Dante, literature and science, and literary encyclopedism.

Bradford Lyau received his Ph.D. in modern European intellectual history from the University of Chicago and has published several articles comparing European and American science fiction. He has taught at various colleges and universities in California and in the Balkans. He divides his time in the business, research, and political worlds. He lives in Albuquerque, New Mexico.

Carol MacKay is distinguished teaching professor of English at the University of Texas at Austin. Editor of two works on Thackeray and Dickens, she is also the author of *Soliloquy in Nineteenth-Century Fiction* and *Creative Negativity: Four Victorian Exemplars of the Female Quest*.

Noah Mass is a Ph.D. candidate in 20th century American literature at the University of Texas at Austin. His work focuses on southern studies, African American studies, ethnic and Third World studies, cultural studies, and issues of regional and transnational identity.

The late **Frank McConnell**, formerly an English professor at the University of California, Santa Barbara, published innumerable articles and reviews, several books of literary criticism, and four detective novels; he also served four times on the committee which selected the Pulitzer Prize for fiction. All of his Eaton Conference papers, along with other essays on science fiction and fantasy, were published as *The Science of Fiction and the Fiction of Science* (2009).

John S. Partington has published five books on H. G. Wells, including *Building Cosmopolis: The Political Thought of H. G. Wells* (2003) and *H. G. Wells in Nature, 1893–1946: A Reception Reader* (2008). He has also published on Sir Arthur Conan Doyle, George Orwell, Woody Guthrie and Richard Coudenhove-Kalergi, with essays on Lorenzo Quelch and Phoebe Cusden in press. He is preparing a volume of critical essays on Guthrie and researching the influence of Clara Zetkin in British politics and the women's movement.

Stephen Potts teaches popular culture in the Department of Literature at the University of California, San Diego. His publications include books on Joseph Heller, F. Scott Fitzgerald, and the Strugatsky brothers, articles on subjects ranging from technology to hero myths, reviews, editorial columns, and fiction.

George Slusser is professor emeritus (recalled) of comparative literature and curator of the Eaton Collection at UC Riverside. His most recent publications are translations/critical editions of Balzac's *The Centenarian* (2006) and J. H. Rosny Aine's *From Prehistory to the End of the Earth: Three Novellas of J. H. Rosny Aine* (forthcoming), both with Danièle Chatelain.

Gary Westfahl, who teaches at the University of California, Riverside, is the author, editor, or co-editor of 22 books about science fiction and fantasy, including the Hugo Award–nominated *Science Fiction Quotations* (2005), the three-volume *The Greenwood Encyclopedia of Science Fiction and Fantasy* (2005), and *Hugo Gernsback and the Century of Science Fiction* (2007). In 2003, he received the Science Fiction Research Association's Pilgrim Award for lifetime contributions to science fiction and fantasy scholarship.

Index